the HIGHLANDER'S *Bride*

AMANDA FORESTER

sourcebooks
casablanca

Published by Sourcebooks Casablanca, an imprint of Sourcebooks, Inc.
P.O. Box 4410, Naperville, Illinois 60567–4410
(630) 961–3900
Fax: (630) 961–2168
www.sourcebooks.com

Printed and bound in Canada.
MBP 10 9 8 7 6 5 4 3 2 1

To those who have encouraged me by their words and their example. And to Ed, who does both.

One

France, 1359

SIR GAVIN PATRICK SPURRED HIS DESTRIER AND RACED into the rising tide of English soldiers with the full knowledge they had already lost. Gavin was a bright lad by all accounts, but even one slow with his sums could readily see that the small force of French and Scottish allies was grossly outnumbered. Again.

A more practical person may have considered a tactical retreat, but the French would fight for honor, and Gavin, being a Highlander, would fight the English any chance he got. Besides, if he led a charge now, he could prevent a rout.

Unfortunately, the French were honorable only to a point and fled as soon as it became clear their advance was a failure. Without order, the knights turned and ran for the protection of the forest, leaving their retreating flank unprotected. It was the worst thing they could have done. One noble continued the fight and was quickly surrounded, unable to flee.

"Hold the line!" cried Gavin to the retreating men. It was a pointless command. The soldiers could hear nothing above the din of their own panic.

Gavin pushed ahead to the surrounded noble. The man was still mounted and fighting hard, but it was a matter of seconds before he was captured or killed. One of the English soldiers grabbed the bridle of the French noble's mount and forced it down. The end of the nobleman was near.

Gavin gave the howling war cry of the charging Highlander. It succeeded in momentarily arresting the attack of the English soldiers, who turned to see what demon was approaching them. Gavin charged forward, scattering the foot soldiers. He grabbed the gauntlet of the nobleman and in one bold move pulled the man onto his own horse.

Gavin spun and galloped back across the field of battle toward a large stand of trees, full of the dense green leaves of spring. The man behind him was leaning precariously and Gavin attempted to hold him with one arm as he urged his mount faster. They must reach the tree line before the English soldiers caught them.

He crashed through some low brush into the forest. The English pursued them into the trees, but here Gavin had prepared a surprise. Arrows rained down from the treetops and the English soldiers dropped and howled. The first wave of English soldiers turned and ran into their own charge, halting their advance.

Gavin smiled, though more in relief than from success. They had turned the English for the moment and prevented them from marching farther, but they were outnumbered and everyone knew it. Without reinforcements, their small force of French soldiers and volunteer Highland warriors would eventually fall.

The man behind him could hold on no longer. Gavin jumped off his horse just in time to catch the falling nobleman. He laid the man on the ground and removed his helmet. The nobleman appeared to be middle-aged, with a well-trimmed, dark beard in the style of the day.

The man gave him a wan smile. "You have saved me, Sir Knight. Pray tell me to whom I am indebted."

"I am Sir Gavin Patrick, of the clan of MacLaren," Gavin responded in French, a tongue he had learned well over the past few years he had spent in France.

"A Scot, are you?" The man's smile grew. "Tonight, you will accept my hospitality. If I do not reward you richly, I do not deserve the name of duc de Bergerac."

❧

Lady Marie Colette, the only daughter of the duc de Bergerac, sat sedately in the ladies' solar with her ladies-in-waiting. By tradition, her four ladies, Marie Claude, Marie Jeannette, Marie Agnes, and Marie Philippe, were there to tend to her needs, but they had been her mother's ladies-in-waiting and had adopted an instructional role after her mother died. They were all old enough to be her mother or her grandmother, and had distinct opinions as to how a lady such as herself should behave.

Colette had hoped when a fifth lady had been added to her entourage, she would be more of a friend to her. Marie Suzanne was indeed young, but at twelve years of age, almost a decade her junior,

Suzanne was hardly a bosom companion. The young girl spent most of her time staring wide-eyed about the room and agreeing with anything her elders said.

All the ladies were at work on their embroidery, one of the few useful arts acceptable for ladies of court. Colette gathered a large sheet of linen about her. She had chosen to embroider a bed linen due to its bulk. Surreptitiously, she pulled a leather-bound book from her workbag, placing it behind the gathered sheet, out of sight from her ladies.

Colette quietly opened her book, careful to take a stitch now and then so as not to raise suspicion. Her ladies would be most displeased if the illicit text were discovered. They did not approve of a lady being taught to read, for everyone knew books would overcome a lady's delicate sensibilities. Colette's educated mother had embraced a more expanded view and once Colette had been taught, nothing could stop her from reading everything in her father's priceless book collection.

Pressed on by a sincere desire to read, Colette had become fluent in many languages. She read stories of glorious battles, myths from the Greeks, and of course, the Book of Hours, her prayer book, the only reading condoned by her ladies. Above all, her favorite stories were adventures of amazing courage and forbidden love.

She secretly turned the page of *La Chanson de Roland*. She had read the heroic adventure so many times she could almost recite it. She longed for her own adventure beyond the reaches of her strict nursemaids, but she had rarely traveled beyond the walls of the castle, and now that the dreaded English were causing havoc in their realm, she never left the castle at all.

She often lost herself completely in a book, but today the story of Roland dying bravely against the onslaught of foreign soldiers caused a ripple of fear to flow through her. Several weeks ago, her father had marched out with his knights to repel the English. He was late in returning. Colette did not wish to consider losing the only parent left her.

A clarion trumpet call gave the signal that the soldiers' return had been seen in the distance. Was her father among them? Colette swooped her book up with the linen sheet and stuffed them both into her workbag, hidden until next time.

"My father, he has returned," she announced, rushing to the door. "Come, let us greet him on the castle walk."

"A lady does not rush about like a common servant," chastised Marie Claude. Stalwart in stature, she was as old as the lines on her face were long. As the eldest of her ladies, Marie Claude's word was law in these chambers.

"And you must wear your headdress and your cloak, my lady," said Marie Jeannette with a scandalized gasp. Her life's work was perfecting the physical appearance of her lady, no matter what Colette's preference might be. Colette was heralded as the most beautiful lady in court, and Marie Jeannette lived on such praise.

"But I am already wearing a veil. Surely I do not need a headdress to stand upon the ramparts. It is a warm day, so a cloak, it will not be necessary," reasoned Colette.

Her ladies stopped her with their shocked expressions. "My lady!" they protested.

Colette sighed. They were right, of course. Everyone in the castle looked to Marie Colette to dress and act in a particular manner. If she should be seen running about the castle in anything less than rigid decorum, it would no doubt cause pandemonium.

"Vexing, forward child, always thinking for herself," muttered Marie Agnes, whose purpose in life was to ensure Colette never forgot her shortcomings.

"Let us pray His Grace has returned safely to us," said Marie Philippe, the only one to grasp what was truly important, at least to Colette, and thus the one who received looks of censor from the other ladies.

Colette relented, allowing them to weigh her down further. "Make haste, if you please." She submitted herself to be further dressed, though she was already warm in a formfitting blue silk kirtle and a brocade sleeveless surcoat, with rich embroidery of golden thread. To show her status, it had no less than a two-foot train, the minimum her maids would allow for everyday use. To this, her maids added a large velvet cloak, lined in ermine.

Colette tried to be patient as her maids pinned on her ornate headdress, a jeweled fillet over the silk barbet, which circled her hair. Her maids were even more chaste, wearing pristine white wimples that encased their heads and wrapped around their chins. Despite the current fashion that allowed unmarried ladies to let their hair flow loose or in two braids, her maids would not allow her hair to be seen in public.

The gown and robe alone were a load to drag around, particularly while keeping her posture rigidly straight, but the ornate golden headdress weighed enough to crush any rebellion from her spirit. It was so heavy it never ceased to give her a pounding head-ache before it was finally removed. She had to move carefully not to tip out of balance and stagger under its weight.

Finally, she was deemed acceptable to walk sedately along the corridors to the castle walls. Even if she wanted to move faster, she was forced to walk slowly, carefully picking up each foot correctly so as not to trip over her fashionable, pointy-toed shoes. It would have been easier to lift the hem of her skirts, but her maids would have been scandalized if she'd accidently revealed (heaven forbid!) an ankle to the public. Thus encumbered, it took great effort to walk down the castle corridor, her five nursemaids trailing along behind her.

Colette was being watched. She was always being watched. So she kept her face placidly calm in contrast to the gnawing worry within. Did her father return? Was he well? Despite the war with the English now threatening their small duchy, her worth was still weighed by her beauty and her comportment. She was not allowed to reveal her fears, so she concentrated on maintaining the illusion of implacable poise.

Her father had marched out with too few men in the hopes of being joined by some landless knights who fought for glory and riches. She thought little of such men who sought their fortune at the misery of others, but she hoped that her father had indeed found help, or he might not return at all.

By the time she gracefully ascended to the ramparts, the soldiers had reached the castle gates. The sun was just setting in the west, casting a warm hue over the valley before her. Colette leaned forward against the cool stones of the tower, searching each figure who entered the gates until her eyes fixed on one man. Relief washed through her. Her father was alive.

She took a deep breath of relief. The air was perfumed with the flower buds of spring. New life emerged on every branch and pushed verdant, tender shoots out of the rich, brown earth. Everywhere around her, life was returning, renewing. Along with it came the sense that her life also would be changing soon. She was not sure whether to look upon this coming change with anticipation or foreboding, but at least she could face the future with her father by her side.

"Tell the steward to prepare for the return of His Grace and our gallant knights," she instructed a page, careful to keep all trace of emotion from her voice. To express relief would be to admit concern in the first place, and that would be unacceptable.

Though she wished to have more time breathing in the fresh air of the tower, she turned away from the glowing sun and walked serenely, with no apparent concern or haste, back down the stone stairs to her father's private solar. She arrived at the solar just as her father's squire was assisting him into the room. Her father reclined gingerly into a chair, pale but with no visible injuries.

Colette wished to run to her father to assist but was mindful of making him appear weak. "Bring wine, if you please, to refresh His Grace after his ordeal," she instructed the squire and then turned to her ladies who were still at her heels. "Thank you, ladies. I will return to you in the solar."

Her ladies gave a low bow to their master and quit the room. They would leave her alone with no man save her own father.

"Are you well?" Colette rushed to her father's side as soon as they were alone.

Her father raised a hand in a weak attempt to fend her off. "I am well, quite well. Took a bit of a blow, but I will recover, I assure you."

Riding off to battle was a young man's game, but Colette bit her lip before she insulted her father by suggesting his youth was behind him. "You are returned to me and I am glad for it." She knelt by his side. She wished to lay her cheek on his hand the way she used to do when she had been small, but she feared her heavy headdress would topple over if she tried.

"And I am so very glad to see you." He gave her a weary smile and sighed deeply. "Though it is not my fortune to keep you by my side. I have been pondering a problem most difficult and today a solution has presented itself. It is time for you to know. I have chosen for you a husband."

Colette stared at her father and slowly rose to her feet. After turning down scores of proposals and allowing Colette to reach one and twenty, well past the age at which most ladies were wed, her father had finally accepted a suitor. But who?

"A husband?" Colette prided herself on remaining composed at all times, but even she could not help the surprise in her tone.

"Yes. You will have the honor of serving the duchy," said her father, avoiding her eye. Something was wrong.

Colette waited for her father to elaborate, but he remained tight-lipped. At length, she could bear the silence no longer. "Will you not tell me which of my suitors you have chosen?"

Colette was much admired in court and her hand had long been sought in marriage. As her father's only child, she stood to inherit a fortune. The duchy, of course, would go to her male cousin, but her dowry was substantial. Yet for her father to choose one suitor would mean making enemies of the others at a time when he could least afford it, so she had remained unwed during their current time of tumult.

"The duchy, it is in grave danger of being captured by the English. We must have more men, strong warriors, if we are to have any hope to turn the tide," her father explained.

"I understand, my father." Her stomach tightened. She hoped his choice was not a certain marquis she had recently met. The man had already buried two wives and drooled slightly when he stared at her.

"We all must do our part." Her father finally turned to her with sad eyes.

"But of course." She was resigned. She would wed the drooling man.

He took her hand and held it tight. "Faith child, but I would not do this if there were any other way."

"Who is the man?" Colette whispered, fear hushing her voice.

"He is a knight from Scotland—"

"Scotland?" Colette could not keep from crying out. "That barbaric country?"

He squeezed her hand, his eyes pleading. "At least I will know you are safe, far from war. You would not deny your father that comfort, would you?"

Her cousin entered the solar, no doubt interested to see if he was closer to inheriting the duchy. Her father dropped her hand. The conversation was over. Colette curtsied and quit the room, still shaking from the sudden news.

Her father wished to keep her safe, but she would not flee before their enemies. No, it was time to be brave.

She, marry a barbaric Highlander?

No.

Never.

Two

IT HAD BEEN A LONG DAY. GAVIN SENT THE DUKE BACK to safety with his men and continued to help others escape the English horde. Though the English had been turned and their advance halted, it had not been without cost. Many French troops lay where they fell, never to rise again. As the grim task began of picking through the bloody aftermath to claim their dead, Gavin bent his head to pray for the departed in battle.

Gavin's reasons for traveling to France from Scotland to fight against the English were a tangled web of desires and obligations. His personal quest had been unsuccessful, though he'd known he had little chance of success from the start. Perhaps it was time to travel home to the Highlands and set his eyes on his mother again.

Though his adventure had not brought the riches that were the dream of every young man, he had been knighted on the field of battle and was still in possession of his arms and legs. He shook his head, surveying the carnage before him. He could still draw breath, and that was fortune enough.

Sir Gavin rode toward the castle of the duc de Bergerac, nestled comfortably in a bright green valley. The castle boasted four towers and was painted a gleaming white with golden trim. It was an enchanting sight, awash in the warm light of the setting sun.

Gavin was greeted at the gates and shown into an elegant chamber to wash and prepare himself for the feast, already well under way. Faint strains of music floated through the castle corridors. Gavin was squired by one of the pages, who assisted him out of his armor and brought him a borrowed but fine surcoat of the bluest silk. It did not quite fit Gavin's broad shoulders, but the page shrugged and said it was the biggest he could find. Gavin struggled into it. He sometimes felt a bit of a giant, being taller and broader than most men he met in France.

Thus civilized, Gavin was led into the great hall. He had thought himself immune to the wealth and opulence displayed by the French nobles, but this hall was beyond any he had yet seen. Painted in bright colors, accented in gold leaf, the walls were ablaze with grand scenes of glorious battles. Tapestries hung from the walls, awash in bright gold thread, such that they shimmered in the candlelight. The hall was filled with tables of elegantly attired courtiers, who were only diminished by the nobility's resplendent display at the high table. Never had Gavin been presented with such an array of rich fabrics, rich food, and rich people. All were feasting and making merry.

Gavin had been pondering the meaning of Bergerac's words regarding a generous reward. He would have settled for a balance in coin instead of the lavish spread before him. Gavin surveyed the scene with mild disapproval. The countryside of France was being ravaged, the common people suffering, yet the nobles continued to feast. If the amount of coin spent on daily excess was put into the war effort, France might not have been losing so badly. If half of those finely dressed lords would trade their robes and ridiculously pointed shoes for a sword and harness, maybe the outcome would be different.

He drew closer to the high table and a lady caught his eye. In truth, he stopped walking and gaped at her like some green lad. She was simply the loveliest lady he had ever seen. She was draped in finery like all around her, but she needed none. Her beauty shone without need of adornment. Her skin was smooth and flawless, her eyes the stunning green of a new leaf. Her lips were full and rosy. She was richly adorned in gold and silk, with an elaborate headdress, yet it was her bright eyes that captured his attention.

She turned her head slightly and caught his openmouthed stare. She raised a thin, dark eyebrow, looking down her perfectly proportioned nose at him. He flushed at being caught gaping and forced his feet to continue moving forward. He cursed under his breath for making a fool of himself before such a beauty.

Bergerac noted Gavin's arrival into the hall and graced him with a smile. He stood, goblet in hand, and all the courtiers stood with him, silencing their conversations in honor of the duke. "Come, *mes amis*, let us drink to the health of the honorable knight who saved me from falling into the hands of our enemy.

He has come from the wilds of Scotland to help us to remain free from English tyranny."

The young lady's face revealed a moment of surprise or alarm, her eyes opening wide, but she quickly achieved a look of utter implacability once again. The crowd raised their glasses and drank deeply of fine wine. The young lady held out her glass and drank but did not raise it to him as the others had. Her face remained impassive, utterly unimpressed by his feats of heroism. Gavin had never considered himself a vain man, seeking the good opinion of others, but he was disappointed he had not been able to impress the beauty before him.

He was led in honor by a page to the high table, to sit beside the duke. A rich noble was asked to move aside and gave Gavin a look of sheer vitriol, but Gavin took it in stride. The only disappointment to his placement at the table was that the lovely lady was seated on the other side of Bergerac, making conversation with her impossible, though the coldness in her eyes had in no way invited his attentions. It would be best to forget such a creature, but he would have enjoyed the view, gazing at her during the feast. Such a thing of beauty must be enjoyed.

The feast went on for hours, long past the hour when Gavin's sore muscles would have enjoyed some rest. He wondered at Bergerac's endurance, though by the amounts of wine he consumed, his vigor was definitely enhanced by the numbing effects of his chosen libation.

Eventually, the celebration waned and the duke ushered him aside to a richly appointed chamber, even finer than the great hall, if such a thing could be believed. The furniture was ornately carved and gilded with gold leaf. Everywhere Gavin looked, he was dazzled.

"Sir Gavin, you are a true knight, brave and sure," Bergerac declared. Though Gavin was fluent in French, the duke spoke to him in English, a tribute of respect. "Your bold action saved my life on the field of battle. You must allow me to bestow upon you a boon to show my gratitude, though I know that nothing I can ever do will repay you. I shall forever be in your debt."

Gavin bowed and came up smiling. Now he was getting to the important part of the evening. "Yer graciousness to this humble knight is more than enough thanks." Though if the duke was prepared to offer him something golden in return for saving his life, Gavin would be most pleased. He swept his gaze from the golden candelabra to the golden chalice on the table. Either would do. Both would be better.

"As a true knight, you would never accept a monetary offering and I would never impinge upon your honor by making such a gauche offer," continued the duke.

Gavin's smile tightened. *Go on, insult me wi' yer riches.*

"To demonstrate the full measure of my appreciation, I present to you my daughter and only child, Lady Marie Colette."

On perfect cue, the beautiful lady from the feast entered the room. Lady Marie Colette possessed the most shocking beauty the world had ever known. Gavin's mouth went dry as he glanced from his host to his daughter—the renowned beauty Marie Colette. The rumors of her pleasing appearance did not disappoint. She was exquisite. Her bright green eyes captured him, a stark contrast to her pale skin and rose-petal lips. Her high cheekbones and delicately carved features were a delight to behold. Her figure, complemented by the blue silk gown of the finest quality, was a study in perfection of the female form. The gown itself was richly adorned with a brocade surcoat with so much gold thread embroidery it must have weighed at least two stone. He could not tell the color of her hair, for the golden headdress covered it entirely, yet still revealed a fashionably high forehead.

Gavin had no particular interest in marriage, but one look at Marie Colette and all objections to the marital state vanished. The lady inclined her head and Gavin swept her a bow, hoping to impress.

"My daughter, she is lovely, no?"

"Aye, Yer Grace, quite lovely," answered Gavin, his eyes only for Marie Colette. His smile was not returned and instead something akin to panic shone in her eyes, though the rest of her face betrayed no emotion.

"Can I call upon your honor as a knight to protect my daughter no matter the cost?" asked Bergerac.

"I would protect her wi' my verra life," answered Gavin. For such a prize, he would do anything; surely any man who could draw breath would do the same.

"Excellent! You will guide her to the Highlands, yes?"

The Highlands. Home. Bergerac wished Gavin to wed his daughter and take her to Scotland? Gavin was surprised, but the duke must wish his daughter to be safe, away from the war that ravaged the land. He did not have to consider his answer.

"Aye," said Gavin. "I will do as ye wish."

"You, sir, are indeed the very model of a true knight." Bergerac nodded in approval. "I will bring the necessary documents to you." The duke left the chamber with a wide smile.

Gavin was left alone with the lady he would marry. She was like a perfect statue, beautiful and poised. Yet as soon as her father left the room, the veneer of detachment fell and her eyes narrowed in shrewd intelligence. She approached fast and spoke low.

"How much for you not to marry me?" Her voice was lower than Gavin expected, sultry and rippling with promise. And yet…what did she mean, *not* to marry her?

He must have paused too long in his reply for she repeated herself, this time in English though with a seductive French accent. "How much coin for you to wed me not?"

Gavin was surprised she could speak in his tongue. He was even more surprised at her request. This Lady Marie Colette was no statue to be admired from afar. This Lady Marie Colette was fierce and bold, and all the more beautiful. He took a step back. "I…I beg yer pardon?"

"You have had dealings with my father; now you will have dealings with me. He has offered you much, no? I have in my power the ability to make you a very rich man. I ask you again, how much to *not* marry me?"

Three

COLETTE HAD ONE CHANCE. SHE NEEDED TO SECURE the Highlander's agreement to decline marrying her, and she needed to do it quickly, before her father returned. She had never before defied her father, but if he thought he could protect her by sending her far away, to Scotland of all places, he was much confused. She would stand by her father and her people, no matter how many English soldiers were at the door.

"Ye dinna wish to marry me?" Sir Gavin seemed confused regarding the basic facts.

"No, I do not," said Colette in a deliberate tone, speaking her best English so he could comprehend. She hoped he was not entirely feebleminded.

In truth, he was a fine specimen of a man. She was fair enough to admit it. He was a young man and built on a large scale, towering over most men. He had broad shoulders and a muscular chest, well-defined beneath the formfitting surcoat. His dark brown hair hung down to his square jaw and had a bit of a thick wave to it. He was clean shaven, a surprise considering he was a barbaric Highlander.

"I have heard rumors o' yer beauty, but they were untrue. Ye're more lovely than anything I heard described." He spoke in a rich tone with a lyrical accent, pleasing to her ears.

She almost wished he would speak more so she could listen to his voice. However, if he thought he could win her over with compliments, he was much mistaken. She had been told so often she was beautiful that the words no longer had meaning. Moreover, she found the people who flattered her often wanted something from her. Some wanted money, others her favor, and others, men primarily, wanted to possess her, as if she were nothing more than an attractive object to decorate their surroundings and warm their beds.

"Please understand. It is impossible for me to marry you. But if you make an arrangement with me now, you will not leave empty-handed. Name your weight in gold to walk away." Her heard pounded to make such a blunt offer. Her maids, had they been present, would have collapsed of apoplexy to hear her, but Colette was determined. She would not leave her home. She knew these foreign fighters were primarily interested in fortune, so she offered him riches to get him out of the way as quick as may be.

Gavin's eyebrows rose, and she feared she had offended him. In truth, she would never have made such a crass offer to a French knight, whose honor would have been greatly impinged, but Sir Gavin was a foreigner. A Highlander. Were they not only here to make a profit off others' sad circumstances?

"Forgive me if I have offended ye, m'lady." Sir

Gavin bowed as well as any courtier. "As to yer offer, ye may keep yer riches. Yer wealth is o' no interest to me."

Colette was confused. Why did he refuse? Did he doubt her ability to provide him with ample fortune? She glanced at the door, worried her father would return soon. She was running out of time. "Sir Knight, mayhap you are not aware that my mother, she was very wealthy before she married my father. Her riches are now my own to do with as I like. If you make an agreement with me now, I can make you quite comfortable."

He shrugged and walked to the window of leaded glass, looking out onto manicured gardens illuminated in the moonlight. "Ye shame me into confessing I had come today for some hope o' reward. It does no' make me a worthy knight, I fear. But even wi'out much honor, I still will no' take the fortune of a lady, nor would I force anyone to marry me." He spoke in a careless manner, as if all she had offered him was as nothing to him.

Colette released a breath she had not realized she was holding. Had he just agreed not to marry her? Would he simply walk away? "So you will tell my father you will not marry me?"

Gavin turned to her, a smile playing about his lips, which gave Colette the distinct impression he was not taking the situation as seriously as she thought it deserved. "I am yers to command. If ye wish me to leave, I will go."

Relief washed over her. She would not be banished to the wilds of Scotland with some strange, albeit attractive, man. "Thank you, Sir Knight. My father, he wished to protect me by sending me far, but I cannot see myself in such a wild, foreign place. We would be most unequally yoked."

Gavin leaned a shoulder against the stone wall and stared out the dark window into the night. "The Highlands are a rugged place compared to here, and my home is no' nearly as grand. 'Tis, in truth, no more than a farmhouse. The green valley around it is good for planting, wi' dark, rich earth that feels good in a man's hands. Above are the high peaks o' the Braes o' Balquhidder. Carved into the very rock itself is Creag an Tuirc, the tower house o' Laird MacLaren, my uncle. 'Tis a wild place, but in the evening, when the sun's rays touch the high peaks, setting them aglow with the fiery light, 'tis so beautiful it robs yer breath. No finely decorated hall or richly appointed chamber could ever compare."

Colette opened her mouth but no words came. Who was this man?

He turned back to her, appraising her finery with a critical eye. "Someday, God willing, I shall take my bride there, a bride who chooses me above all men. We will no' be surrounded by courtiers or pageantry or fancy clothes or ridiculous pointed shoes."

Colette swallowed, heat creeping up the back of her neck. Had he seen the points of her shoes?

He stepped close to her, moving with a fluid grace that made her heart beat faster. "In the Highlands we dinna have all yer comforts, but what we do have we hold fast and fiercely defend."

He was so tall, she had to tilt back her head to

see him, putting her headdress dangerously out of alignment. "What do you have?" she asked in a voice barely above a whisper.

"Freedom. We have freedom. No one to order ye about. No one to say what ye can or canna do. Ye can wear what ye wish, eat what ye wish. Ye can ride a horse as long and as fast as ye wish. In the Highlands, m'lady, ye would be free."

Free? She stared up at him. He dangled before her the one thing all her riches could never buy. He offered her freedom.

He leaned nearer and her eyes fell to his lips, which inexplicably appeared soft. She could not help but to lean closer toward the irresistible pull of his inviting lips. He also moved closer, bending down slowly so that their lips drew dangerously close. She breathed in the scent of him, an intoxicating mix of wood smoke, fine wine, and pure man.

"Here, I have brought the parchment for you to seal our accord." Her father strode back in the room, fortunately distracted with his scrolls as both Colette and Gavin jumped away from each other.

The duc de Bergerac spread a scroll out on a table to show them. Colette frowned. It was a marriage contract for her, but Gavin's name could not be found.

"This is the accord I have made with Kenneth Mackenzie, Baron of Kintail," said her father.

"I beg your pardon, but…" Colette swallowed, trying to gather together her swirling thoughts in order to form speech. "You made an accord with whom?"

"The Baron of Kintail. Sir Gavin, are you acquainted with him?"

"I...I ken him by reputation," said Gavin. The careless smile was gone, replaced by a thin line. He glanced at Marie Colette, one eyebrow raised. They had both made the wrong assumption. He wasn't meant for Colette at all.

"We have come to an understanding in the marriage arrangements," continued her father, directing his comments to Sir Gavin. "The accord has been several months in the making, but it is now settled. He will send troops, for you are well aware of how we are most desperate for reinforcements. In exchange, I have offered my daughter's hand in marriage along with her dowry."

"Father, may I beg a private audience?" asked Colette quickly. She needed to talk to him, to try to undo whatever arrangement he might have made. She could not be banished to a frozen wasteland of the north. She would not leave her people in their time of need. Surely there must be some other way.

Her father refused to look at her and focused his attention on the scroll. "The warriors have already been sent. They are on their way."

Marie Colette closed her eyes for a moment and took a deep breath. There was no way out of this accord. She was trapped. "I understand."

"I hope I have done right by you." Her father shifted his gaze to her, his eyes pleading as if for forgiveness. "I...I needed to protect our people and see you safe."

Colette squared her shoulders, pausing for a moment to ensure her voice would not betray her emotions. She needed to fall back on her training. She needed to say the right things without burdening the two men before her with her sudden desire to burst into tears. "You have done what you thought was right, and so your actions are just. I am pleased my life may be lived in service to my people."

Her father turned to Gavin. "There has been only one problem with this plan. Who would protect my daughter as she traveled to Scotland? When you saved my life with such great bravery, I knew you to be the most courageous of all the knights. Since you have proven your worth, and since you know your way to the Scottish Highlands, I have decided to give you the inexpressible boon of serving as my daughter's guide and guard on this arduous journey. Thank you, Sir Knight, for agreeing to take my precious daughter to the land of your birth, to Scotland and her betrothed."

There was no way for him to refuse. "Aye, Yer Grace. I will see her safe."

Colette suspected her father had intentionally misled him to garner his agreement to the plan. Gavin's tight lips and false smile told her everything she wanted to know. He did not wish to escort her anywhere.

They were both going on an unwanted journey.

Four

COLETTE WAS STILL SHAKING WHEN SHE REACHED HER private chambers. The unfortunate tidings of her betrothal were soon related to her ladies-in-waiting, and the news spread throughout the castle like the pox, afflicting the courtiers before they reached their beds.

The unexpected news was not well received by her ladies. They all became distraught and several wept openly, for as her ladies, they would be required to journey with her. Her banishment was their own.

Colette wished nothing more than to join their loud lament, but she held her anguish tight inside. *You are the brightest ornament of court. You must always act in a manner becoming your station or you will be a discredit to your father,* her mother's instruction rang in her head. The teachings of her mother were all Colette had left of her, so she clung to them with an adamantine will. Besides, she was not expected to have any thoughts of her own, save how she could serve first her father and then her husband. She was not allowed to betray dismay at her father's plan for her life.

Colette held still while her ladies pulled and tugged,

extricating her from the punitive headdress. It always gave her a headache, but tonight her head pounded in pain. Marie Jeannette was not attending her work, most likely too distracted by her own distress. Tears sprung to Colette's eyes when the headdress was pulled off before all the pins had been removed, taking with it several strands of her hair. Colette knew better than to complain. Jeannette and Agnes had wished to shave off her hair entirely in preference to wigs, which they argued were easier to manage. Colette firmly refused.

With the help of her ladies, Colette was finally set free from her tight kirtle, and she took a deep breath for the first time in hours. Though they continued to perform their office, none of her ladies met her eye, so focused were they on their own distress.

"She must have done something wrong to be banished," muttered Agnes in a tone Colette was supposed to pretend she did not hear.

Colette sighed. Her mind was in turmoil, trying to devise a plan that would provide the warriors her father needed to protect their people but would not require her to leave her homeland. Her head spun from the effort.

After their initial shock, her maids attempted to regain their composure. Little Marie Suzanne, however, could not stop the tears from running down her cheeks. As soon as she brushed them away, more fell. Colette's heart went out to the young girl.

"Suzanne," Colette called her forward. "I wonder if you would do me a great favor."

Suzanne blinked away the tears. "As you wish, my lady."

"My falcon, Algon—I fear he would not fare well

on our journey." Colette, as with many ladies in court, had a prized hunting falcon who was quite dear to her. "Would you be so good as to leave my service and return to your excellent parents with Algon so I will be at peace, knowing he is in good care?"

The young girl's eyes widened and more tears spilled, though this time a smile broke on her face. "Yes, oh yes, my lady. It would be my honor."

"It is decided then." Colette gave her a nod in return. She could do nothing to save herself from her fate, but at least she could spare the youngest lady in her care.

"It is time for prayers, my lady," said a stern Marie Claude. Colette's other ladies were thin lipped and solemn. They knew there would be no reprieve for them.

Colette opened her small Book of Hours, the prayer book that had been her mother's. It was finely decorated with the Bergerac heraldic crest on the leather cover and had a nice illustration of Saint Francis of Assisi on the first page. She turned to compline and led her maids in prayers. With all the emotions of the day, she could barely focus on the words.

"Good night, my lady," Marie Claude said in chilling accents, assisting her into the tall bed, big enough for an entire family. The ladies closed the thick velvet curtains against the cool night air and set out their pallets around the bed. Colette was surrounded by her ladies yet quite alone. She could hear them talking amongst themselves, lamenting their fate. Colette wished to join them, but she knew it was not allowed.

Colette fought against tears. Tears marred the face and her appearance must always be flawless. She had learned to cry on the inside, where no one could see.

She calmed herself with the thought that though she was being banished, sold in marriage to some barbarian in the frozen north, she would not leave without her comforts. She still held great fortune in her own right, in addition to her dowry. Her mother's fortune in jewels, clothes, furnishings, art, tapestries, horses, and all the rest would be coming with her. She may be banished from home, but she would take as much of home with her as she could. It was her only comfort in the entire sad affair.

She wondered what her new life would bring. As her mind drifted, her thoughts returned to Sir Gavin, the large Highlander she would not marry. Other men had fawned over her and flattered her, but he was the first one to offer her something she truly wanted—her freedom.

It was the one thing she would never have.

⤞⤝

Gavin rode down the dusty road in the early morning light, returning to the castle of the duc de Bergerac. He had scouted the road ahead, finding the safest route. The original plan was to leave at the end of the month and travel during summer, when the seas would be at their most calm. The English, however, were busy making mischief, taking coastal towns and causing Bergerac to hasten their departure, before it was too late to escape.

The last thing anyone wanted was to have the substantial dowry of Lady Marie Colette carried away by the English. They would no doubt take Marie Colette too—and kill Gavin to do it.

It had not taken long for Gavin to set his affairs in order. As an itinerant knight, he had little to do but arrange for his squire. Gavin also sent a missive back home to let his mother know that he would be returning. At least one person would be pleased with the turn of events. Two, actually.

His stepfather, Sir Chaumont, was a French knight. Years ago, Gavin's uncle, Laird MacLaren, had joined forces with the French to fight against the English in the seemingly endless war. Sir Chaumont and MacLaren had forged a friendship and Chaumont had traveled with him to Scotland. After meeting Gavin's mother, Mary, Chaumont had decided to stay.

Three years ago, Gavin and Chaumont had been sent to France on an important errand for the church. Once completed, Gavin had decided to stay and make his fortune.

Chaumont had made weak attempts to dissuade him, mostly on behalf of Gavin's mother. Yet Gavin could tell Chaumont was proud of him and did not push too hard. Chaumont understood what his mother did not—that a man, especially a young man, needed to be tested and tried in order to become a man he could live with for the rest of his life.

The past three years had done just that. He had arrived in France at the tender age of nineteen. He was now twenty-two and had grown considerably, in height and strength, but also in worldly knowledge. Most of all, he had learned the pointlessness of war, especially this conflict between England and France, which stretched beyond the generations.

His only regret in leaving was that his own quest

had been unfulfilled. He had searched and searched, but what he sought could not be found. He slowed his mount to a walk, taking a moment to appreciate the colorful fields of the countryside. From his tunic, he pulled a simple gold band he wore on a chain around his neck.

"I'm sorry I failed ye," he whispered and kissed the band. He kicked his horse into a cantor and proceeded down the road. His quest was left undone, but it was time to leave. It was time to return home.

Gavin returned to the castle to find it in utter uproar. He had hoped to travel quickly to the appointed rendezvous near Bordeaux, along the Garonne River. He had a vague understanding that French nobility would not travel light, but he was shocked at the crates and trunks lined up in the courtyard, stretching around the corner of the wall, out of sight. Stacked next to these were what looked to be the furnishing for an entire castle: tables, chairs, even a massive bed was carried out into the courtyard and prepared for travel.

Gavin shook his head in disbelief. Courtiers, servants, and guards ran about carrying items this way and that. Candlesticks, gold plates, silver challises, even armloads of glass goblets were being wrapped in linen and packed in straw. Did Bergerac intend to send his daughter with a flotilla to carry all her worldly goods?

He looked around to discuss the matter with the duke, but he was notably absent. Instead, Lady Marie Colette was standing like a queen on a raised platform, overseeing the massive production with a critical eye. She gave no direct commands but spoke quietly to one of her ladies-in-waiting who ran around conveying her wishes to her servants. Gavin strode up to her, finding he needed to look up at her on the platform.

"Ye canna take all this lot to Scotland." He spoke to her directly.

One of Marie Colette's ladies gasped and put her hand over her mouth.

Undeterred, Gavin continued. "There is no way to travel wi' all this wi'out arousing the notice of our English friends. We need to travel quick and light to get ye safely to Laird Mackenzie. Ye canna bring it all wi' ye."

Marie Colette's bright green eyes flashed. She had heard him at least. She did not speak to him however and instead whispered to the maid beside her.

"My mistress wishes to convey her thanks for your concern," said the elderly lady-in-waiting with clear disdain in her tone. "But this is her dowry and her inheritance. It must come."

Gavin did not attempt to hide his displeasure. Who was this lady who thought herself so beyond her company that she would not even speak to him? She had spoken directly enough when she was trying to persuade him not to marry her. At least he had escaped having to marry this arrogant heiress.

Gavin ignored the maid and directed his comments to Marie Colette. "I ken this is yer dowry. But there be no way to haul it all to Kintail. I assure ye, Scotland may be far, but we do have beds."

Marie Colette looked down her thin nose at him, raising one long eyebrow. "Tell the master of the guards to be sure to pack his saddles." She spoke to one of her maids but in a voice loud enough for Gavin to hear. She turned her back on him.

Gavin was not known for being short-tempered. He generally approached life with good nature and patience, but even he had his limits. He clenched his teeth to avoid telling the lady exactly what he thought of her. Instead, he spun on his heel and searched out her father. Only the duke could put an end to this madness.

He found Bergerac in his chambers with a bottle of wine in one hand and several empties around him. "About yer daughter," began Gavin.

"She is so beautiful. So very beautiful." Clearly the man was experiencing the full effect of his drink.

"Aye, a bonnie lass. But I need to speak to ye about the amount o' baggage—"

"Her mother, she was a beauty, no? So beautiful."

"Yes, quite." Gavin glared at the duke. "But we need to discuss the travel arrangements. We need to move quickly to avoid detection. We canna be safe wi' so many wagons o' goods."

"So lovely—"

"Bergerac!" Gavin was losing patience. "She is packing too much stuff!"

The duke turned to him as if seeing him for the first time. He nodded slowly and took another long drink. "Too much. She will not be able to get it all through. You are right."

"So tell her to stop packing."

He shook his head. "That I cannot do. The accord was made for the dowry to be delivered, and as for the rest, it is her due."

"Even if we could get it all to the ship, I doubt it would fit in the hold. It will be left on the shore."

"Leave it." The duke raised a glass. "To your health."

Gavin stormed out of the great hall to the small bedchamber he'd used during his stay at the castle. He was not sure who he was angrier with—Marie Colette for trying to take the castle with her, or her father who indulged her and thus allowed her to meet with disappointment, as long as he did not have to be the one to bear the bad news.

In contrast to his French friends, all Gavin brought with him could be carried on his horse. He grabbed his few belongings, which could be easily stuffed into his saddlebag but stopped, considering his options. With determination, he stripped out of his tunic, doublet, hose, and breeches, until he was standing in nothing but his linen shirt. He pulled out his large plaid. If he was going home, it was time to become the Highlander he was.

Five

As Gavin predicted, it took a long time to get everything loaded into carts and wagons, and the plan of an early start was long gone by the time the caravan was finally assembled. Gavin kept out of the way, resigned to let the travesty play itself out.

Finally, the entire population of the castle, and possibly the duchy, assembled to bid farewell to Lady Marie Colette and her entourage. Gavin stood at the back of the crowd, simply observing the spectacle. Marie Colette emerged, wearing a plush fur robe clasped at the shoulder. It might have been appropriate for winter, but other than being an impressive piece, it had little functionality on such a warm day.

She approached her father and curtsied low to him. In a formal show of fatherly affection, he nodded his head and offered his hand to help her up. She rose with a fluidity Gavin would not have thought possible while wearing such a heavy cloak.

"My daughter, my heart, our salvation—it rests in your beautiful hands," cried the duc de Bergerac. "We thank you for the sacrifice you make for us, to leave home and hearth and travel to the far reaches of the known world to the land of the Scots."

People wept as if she was being banished to a barren wasteland. Gavin wanted to defend his homeland, but he held his tongue. This would most likely be the last time the duke would see his only daughter. They could have their moment.

"May you brighten your new homeland with your gifts and your beauty, though we know you will pine for us for your lifetime, as we will carry the sorrow of your loss forever." Bergerac cast Marie Colette in the light of a martyr.

"I will grieve the loss of my people all my days." Marie Colette spoke in a husky voice. If it were not for the perfectly placid face, Gavin might have suspected some deep emotion on her part.

Bergerac now presented his daughter with his farewell gift. "I give you these common implements and instruct you to humble yourself before your husband and cook him his first meal yourself, alone." He gave her a black iron ladle, a long-handled slotted spoon, and a long iron spit.

Gavin was more than a little surprised at his instructions and the gift. He would have expected the parting gift to be something more sparkly and less utilitarian. Marie Colette also appeared a bit surprised by the gift, her eyebrows raising. She accepted the iron utensils and Gavin saw her stagger under the weight of the three implements. She clearly needed to do some cooking to build her strength.

"Promise you will do this for me, my daughter," said Bergerac, his voice demanding.

A tiny frown of confusion flashed across her face then disappeared. "I swear to you, my father, it will be done." She handed the items over to be packed with the rest.

Gavin sighed audibly. More things to carry.

"And now with Sir Gavin to guide and protect you, I wish you a journey most blessed, my precious daughter." Bergerac kissed first one then the other of Marie Colette's cheeks.

Gavin decided it was time for his part in the human drama and stepped forward to lead the charge—or rather the slow amble out of the castle gates. With great ceremony, cheering and sobbing courtiers, horns blaring, and drums pounding, Marie Colette strode majestically across the courtyard on the arm of her father.

She caught sight of Gavin and her eyes flashed. He walked up to her as she approached the waiting horses. The duke stepped forward and offered Gavin his daughter, the symbolic gesture that now Marie Colette was Gavin's responsibility.

"Lady Marie Colette, my precious daughter, I now leave in your care, trusting you will do all that is right to protect her safety." Bergerac nodded to him and Gavin bowed in return and accepted the hand of Marie Colette on his arm.

Bergerac left them to make a show of inspecting the preparations, leaving Gavin and Colette to make their way through the cheering crowd to the horses.

"What are you wearing, Sir Knight?" Marie Colette hissed at him.

"My plaid. 'Tis the common dress o' the Highlander and practical for travel," returned Gavin, ridiculously pleased at having goaded her into speaking with him directly.

"No, no, no, it is appropriate for nothing. I can see your legs for you forgot to wear your hose!" She did an admirable job of speaking out of the corner of her mouth without appearing to be conversing. No one who watched them would know she was speaking to him.

He leaned closer and said in a conspiratorial tone, "Highlanders wear no hose, m'lady."

He should not have, but he took enjoyment at the way her jaw dropped open. She was so tightly controlled; it took a lot to break through the cool mask she wore. The fact that his naked legs could crack her composure made him happier than it ought. Why should he care what she thought?

Marie Colette was led to a mounting block and easily stepped up to take her seat on a large, ornately decorated saddle atop an ornately decorated beast Gavin supposed at one time had been a horse. He was a little surprised that she rode astride, though only a keen eye would have caught it, for her lower extremities were quickly covered by her sumptuous gown and her luxurious, long fur cloak. He would have been concerned she would overheat in such a warm cloak, but she was much too cold for concern.

Gavin glared at the long line of wagons, carrying enough belongings to outfit a small town. Lady Marie Colette could not leave her home without an entourage of four ladies, twenty soldiers, and a veritable army of stable hands to lead a long line of wagons. Gavin turned around, refusing to count. He didn't want to know. Instead of consolidating her efforts,

Gavin was convinced she had added more things to her list. If she left a single piece of crockery behind, he would have been very much surprised.

Her grim-faced maids sat sidesaddle on smaller (naturally) horses being led by grooms. The ladies wept openly and waved their handkerchiefs to their families, who were crying at their departure. It was a touching moment. Yet Marie Colette remained unmoved. No tear of feeling rolled down her cheek. If he had not known firsthand that she did not wish to leave the castle, her serene face would have revealed nothing. She was a cold one, this Lady Marie Colette.

They walked out of the castle gates at a painstakingly slow pace. At this rate, the sun would be high before they even left the castle. Considering all they carried, in such an obvious manner, Gavin worried they would soon become a target for thieves. Surely it would not take long before such a bounty of wealth was recognized and attacked. And at their current pace, they should be prepared to hand it over.

"We need to mount up everyone. We need to ride and cover ground," Gavin demanded to the captain of the guard.

Captain Perrine slowly shook his head. He held himself with rigid posture, the perfect picture of an experienced soldier with a pointed, black goatee. "I take my orders from Lady Marie Colette."

Gavin sighed. It was time to have another discussion with m'lady. He rode back to the middle of the long line, to speak to Marie Colette. She was perched like royalty high on her massive horse, surrounded by her ladies. Despite his growing irritation with her, he could not help but recognize her beauty. His job would have been easier if she were not quite so attractive.

"We need to move faster," he demanded, pushing such traitorous thoughts aside. "We are at risk for attack parading this much wealth throughout the countryside."

"Not everyone has mounts," she condescended to respond. "We cannot move any faster."

"Those who walk now could ride in the wagons," suggested Gavin.

"It would be unseemly for the guards to be carried in a wagon like common goods," exclaimed Marie Colette.

She was right, of course. He would prefer to walk then sit in a wagon, but he couldn't shake the feeling they were putting themselves in danger by slowly meandering through the countryside with such an obvious display of wealth.

"Understand this." Gavin stared deep into her smoldering green eyes. "I have agreed to protect ye and see ye safe to yer affianced husband. I hav'na agreed to protect the entire contents o' Bergerac Castle ye packed wi' ye."

"Thank you for making your opinion so clear. I shall not look to you for help if a time of crisis arises." She turned her head away, dismissing him.

Gavin clenched his teeth to prevent anything he was thinking from emerging from his lips, and kicked his mount to ride away. He was once a mild-mannered lad. What had happened to him? French aristocracy, that was what happened. Now he understood why his uncle MacLaren returned from France with such a sour disposition.

Gavin could not wait for this journey to be over.

Six

COLETTE WAS HAVING A DREADFUL DAY. FIRST, SHE had to say good-bye to her father, to everything she had ever known, in the public courtyard with hundreds of witnesses. Second, she had to do so without betraying any emotion of her dreadful loss. Propriety dictated that she must avoid any public display of emotion. She needed to maintain appearances, to remain calm and strong, though inside she was crumbling apart.

They ambled slowly down the dirt road, giving rise to her concerns over the large number of wagons required to haul her dowry. How was she going to take all these things with her? Her father had pledged much to the Baron of Kintail, and she must take her own inheritance. It was her only source of security in a strange land. Besides, to leave behind her mother's things was unthinkable. But how would she transport all these goods to the wilds of Scotland?

She should have known better than to expect her Highland guide to help her. Instead of providing any assistance, Sir Gavin only pointed out the obvious, telling her that they were too heavily laden and that they would most likely become the targets for thieves and robbers, not to mention the English.

What was worse, he spoke to her directly. Did he not know that she was not allowed to speak directly to men in public unless chaperoned by her father? It was considered most unseemly. He seemed to have a complete disregard for protocol! Instead, he demanded and challenged, upsetting her maids even more than they already were by placing unneeded worry in their minds. She prided herself on being in control in any situation, but he stomped through her neatly arranged plans, leaving disaster in his wake. If she did not require his services as guide, she would have dismissed him from the party.

The sun climbed high in the sky as they plodded along the dusty dirt road. Colette longed to take off the warm fur cloak but could not do so without offending Marie Philippe, whose family had given her the cloak. So she held her head high and ignored the sweat running down her back and the dust in her face. Ladies did not cough or sweat.

Sir Gavin rode by, followed by the titters of her maids. She was shocked by his half-dressed appearance. Was he trying to insult her by wearing so little? Could the men in his homeland truly walk about without proper clothing? Would her own future husband be so indecently attired? The thought gripped her with fear. No, it could not possibly be true.

Gavin galloped up the road and then back again. He did not stay in his place like everyone else. Sometimes he was in the front. Sometimes he rode in the back.

He made a mockery of her assigned order. It was most disconcerting.

He passed her once again and she followed him with her eyes. He was a magnificent man astride a horse, now with even more of his bare legs showing. It was positively indecent, probably immoral, and altogether uncivilized, but she could not help but turn her head to watch as he passed. She was rewarded with a glimpse of his thigh. More sweat rolled down her back.

She was not the only one who noticed him. Even though all were at least twenty years her senior, her ladies watched him with eager eyes and commented on his carriage, his visage, his horsemanship, and of course, those dratted bare legs. Their voices lowered to a whisper, followed by an uncharacteristic giggle from Marie Jeannette. Had Gavin driven her ladies mad? She knew they were speaking of things they ought not, and truth be told, some of her own thoughts made her blush.

Sir Gavin was a fine man and there was no denying it. Their time together in her father's chamber came to mind more often than it should. It was most fortunate, she told herself, that she was not required to marry the man. And yet she began to wonder what would it be like to be this man's wife. He was young. He was attractive. There was no room for complaint, at least in regards to physical attributes.

Of course her marriage would not be based on any such things. All she knew of her future husband was that he was forty-eight years of age, and that his first wife had died, leaving him a son and heir. She had tried to ascertain a description of his appearance, but unfortunately this was not a concern in forming the marriage contract. Marriages between members of the aristocracy were based on important matters such as wealth and power. Marriage was a matter of business. Human affection had no place in such arrangements.

Sir Gavin rode by once again, slowing down to ride beside her. "I dinna like what I see here," he muttered in her general direction.

Colette looked about and noted with displeasure that people were taking notice of the procession. People working in the fields stopped to watch them, whispering to each other. Others ran ahead of them, and still others ran off to parts unknown, probably to let their friends and neighbors know of a huge procession of riches slowly meandering down the road.

"These are our people. We are still within our borders. We are safe here," Colette said with what she hoped was firm confidence.

"We shall soon leave the security o' yer borders." With that parting shot, he galloped back to the front of the line, leaving Colette to admire his straight back even while silently cursing his name.

Several hours later, they were well outside the borders of the duchy. The road was bordered on both sides by thick forest. Sunlight filtered down through the green boughs of the trees in shafts of light. The birds had been twittering happily but had fallen silent, as if the forest were holding its breath, waiting for something to happen. Colette glanced around at the dense forest, but could see nothing amiss.

Suddenly, Gavin raced toward her and pulled up

short. "Thieves!" He shot her a glare as if the imposition was entirely her fault.

"If we are under attack, perhaps you should make yourself useful and do something about it," she said through gritted teeth, irritated that he blamed her for the situation and even more irritated that he had been right all along.

"As ye wish." He pulled a large broadsword from a harness he wore on his back and charged an approaching would-be marauder, who jumped out from the trees.

Gavin's war cry was so loud, so inhuman, Colette herself wanted to run in fear. She actually felt sorry for the thief, who dropped his short sword and ran screaming into the forest.

"Captain Perrine, send eight soldiers to the front, eight to the rear, and the rest of ye protect the ladies," shouted Gavin, and he charged another thief, scaring the man back to the woods.

Perrine glanced at Colette and she gave a nod. When it came to warfare, there could be no question Sir Gavin was the best one to lead. More brigands appeared from different sides of the road. Captain Perrine and his men obeyed Gavin without hesitation.

The thieves charged from all directions and Colette quickly gathered her maids to her. Marie Philippe cried out in fear. All her ladies appeared terrified. Her guards drew their weapons and stood in a circle around her and her maids.

"Be not afraid," said Colette over the din of the attack. "Sir Gavin will not allow us to come to harm." At the invocation of his name, her ladies appeared to be reassured. She was surprised they had such reliance on him though he was a foreigner and but a stranger to them. And yet Colette also had placed her safety in his hands, not those of her captain, whom she had known all her life.

Gavin chased away the attacking knaves with ferocity. He was an imposing man when he wished to be, there could be no denying. Colette could not help but watch him with something between terror and admiration.

At first, it appeared that the onslaught would be short. The thieves charged from all directions but broke off before they actually made contact with the soldiers, disappearing into the forest.

"Dinna follow them off the road!" commanded Gavin, racing up and down the line, shouting orders and scaring off the thieves. Colette could see their attackers were not particularly brave, only greedy. They were interested in easy pickings and were quickly chased away by a soldier with a mace. They ran even faster from a Highlander brandishing a broadsword. A group of bold marauders charged her soldiers, who held their ground. The knaves appeared to be running away but circled back and charged from the other side. Her soldiers met the attack and raced around them, preventing them from escaping back into the forest.

The foolhardy marauders instantly surrendered, throwing down their weapons. Her captain was unsympathetic and raised his sword for a death blow, harsh justice for the knaves who threatened her.

"No!" she cried. "They are naught but young lads." For the raiders before her were barely in their teens.

Her captain scowled but turned to take the youths as prisoners. The guards being momentarily occupied, another group of raiders rushed for them. Colette thought they had come to rescue the young men but, instead, jumped on one of the wagons, tossing the driver from the cart. The knave grabbed the reins and rode off with the entire cart into the forest.

"Wait! Stop!" she cried.

"It shall be retrieved," cried one of her soldiers, and several of them raced into the forest after the wagon. Colette feared this was precisely what Gavin had instructed them all to avoid, but her attention was drawn to the semiconscious man who had been thrown from the cart.

She swung down to the ground from her mount, a move she had never done before without a mounting block. She feared she was hardly graceful, but desperate times demanded desperate actions, so she dismounted her beast without the usual assistance, gravity insisting where she was hesitant.

She knelt down by the side of the injured man, removing her great fur cloak and laying it over him. She pressed her handkerchief to his forehead where he was bleeding. His eyes fluttered.

"Are you well?" she asked.

The man's eyes went wide, clearly surprised to find himself within inches of her face. "Yes, my lady, I am well. I am sorry to have failed you."

"Do not trouble yourself. I am only too glad you are not more seriously hurt."

"My lady," rasped the man. "Please, you must get off the ground. It is not safe."

With the commotion around her, Colette could see the man spoke the truth. It was not safe for anyone on the ground.

"My ladies!" called Colette, and her ladies moved their mounts around the injured man. "I must mount again," she said, grabbing the pommel of her saddle and attempting to physically hoist herself up into the saddle without a mounting block. She was completely unsuccessful. Another wagon was close, so she climbed up on the back to gain the proper height. It was a rather undignified maneuver, but knew she must regain her mount.

Suddenly, the cart lurched and she fell back into it, hitting her head on the edge of a trunk. Pain seared through her left temple and her vision narrowed, the gray, fuzzy edges closing in on her sight. *Thieves are taking the wagon. I must get out now.*

The hazy edges of her vision grew until all went black and she drifted into nothingness.

༄

Gavin had been expecting an attack. When it came, he quickly put into action the plan he had been considering during the long ride. Despite his initial disagreement with Captain Perrine, once approved by Lady Marie Colette, the captain followed orders without complaint. Their attackers were opportunists, looking for easy pickings more than wanting to actually engage in a fight. Had some of the soldiers not given chase, they would not have lost two of the wagons. Once they had their prize, the robbers broke off the attack and disappeared back into the woods.

Gavin stared at the hole in the forest where the missing wagons had gone. He wondered if he should bother going after them at all. If the thieves kept them, it would be less baggage to defend.

Despite the end of hostilities, Lady Marie Colette's ladies shrieked and carried on in a disturbing manner. Gavin glanced around for Marie Colette but could not see her. "Ladies, please," he said, gathering his patience so as to speak in a calm and rational voice. "The loss of a wagon or two is hardly worth this commotion. Let us continue wi'out it. Where is yer mistress?"

"That is what we are trying to tell you," sobbed one of the ladies. "Lady Colette fell in the wagon. She's been taken!"

"She fell in the wagon?!" Gavin cursed in his native Gaelic tongue as only a man raised in the Highlands could do. Considering how upset the ladies already were, it was a good thing they could not comprehend what he was saying.

"Which way?" he demanded.

The four ladies all pointed the same direction into the forest. Gavin dug his spurs into the side of his horse and bolted into the trees, after the wagon. He bounded through thick underbrush, following the trail the wagon left.

How could she fall in the wagon? Troublesome lass. Why had he ever agreed to do this? And yet, if anything happened to her... He spurred his horse faster, not able to even finish the thought without his stomach clenching into a sick knot.

It did not take him long to find a small clearing where the ruts told him the wagon had stopped, but all was gone—not even the horses were left. Marie Colette was nowhere to be seen. He slung himself down in an easy motion and inspected the ground, reading the tracks. His worst fears were realized. Tracks of the fleeing raiders rode off in all directions. Most likely, they had grabbed what they could from the wagon and fled. The wagon itself had also been rolled away.

Marie Colette had been abducted.

But which way? What if he could not find her in time? He gritted his teeth against the slither of fear. He must act now and fast. If he was to abduct a lady, he wouldn't keep her in a cart. He'd get her on horseback and as far away as possible. He picked one of the tracks and raced after it.

Seven

COLETTE THOUGHT HER DAY COULD NOT GET WORSE. She was wrong.

The cart rattled, jarring her aching head. Colette put a hand to her head, wishing she could remove her heavy headdress, yet in her current situation, she dared not. She did not feel any blood, which she considered a good sign.

She attempted to sit up in the fast-moving covered wagon, bumping along, bouncing her on top of the trunks and crates. She needed to get out of the wagon before she was discovered. It was difficult to move while being jostled to and fro atop several large trunks, but she slid herself to the back with the idea of jumping off. With a jerk, the wagon came to a stop.

The canvas was pulled aside and Colette was face-to-face with the thieves. The men had scarves covering most of their faces, but their eyebrows raised and their eyes widened to find her in the cart. For a moment, all was still. No one said a word. Her heart refused to beat. Then one of the men cursed, breaking the spell.

"Grab the trunks. Hurry!" demanded a tall man.

"What about her?" asked one of the thieves.

"Leave her! They will be after her. Look lively now!"

The men swarmed around the wagon, reaching in and grabbing the trunks, removing her things.

"No!" she commanded. "You may not take these things. Stop now! Those candlesticks belonged to my grandmother. Oh!" She was unceremoniously dumped onto her backside when a man grabbed the crate on which she was sitting.

It took less than a minute for the vultures to pick the wagon clean. Colette could do nothing but watch with fear, horror, and frustration, unable to stop the carnage.

"Wait! What about me?" A thin man in a stained blue doublet and red hose ran up to the wagon, putting one hand on the back of the wagon and the other around his middle, bending over to catch his breath.

Though his face was mostly covered, Colette could still see the captain of the thieves roll his eyes.

"We left you the best part, Clyes. The princess!" The thief mounted in a flash, and he and his men disappeared into the forest.

A heavyset man lumbered up behind the wiry man. "Did we get us the treasure?" he asked, looking toward the treetops as if riches were going to rain down on him.

"We got ourselves a princess," said Clyes, a thin man of objectionable hygiene.

"She's real pretty. What are we going to do with her?" asked the large man.

"I am not a princess," corrected Colette, feeling the need to join the debate now that her future was being discussed. She scrambled up to a standing position, though she was forced to stoop somewhat due to the canvas covering the wagon. "I request that you return me to my people on the road." She used her most imperious voice, hoping to impress the two ruffians into doing what she asked.

"You are not a princess?" asked the large man, disappointment on his face.

"No."

"But your father, he is rich, no?" Clyes asked.

Never in her life had Colette been asked a more impudent question. She swallowed down a retort. She needed these men to either help her or at least not prevent her from following the ruts of the wagon back to the road. "I have means to reward you both for my safe return to the road."

The men exchanged a glance. The thin one nodded. "We will drive you back, my lady." He gave her a crooked smile. The large one removed his cap and nodded furiously.

"Thank you." The men walked around to the front of the wagon, and Colette sank down to sit on the wooden slats as gracefully as she could. Thick curtains hid her from view of the men in front, and she was relieved to have a moment of privacy in which to try to calm herself from the unwanted excitement. At least she was going back to her people. She lost a wagon of goods, but it could have been worse.

The wagon brushed through thick foliage, rocking over unsteady ground. Since no one was watching, she leaned back on the side of the wagon and closed her eyes for a moment. She had always loved reading about great adventures, but now that she found herself in the midst of one, all she wanted to do was return home.

The cart came to a stop with a jerk, and she opened her eyes, unsure how much time had elapsed. She pulled herself up and climbed over the back of the wagon, anxious to return to her people, but when she looked around, she realized she was not back at the road but instead in a small clearing surrounded by dense forest.

She walked around to the front of the wagon and was further surprised to see not two men driving the workhorses, but two men detaching themselves from the harness and no horses at all.

"They took the horses," mumbled the big man as an explanation.

"Where did you take me?" asked Colette, a knot of fear twisting her stomach.

"You said there was to be a reward." The wiry man walked up to her, a glint of avarice in his eye.

"If you returned me to my companions on the road," said Colette, emphasizing the important part of the proposed deal. "Where am I?" She hoped she sounded less frightened than she felt.

"You are most welcome to my humble home," said the thin man with a sweeping gesture to a hovel at the edge of the clearing. The hut was short and squat, dug partially into the ground like a fat mushroom. To say it was humble was to elevate it considerably.

"Your hospitality is most appreciated, but now I must return to my companions. They will be concerned for my welfare." She was growing concerned for her own well-being. She glanced around at the trees, hoping her maids and soldiers would burst out at any moment, but she was alone. She had wished many times to have some freedom, but at this moment she would have welcomed being overprotected.

"Sometimes these rich men, they do not like to pay after you give them what they want, no? They must pay before you return." Clyes ran his hand through greasy hair.

She gasped. "You are holding me for ransom?"

"They make us rich, and then you go back," explained the large man, as if she was unclear on the concept.

"You are making a mistake most grave if you do not allow me to return to my people at once," she demanded, her heart pounding. She considered running into the forest to escape, but in her unwieldy velvet gown and heavy headdress, she could hardly hope to outrun these two men. Besides, she did not know which way to go.

The large man glanced at Clyes with uncertainty. "Maybe we should give her back?"

"No!" hissed Clyes in an undertone to his friend, though Colette could hear him plainly. "This is our one chance to be rich. Would you let it slip away?"

"My guards will come for me," declared Colette, folding her arms before her as much to protect herself as to keep her wildly beating heart from leaping outside of her chest.

"They will give us a whole wagon full of treasures, no?" Clyes was telling his partner, not listening to her at all.

"No! If you do not release me immediately, your only hope is that my father shows leniency in the manner of your death," she declared, but the men seemed to have fallen under the stupefying prospect of unfathomable wealth.

"Please do come inside," said Clyes, beckoning her toward the hut. It was a bold, or rather foolhardy, decision to take her to their own home, but she supposed thieves were not the cleverest of creatures.

Colette did not wish to enter the disreputable dwelling, but she had few options. She hoped she could convince her bumbling abductors to release her. It was with some foreboding that she entered the hut, having to stoop down so as not to scrape her headdress on the door frame.

"Brought you a visitor, I did," announced Clyes, following her inside along with his friend.

A woman turned around, small and squat like the hut itself, with black hair sticking out at all angles. "What is it? Who is that?" demanded the diminutive woman in a sharp voice.

"Never asked her name," Clyes mumbled, rubbing the back of his neck.

"You invite some high and mighty mademoiselle into my home and you do not even know her name?"

"What's your name, lady?" asked the rotund man without ceremony.

Marie Colette held herself as high as she could without hitting her head. She paused, waiting for everyone's attention in the room, and then she spoke with the voice of authority. "I am the daughter of the duc de Bergerac. I have been sent by special envoy from His

Grace. Even now his soldiers are in pursuit of me. You will trust me when I assure you that they will find me and will not take kindly to me being held for ransom. I suggest you take this moment to say your prayers since you will most surely not live to see the morrow."

Her three captors stared at her. "You stole the daughter of a duke?" The woman's jaw hung open.

"They are searching for me now. It will only be a matter of time before they arrive," confirmed Colette.

"You are as foolhardy a knave as they come. Why would you bring her here?" The lady of the house raised her iron spoon and came after Clyes with a shriek. He and the large man took flight, though there was very little place to go within the hut, so the three of them ended up running around Marie Colette like some crazed Maypole dance.

"Calm yourselves!" Colette had intended to put fear into her hosts in order to secure her release, but this madness was intolerable. "If you please, madam. If you would stop running for a moment."

Instead of ceasing her hostilities, madam grabbed a knife and brandished it menacingly. "I'm going to cut up your fool self and feed you to the pigs!" she threatened Clyes.

"But, dearest, we don't have any pigs," whined Clyes.

Colette wondered why, of all the things he could have protested at that moment, it was the lack of pigs he chose to highlight.

"Madam, is this man your husband?" asked Colette, trying to gain some control of the situation.

The woman paused a moment but did not lower the knife. "I suppose it is so. We share a bed and I feed him, so I guess that makes him my husband. Though he is a great imbecile."

"You have my condolences," said Colette, much in agreement. "Now if you will simply let me be on my way, I am willing to forget the whole affair ever happened."

"On my honor, your duchessness, you be too good to us," cried the stout madam. Without warning, she dropped her knife and rushed at Colette, throwing herself around her waist and sobbing into the velvet.

Colette had never been so attacked nor so demonstratively adored. She patted the woman's head awkwardly, wishing the mistress of the hovel would express her appreciation in some other manner. When Colette was finally able to disentangle herself from the effusive thanks of the sobbing woman, she glanced with trepidation at the velvet gown Mary Jeannette had spent countless hours making. There was no hope of trying to cover the stains. Colette sighed, knowing that not even abduction would save her from Marie Jeannette's wrath.

"It is not as bad as you say," defended Clyes, scratching his grimy hair. "I still think it would have worked."

He was silenced by an icy stare from his wife, who returned to wailing into Colette's skirts.

"My dear madam, please do calm yourself. I see that you have made an unfortunate choice in husbands, but you still have your lovely home, no?" Colette struggled to find a bright spot in this woman's drab existence. All this woman had to look forward to was to live in squalor with a fool for a husband. The least Colette could do was to give her some hope.

Colette took a jeweled pin from her gown and pressed it into the woman's hand closing the dirty fingers around it. "Now you take this," she whispered conspiratorially into the woman's ear. "And you buy with it some pigs. And if your man ever gives you trouble, you go ahead with your first plan."

The woman smiled at her and hiccuped, a wide grin gracing her dirty face.

An inhuman roar ripped through the hut along with the grinding blast of splintering wood as the door itself was torn from its hinges. An enormous man brandishing a large sword stood in the doorway.

Sir Gavin had arrived.

Colette knew that Sir Gavin was a large man, but in the small confines of the humble hut, Gavin was a monstrous man. Mountain trolls might have been of smaller stature. He not only filled the entire doorway, but stooping low to enter, he took up at least half of the hut's space as well. Sir Gavin was built of impressive proportions.

"Release Lady Mary Colette or ye'll die where ye stand," commanded Gavin.

The two men and the unfortunate woman screamed in terror and all tried to hide behind Marie Colette, reaching out to grab on to her velvet gown, which at this point was a complete loss. The hapless thieves begged her to intercede between themselves and what could only be a giant of mythic proportion.

Marie Colette prided herself on the ability to remain calm in all situations. But this was one that she never encountered in all her life. In truth, when she woke up this morning, she in no way foresaw that she would, mere hours later, be standing in a squalid hut with three persons of the most dubious character cowering behind her, facing Gavin Patrick with eyes blazing, sword raised, coming to her rescue. Not one of her heroic tales ever described such a ludicrous scene. It was a situation so absurd that a bubble of mirth simmered to the surface.

Colette tried to contain herself. It would be most unseemly to laugh at a situation of this gravity. After all, she had been abducted. She was being held for ransom in this squalid hut. Never mind the fact that she had essentially already extricated herself from the situation.

The combination of the raw emotion of the momentous day mixed with the utter ridiculousness of the situation was a force even Marie Colette could not fight against. She desperately stifled a laugh. She giggled. She snorted. And then she laughed out loud until tears ran down her face.

Sir Gavin Patrick stared. Her two abductors stared. The mistress of the house stared. And everyone took a step back from what could only be a madwoman.

It only made her laugh louder.

"Are ye quite well, m'lady?" Gavin now had backed up so far that he was standing outside the hut, his head no longer visible due to the low-hanging eaves of the thatched roof. Her vantage of the headless Sir Gavin was a new point of hilarity and Colette only laughed harder.

"Perhaps we should leave?" suggested Gavin.

Marie Colette, without a shred of dignity left, struggled out of the hut, trying to contain her inappropriate mirth. She placed her hands over her mouth, forcing herself into better regulation. She must stop this. She could not go on cackling like some crazed fiend. In her head, she could hear her maids reprimanding her to stop at once.

She took a gulp of fresh air, hoping it would restore her sanity. "I fear I have gone quite mad."

"Aye, m'lady. I fear that as well." It was the first time Gavin had agreed with her, and only that she was not well in the head.

"Pay me no heed, I beg you, Sir Gavin. It has been a trying day and I am not myself. I shall soon recover, I am sure."

"This day has definitely been…different." The corners of Gavin's mouth twitched up.

Colette became fascinated with that mouth. It was a fine, wide mouth, supple, and ever moving. What could a man like that do with a mouth like that? Colette pushed aside the question as another manifestation of her current madness.

"I have never been abducted before," explained Colette. "But if I ever was, I had supposed the thing would be done with more finesse and less stupidity."

The edges of Gavin's mouth which had threatened amusement now brightened into a wide smile, revealing straight, white teeth. "I see ye're less concerned with the fact that ye were abducted, but rather that the thing was done poorly."

"I am the daughter of a duke. I have high expectations of everyone around me."

Now Gavin started to laugh. And with his laughter, she could hardly contain her own. So they both laughed. It was a huge relief; the worry, the nerves, the fear, the grief, the absurd ridiculousness of the entire situation, it all came out in laughter and tears with a man who was not judging her but merely laughing with her.

Something within her tightly guarded heart cracked open, and she felt the wind on her face and smelled the fragrance of the pine trees around her as if for the first time. She felt as though she had awoken as from a long, dark sleep. She had never felt so alive. And she had never before seen a man more handsome nor more perfectly built than Sir Gavin.

With that thought, her mirth ended. She was not free to love as she pleased. She was not free at all, for she was bound in marriage to save her people. It would not do to be too alive, to hope for things that could never be hers. It was a most sobering reflection.

Colette took a deep breath and blew it out again. "We should return. My people, they will be concerned for me."

"Aye, m'lady." Gavin's laughter died away, but the humor remained in his eyes, and despite everything, she liked it there. She enjoyed laughing with him, sharing something that had more to do with who she was, not what she was. It was refreshing since she had so few interactions that did not revolve around power or position. She knew this moment, for good or for ill, would be one she would treasure.

Gavin led her to his horse, a tall, prized destrier. He knelt by the side of the sleek black horse and held his hands out to her, palms up, as in supplication. It took her a moment to realize what he was doing. He wished to help her onto the horse, but putting her foot in a man's hands to be tossed into a saddle, *his* saddle, seemed strangely intimate.

"Ye'd like to stay here, m'lady?" Gavin's eyebrows raised as he knelt before her, his hands raised, waiting for her.

"No, no, not at all." She could not sit in his saddle on his horse, could she? "What about the wagon? Could you not take me back in that?"

"I could if I had something to pull the wagon."

"Your horse perhaps?" she suggested.

"Och, what are ye thinking, lass?" Gavin stood, aghast. He smoothed the nose of his impressive horse. "She dinna mean it," he whispered to the beast. "Pay her no heed."

Colette sighed. Just like people, horses were divided into different classes. A warhorse would never pull a cart any more than a packhorse would be ridden into battle. She supposed she should not have even asked.

His horse soothed, Gavin once again dropped to one knee before her. "He is still willing to let you ride, unless you would rather walk."

"It is a kindly offer," she murmured, but still she hesitated, as if she knew that this act would change things. It would be the first time they touched—the first time she ever touched a man not her own father. Even such a commonplace, remote touch as to put the sole of her boot in his hand was still contact. She gritted her teeth to gain better control of herself. She must be going soft in the head. Perhaps this laughter had loosened something that was supposed to be tight. Why was she thinking such nonsense? She stepped forward and put her foot into his hand.

He did nothing. He continued to kneel there, one eyebrow raised.

Heat slithered up the back of her neck, and she feared her cheeks revealed a telltale sign of pink. Why was he not helping her into the saddle? "Well? Were you going to help me?"

"Well, unless you would like to sit backward in the saddle, m'lady, I suggest ye put yer other foot in my hands."

She really did blush then, much to her dismay. Drat that man. How could he be so unfeeling as to make her feel such embarrassment? "Yes, of course," she said sharply, removing her foot and replacing it with her other. More concerned with her own embarrassment, she was caught unprepared as he tossed her up into the saddle, and she pitched precariously, almost falling off the other side.

He leaped up and grabbed her around the waist, pulling her toward him, righting her in the saddle as he stood beside her.

"Oh! I am fine, thank you. No need to—oh!"

Not content with simply settling her in the saddle, he swung up behind her, reaching around to grab the reins.

It was too much. She had never been this close to anyone in her life. Ever. She had never been held or cuddled, at least not that she could recall. And this was not just anyone; this was a wild, broad-shouldered, square-jawed Highlander. He did not belong in her world, nor she in his. And he certainly had no right to put his arms around her in a most intimate manner.

"Release me at once!" she cried, leaning forward to try to prevent herself from touching him. It was a pointless endeavor.

"It is not my intent to abduct you," rumbled Gavin's low voice from behind her. She could feel the vibration of his chest when he spoke. "Would you rather walk?"

"No...I...I thought you would." He should be leading the horse, not mounted behind her. It was beyond anything she had ever experienced or even considered. It had never occurred to her that he would take such liberties.

He merely chuckled. "I warrant ye did think I'd be walking my own horse. Sorry to disappoint, but we have tarried too long. Yer abductors were fools, but there are others who winna be so easily thwarted. We will both be safer wi' ye back wi' yer people."

She was about to command him to dismount when she realized two important things. First, they did need to be on their way out of the forest as quick as may be, and second, Sir Gavin was not under her command. She feared this man was not under anyone's command but his own.

Without waiting for her to make a more articulate reply, he clicked and his large horse leaped into action, and before she could say anything, they were crashing through the forest at top speed. Out of a sheer desire to live through the day and not fall off the large beast, she stopped trying to lean away from him and nestled back between his arms.

They were touching, moving together with the fluid movements of the impressive mount. Heat exploded through her. She feared her body was burning with embarrassment and, even worse, desire.

Desire?

She gulped air. She had no right to be enjoying contact with this man. What was wrong with her? Perhaps she had hit her head harder than she thought?

"I fear I may be concussed," she murmured, half hoping it to be the case to explain this strange reaction.

"What was that?" he asked, slowing to wind his way around several large trees.

"My head. I fear the bump has left me daft."

"Ye're injured?" he asked, a tinge of anxiety to his tone. "Why dinna ye tell me? Where are ye hurt?" He slowed to a stop and attempted to remove her headgear, which only succeeded in pulling her hair.

"Ow! Stop at once. I am fine. My ladies can attend me. If you please, you will not touch me."

Gavin dropped his hands at once and nudged his mount to move again. "Aye, as ye wish."

"It is not that I do not appreciate your assistance," Colette felt compelled to add. "It is only that I am not accustomed to being so close to a man."

"Understandable. Pretend I am one o' yer maids."

Gavin one of her maids? She doubted anyone had that much imagination. "Never have I been this close to them. Or anyone." She tried not to allow her thighs to touch his, but with the movement of the horse, it was difficult. It was fortunate that, sitting behind her, he could not see the furious blush that seared across her face.

"This may hurt my male pride, but pretend I am naught but yer own dear mother."

"Not even my mother ever held me this close," admitted Colette.

"Truly? My mum was forever hugging me and

kissing my cheeks. I thought all mothers were alike in this."

"I was raised a little differently." Colette shifted again, not sure if she was more uncomfortable with the seating arrangement or the topic. Despite the unusual emotions it evoked, she did not wish to stop. "As my father's only child, there were expectations of how I was to appear and how I was to behave. Demonstrative displays of affection were not allowed. I believe I was intended to be more…decorative."

Gavin said nothing for a few moments and his silence stretched out like a rebuke. What was she thinking to say such candid things to this man? "Ye are a verra bonnie lass, I'll no' deny it," his deep voice reverberated through her. "But none o' God's children was put here to be merely ornamental."

It was a blessing he could not see her face, for she feared her detached facade broke. Her jaw dropped and she may have even broke into a wide smile, tears springing to her eyes, before she could get herself under tighter control.

She was spared the difficulty of making a response by their sudden emergence into a wide field. Gavin urged the mount faster, and the horse broke into a run, forcing Colette to hold on to the saddle to prevent herself from falling off. Even as she clutched the pommel, she knew with Gavin's two strong arms around her, he would not allow her to fall.

Suddenly, they pulled up short beside a gnarled tree on the other side of the field. To her surprise, Gavin jumped down from the horse and strode to the odd-shaped tree. He glanced northward toward the bluffs that looked down upon the valley field. "Nay, it canna be."

"What cannot be?" asked Colette, genuinely confused and strangely missing the warmth of his physical presence.

"I must ask to take your leave for a moment," he said in a gravelly voice, his eyes never leaving the high bluff above them. "I must climb to the top of this bluff and will return shortly." His face revealed nothing of his thoughts, unusual for such a generally expressive man. If his face was shuttered, he must be hiding something.

"What is wrong, Sir Knight?"

His eyes met hers. "I have found my father."

Eight

THIS WAS IT. THIS MUST BE THE PLACE CHAUMONT described. The place he had been looking for these many long years. The gnarled tree, the wide field, the bluffs beyond—it must be the place.

"Your father?" Lady Marie Colette looked around, confused.

He did not have the words to explain. "Wait here," Gavin demanded tersely. This was something he needed to do alone.

"But we must return to my people. You yourself said it was most urgent."

Gavin stifled a groan. He supposed she was right. "Aye, but this is something I must do. Ye best follow me, for I canna leave ye here in the open."

"Wait! We must return at once!" Marie Colette's frown did nothing to diminish her beauty. She was a siren, no matter how much her fine eyebrows scrunched together in annoyance.

"I must do this." He met her gaze, hoping to convey all he could not say. It was unfortunate timing, but he had searched for this place for years. It was his quest, his reason for remaining so long in France. He could not even think of leaving.

Without another word, he turned and ran up a steep path that led to the top of the bluff. Behind him, the muted clops of his mount on the hillside told him Marie Colette was following. He should have been irritated that at this most personal moment of the end of his quest he was not able to be alone, yet he was strangely comforted by her presence.

At the top of the steep embankment, he paused to catch his breath, gazing out over the lush, green valley below. It was exactly as Chaumont had described. Could it truly be the place?

His heart beat pounded in anticipation. He turned and caught Marie Colette's eye. He expected her to be furious with him for delaying them, but instead her eyes showed only confusion and concern.

He turned away. He must attend to his search. Tall grass covered the bluff, swaying in a rhythmic pattern with the gentle breeze. He strode through the overgrowth, the cool fingers of the blades of grass brushing his bare legs. He pushed the grasses aside, searching for the spot. It had been many years; it would surely be overgrown. Or maybe this was not the place at all.

"For what do you search?" Marie Colette asked. It was a fair question, but one he could not yet answer.

He hastened his search. Perhaps he had been wrong. Perhaps this was not the place. He waded through the tall grass until his boot hit something hard. He bent down and found a large rock. Brushing aside the grasses, he found a pile of large rocks.

Was this it? Had he found it at last? He began

to furiously pull out the grasses and weeds that had grown around and among the stones.

"What have you found?" asked the lady, still mounted behind him.

He continued to pull away the grasses until he came to it. The hilt of a dagger stuck deep into the top of the rock mound, just as Chaumont had said, the dagger becoming the cross for burial. He took a deep breath. His quest was complete.

"My father." His voice cracked and he could say no more. At last, he had found his father's grave.

With a swish of her skirts, he heard her dismount. To his surprise, Lady Marie Colette, daughter of the duc de Bergerac, knelt beside him and began to help pull out the weeds.

"Ye'll ruin yer gown and yer gloves," he said, taken aback that she would lower herself to conduct such labor.

"No matter. They are already ruined," she said in a logical tone.

They worked together, side by side, he acutely aware of her presence. She did an admirable job, though he would wager she had never condescended to do anything as menial as weeding before. When they were done, a pile of large stones had been revealed, capped with the dagger thrust down between them. His father's dagger.

Gavin stood and returned to his saddlebag, pulling out the small marble slab wrapped in linen he had carried many a year since coming to France. He walked back and placed the plaque on the stone gravesite, arranging the stones to hold his marker secure.

Sir James Patrick
1317–1346

He knelt and prayed before the gravesite of his father, something he had wished to do for a long time. He placed his hand over his heart and felt his father's ring hanging there beneath his shirt. *Rest in peace, my father.*

Marie Colette slipped a hand into her kirtle and produced a small book, which must have been kept in her purse tied under her skirts, as was common for ladies. "Would this be of service to you?" She held out a Book of Hours.

"Aye, it would. I thank ye." She was being exceptionally kind. He did not know what to make of it. He brushed the confusing thoughts aside, focusing on the prayer book. He turned to the page for the Office of the Dead and prayed silently for his father's soul, along with thanks for being allowed to find his resting place.

Lady Marie Colette sat serenely beside the grave marker, her legs tucked neatly beneath her skirts. When he crossed himself, she did as well. He appreciated her understanding and her willingness to wait patiently for him. He had thought her haughty and arrogant and rather spoiled. The understanding lady beside him was none of those things.

He handed the prayer book back to Marie Colette. "Thank ye for yer help." He wanted to say more but had not the words to express it.

"It is nothing. This is the grave of your father, yes?"

"Aye. I have searched for the gravesite of my father since I have been in France. After three years of failure,

I had given up my quest. I gives me great peace to ken that my father's place o' rest is no longer unmarked."

A fine eyebrow raised. "I am glad the place is found to you. But how did your father come to be buried here?" Her eyes were a bright green, filled with compassion. A man would do much for such eyes.

"My father and my uncle, Laird MacLaren, traveled to France when I was but a lad to help France fight against the English who sought to claim their land. They were successful in their efforts and both were knighted for bravery on the field of battle."

Gavin pointed to the date on the stone of his father's death. "On this day, in the field below, my father fell in battle. He was buried in haste, for MacLaren soon discovered that they had been betrayed to the English. My father had died in vain. MacLaren and Chaumont found themselves surrounded by enemies, and they were forced to leave the country at once. There was no time to place a proper monument. That honor was left to me."

"I am sorry for your loss and the betrayal of your father." Marie Colette's eyes were softer than he had ever seen them. "Who is this Chaumont of whom you speak?"

"Sir Chaumont is a French knight who befriended MacLaren and my father. When MacLaren returned to Scotland, he came too. When he met my mother, he stayed." Gavin could not help a small smile at the thought. He had been a young lad when he first met his stepfather, and he had admired Chaumont from the start.

"So Sir Chaumont married your mother?"

"Aye. They were wed and Chaumont has acted as

a good father to me. Yet as I grew, I wished to better know my sire. He left when I was but a wee lad, so I have but poor memories o' him. It is a weight off my soul to know I have paid my respects to my father."

Marie Colette lifted her hand as if to place it on his shoulder before thinking better of it and awkwardly placing it back in her lap. "This morn, before the sun rose, I visited my mother's grave and placed flowers for the last time."

"Your mother has also passed?" Gavin asked. He supposed he could have discerned it, since he had not met her mother. He realized how little he actually knew of the lady before him.

"Yes, it was many years ago now. The great plague passed through the land and so many of our people died. She was told to stop providing sustenance for the poor, but she said it was her duty and would not shirk it. She was struck down so fast. I remember being told one night that she was ill, and by sunrise she was gone."

"I am sorry for yer loss as well." He wanted to reach out to her but knew not how. The more she shared, the more he realized his assumptions about her had been wrong.

"I was but ten years old when she died." Colette looked down and smoothed her skirts. The spring wind played with the grasses and rustled the bright green leaves. "We shall never stand beside them again," she added softly.

"We shall, in the end times," said Gavin with confidence.

"*Oui*. This is the teaching of the Church. I know it"—she pointed to her head—"but sometimes it is difficult to know it." She pointed to her heart.

"Through faith there is hope, and without hope, life would be unbearable." He spoke with conviction. He had seen fellow soldiers try to live without hope, poor miserable sods.

"Hope can be difficult when the path before you is so uncertain." She turned her head to the wind, a deep sorrow in her green eyes.

He felt for her. She had a difficult journey before her into an unknown land. He struggled to find some words of comfort to give to her. "When our path is rocky, it is even more important to hold on to faith, to hope."

She nodded but said nothing. He could tell his admonition had not helped and felt compelled to try again.

"Even though our parents are no longer present, still we carry them with us. They are in our thoughts and hearts forever. Sometimes a physical remembrance can help." He put a hand on the hilt on his sword. "My father's sword."

Colette gazed off in the direction of the road. From their vantage point atop the bluff, the tops of the wagons were just visible in the distance. "My dowry, my mother's things. Each one holds a memory for me. Each one is a piece of her."

"Oh," said Gavin, feeling the weight of his insensitive words earlier that day. "I apologize for…" He did not know how to express what he wanted to say. How would he feel if he was told to discard his father's belongings? What would he do if he was forced to leave his home and marry some stranger in a strange land? He realized he had judged the lady before him too harshly.

"Lady Marie—" he began.

"Colette," she interrupted.

"I beg yer pardon?"

"Every lady in my family and all my ladies-in-waiting are named Marie after our Holy Mother," she explained, returning to her cool, logical tone. "My mother was Marie Hélène. My maids are Marie Claude, Marie Jeannette, Marie Agnes, and Marie Philippe. So many Maries, we have taken to calling ourselves by our second name. I am known as Colette."

"Lady Colette." He paused. Her name felt good on his lips. "I fear I owe ye an apology. I dinna ken the meaning of the things ye carry. And yet..." He broke off once again. He did not wish to be unkind, but there were certain realities to trying to transport so much.

Colette picked a blade of grass and played with it, running it up and down the velvet fabric of her kirtle. For some reason, he found the careless gesture alluring.

"And yet we are heavily burdened, putting ourselves at risk," Colette finished for him. "But much of it is the dowry promised to my future husband and the other is my mother's inheritance, mine in my own right."

"Much of it is housewares," Gavin said gently. "Yer husband will no doubt already have these things. Ye winna go wi'out."

"But that is the point." Colette met his eyes. "My husband will have these things. They will not be mine. When he dies, everything will go to his son. If I wish to leave any legacy to my own children, I must take it with me."

Gavin paused. He had never thought of how difficult things could be for women. Their claims on land or property were always supplanted by the claims of men, unless specifically dictated by contract. Lady Colette was right. If she left behind any of her things, she could never acquire them again.

Gavin ran his fingers through his hair, thinking hard. "Ye make a fair point, m'lady. We shall have to do what we may to take as much as we can. Though I beg ye to consider, some things should be left behind." He gestured to his father's dagger, struck into the grave marker.

Colette's smile was beautiful to behold. It was wide and lit her whole face, her bright green eyes gleaming. "Thank you, Sir Gavin. I know if you will help me, we are sure to manage."

"I...I... That is to say," stuttered Gavin. She was simply too beautiful to look upon without his tongue stumbling over his words and his mind going blank. He struggled to keep his thoughts in order and not appear foolish before her. "'Tis a difficult journey. I canna say whether we will be successful."

"I ask only that you try. My grateful thanks to you, Sir Knight."

Gavin had the feeling he had exchanged one impossible quest for another. He stood before he could be charmed into agreeing to goodness only knew what else. She had a face that made a man want to consent to anything. He would do well to remember that she was promised to another man. She was not his and never would be. Any other feelings would only lead to disappointment.

He held out his hand and she accepted it, putting her gloved hand in his and allowing him to help her up. He squeezed her hand gently and then dropped it, remembering the need to keep his distance.

He bowed his head to his father's resting place, grateful he had been given the chance to find it. His father's grave would not lie unmarked and unknown. It gave him peace.

They walked back to the horses and Gavin once again knelt before Colette to help her into the saddle. She paused but this time quickly lifted the correct foot, and he tossed her easily up into the boxlike saddle. He recognized that every time they touched, even in such an insignificant way, he longed for more. He needed to remember his task was to transport her and her things. Nothing more.

This time, he did not mount his horse but grabbed the reins and led the beast down the slope. It had been a mistake to ride with her before, every inch of him coming alive with her pressed against him. He needed to eliminate all such treacherous thoughts. She was much too attractive for her own good, or at least his own good. It was best to keep out of her presence as much as possible. She would return to the company of her ladies and they would continue on their journey.

The less he saw of her, the better.

Nine

COLETTE HAD ANTICIPATED SIR GAVIN WOULD RIDE
with her back to the road, but it was not to be. Instead,
he led his mount with her on it back to the waiting
caravan to the cheers of the guards and ladies. All
appeared appropriate and as it should be. Colette was
much fussed over by her maids, particularly after the
unfortunate story of her kidnapping had been revealed.
She wished to say something to Gavin, with whom
she had shared much, but he quickly disappeared to do
whatever it was he did to ensure their safety.

Marie Claude appeared satisfied that Colette had
returned and had nothing more to say on the matter;
Marie Jeanette cried over the ruined state of her gown,
while Marie Agnes blamed Colette for being abducted
in the first place. It was only Marie Philippe who,
tending to the bump on her head later that night, gave
her a welcome embrace when none of the other ladies
were looking. Colette appreciated Philippe, though
wished her support could be more overt and less
cloaked in secrecy. Colette did understand Philippe
would be criticized by the other ladies for anything

that appeared to be coddling, an irony since most people who saw Colette from afar most likely thought her spoiled.

Despite all the turmoil in her life, Colette's thoughts seemed to revolve around a certain Highlander. She did not know if it was the shock of being abducted or the trauma of leaving her homeland, but she had never sat on the grass and talked to a man. Considering her overly restrictive upbringing, she had never even sat on the plain grass before. Despite this or perhaps because of it, she had conversed in a most friendly manner with a half-dressed barbarian she hardly knew. Even worse, in the course of one conversation, she had revealed to him struggles she had never told another soul.

They traveled only another few miles that day, to an open field large enough for the company to prepare camp. Gavin was true to his word and began to bark orders to help them travel without further molestation. All liveries would be hidden and the wagons had their heraldic crests pried off and mud splattered on them to appear dingy and unappealing.

After a long night attempting to sleep on a regular pallet (her ladies requested her great bed be assembled but this was denied), Colette awoke stiff and momentarily confused as to where she was. She sat up with a sigh. It was no dream. This was truly happening to her.

She reached for her Book of Hours. Even if her life was no longer recognizable as her own, she would still begin her day as she always had, with the reading from her prayer book for Lauds.

"*Ego enim scio cogitationes quas ego cogito super vos, ait Dominus, cogitationes pacis et non afflictionis, ut dem vobis finem et patientiam,*" she read to her ladies and then translated, for none of them spoke Latin. "It is from the book of Jeremiah, 'For I know the plans I have for you,' declares the Lord, 'plans to prosper you and not to harm you, plans to give you hope and a future.'"

Colette paused. A hope and a future? Was that not what Sir Gavin had spoken of yesterday, the importance of holding on to hope? She breathed deeply. Perhaps there was a hope for a future in this wild Scotland after all.

It was time to embrace her future. She gave her ladies firm instructions to dress for concealment rather than show. Her hair was braided more simply into a herringbone pattern and tucked completely under a plain linen wimple. Over this was placed a less elaborate headdress. She advocated for none, but Jeannette went into vapors and Colette relented. Her gown was simple and more flowing, allowing for more freedom of movement and breathing. She had never before worn such plain fabrics and it was a relief. She was draped in a plain brown cloak and saw that her mount had been prepared with a simple leather saddle.

Her pleasure at successfully taking measures to blend in with the populace was short-lived. Gavin strode up to her with his long legs, his eyebrows clamped down ferociously over his eyes. Her heart beat faster, though whether it was simply from his mere presence or due to the scowl on his face, she did not know.

"I asked ye to be ready early," he chastised.

"It is early," she reasoned. It wasn't even noon.

He raised one eyebrow. "I meant to leave at first light. We need to have everyone mounted. I know this is difficult for ye, but are there some things, maybe larger things of lesser value, that we can trade for mounts for the guards? We could lighten our load and travel more quickly. The sooner we are at sea, the better."

Colette pressed her lips together to avoid an untoward retort. She knew he was making sense, even if it was not what she wished to hear. It was time to start making choices for the good of all. She had lightened her garments and it felt good. Perhaps letting go of a few things would not be so painful.

"*Oui*, Sir Knight. I will show you some things we can leave behind." The words almost hurt, but she managed to speak them.

A few hours later, after Gavin and a few others had traded two wardrobes, a chest, and some other lesser items for traveling horses and saddles in a nearby town, they once again started on the road, less another wagon. They also sent home the injured man from yesterday and as many of the stable hands as could be spared now that they had fewer wagons. She told herself it was for the best, for she knew it was. She had to admit, they were moving more quickly now that everyone was riding.

At a fork in the road, Gavin divided the caravan into two groups. They would travel to the appointed rendezvous spot separately, to avoid attracting too much attention. Colette assisted with the division of the carts, keeping most of her own inheritance with her and allowing her dowry, now the possession of her future husband, to continue on without her. Her ladies and most of the guards remained with her party. It was difficult to allow her things to travel outside her control, but again she knew Gavin's reasoning to be sound.

She spoke to him a few times, always about traveling arrangements. If there had been any connection between them, there was nothing in his words or demeanor to suggest it. She also adopted her public face for conversing with him, but she missed the private moments they had shared. Yet she knew it was better this way. Nothing could be gained from developing some sort of ill-advised attachment to such a man, especially with her future husband waiting for her.

Somehow they managed to make it another day without attack. Gavin continued to ride ahead, around, and behind the caravan to ensure its safety. He was always there to encourage haste when anyone fell off the pace he deemed necessary. By the end of a full day's ride, Colette was saddle sore but admittedly pleased with the progress they had made.

Gavin, however, constantly challenged the needs for multiple tents, demanding the cooking be kept to what was only necessary to sustain life. He might be right, but he was poor company.

The next day he roused them before dawn and had everyone on the road as the first rays of the sun hit their backs, traveling west down the road. Colette managed to keep herself from grumbling, mostly by keeping silent, but it did not stop her ladies from whispering their complaints between one another. They were gently bred ladies, not intended for hard travel, but Gavin was without mercy in pressing them forward.

At last, when Colette despaired Gavin would forget the need for the midday meal, he called the party to a halt.

"Hold back!" he shouted at Captain Perrine. "The town ahead has been attacked. I will scout ahead. Have the rest o' yer men stay and guard the ladies."

"What say you?" Marie Colette rode up to join the conversation. "The town was attacked?" She noticed the smoke rising from the town ahead. She froze, listening for any sounds to indicate a battle was at hand, but all was quiet.

"Aye, recently by the look o' it. English troops no doubt. Village was captured, sacked, and put to the flame."

"Are the English soldiers still here?" asked Colette, catching her breath.

"Nay, they have moved on."

"Heaven protect us!" cried Marie Claude, riding up after Colette. "You have certainly led us into danger," she accused Gavin with a haughty look down her long nose.

Colette wished she had held her tongue. It was hardly Gavin's fault there were English about. The English incursion was the reason she was leaving, after all. "Be there any survivors?" Colette asked Gavin, trying to ignore Marie Claude's rude comments.

"None in the town that I saw. It appears to have been abandoned. Hopefully most left before the English came."

"But is anyone hurt?" Colette pressed. It was her responsibility to care for those less fortunate.

"None that I saw."

"Where is the English army now?" Marie Claude demanded to know.

"I dinna ken, but I intend to find out," said Gavin with grim determination.

"If you do not know where they are"—Marie Claude's words were an indictment against him—"then we must not go on, for we could travel right into their camp! We must stop here for the night."

Gavin pressed his lips together, forming a thin line. He clearly did not think much of the idea of stopping when the English were about, but there was some truth in what Marie Claude said. Without knowing where the English army had gone, they might march right into each other, and that would be disastrous.

"We can take a break for the midday meal, but be ready to ride, for we may need to leave quickly," conceded Gavin.

"We must also look for survivors," said Colette, yearning to ride into the town to be of some help.

"You will come back with me and do as you're told!" demanded Marie Claude.

There was nothing unusual about the tone Marie Claude used; she chided Colette often enough, but Gavin's reaction was immediate. His eyebrows raised high and his mouth opened slightly in pure surprise. Recovering quickly from the shock, his normally pleasant features twisted into something of a scowl. He clearly did not care for the way Marie Claude was speaking to her.

Colette held her back straighter if such a thing was possible with her already perfect posture. She didn't care for the way Marie Claude spoke to her either. She met Gavin's eye and his disdain gave her courage.

She spurred her mount and galloped forward before anyone could say another word.

～∞～

Gavin kicked his mount to follow her. He should have been irritated that she was endangering herself by riding into the town, but after what he'd just witnessed, he could only be proud of her. Somehow in the short time he had known her, he was not surprised by her impulse to help, but he was surprised at her open defiance to her lady-in-waiting, who clearly had been controlling Colette for a long time.

He urged his mount faster until he was riding next to Colette, her chin high, her back straight. "Good for ye, m'lady," he murmured in a voice meant only for her.

A small smile formed on her lips. "I will pay for my rash action."

"Freedom is always worth the fight."

His words earned him a full smile and his breath caught. She truly was a vision to behold. They reached the town together and rode in slowly, her guards following a short distance behind.

"While as a Highlander I do support willful defiance as a general rule, as yer protector, I must recommend ye return to yer ladies," said Gavin.

"If you but knew how angry Marie Claude will be with me, you would understand I am safer here with you." Colette cast him a furtive glance. "Besides, these people may need help."

The town had been put to the flame. A few buildings still stood, black scorch marks on the stone. Anything built of wood had been burned to the ground. Around the main square were heaps of smoldering ash and ruin. It was not an easy thing to see. He wished to protect Colette from it but knew she was strong enough to handle the difficult scene.

They stopped in the middle of the town square. Many of the stone buildings were marred with black scorch marks, leaving nothing more than hollow shells. One of the buildings had been a church, its steeple still rising to the sky. He bowed his head to say a prayer for whatever fate had befallen these people.

In the silence, he heard it. A soft cry. Gavin froze, listening for the small cry again. Was it just the wind rushing through the vacant buildings in some strange manner? But it appeared Colette had heard it too, cocking her head to one side to listen. It came again. This time there could be no mistaking the sound. It was definitely a cry of something, perhaps human, perhaps animal, but something was alive but hurt.

The soft cry came again, and he located its position in the burnt-out husk of the church. He dismounted in a flash. "Stay here," he ordered Colette, though he was not at all surprised when he heard her slip down from her own mount and follow him into the church.

"What men are these English who would put even a church to the flame?" she asked in a whisper.

"I dinna ken," answered Gavin. He wondered who could be so callous as to burn the entire town. He guessed once they had put one part of town to the flame, the fire would have been unrelenting, even to a holy place.

The church was grim. Jagged, black char marks marred the white stone walls. Gavin's boots crunched over black charcoal debris of what were probably the wooden pews. He did not wish to look closely, but he suspected the townspeople who had run into the church for shelter had not survived, overcome by smoke and flame. The smell of charred remains was indescribable, and he struggled not to gag.

"This is no place for ye." He turned to Colette, wanting her to leave this place of death and destruction. Truth be told, he wanted to run away himself.

Her eyes were filled with tears, whether from the smoke or the horror of the place he did not know. She held a handkerchief over her nose and mouth against the acrid stench of the place. Yet there was determination in her tone. "We must find survivors."

Gavin opened his mouth to protest, but the soft cry came again and they both froze in the middle of the church, listening.

They followed the sound of the soft mewling toward the stone altar. No one was there. They shared a look of confusion and began to look about. They found nothing.

"What made the sound?" asked Colette.

Gavin shook his head and sank to his knees, praying for guidance. He had hardly begun when a piece of fabric caught his eye. Under the altar, in a small crevice hewn from the stone, he found a package wrapped in a linen blanket. He gently pulled the package out from under the altar.

"What is it?" she asked, her face dangerously close to his.

He slowly unwrapped the bundle, revealing a most surprising treasure. Two brown eyes blinked back at him. "*Sacre coeur!*" exclaimed Colette. "A baby!"

Ten

COLETTE KNELT ON THE FLOOR BESIDE GAVIN, STARING at the squirming lump, only eyes visible from beneath the wrappings. The baby was alive. Truly a miracle.

Gavin shook his head. "I dinna ken how it survived the fire." He drew back the blanket to unwrap the child, revealing a red burn on the baby's face.

"Poor thing. What a horrible burn," said Colette. The little babe must be in pain.

Gavin unwrapped further, looking for any other injuries, revealing the babe to be a girl. Other than the burn on her cheek, she was unhurt.

"Where is her mother?" asked Colette.

"It appears the poor souls who took refuge here dinna survive."

Colette knew it to be true. She avoided looking at the remains. She needed to get out of this church, this grave. She stood briskly. "The terror, it must have been…" Colette could not find the words.

Gavin rewrapped the babe and stood beside her, holding the baby comfortably in the crook of his arm.

"Let us leave this place." He motioned for her to leave and this time she needed no further encouragement.

Colette took a deep breath once outside the church. It still smelled of smoke, but the air was fresher.

One of her soldiers walked up to them, stepping over broken stones and charred wood that littered the street. His expression was grim, his face pale. "We have searched the village. No survivors were found."

Gavin gave him a short nod. "Bring Lady Colette her horse and escort her back to camp."

The soldier bowed and was gone.

"At least we found this wee bairn," said Gavin. "Thanks to ye."

Colette shook her head. "You were the one who found her."

"In truth, I woud'na have looked but for ye."

Colette gave a small smile. He had given her a compliment, something he did not bestow lightly. It was nice to speak to him again of something other than travel arrangements.

"I will look for someone who knows the family where we can restore this infant." Gavin held out the bundle of baby to her.

Colette froze. She'd hardly seen a baby let alone touched one. What was she supposed to do with an infant? She recognized at some point she would be obligated to bear children herself, but she fully expected that, like her mother before her, she would have nothing to do with the actual care or keeping of a baby. This was the work of servants who were highly paid for the privilege of trying to keep the child alive.

If the child lived to respectable age, perhaps five or six, then he or she would be brought to Colette for an introduction. It was better this way, her mother had explained, for it was too sad to get attached to a small thing that might not live. Better to wait and see if it was hardy, than to expend the energy of developing affection for a sickly babe. Her mother had warned Colette that ladies who had not heeded this advice had died of broken hearts when their tots perished.

And now Gavin was trying to hand her an injured babe.

"I know not how to care for an infant." She drew back.

"Do as best ye can. She must be thirsty. She is no' crying, which makes me concerned. Feed her some water and maybe some porridge and see if she will eat. She looks about six to nine months old to me."

"How would you know her age?" Colette wouldn't know if it was newborn or two years old.

Gavin gave her a wry smile that only enhanced his already attractive face. "I'm the oldest of several siblings. It was only my mum and me for years until she married Chaumont. Then they had two boys and two girls. Naturally, I have had some experience in watching after them."

Colette stared at him. There was nothing natural about it. Ladies did not look after their own babies. Men did not acknowledge their children until they reached an age when they were useful.

"Here, take the babe. She winna bite ye, I pray." He added the last bit as an afterthought and held the wrapped infant out to her. Did babies bite?

"I… But… She is injured." Colette stepped back. She could not care for an injured infant. She could not care for any infant.

Gavin closed the gap between them and thrust the baby into her arms. "Ye'll do well. I will try to find her kin." He spoke to her with a mixture of encouragement and determination. He clearly intended her to take control of the babe.

Before Marie Colette could say another word, Sir Gavin mounted quickly and galloped off. Leaving her with the infant—and a sickly one at that.

Her soldiers found a box for her to stand on, so she could mount her horse, a new challenge holding the strangely quiet bundle.

"Go find me a healer and a wet nurse," she commanded the soldier. She did not share Gavin's confidence in her mothering acumen. She needed reinforcements.

Colette attempted to turn her horse to ride back to camp but found the process of trying to hold a baby while managing the reins to be challenging at best. She managed finally, realizing she needed to press the soot-covered infant against her body in order to keep it secure. It felt warm and oddly soothing as she struggled to ride.

Back at camp, Marie Claude had ignored Gavin's advice to be ready to move soon and had directed the tents to be raised. Clearly, she had no intention of going any farther today.

Colette entered the large, cavernous tent with some trepidation. She had never before been so brazen in disobeying Marie Claude. A book hidden in her needlework was nothing compared to public insubordination. To make matters worse, Colette was returning with an injured infant.

"Lady Marie Colette!" Marie Claude descended on her, fury blazing out of two small black eyes. "What were you thinking, riding off with a man without your chaperone and against my direct orders? You have lost your head, yes? You think you do not need us anymore? Perhaps we shall return to Bergerac and tell him his naughty daughter cast us away!"

"No, of course I do not wish for you to leave," said Colette. She resigned herself to being criticized and guilt ridden for the rest of the night at the very least.

"What is that you hold?" demanded Marie Claude.

"A baby has been found. It appears her parents died in the fire. Sir Gavin has gone to look for her kin." Colette was happy to change the subject. "Someone should look after it," she added, holding out the grimy bundle.

If she hoped her ladies would delight in caring for a dirty, injured infant, she was to be disappointed, though in truth she had no expectation, especially considering the state of war between herself and Marie Claude. They all looked at her much as she had looked at Gavin when he'd suggested that she care for it. Her maids had dedicated their lives to the service of their mistress and none had married or borne children.

Marie Claude folded her arms across her chest. "You see what trouble you find when you do not heed your elders?"

"Wicked, headstrong girl. I should not be surprised if it has the plague, brought here to kill us all," added

Marie Agnes, who could not resist the urge to chastise, using the gloomiest terms possible.

"The babe has not the plague. Her face is burned, is all. I request your services in this matter," said Colette with more nerve than she usually had. Something about this journey made her less cowed by her overprotecting ladies. She did not try to hand the babe to Marie Claude but did thrust it onto a horrified Marie Jeanette.

Marie Jeannette took it reluctantly, holding the infant at arm's length. She gave it immediately to Marie Agnes, who shoved it into the unwilling arms of Marie Philippe.

Colette could hardly blame them. The baby was dirty and her face was scarred, such that it was difficult to look upon.

"What shall I do with it?" cried Marie Philippe.

"She needs care," answered Colette, hoping one of them would have a suggestion. None of her ladies appeared to have anything but revulsion for the child.

Once again, Colette felt pushed into unfamiliar territory. She had been briefly proud of her ability to stand up for herself and adapt to the journey, but taking care of an orphaned infant was not something she was prepared to do.

She blamed Gavin for putting her in this situation, though in fairness it had been her idea to look for the wounded. She had an unsettling feeling of being somehow deficient because she could not cradle the baby as easily as Gavin. Whoever heard of a knight taking care of a baby or helping to raise children? Scotland must be a wild and strange place.

The new thought came to mind, unbidden and unwelcome. What if her new husband expected her to actually care for the infants she would be obliged to produce? What if she must feed them and clothe them and clean their little bottoms? She clenched her jaw against the mere thought. Might she actually be expected to put a squalling infant to her own breast?

"You called for a wet nurse, yes?" A solidly built woman stood at the entrance of the tent.

"Yes, please do come in," said Colette with relief. Marie Philippe thrust the babe at the woman immediately, and they all took a step back, just in case the woman felt inclined to try to pass the child along.

The woman was clearly comfortable with infants and put the babe to her breast. The baby revived at the prospect of food and nursed hungrily. Colette averted her eyes but was a little envious of the ease with which the woman handled the tot.

After the baby had her fill, the woman cleaned and bathed her, taking special care with the burn. "Poor little love," clucked the woman. "She will be scarred all her life."

"So she shall live?" asked Colette cautiously, handing the woman some clean linen for the babe.

The woman paused. "With the right care, it is possible." She smoothed a salve on the baby's face and then handed Colette the jar of the ointment. "Keep the wound clean and put this on it a few times a day. The babe is old enough to eat porridge and drink the milk of a goat or cow." The woman attempted to hand the baby back to Colette, but Colette stepped away.

"You are not leaving me?" asked Colette, truly alarmed.

"I have children of my own and many to care for after the recent attacks," explained the woman.

"Here is payment for services rendered." Colette nodded to Marie Claude who counted out a few coins and handed it to the wet nurse. "You will be rewarded even more handsomely if you would but remain until the babe's kin can be found," Colette pleaded, desperate to keep the woman.

The woman shook her head. "I've other folk who need my help. Would not be right to think of my own gain while others suffer because I would not help. Hope you find her kin soon. Here is the babe. *Bonne chance.*" With that, she handed the baby back to Colette and turned without ceremony, leaving the tent.

Colette attempted to hand off the infant to one of her maids, but they were all suddenly quite busy at their various tasks, bustling about the tent, preparing for the evening meal. She was stuck holding the babe, waiting for Gavin to return. At first she held it out at arm's length, but the babe squirmed, unhappy in the position. Remembering what Gavin had done, she tucked the little thing in the crook of her arm and held her close to her body.

The child closed her eyes and drifted to sleep. Colette held the warm bundle, cuddled up to her. Maybe the little one was not so bad now that she was clean and peaceful.

Everything went well until it came time sit down for their supper. At first, the babe made a soft sound, one that could be easily be ignored. Within minutes, however, the child was howling and everyone was in an uproar. Colette placed the tot on a cushion, not sure what she had done wrong. She and her maids crowded around the infant, trying to cajole it to stop its incessant caterwauling.

"Make it stop!" demanded Marie Agnes.

"Someone should pick it up," suggested Marie Claude.

Marie Jeanette proved her courage by lifting the bundle. The babe stopped for a moment, looking expectantly as Jeanette held her at arm's length. Within moments, the baby took up a horrible wail again and Colette fought the urge to stick her fingers in her ears and run from the tent.

Jeanette handed the baby to Marie Philippe, who began to cry herself.

"If you please, stop this noise!" commanded Colette. It worked on neither of them.

"Are ye ladies unwell?" called Gavin through the side of the canvas tent.

"Sir Gavin!" called Colette. "We are in need of assistance, if you please to come in at once!"

Despite inviting a man into their private tent, not one of her maids complained. Gavin entered, amusement twinkling in his eyes at the clear distress that one howling infant had given five grown women.

"This child, is she dying?" asked Colette anxiously.

Gavin only smiled. "Got a healthy set o' lungs on her." He reached out his hands and Marie Philippe was only too willing to shove the infant into his arms. He tucked the infant in the crook of one arm in a confident motion and jiggled the baby a bit until she stopped her crying.

"Probably a wee bit hungry." He walked to the table, set for their meal, and dipped his little finger into a bowl of porridge, placing his finger into the baby's eager mouth. Colette was not sure if she should be fascinated or repulsed as she watched him feed the tot. The baby was soon happy and drifted back to sleep.

Colette was amazed Gavin could so easily calm the distressed child. She was not sure if she was impressed by his skill or irritated at how inept he made them all appear. "Her family, did you find them?" asked Colette, getting back to the business at hand.

The humorous glint in his eye faded. "Unfortunately, they perished in the attack."

Colette's heart sank. "But this is terrible. What shall become of this child?"

"I've heard of a home a few miles away that takes orphans. I hope the baby will be safe there," said Gavin.

"Good. I am glad the matter is settled." She had a sudden impulse to say good-bye to the babe but resisted. She should not get attached. She cleared her throat. "Here is a jar of ointment for her face."

Gavin took it with a soft smile. "Thank ye."

Colette followed him out of the large canvas tent, unable to stop from following such an attractive smile.

"I knew ye could care for the wee bairn," said Gavin with another one of his warm smiles.

"I did not, I fear. I called a wet nurse," Colette confessed.

"Wise. Ye did well."

Colette should not have let his praise warm her heart, but it did. "Thank you for finding a good home for this one. She should not survive the fire only to perish of neglect."

"Aye, we must find her a good home t'be sure. Trouble is, many good folk have fled from the English incursions."

Colette leaned in to look upon the babe asleep in Gavin's arms once more. She glanced up at his face and was suddenly aware of how close she had come to him. She should have backed away immediately, but she could not. Here was what she wanted—a tall, strong man, fierce in his protection of her but willing and capable of caring for even the littlest one in their midst. He was a true knight of the chivalric code. And he was wickedly handsome.

She jerked back and cleared her throat, wishing she could as easily clear her mind. "The English camp, did you find it?" asked Colette, trying to return to the subject. Besides, she had no wish to be taken hostage. Again.

"Aye. Their camp is miles away to the south. I hope we shall avoid them. We will stay here tonight."

"Thank you for all your help to us," said Colette warmly.

"Only doing my duty," said Gavin, but his smile showed he appreciated her praise. "Sleep well. Let us hope the morn will bring better tidings." He voice was low and the seductive lilt of his Scottish tongue swept over her sweetly, like a cool summer breeze.

Colette stood in the doorway of her tent and watched, unable to turn away, as he rode down the dusty road, the babe nestled in the crook of one arm. She had not thought such a man could exist.

Eleven

MADAME ALISOUN WAS DRUNK. AGAIN.

Pippa was never sure if she preferred Madame drunk or sober. At least with drink, there was a chance she would pass out. And that was how Pippa liked Madame Alisoun best.

Madame Alisoun downed another bottle and tossed it to the side. She had chosen an odd name, for she had never married and the only genteel thing about her was her aversion to work. Work was what Pippa and the other girls were for.

A knock on the door brought a chill to Pippa's heart. Madame Alisoun answered the door with a slippery smile and welcomed in a well-dressed man. Pippa watched the proceedings from behind a tattered curtain, which divided the main room of what had once been a respectable farmhouse.

"Pippa, bring out the girls!" demanded Madame.

Several young girls crowded around Pippa, their eyes wide. They ranged in age from six to twelve years. Pippa, at seventeen, was the oldest. She was old enough to escape Madame Alisoun, but she refused to leave the young girls behind. What would happen to them without her? She shuddered at the thought.

"Do not fear. We will take care of him as we have the rest." She held out a little bottle of tawny liquid and dropped it back into her pocket.

Pippa led the girls out before the man, who looked them over with a critical, if slightly inebriated, eye.

"That one." He pointed at Emelye, a ten-year-old with large blue eyes and a creamy complexion marred by the garish red rouge Madame Alisoun applied.

Emelye looked up at Pippa, her eyes widening even more. Pippa gave her a confident nod. Emelye led the man to a small chamber, barely large enough to hold a bed. Pippa prepared a glass of wine with a liberal dose of the contents of her small bottle.

"For you, good sir, compliments of the house." Pippa entered the room and handed the man the glass.

"Ah, this best be good." He grabbed the glass and drank it down in a single gulp. "I'm paying good coin for this."

"Then let me prepare this girl for your comfort," Pippa said, without revealing too much of a growl. She grabbed Emelye's hand and led her from the chamber.

"Do you think it will work?" whispered Emelye anxiously.

"It has never failed me," Pippa whispered in return.

"Here now. I want my girl now!" The man emerged from the room, swaying on his feet.

"Run!" hissed Pippa to Emelye. She thrust herself between the drunk man and the young girl. He grabbed her and tried to toss her aside, but Pippa grappled him to the ground. They struggled until the man's limbs grew weak and he lost consciousness, snoring loudly.

Pippa sat up, gasping at his side.

"Are you hurt?" asked Emelye.

"No, I am fine," said Pippa, ignoring the bumps and bruises. "Let us strip him naked and lay him on the bed. Make him think he had quite the time, yes?"

"Do we take his purse?" asked the youngest girl, jangling the pouch in her hand.

"Of course," answered Pippa. "Fool jackanapes deserves what he gets. Madame Alisoun will make up some excuse to charge him more."

Pippa went about her work roughly. She cared not for the likes of men. They were all the same and all bad.

※

Gavin rode down the dusty road, the baby sleeping comfortably in the crook of his arm. The setting sun hastened his pace. The hour was late, and he needed to quickly find a home for the babe and return to camp. News had reached him that the English were taking more control of the coast, which could be disastrous to their plan of leaving by ship.

With this many English soldiers mucking about, it was only a matter of time before the whispers of an enormous fortune being driven down the road would reach their ears. Gavin had no illusions about his ability to defeat an English army intent on claiming an easy prize.

Gavin had heard tell of a woman who took in orphans. She was not far and it seemed the quickest way to rid himself of one difficulty. In truth, his mind was far from the small, wiggling bundle and more on the difficulties of having to try to find a way to get Colette and all her belongings into Scotland.

Gavin was so intent in all his musings that he almost missed the humble cottage by the side of the road. It was a strange little place. There was one main cottage, which must have been a farmhouse at one time but additional rooms had been added onto it. Each addition was made of slightly different construction, giving the house a disjointed feel. A rickety gate surrounded the house and an untended garden. A red silk banner was raised on a pole, flapping in the wind. Gavin was not sure what to make of the place.

Gavin dismounted, wrapped the reins of his destrier around the rickety gate with a flick of his wrist, and strode toward the main door, baby in hand. The door was flung open before he got a chance to knock. A woman stood at the door with greasy blond hair, a sharp mouth, and owlish eyes.

She looked him up and down and gave him a smile that was so cold he almost shuddered from the shock. "Welcome, welcome, good knight." She rubbed her hands together. "I am Madame Alisoun. What will be your pleasure today?"

Though she beckoned him inside the house, Gavin's feet refused to move. His very soul fought against entering and he was quite sure that this baby was not going to be left in her care. "Forgive me, madam, I have clearly come to the wrong house. I wish ye well. Good day." He turned to leave, but she grabbed his arm.

"No, good sir. Do not leave so hastily. I see you wish to have the finer things in life, no? Be not fooled by appearances. We can give you anything you wish."

Gavin slowly turned to her. What he wished was for her to release his sleeve. A part of him wanted to make a run for it and ride back down the road, never looking back. But another part was afraid there was something here that needed to be revealed, something very wrong, which, if he did not investigate, would never be corrected. "And what, madam, do I desire?"

Her calculating smile widened. "But, look here, you brought us a present. If you please, do step inside. We can help you with this bundle if it be a girl bundle."

"Ye only take girls?" Gavin was suspicious.

"Quite so, sir. Of course you would not want to leave this baby unprotected, uncared for. An arrangement most beneficial can be made." She reached out for the child, but Gavin held the baby fast. He was not going to allow this woman of dubious intent to touch the child.

She gave him another cold smile and led him into the house. The main room was something odd. Dingy red drapes had been hung about the room, concealing much from view. The woman clapped her hands and out came three young girls.

The oldest might have been in her older teens, with the other girls progressively younger. The eldest girl stood in front, as if to protect the younger ones. Their hair was unkempt and their cheeks and lips had been rouged. Gavin's stomach took an unpleasant lurch. He was very much afraid of where he had landed.

"Will you not sit, Sir Knight?" purred Madame Alisoun, pointing to a bench covered in velvet cushions with suspicious stains. "My girls, they can entertain you while we consider the price of caring for the precious baby."

"So ye sell yer services to take care o' young girls," Gavin stated coldly. There was nothing in this world that could induce him to sit on one of the benches. "What else here is for sale, madam?"

The woman's eyes turned from deep round orbs to narrow slits. "Anything you see that you like is for sale."

Gavin took two large steps toward her, hardly able to contain his own fury. She took a step back, her eyes flying wide once more. "Aye," he said with a growl. "Let us do business."

❧

Gavin rode back down the dusty road, the baby still cradled in his arm. It was night, his way lit only by the light of a half-moon. Though anxious to return to camp, he did not travel faster than a leisurely walk. Behind him a parade of five young girls followed him. The rescue had cost him all his coin and had left him saddled not only with one infant but five girls ranging in age from teens to six years old. He'd made a deal with Madame Alisoun and had not left the house as well as he had found it. She was greatly displeased to be deprived of her only source of income, but he very much insisted.

After their liberation, the girls all looked to the eldest, as if waiting on her decision as to whether or not to go with him. The teen, Pippa she called herself, held a knife almost hidden in the folds of her skirt.

"What you want with us?" she demanded.

"I wish to find ye all a safe home."

Pippa gave him a shrewd look, her eyes blazing, but accepted his offer of freedom. "I will come with you because I like how you redecorated the house." She glanced at the havoc he had wrought. "But if any part of you touches me or the girls, I will cut out your gizzard and eat it for supper, I swear it will be so."

He gave the fierce creature a quick nod. He had no interest in coming anywhere near any of them. And yet he could not leave children in such a state.

The girls followed Pippa, looking rather bewildered, but very willing to leave the house. He needed to find homes for them, homes where they would not be subject to ill treatment, and he still needed to get Lady Colette and all her belongings and all her maids and all her soldiers to Scotland. Oh, and he still needed someone to care for the baby.

Gavin ran his hand though his hair in the distracted manner he had seen his uncle do many times. He had not understood the gesture when he was young. He did now. It had not been an easy day. But then again, he glanced back at his dazed charges, considering what others had endured, he could not complain.

He shook his head, trying to imagine what the captain of the guard or Colette would say to this strange addition to their party. He had gone to relieve them of one baby and was returning with an entire nursery!

He knew he was not making their journey any easier. He was supposed to be the knight who took care of things, ensuring their journey was a success, but instead he was adding complications and delay. He did not relish appearing incompetent in Colette's eyes. But maybe, if he could quickly figure out a place the children could go, Colette would never have to know.

Twelve

MARIE COLETTE LAY AWAKE ON HER COT, WAITING FOR the return of Sir Gavin. He had not returned as soon as she'd expected. How long could it take to drop off one baby? Why she should be waiting for his return she did not know. It could not possibly be that she was concerned for his safety. He was quite capable of taking care of himself. Nor did she fear that he would abandon them. She knew in her heart he was a man of impeccable honor.

Despite telling herself firmly to go to sleep, she lay awake, listening for his return. Her maids lay around her asleep, guarding her as they were trained to do. Colette closed her eyes, folded her arms over her chest, and willed herself to sleep, but slumber is a fickle bedfellow and always runs away when actively sought.

Finally, she heard a rider approaching, but at first she did not believe it to be Gavin, for the horse came slowly, at a sedate walk. Gavin never walked his horse anywhere but galloped hither and yon wherever he went. As she listened intently, she heard the rumble of a low voice with a tone and tenor that could only be his. What had kept him? *Something must be wrong.*

Without considering the ramifications, she slid noiselessly from the bed and pulled on her silk robe, wrapping it around her. She wore her sleeping wimple, a plain white linen veil that covered her head and neck. Even in sleep, propriety had to be maintained. She tiptoed carefully around the sleeping forms of her maids, searching for a pair of slippers, but with only the moon illuminating the walls of the canvas tent, she was unable to find them. She gave up and stealthily crept around her maids, careful not to wake them.

She slipped out the tent and stopped at the shock of the cold grass on her bare feet. She tried to remember the last time her bare feet had touched the earth, but she could not recall. She must have been very young, or perhaps it had never been allowed. She scrunched her toes into the cool grass, relishing the feel of the earth between her toes. What would her ladies say if they saw her dirtying her feet in such a manner?

She wrapped her robe around herself tighter against the chill of the evening and walked quietly toward the sound of the male voices. It was a calm night. The waxing moon hung low in the night sky and a myriad of bright stars twinkled above her.

When the rumble of voices became discernible words, she stopped behind one of her wagons. Since she had already broken every rule by walking about barefoot, unguarded at night, she reasoned she might as well toss aside every stricture on her conduct and eavesdrop shamelessly on the conversation.

"Not sure what you expect us to do with them." Captain Perrine spoke to Sir Gavin in a harsh whisper. "The English, they are on the move. This will only slow us down further, no?"

"I ken this comes at a bad time. But I coud'na leave them in such a shameful condition. As a Christian and a knight, my conscience bade me act. I did the only thing I could," said Sir Gavin with his enticing, lyrical voice.

"I do not wish you to think me an unfeeling man. I have children of my own. But I fear we have more than we can handle simply trying protect our lady, let alone take care of anyone else."

"Aye. That is why I hoped to find a solution soon. Tonight if possible. Do you know of anyone, anyplace that might help us?"

"I do not know. Perhaps Lady Colette—" suggested Captain Perrine, but Gavin cut him off.

"In truth, I was hoping no' to involve her."

What were they talking about? What was Sir Gavin trying to keep from her? It was time to be bold. She held her head high and walked into the moonlight toward the two men. She hoped that they would not notice her bare feet. It was easier to hold herself with aristocratic hauteur if they did not see her bare toes wiggling in the dirt.

One look at the men's faces as she approached told her that her bare feet would be the least of anyone's concern.

"My lady!" Captain Perrine gasped. "Is anything amiss?"

"No, all is well, except Sir Gavin returns to camp at a late hour. What has detained you, Sir Knight?"

Gavin and her captain exchanged a glance, as if trying to decide how much they should reveal. Marie Colette ground her teeth. She hated to be treated like some sort of insipid piece of fragile glass that might shatter at any moment. She knew her practiced composure made people conclude she never had a care in the world. No one could know the pain it caused nor the strength it demanded to maintain such a serene facade.

"Go to bed, m'lady. There is naught to concern ye now." Gavin's voice was tired.

"The babe you still carry in your arms," observed Marie Colette. "I thought you had found someone to take the infant."

"The woman proved woefully inept. In truth, instead o' finding a solution, I found more troubles, but this is my problem to solve."

It was then that Colette noticed them. Five girls were huddled toward the end of one of the wagons. "You sought to give away a babe and returned with five more instead?"

"It was an unavoidable circumstance. Naught to concern ye." Gavin shifted from one foot to the other, clearly uncomfortable with the conversation.

"Of course this concerns me!" declared Colette. "Sir Gavin, you cannot traipse about the countryside collecting waifs you find along the way. You must return them to their families."

"If they had families, I woud'na be collecting them at all."

"Are we now to serve as an orphanage? What is to become of them?" Colette did not know what to think. She wished to help anyone who needed it, but she feared they may only bring these children into more danger by adding them to their party.

"What would ye have me do? I coud'na leave them." Gavin's eyebrows clamped down over stern black eyes.

"But how are we to help them?" she asked.

"I dinna ken" was his only answer. He ran his fingers through his hair in a distracted manner.

"We cannot take them with us to the Highlands. I do not know what you think we can do for them," continued Colette, appealing to reason.

Gavin's shoulders slumped, but a certain set to his jaw indicated he did not appreciate her pointing out the facts before him. "If ye are worried for yer own inconvenience, let me assure ye, I dinna expect ye to care for them."

Colette flushed warm in the cool night air, anger rising within her. "But why ever not? Let us start a home for wayward children. It will be most delightful to arrive on the doorstep of my husband with an entire brood of children, no? It does a lady's reputation much good to surround herself with infants and young children of unknown parentage."

"Ye'll find in the Highlands, we have much different ideas o' how we treat each other, m'lady. We dinna walk by the poor and the needy wi'out extending a hand," Gavin responded coldly.

Colette gasped at his rude comment, especially after she had cherished his praise on how she had tended the infant. "How do you propose we help them? By including them in our party, we will travel slower, putting not only ourselves but them at risk too."

"The only thing making us a target for English attack are all these wagons full o' riches."

His words stung. Colette thought he'd understood what her inheritance meant to her. "These are my mother's things," she said through gritted teeth.

"They are things!" Gavin gestured wildly with his free hand in an exasperated manner. "Ye put yerself and everyone at risk, clinging to these belongings."

Colette held her head high, her back straight. She would not let him see how his words struck her harder than a physical blow. He had agreed to help her, but at the first sign of difficulty, he threw it back in her face.

Colette pulled her wrap around her closer, aware of many sets of eyes. Captain Perrine was watching them. The orphans were watching them. The night stars were watching them, and she felt the judgment of all the heavens upon her.

"Thank you for your candid opinion regarding my marriage contract. I appreciate how boldly you have shared it with not only me but so many of our traveling companions. Since you have declared this is not my concern, I will allow you to tend to it and we can continue this edifying conversation in the morn." She spun and stalked off, intending to go back to her tent.

A plaintive groan arrested her in her tracks. "Wait!" called Gavin, catching up to her. "I was wrong. I shoud'na have spoke to ye such."

Colette did not turn around, not trusting herself to keep her temper.

"A word in private, if I may?" he asked, his voice once again soft and low, though with a sliver of anxiety. It was for this reason alone she gave a quick nod and walked off behind one of the far wagons so they could speak without an audience.

"It was not right for you to speak to me such before my guards and certainly not before a passel of orphans you found by the side of the road," began Colette.

Gavin sighed and leaned a shoulder against the wagon, the tightly wrapped babe still sleeping in one arm. "Ye're right."

"And this is my journey, my people. If you wish to add to our party, you must ask me first, not dismiss me and tell me it is none of my concern."

"Aye, ye're right again."

She stared at him. Of all the things she had thought he was going to say, an acceptance of blame was not one of them. She had been ready for a fight, but now she did not know what to say.

"I shoud'na have said… Och, I shoud'na said most o' what I just said. My mum would box my ears if she could have heard me," Gavin acknowledged with an easy humility that only betrayed his strength. "In truth, I would feel better if ye did it for her. I'm man enough to admit I deserve it."

Colette could not help a small smile at the thought of doing Gavin some well-deserved harm, but she demurred. "You hold a child, and I could never hurt an innocent."

"Ah, now ye have saved me, wee lassie," Gavin said to the sleeping baby. He looked up at Colette with eyes bright in the moonlight. "Ye're also right about the orphans. We canna care for them, but I dinna ken what else to do but take them wi' me."

"Yes, well…yes." She did not know what to say to a man who agreed with her.

"I found the girls in the care of a woman o' vicious character," Gavin explained. "It was a house of ill repute, I am sorry to say. She was willing not only to take the baby for coin, but she also offered me carnal knowledge o' her young charges for the right price. It was impossible for me to leave them in that situation."

Colette's heart sank. "They were being… But they are only children!"

Gavin gave her a grim-faced nod.

She could not imagine anything so despicable. "Why did you not say so in the first place? I cannot imagine anyone could be so cruel as to misuse a child. We must see them to a safe place."

"Thank ye." Gavin closed his eyes for a moment, then opened them again and gave her a warm smile.

"But why did you wish to keep this from me?" asked Colette.

Gavin sighed. "I was supposed to fix the problem, no' come back wi' more. I dinna ken how to solve this situation, and I dinna wish ye to think me less than capable. I fear it made me irritable."

"This is not your fault, unless having a tender heart is a crime. But we must work together if we are to find some solution," said Colette, stepping closer, her anger appeased.

The smile Gavin gave her warmed her down to her bare toes. "I hope so, though wi' many o' the folk around here reeling from the losses incurred from the English, it will be difficult to find families willing to take them in."

In a flash, Colette knew what must be done, but she could not bear to speak the words. "An idea, it has come to me of how we may solve many of these problems, but let us wait until morn to discuss it. Call the children and let them sleep in the protection of my tent."

Gavin's eyebrows rose, for it was an uncommon privilege for a lady of her rank to invite such people into her own tent. He stepped closer, a smile playing on his lips. "I am so glad we had this talk, m'lady. And that you decided on counsel rather than doing me violence."

She moved toward him and placed her hand on the head of the sleeping baby. "You can thank your young friend here for your protection." She stroked the soft head of the sleeping child, then slid her hand up, onto his muscled arm. She had wanted to do that for so long, she could not hold her hand back and was rewarded with the feel of rock-solid muscle. "You are a strong man, Sir Gavin. It would be a shame to best you before others, no?" She spoke in jest to cover her thrill in shamelessly feeling the man's muscles.

He placed his free hand over hers, moving even closer toward her. She had to tilt her chin up to see into his eyes.

"Ye can wound a man wi'out touching him. Dinna doubt yer power." Gavin gently took her hand and pressed her knuckles to his soft lips.

Heat raced from his touch, down her arm and to the core of her being. How many courtiers had brushed their lips against her fingers? Yet none had ever gave her such a tremor of excitement.

He handed her the baby, and she leaned even closer to accept the child. The closer she was to him, the harder her heart felt compelled to beat. Instinctively, she backed away, taking the babe with her, yet she regretted their lack of connection. He stepped back, giving her a formal bow.

"Good night, Sir Knight." Her mind spinning, she turned and fled back to her tent.

Thirteen

COLETTE SLEPT POORLY, IN PART DUE TO THE UPROAR bringing five girls and a baby into the tent caused with her ladies, and in part due to her mixed feelings regarding Sir Gavin. She had never been so attracted to a man. It was unacceptable, and she wished to blame him for her confusing feelings but feared it was her own fault. What was she thinking, running her hand up and down his arm like a common harlot?

It was at least an hour before dawn when she gave up any hope of sleeping and once again crept out of the tent, though this time it was light enough to find slippers. It was strange how freeing one simple act of rebellion could feel. She strolled through the lush, tall grass, beads of dew shimmering on each strand. She ran her hand along the wet tops as she brushed through until she reached a small rise. She was not foolish enough to wander far, just enough distance to regain perspective on a world gone sideways.

The sky grew lighter in the east, at first nothing more than a gray smudge but gradually blossoming with pale pinks and oranges until the sky was painted brilliant colors with the promise of a fresh new day.

She opened her Book of Hours and read the passage from the book of Isaiah. *Ne memineritis priorum, et antiqua ne intueamini. Ecce ego facio nova, et nunc orientur, utique cognoscetis ea; ponam in deserto viam, et in invio flumina.* She pondered the verse, translating to herself. "Forget the former things; do not dwell on the past. See, I am doing a new thing! Now it springs up; do you not perceive it? I am making a way in the wilderness and streams in the wasteland."

Her old life was past. Was she holding on to her former existence? The plan she had considered the night before crept back to mind. Was it time to let go? This new life was different from anything she had ever known. A single tear fell, and she let it roll down her cheek. She could not remember when she had last allowed herself to shed tears. Everything was changing. And yet the Scriptures also spoke of a way in the wilderness. She shook her head. If there was a way, it was difficult to perceive.

"My lady?" Gavin's voice sounded from behind her and she quickly wiped the telltale tear from sight.

She took a moment to ensure she was composed and turned to face him. "Yes, Sir Gavin? You are an early riser."

He strode up the rise to stand beside her. He was at home in the pale light of dawn, earthy and raw. "Coud'na sleep for thinking." He frowned at her. "Why are ye not in yer tent?"

Colette could not help but smile. He spoke as if she were a misplaced object. "Ah, you have caught me in the act of making my escape most desperate."

Gavin gave her an easy smile. "Anyone wi' any sense would leave this outfit."

"Shall you be leaving then?"

Gavin shrugged. "I'm a Highlander. Got no sense."

"I am very sorry to hear it."

Gavin sighed, the quick humor in his eyes turning serious once more. "I wish I had an answer for the bairns I saddled ye wi' and a way to get ye safe to yer ship."

The sun's rays crept over the horizon, bathing them in a shaft of orange light. It was a new day. The old was past. Tomorrow was yet to come. Though it was sad to leave behind the old, Colette had a tingle of excitement at beginning her own new adventure. Like the fearless heroes and heroines of her beloved books, perhaps it was time to take her future more firmly in hand. "Take me to the nearest township. I know what needs to be done."

She took a deep breath of the clean morning air. It was time. Everything must change.

❧

Gavin prided himself on being able to deal calmly with whatever life brought his way. He was not one to dwell in anxious thoughts. However, the prospect of keeping Lady Colette safe, protecting her vast wealth, and now finding a suitable arrangement for a wagon full of urchins did give rise to a bit of worry. Add to that the growing fear of an English attack and Gavin was becoming uncharacteristically nervous.

He rode up and down the road, scanning for any sign of attack. The English were nearby in large numbers and could decide to go anywhere, even straight into their path.

Another distraction was Colette herself. He had expected her to dissolve into hysterics by now, but she had remained remarkably implacable, seeing to the care of the children and directing her ladies to be helpful. He was not sure whether it was her acceptance of the orphans or her ability to stand up to her outraged ladies-in-waiting that impressed him more. Most disconcerting was her undeniable beauty. She was a handsome woman at any time, but this morning, when the sun's rays had shone on her face, she had glowed like an angel. He feared the image would be forever seared into his memory.

As requested, he found a township along their route that was not occupied by the English. Many of the townsfolk from the destroyed town had taken refuge there. Why she wished to stop he could not say, though he guessed she might wish to buy more supplies for their growing party.

After they had been in the village for about an hour, he grew restless. He wanted to get back on the road. Staying in one place left them vulnerable to being surrounded and attacked. He noted with impatience that Lady Colette was in deep discussion with the mayor of the town and his wife. What they were discussing he did not know nor did he care, for he was only interested in how soon he could get her back into the saddle.

Much to his displeasure, he noted tables and benches were being brought into the open square in the middle of the town. They were beginning a meal. He groaned audibly. They had no time for this. What could she be thinking?

Gavin gave word to the guards to prepare to leave and walked toward Colette to get her moving again. No matter his feelings, his job was to get her safely to Scotland and he would see it done.

He was surprised to see the children walk toward Colette, brought forth by her ladies-in-waiting. The children had been riding in one of the wagons with a few of her ladies and had been transformed. The children's garments, originally rough and soiled, had been replaced by beautiful ones of silk and fine linen. Colette must have directed her maids to quickly alter her own gowns for the children. He stopped short, wondering what she was doing.

Colette held out her hand to one of the girls, who walked forward and took it with a smile. "This is Emelye," said Colette with a nod of approval. "With all of the battles our country has endured, many of our children have been left homeless and without protection. These poor orphans, they have been adopted by a close friend, who has provided them with dowries for the family who would take them and love them as all God's children should be."

"Oh!" cried the mayor's wife. "What a little angel she looks. I have always wanted a little girl, and the Lord has blessed me with five strapping boys." She smiled and her eyes never left the face of the child.

"You said something about a dowry?" The mayor did not appear to be as delighted with the idea of a daughter as his wife was, but he was certainly interested to hear what she brought to the table.

"Yes, quite," said Colette with a winning smile. "She has been given a dowry of thirty yards of silk, two gold candlesticks, a feather mattress, and an engraved wood bed frame."

Gavin gasped. What was she doing? She was giving away her own things in order for the children to be adopted. He vaguely recognized that his chin had dropped almost to his chest, but he could do nothing to bring it back. He was astounded. Marie Colette, whom he had been convinced would hold desperately to her possessions even if it meant her own demise, was giving away her things to help a young orphaned child. And he was finally rid of that enormous bed!

He had thought Colette was the most beautiful woman he'd ever seen, but now she was even more striking. She turned and caught his eye, a slow smile spreading across her face. She was stunning. His knees gave way and he stumbled forward, catching himself on the edge of the table. He wanted to return the smile, but the power of the emotion coursing through him would not allow it. He must get away. It was wrong to feel this powerful an attraction toward an engaged lady under his protection.

He spun on his heel and walked away.

It wasn't until he reached the wagons and watched one being unloaded that he fully recognized the magnitude of her loss. He knew what this meant to her and yet she gave it away with a smile. Just how much of herself did this lady hide from view? None who looked at her would guess the enormity of her sacrifice. Yet he knew.

Was there anyone else who recognized what courage and pure charity of heart this took? He watched her ladies squabbling and complaining as things were being removed. Her ladies didn't understand, that was certain.

It was a special gift, this glimpse of herself that she had given him. But what was he to do with it?

Fourteen

OMINOUS DARK CLOUDS ROLLED IN FROM THE WEST. IT would probably rain soon, a perfect match for her current mood. Colette sat at the table beside the mayor and his wife and gave away large portions of her inheritance in order to find homes for the waifs. As an added benefit, the things she gave provided practical assistance to many families who were now refugees in their own homeland after the English had burned their town to the ground.

Despite the good she knew she was doing, it was difficult to hand over her mother's things to strangers. There was not a gold goblet or velvet chair that did not hold some cherished remembrance. She wished to cry, to mourn the loss of each item, but she would not shame the memory of her mother by making such a display in public. So she smiled through the entire arrangement without betraying the emotion it cost her to do so. She was successful in her efforts, yet the one person she thought would be pleased had merely glowered and walked away.

She had not realized how much she had been

anticipating Sir Gavin's favorable response. It was to be the one consolation for her sacrifice. She watched him edge closer to the proceedings and noted his surprise at her intentions. She had expected him to catch her eye with a smile, or at least look pleased, but she was rewarded with nothing but a scowl. She felt cheated.

Colette directed her attention back to her work and was able to find homes for all the girls save the infant. No amount of gold could make up for the disfiguring scar across the child's cheek. Colette heard a whisper of "devil mark" slither through the townsfolk, and none would touch her. It did not help that Philippa, the eldest of the rescued waifs, held on to the baby with fierce protection and glared at anyone who glanced in their direction.

Philippa, or Pippa as she called herself, had come to Colette a dirty thing with straggly brown hair and a filthy gown. After a rather uncomfortable confrontation with Marie Claude, in which Colette insisted her ladies provide assistance no matter how unpleasant the work or ungrateful the recipient, much work had gone into freeing the teen from her filth.

Remarkably, Pippa emerged a handsome creature with dark brown eyes and beautiful brown hair that fell in natural ringlets. At seventeen years, she was a ripe age for marriage, and Colette was certain she could see the thing done if Pippa could manage to divest herself of her scowl.

It was time to find a suitable situation for the irritable teenager. Colette leaned to the side to speak to the mayor's wife privately. "I also have Philippa here, a lovely girl and good with children, yes? She would make some man a very capable wife."

"Yes, of course," said the mayor's wife, smiling. Her focus was primarily on the new child she had just adopted. "I shall direct my husband."

It did not take long for several men to approach their table and take up seemingly innocent conversations as they took note of a scowling Pippa. Unfortunately, the recalcitrant teen noticed them as well and was instantly suspicious.

"These men, what are they doing here?" she asked in a voice not as hushed as Colette would have preferred. "I am too old to be put in some home, no?"

"But of course. That is why you must be married," whispered Colette in a practiced undertone.

"Married?!" Pippa squawked in a loud voice.

"Hush!" Colette spoke without moving her lips and gave young Pippa a searing glance. The young girl slouched and cast a sullen look to all about her.

Colette took a deep drink from her goblet before turning to the rather surprised faces of the mayor and his wife. The mayor was the first to recover.

"And what of her dowry?" he asked.

Colette paused. She wished she could discuss the matter privately, without Pippa being present. Dowries and marriage contracts should be negotiated by fathers behind closed doors, not in the town square before the maid in question.

Colette leaned toward the mayor. "Her dowry will be more than adequate."

The mayor leaned toward her. "And what do you consider adequate?"

Pippa also leaned in. "What are you all whispering about?"

Colette turned to Pippa and spoke in what she hoped was a reassuring tone. "A dowry is being provided for you. You cannot marry without one. You would like to be married, no?"

Pippa screwed up her face into a look of disgust. "Married? Why would I want that? And why must I give some man something to marry me? At least with Madame Alisoun, the men paid me."

"Philippa!" Even Colette could not restrain her tongue.

"You tell these men I am not for sale!" demanded Pippa.

The mayor gasped. His wife dropped her goblet, splashing wine on her gown. Such was her shock that she hardly noticed.

"Take the babe and go wait in the wagon," Colette instructed Pippa. Any hopes of marrying her off respectably were dashed. "Thank you for your hospitality," Colette said, addressing the mayor and his wife. Colette rose from her seat with a poise she did not feel. It was time for a hasty retreat.

Colette walked out of the square to the outskirts of the town where her wagons, or what was left of them, were waiting. "Repack the wagons to travel with as few as possible. Leave those unused behind," she directed her guards.

The wind blew a chill on the back of her neck. The weather was turning. She walked into the wind, relishing its biting sting. Despite Pippa's clear lack of grace or tact, her statements struck a tender nerve within Colette. Though she had nothing, Pippa would not trade her freedom for safety or security. She was not for sale.

But Colette…apparently, she was.

Odd how an orphaned waif could demand more from life than Colette herself. And why, now that she was thinking of it, did Colette have to bring a large dowry with her to entice a man to marry her? Was she not good enough on her own?

Colette stared into the dark clouds of the approaching storm. She had every advantage, but still she had less freedom than the average urchin. Her new adventure did not seem so glorious as it had earlier that morning.

"Why did ye do it?" Gavin was at her side.

Colette jumped a little at his sudden appearance, even as her heart beat a bit faster. She did not feel equal to crossing swords with Sir Gavin at that moment. "You told me to give my things away, no? Now I have done so while finding homes for the orphans and assisting those who had lost much when their town was destroyed. I thought you would be pleased."

"But those were yer mother's things. Ye gave them away wi'out letting anyone see the pain it gave ye."

Colette took a sharp breath. He saw too much. "There can be no purpose in distressing those around me."

"I ken what it cost ye to do this today," Gavin said softly, his eyes warm with sympathy. "I thank ye for it. Ye may have saved this journey from capture and ye certainly gave the bairns, and those who took them in, a better life."

Colette tried to give him a controlled smile, but her lips trembled and the practiced, cool facade crumbled. This man saw through the disguise. This man understood her sacrifice. "I saw you leave the square. I thought you were displeased."

"I was surprised is all." Gavin looked away and cleared his throat. "I hope I have recovered from my shock enough to say how greatly I appreciate your efforts. Ye're more than I expected and stronger than I thought."

His kind words slid past her defenses and hit home in a manner harsh words could not. "Thank you." She turned and hastily wiped away a tear. It would not do to cry, and yet grief for all she was leaving behind bubbled up within her. Her family, her home, the only life she had ever known—it was all gone.

He drew nearer, standing between her and her people, who were preparing for travel. "No shame in crying," he said softly.

But Colette did not wish to cry, especially not before Sir Gavin. She kept her back to him and had almost gotten herself back under control when he put a warm hand on her shoulder. Heat flowed through her, warm and sweet, at the mere touch of his hand.

"Ye did well, but I am sorry for yer loss." Gavin gave her shoulder a slight squeeze.

It was too much. Colette could no longer hold in the emotion. Tears streamed down her face—tears that had been waiting years to be shed over the loss of her mother were finally allowed to break free. She took a ragged breath, and before she knew what was happening, she was wrapped up into the strong arms of her Highland guide.

She should have struggled to break free, but instead she gave in to grief and sobbed onto his broad shoulder. He held her gently and made calming noises in some language she did not understand. He blocked her from view, and Colette knew he was intentionally protecting her from prying eyes.

"I do apologize. I cannot understand what madness this is," Colette murmured, when she could once again speak.

"Ye've lost much. There's no need for apology." He gave her a gentle squeeze before letting go. She longed for more of his warm embrace.

"I fear I look a sight," she wiped the tears from her swollen eyes.

"Ye're always beautiful to me." He leaned toward her, his face dangerously close to hers.

Her heart beat fast. Her lips parted as she stared up into his handsome face. His eyes, which had always seemed warm to her, now burned with intensity. She drew herself closer to him, wrapping her hands around his neck, rising on her toes to be closer still.

A cold splash of water fell onto her nose, bringing her back to her senses. "Oh!"

Gavin stepped back and cleared his throat. "The rain is come," he observed, staring up into the offending clouds.

More splashes on her cheeks told her it was so. A call came from the camp; the wagons were ready to leave. Gavin gave her a quick nod and escorted her to her mount.

The old was being washed away. It was time to move into the new.

Fifteen

Pippa pulled a wide hood over her head as the rain began to fall with decided rapidity. She sat in the front of a wagon, holding the baby, whom she had finally rocked to sleep, while Lady Colette and her maids rode before her. Pippa wiped her nose on her sleeve, sniffing loudly. She thought she had cried all her tears, saying good-bye to the young girls she had fought to protect. But still more came. The babe also was squally, and so they had both cried together. They were a sorry lot.

Despite her sorrow, she was grateful to Sir Gavin and Lady Colette for doing in two days what she had not been able to do in a dozen years. They had rescued the girls and found them all good homes. Pippa recognized the great lady had given away her own things to serve as a dowry for the children. Their party was now considerably smaller, just two wagons, the lady's guards, and her ladies-in-waiting. Sir Gavin rode in front and around and behind, always watchful and ready.

Pippa was not sure what to do with herself now. While she appreciated Lady Colette's efforts to find homes for the young ones, she was not about to be sold off in marriage, no matter how well intended. If she were to ever marry, which did not seem likely since she had no dowry and had a healthy dislike for most men, she would be the one doing the choosing.

But what now? The great lady was leaving France, and Pippa must do something with herself. She had no fear of work and wondered if she might get hired as a maid, though they would no doubt ask questions of where she came from, which would be difficult to answer. The one thing she would not do was go back into the life she had escaped. For the meantime, she was content to stay with Lady Colette and Sir Gavin as long as they continued to feed her.

The rain began to pound down harder, and Pippa lowered her head so her hood protected her face and the baby from the weather. They rode on for hours, past the sunset and on into the dark evening. The rain was unrelenting and Pippa began to fear they would ride through the night.

Finally, Sir Gavin rode up beside Lady Colette. "There is an inn ahead. We should stop for the night."

Pippa sighed in relief.

"We cannot go much farther," said Lady Colette, though her perfect posture had not slacked one inch since the beginning of the ride.

"Aye, and wi' every step, we draw closer to the English army," said Sir Gavin. "They're strong along the coastal towns. We would do well to stop here and determine how we are to proceed. Bordeaux isna far now."

"I am certain we could all use some rest," said Lady Colette.

Both Lady Colette and Sir Gavin held back a bit and to the side until they were next to each other and a bit apart from the others. Pippa wondered if they realized they did it.

"When we arrive at the inn, please dinna reveal yer true identity. It woud'na be safe," said Sir Gavin, gazing at the great lady, particularly when she was not looking.

"I understand," answered Lady Colette, stealing glances at the knight beside her when he turned away.

"We'll say we are a family of merchants. That will explain the wagons and the number of us," said Sir Gavin.

Lady Colette nodded.

Pippa expected him to gallop off immediately, as he always did with anyone else, but he did not. Instead, he rode beside Lady Colette for a while, even as the rain began to pelt down harder. Pippa wondered at this. She had been told Lady Colette was on a journey to meet her new husband in Scotland, so she did not understand the longing looks Sir Gavin and Lady Colette were casting each other.

Something interesting was going to happen. She could feel it.

❧

It was with no small amount of relief that Colette arrived at the inn and was assisted from her mount by Sir Gavin while Captain Perrine prepared for their arrival. She was pleased to be off the horse and even more pleased to have Gavin's hands around her waist. Their eyes met in the dark, lit only by the lantern on the inn door. Neither spoke.

Gavin suddenly released her and cleared his throat. "Must see to the horses," he said, a hint of a smile about his mouth, and strode off into the darkness.

She pushed all thoughts of Gavin from her mind and focused on the inn. The prospect of going somewhere warm and dry was a welcome one. While she gritted her teeth against any complaint, her ladies did not feel such compunction. The past several days had been difficult for them, and they were not beyond letting this be known to anyone who stood close enough to hear. They were displeased about the long rides, they were displeased about the weather, they were displeased about the accommodations, and though not spoken freely, Colette knew they were increasingly displeased at having to accompany her into the wilds of Scotland.

The inn was a modest one and did not support private dining accommodations, so they were all required to eat in the public room. Given the inclement weather, the main room was crowded with people seeking refuge from the cold and damp. Her captain secured a table in the corner, and Colette was ushered there with her maids, their mouths tight with indignation. Colette struggled to keep her face serene. When the food arrived, plain but hearty and plenty of it, she threw aside her usual reserve and ate a substantial meal. Her weary ladies took her suggestion and also ate well.

The mistress of the house, a plump lady with a generous bosom and rosy cheeks, came around the table. "I trust you have found the meal to your liking."

"*Oui*. It was very good. *Merci*." Colette gave the landlady an approving nod of her head.

Gavin entered the inn with his characteristic pleasant demeanor. He called for a pint of ale and all eyes followed him as he strode across the room. Colette watched as well. He had an easy presence about him— something akin to a puppy who did not realize he had grown to be a large dog, still retaining his playfulness.

"Well now, he is a handsome man and no mistake." The landlady put a hand over her ample cleavage and sighed.

Colette frowned. She did not approve of Gavin being ogled in a public room.

The landlady caught her look of disapproval and apologized hastily. "I am begging your pardon, m'lady. Is he your husband or your betrothed mayhap?"

"No." *Unfortunately not.* Colette pushed the treacherous thought away with all the others.

"A Scot, is he?" asked the inquisitive landlady.

Colette wished to ignore her impudence, but she reminded herself they were trying to blend in as merchants. Besides, there was no way to hide his accent nor his peculiar mode of dress. "But of course. He is our guide."

The calculating smile returned to the landlady's face. "I see, I do. So he is a tradesman and a wealthy one I wager. Free for the taking, is he?"

"No!" The denial emerged forcefully from Colette's lips before she could consider why she was denying it. "He is spoken for." She was not sure why she said this since she knew he was very much unattached. Yet she was adamant to fend off any sort of liaison with anyone he would find at a public inn. Except herself...and that was another thought to be stuffed away.

"Too bad," said the landlady. "The good ones, they are always taken, no?" She gave Colette a conspiratorial wink. "And who is this lovely little one?" She smiled at Pippa, who was holding the baby.

"She belongs to her," said Pippa, pointing at Marie Colette in a manner so outside the usual courtesy with which Colette was accustomed to being addressed that she was rendered speechless. At least no one would believe she was aristocracy with such colorful traveling companions.

"Ah, so you are a new mother." The landlady beamed at Colette. "There is no better time in life, no? Which of these men is your husband?"

"None," declared Colette and then realized at the askance look on the landlady's face that she needed to make some explanation. "The child's father died in an attack by the English. The town was put to the flames. The babe barely escaped with her life."

"Ah, so sorry you lost your husband. I lost my poor Henri only last winter. Now I am on my own with this inn to run all by myself. Not that I am complaining, but I do understand your loss."

Colette said nothing, deciding it would serve no purpose to correct the woman's misunderstanding. She did appreciate the sentiment. She had lost people she loved, though not a husband.

"Poor babe." The landlady bent closer in order to see the tot, her bosom quivering dangerously, ready to spill out of her bodice at any moment. "I see the child got a taste of the flames. Too bad she is so disfigured. It is a face only a mother could love, no?"

Of course it was nothing short of the truth, but Colette bristled at the comment. "Quite," she said in a tone so cold it could have given the landlady frostbite.

"You have a pleasant evening," said the landlady with a smile, not noticing the chill in Colette's tone. The woman sidled away back into the kitchens.

"Can you believe her cheek?" hissed Marie Agnes.

"Unbelievable that she would consider herself worthy of addressing you, my lady," said Marie Jeanette.

"She only spoke the truth," defended Pippa, who was sitting at the end of the table slightly aside from the others. "The babe's face is scarred. And you have all been whispering about Sir Gavin and his naked legs. You think it's better to whisper something in private than to speak the plain, simple truth?"

The distinguished ladies-in-waiting raised their delicate eyebrows and as one turned their backs on the unwanted orphan and continued the rest of their meal in silence.

Taking command of the infant, Colette was determined to do right by the creature, no matter how unappealing she appeared. Colette fed the child porridge, milk, and small bits of biscuit from the table. Afterward, the baby whined, whimpered, cried, and finally screamed as Colette and her ladies passed the infant from person to person each trying unsuccessfully to calm the babe. Colette spoke firmly to the infant, demanding the child to stop crying at once, but to no avail.

The baby wailed until Pippa placed the babe over her shoulder and gave her a few gentle thumps between the shoulder blades. The babe made a most disagreeable noise, but then smiled and was content.

From that moment on, Colette and her ladies resigned the babe to Pippa's care.

Raised voices caught Colette's attention. Despite the lateness of the hour, other weary travelers found rest at the inn, but two appeared to be making a hasty departure.

"Come back!" shouted the landlady, waddling after two young men who were heading to the door. "You need to pay your shot! You drank four bottles of my best wine."

"And who is it that is going to make us?" taunted one of the man. "You are so fat, you can't even catch me!" He laughed in her face and strolled out the door even as tears ran down the landlady's face.

Gavin was up and out the door before Colette could express her outrage. A loud crash, some banging, a yell, and a muffled yelp came from outside the door. All was silent for a moment, and Colette feared the rude men had hurt her Gavin. Colette stilled. *Her* Gavin?

Gavin strolled back into the inn with a wide smile and both of the men in a headlock, one head under each of his muscular arms. "Sorry, madam, these men have something to say," he addressed the landlady with bright, good humor.

A few squeezes of the headlock and both men began to express their most humble, heartfelt apologies. They reached for their purses and produced more than their fair share of the evening's fare.

"Thank you," said the landlady to Gavin once he had released the objects of his instruction and they had run from the inn, lighter in purse but wiser in worldly knowledge. The landlady beamed at him, adoration in her eyes. "Thank you, kind sir. Thank you!"

Gavin tried to wave off the compliment but the landlady embraced him, drawing him into the fleshy abyss of her cleavage.

"Yes, thank you, Sir Gavin." Colette strolled up to them, not sure what exactly she was doing but needing to get Gavin's face out of the landlady's ample bosom.

"Yes, indeed, I thank you greatly! If I can ever give you a good turn, do let me know." The landlady released Gavin and gave him a wink before moving back into the kitchen.

"You have a new friend," said Colette dryly.

"Aye, a little friendly suffocation," answered Gavin catching his breath.

Colette could not squelch a smile.

"Ye should get some sleep. I'm so tired, I hardly know what I'm about," said Gavin with a drowsy smile.

Colette found his heavy-lidded expression and half grin made her a bit weak in the knees. She wanted to believe it was nothing more than her own fatigue.

He stepped closer to her and spoke in a voice none but she could hear. "I want for naught but a warm bed, but I warrant I should ride down to Bordeaux now, since it's night, and make sure our path is safe for the morrow. If all goes well, we shall leave wi' the tide." Though he spoke of nothing but their plans for travel, a quiver of something dangerous came alive within her.

"How very kind and thoughtful you are," said Colette in a soft voice, meant only for him.

"Would ye care to thank me as another did?" asked Gavin, an impish glint in his eye.

Colette gasped at the suggestion, though she had the sudden compulsion to laugh at his audacity. "Thank you for sparing me any concern for your fatigue. I see you are quite energetic, enough for more adventures tonight. *Bonne chance*." She turned and led her ladies up the stairs but gave herself away by turning back to steal another glance at Gavin.

He was watching her.

Considering the number of people taking refuge in the inn, only one room was left available. Gavin arranged for places in the stable and the common room for himself and the guards. Colette, her maids, Pippa, and the baby would be forced to share the room. Colette could see at once that they would have to sleep in quarters closer than they would have liked.

Colette settled in among the pallets of her ladies-in-waiting, trying to get comfortable in a small, hard bed. Gavin may have chastised her for trying to take her featherbed with her, but anyone who had slept on a featherbed would understand its value.

Colette had finally drifted off to sleep when a sharp rap at the door woke them all. Marie Philippe, who was lying closest to the door and had grumbled about the cold draft, rose and put an ear to the door. "Who is it?"

"Sir Gavin to speak with Lady Marie Colette."

A quiver of excitement hummed through Colette's body in a most disconcerting manner. Colette wished that she would cease this inappropriate response anytime he was near. It was most disagreeable and somehow she was sure it was his fault.

Marie Philippe turned to her with wide eyes, whispering, "We cannot let him in, m'lady. He's a man!"

"Very much so," whispered Marie Jeannette, followed by tittering of the others.

Colette rolled her eyes. Who would have thought women old enough to be her mother would be so smitten with Sir Gavin? Of course, her own heart picked up its beat at the sound of his voice, so apparently the malady was contagious.

"If he is knocking on the door at this hour, then he has something of import to tell us. Find me a dressing gown and I will speak to him," said Colette, trying to sound impartial.

Gavin was told to wait a moment and her ladies all got up from their pallets and made a bit of a commotion as they quickly dressed her in something they deemed appropriate. Her hair was already in her sleeping wimple but they insisted on her wearing another headdress and ornate dressing gown. Colette was only concerned that they be done and quick about it, for she was certain Gavin would not knock unless there was some trouble that could not wait till morning. Though she had eaten well that night, a gnawing grew in the pit of her stomach.

Finally, the door was opened and her maids stood in two lines before her, presenting her formally, while Pippa held the baby to the side. Gavin looked a bit taken aback at such a formal presentation but glanced up and down the hall, gave a slight shrug, and entered the room, closing the door behind him.

"Forgive my imposition into yer private quarters, m'lady. I fear I have tidings that cannot wait till morn."

Marie Colette raised her chin, determined to take whatever news he should tell her with a poise and reserve that would make her mother proud. "Thank you for your consideration, Sir Gavin. Please do tell me what tidings you bring."

"Bordeaux has been taken by the English. The ship that was waiting for us in the harbor has also been taken. I fear we will not be able to travel to Scotland by that route."

Her ladies gave a collective gasp. She held out a hand to silence them. "This is indeed unfortunate. How do you suggest we make our way to Scotland now?"

"I took it upon myself to try to find another ship. We are fortunate in that the landlady here has a brother who is a captain of a merchant ship. He is to set sail tomorrow on a mission o' trade with Scotland. Wi' yer permission, I will arrange for us to travel on that ship."

"Very well done, Sir Gavin. I am glad that you have found alternate accommodations for us. Please do make these arrangements," said Colette, relieved Gavin had been able to so quickly find alternative means of travel.

"Unfortunately," continued Gavin, shifting a bit and glancing at her ladies and back to Colette, "the St. Olga is a smaller vessel and accommodations will be quite cramped. When I spoke to the captain, he said only two small cabins could be secured. I fear ye and yer ladies woud'na all fit into them."

"What do you suggest? How are we to travel?" asked Colette.

"The men can sleep on deck or in the hold below. I fear that some of yer maids will have to sleep in that manner as well or can take turns sleeping in the cabin."

This pronouncement brought even more gasps and cries from her ladies. "My father was the Lord Chamberlain of the duc de Bergerac. I shall not sleep in the hold with seafaring men!" gasped Marie Claude.

"Nor I!" exclaimed Marie Jeannette.

Marie Colette held up her hand once more to silence her maids. A mutiny was on her hands. She glared at Gavin but he continued giving his bad news.

"And one more thing. Unfortunately, the English have heard reports of a wealthy heiress traveling these parts in a large party intent to go to Scotland. It is well we did not announce our presence. Many here have English leanings, and I fear if anyone realizes ye were the lady they sought, ye woud'na be allowed to escape. The landlady here has been most helpful, but her brother has allied himself wi' the English, and I fear she also has English leanings. Forgive me for taking liberties, m'lady, but I felt it best they considered ye betrothed to someone local."

Marie Colette grew suspicious. "What did you tell them, Sir Knight?"

Gavin shifted again on his feet, glanced down and then back up at the ceiling, avoiding her eye. "I told them ye were a young widow, traveling wi' her cousins and her baby, and promised in marriage to…" Gavin's voice failed him.

Marie Colette stared at him. "And who, pray tell, is my affianced husband?"

Gavin gave a little cough and turned a slight shade of red. He stared at the ceiling. "Dinna quite think it through before I spoke, ye ken. Had to say something."

"Yes, I quite understand. Who is my new husband?"

He brushed his hair back with a sweep of his hand and shrugged apologetically. "No' many options, ye ken."

Colette waited.

"It's me."

Sixteen

GAVIN KNEW HIS ADMISSION THAT HE HAD TOLD THE landlady and her brother he was to wed Lady Colette may have come to her as something of a shock. However, he was unprepared for the magnitude of her reaction. She went utterly white. She stepped forward until he was forced to open the door and step outside the room to make way for her. Without breaking eye contact and without saying a word, she slowly shut the door in his face.

Gavin sighed and sought his own bed. Unfortunately, his uncomfortable sleeping arrangement in the stable was shared by a playful goat. It was a long night. The next morning, he had hoofprints on his face and a goat-sized bite out of the end of his plaid. His new friend taunted him with a goatish grin. He was not amused.

Gavin strode into the inn and took the stairs two at a time. He was anxious to see Marie Colette and gauge her reaction to the situation after she had gotten a night's sleep. Hopefully she had fared better without a goat.

He slowed as he approached her door, and though it

was poor manners, he could not help but overhear raised voices coming from the cracked door of their room.

"I beg you would reconsider," said Lady Colette with an anxious tinge he did not like to hear in her voice.

"There is naught we can do under the circumstances," retorted the voice of Marie Claude. "It gives us no pleasure to come to this unfortunate conclusion, but you give us no choice."

"Surely something can be arranged," appeased Colette.

"I, for one, will have no more to do with this ill-fated adventure," came the sharp voice of Marie Agnes. "You have become quite headstrong in the past few days. It has been most disappointing."

Gavin knocked on the door and strolled in without waiting for a reply. "For my part, I have been rather impressed with Lady Colette o' late." Gavin winked at Colette when he said it. Cheeky he knew, but she gave him a faint smile, indicating his words were not unappreciated. "Good morn to ye all. What seems to be the trouble today?"

Marie Claude turned to him with disdain. "My good ladies and I have given your words last night great thought. It is with immense sorrow that we fear we shall not be able to accompany our great lady on her journey most arduous." The lady held herself with a haughty rigor, daring him to voice complaint.

"Ye're telling me that ye're going to abandon yer lady at the hour o' her greatest need?" If they thought Gavin was going to put this into polite terms, they were very much mistaken. He tried to catch Colette's eye, but she turned away.

The ladies-in-waiting gasped as if he had struck

each and every one of them. If he had been a different sort of man, he might have done just that.

"Never would we abandon our lady in the hour of need," cried Marie Claude, her nostrils flaring. "It is most unfortunate, most unfortunate indeed, that we are prevented from being able to follow our lady because her ship has been taken and there are no accommodations for us in this new boat you have found. Had you been able to secure a ship that would accommodate us, we would never have been brought to this most distressing position."

So it was his fault, was it? Gavin was having none of it. "Mayhap if any one o' ye had half the backbone that Lady Marie Colette does, ye woud'na feel the need to turn tail and run back home as cowards. But if ye want to go, then go. If that is all yer loyalty means to ye, then ye're no' worth the bother ye cause to take ye with us." He enjoyed the looks of shock and horror on their faces.

"How dare you?" seethed Marie Agnes.

"I speak as I find," said Gavin placidly, reining in his irritation at these fickle ladies who would abandon their mistress. His grasp of protocol was shaky at best, but he did know the lady could not travel alone without some sort of feminine companion. What were they going to do now?

"Well! I believe there can be nothing more to say," declared Marie Claude. She turned to Lady Colette's sad face, her lips trembling for a moment. Marie Claude pressed her lips together and the moment passed. "I wish you a safe journey and a blessed life, my child." She turned to leave, followed by the other ladies.

Colette looked from one lady to the next, but all were resolute save the wide, hesitant eyes of Marie Philippe. "Marie Philippe," whispered Colette. "Please, do not go."

Marie Philippe looked from Colette to Marie Claude and back, her face twisting in anguish. "I am sorry, my dear. I must go with them." She followed the other ladies out of the room but then ran back and gave Colette a warm embrace. "I am sorry, my little love. Peace be with you." She turned and hastened after the other ladies.

"And also with you," replied Colette duly in response.

Gavin did not know what to say. Colette appeared smaller, more vulnerable without the constant presence of her ladies. "I am sorry. Can I do anything for ye?" asked Gavin feebly.

"No, I wish for a moment alone, if you please," said Colette in a tired voice.

Possibly sensing the unhappy atmosphere of the room, the baby began to cry, and Pippa took the opportunity to leave with the babe.

"As you wish." Gavin did not know what else to do, so he followed the ladies and arranged for their safe return. Of course they could not travel back alone, so he spoke with Captain Perrine to send half of the soldiers back with them to ensure their safety. It also lessened their presence, which, considering their desire to go unnoticed, was helpful. A small voice within him said he should first ask Colette before making such arrangements, but he felt he needed to take things in hand.

When all was completed, and the maids and their

guards had left, Gavin returned to speak to Colette. Poor lass, how was he to comfort her now? He knocked on the door and it was opened by Pippa, holding the baby. He was a little surprised, for he feared Pippa might have left entirely, but she had returned and he hoped had been some comfort.

Marie Colette was sitting in a chair by a narrow window, a shaft of a golden sunlight forming a bright rectangle on the floor by her feet. She wore a gown of flowing blue silk and a crisp white wimple covered her head. She did not turn when he entered the room but continued to stare out the window, her chest slowly rising and falling, as if it was all she could do to focus on her breathing.

Gavin stood silently, wondering if he should say something first or wait for her to acknowledge him. She gazed out the window with a look of such beautiful sadness that he wished to take her once more in his arms. Yet with the audience of Pippa, he remained apart. He had no right to embrace her, but his desire could not be ignored.

Colette turned to Pippa and with a small nod dismissed the girl and the babe. Pippa left, shutting the door behind them. Gavin knew under no circumstances should he be alone with Lady Colette, particularly in a public inn, and her willingness to meet him in such a manner spoke to the desperation of the situation.

"I'm sorry, m'lady," said Gavin softly. "They were no' worthy o' ye." He was surprised at how much he felt those words.

"I could not expect them to stay under such

conditions, though I had not anticipated their loss."
She leaned forward and the shaft of sunlight caught
her face, illuminating her smooth complexion. The
exquisite sorrow of her expression caught his breath.

"Ye're more charitable than I, for I believe 'tis their
duty to stay with ye, and no' run at the smallest hint of
inconvenience. Ye're well rid o' them."

Colette turned to him, the spark in her eye reig-
nited. "It is uncharitable for you to say so, Sir Knight."
Her words may have sounded harsh, but the small
smile about her lips told him she was not unapprecia-
tive of his defense.

"I speak only the truth as I see it, m'lady. Ye
deserve better." At his pronouncement, he was
rewarded with a small smile, which warmed his
insides in a ridiculous manner. He liked to see the
spark back in her eye. If irritating her was the price
to do it, he was her man.

"I should not like to quarrel, so I shall be forced to
agree with you. However, this does create a situation
for me most tenuous. I must continue on to meet my
husband, but it would be unseemly in the extreme to
arrive without my maids by my side."

"Aye, that is a problem." Gavin sighed.

"And as I have had much time to think on your
words from last night, it occurs to me that there is
another difficulty," admitted Colette. "I told the
landlady we were not betrothed."

"Och, what did you do that for?" Gavin hit his
forehead with the palm of his hand.

"Why would I tell her otherwise?" She raised an
eyebrow. Much to his irritation, it only enhanced her

beauty. "I had no idea you would come up with such a preposterous plan."

"Have ye a better plan, m'lady?" he challenged, purposely baiting her to see the light in her eyes rekindle.

"Me? Is it not you who are supposed to find a safe passage to Scotland?" Her eyes narrowed and he greatly preferred it to the defeat he had seen in her smoky, green eyes only a moment before. He would rather see her fight, even with him, than be sad.

"'Tis hardly my responsibility to keep yer maids by yer side. They are naught but petty, selfish, spineless fools who abandon ye at the first sign o' trouble," he said, knowing it would anger her further.

"Traveling to Scotland with no more dignity than a pig lashed to the deck is not to be tolerated. My ladies had but little choice," defended Colette, standing defiantly. At least now she was fighting back.

"It could no' be helped." He gestured with his hand like swatting a fly. "I saw them safely off on their journey back home."

Colette's eyes widened. "They have left?"

"Aye." Gavin knew he should tell her about the guards too, but his tongue grew heavy in his mouth.

"I thought they would come to say a final farewell," she said softly, placing a delicate hand on her chest.

Gavin's anger burned against the maids who had abandoned their mistress. "They are unworthy o' ye. I sent them home with some of the guards to ensure their safe passage."

"My guards?" Her eyes narrowed.

"Aye." He swallowed hard. If his plan was to anger her, this would surely do it. "The ladies coud'na travel wi'out some protection."

"No, of course they could not. But it is for me to decide how to ensure their safety. You have no right to order about my guards."

"I did what I felt was right," he defended.

"But it was not your prerogative to do so." Her green eyes flashed. "These are my people. They take orders from me, not you. You are a hired guide, nothing more."

His plan may have worked a little too well, for now her anger fanned the flames of his own. "Hired? M'lady, let me disabuse ye of any notion that I have been compensated for my part in this journey. I am on this errand out o' the pure goodness o' my soul."

"I would not keep you here one moment longer than you wish." Her voice raised with every word, although she managed to keep her tone low.

"Believe me, m'lady, I have considered what a relief it would be to divest myself of this whole affair." He stepped closer, pulled by a powerful attraction.

"Then I dismiss you from my service." She held her head high, her shoulders back. "I thank you for your service to my family, and I wish you the best for your future." She made an elegant sweeping gesture to banish him from the room.

Instead of leaving, Gavin stepped forward. "If that is what ye wish, then it is what ye shall have. I can do no more than my poor best." The wild, fey creature before him was the most beautiful, most captivating, most desirable lady he had ever beheld. He may have started this fire, but now it was raging beyond his control.

Instead of backing away, she stepped toward him, the air between them crackling. "If this is your best, Sir Knight," she said in a silky tone, "I tremble lest I see your worst."

She was standing so close he could see her chest rise and fall quickly, belying the outward calm she strove to display. He had always considered himself an even-tempered sort of man, but this infuriating woman aggravated and aroused him in a way none ever had.

"Ye have dismissed me from yer presence and I have no choice but to leave, m'lady. I wish ye a safe journey. *Adieu*." He leaned down with a scandalous familiarity and kissed first one cheek and then, slowly, the other.

He did not back away nor did she, and they paused, their faces inches from each other. He expected her to back away, but instead she raised her chin in defiance. Her full, red lips pulled him toward her. This would be his farewell. This was his one chance.

Alarm bells rang through his mind, but he was thinking with a different organ altogether. He leaned even closer, his lips a whisper from hers and stopped. She closed the gap, her soft lips brushing against his. Lightning jolted through him, his body aflame with desire. He pressed his lips to hers and attempted to put his arms around her, but all of a sudden she gave a sharp inhale and jumped back, looking toward the door.

Pippa stood in the doorway, her mouth hanging open.

Seventeen

SHE KISSED HIM.

Kissed him!

Colette's body hummed with the excitement and pure pleasure the feel of his lips had wrought. Even though she'd jumped back when Pippa opened the door, she could still feel his strong arms around her.

"I'll come back later." Pippa gave them a knowing smile and closed the door once more.

Colette could not look at Gavin, but she could feel his gaze on her, heating her through to her core. What was she to do now? This madness was nothing she ought to feel, nothing she should ever feel. And yet now that she had a taste of what was denied her, she could not help but want more.

Much more.

"Forgive me. I had no right," Gavin said softly.

Colette shook her head, averting her gaze out the window. She could not look at him without wanting to press herself against him once more. "I cannot account for my actions."

"It has been a trying day and a difficult journey.

I should have consulted ye before dismissing half yer guard."

"And if ye had, the outcome would have been the same, for it was the only thing that could be done." Colette took a breath and, drawing on all her practice of hiding her true feelings, turned to him as if nothing had passed between them. "Is there any manner by which to travel to Scotland other than this ship you found?"

Gavin cleared his throat, though his eyes still smoldered. "Yer ship has been taken and there is no other captain willing to sail to Scotland. Even if we could commission a larger vessel, we would surely attract notice, and ye may be discovered. The English are searching for ye. Whatever we do, we canna tarry."

"Then travel we must on this ship, under the guise of being merchants. We shall hope no one challenges our lack of nuptials." Even the thought of wedding Sir Gavin made her heart pound.

"We should leave as soon as possible." He turned to leave but paused at the door. "But we still have the problem o' ye traveling wi'out a maid."

"I'll do it." Pippa opened the door and entered the room, the baby on one hip.

"Were ye eavesdropping?" Gavin frowned.

Pippa nodded enthusiastically. "Interesting things happening in here." She could not look less like a lady-in-waiting. Her brown ringlets flew wild, her dark eyes were determined, and her mouth permanently set in something of a scowl. There was nothing of the soft femininity of a lady of court about her. Yet Colette had to acknowledge that Pippa would fare better on the journey than any of her gentile ladies.

"That is very kind of you, Pippa, but I fear that there are certain requirements to be a lady-in-waiting," said Colette gently.

"Thought I'd offer," said Pippa in a sullen tone. "Me, I can do anything I set my mind to, and it doesn't look like your fancy ladies had much backbone to them. There's nothing I fear."

Colette glanced at Gavin, uncertain as to how to proceed. Pippa was unsuitable, but she was the only one they had left. "What of your family? Are there none who would miss you if you never returned?"

"Got no family, my lady. If I did, I wouldn't have been in such a damned place."

"How colorfully spoken, my child," said Colette.

"You don't want me because I cusses a bit. Can't say as I can change, but I can try. So you want me for your maid, or no?" Pippa stood, her feet planted on the floorboards shoulder width apart as if prepared to fight.

What other choice did she have? "*Oui*, I would be quite pleased to accept you, as I have none other. But you must apply yourself," admonished Colette.

Pippa smiled and gave her a clumsy curtsy. "I'll serve you well, will I."

One problem solved, Gavin bowed to her and Colette nodded in return. She did not know what to say. He paused as if wanting to speak but glanced at Pippa and shut his mouth. He bowed again and proceeded to walk down the hall.

"What can be done for you, my lady?" asked Pippa.

"You may begin by packing this trunk. We need to depart before anyone decides a betrothal is not sufficient and plans for me a wedding."

Gavin's footsteps in the hall suddenly stopped.
Had she said *wedding*?

⅋—ʞ

Gavin rode hard to Bordeaux to make the final
arrangements. Despite the distraction of all that needed
to be done, the kiss still held his body ablaze. He knew
that single kiss would linger on his lips forever.

Gavin ruthlessly pushed such thoughts aside. He
needed to focus on the problem of escaping France.
He found the other half of their party that had been
sent on ahead with part of Lady Colette's dowry. They
were hiding beside the river outside of Bordeaux, a
few wagons lighter than when they had started. They
had endured their own misadventures with thieves
and bandits.

Gavin finalized arrangements with the captain of
the *St. Olga*, spinning a story that he was a merchant,
traveling to Scotland with his goods for sale, along
with his family and some business associates. The
captain accepted the story and was pleased with the
compensation offered. They would leave with the tide
that evening.

The flat-bottomed *St. Olga* floated stalwartly in
the harbor. She was by no means a fancy vessel, but
one used to hard work and honest labor. It was hardly
a suitable vessel for the daughter of a duke, but his
choices were limited.

Gavin tried to keep his thoughts focused on his
pressing responsibilities, but once everything had been
attended to, his mind wandered into dangerous territory. Marie Colette's perfume still haunted him, the

feel of her lips lingered on his. He had broken every rule by kissing her, and truth be told, all he wanted was to do it again. How was he to survive pretending to be betrothed to her? At least he would not have to pretend attraction; it was all too real.

Gavin returned to the inn only to find more trouble had arrived. English soldiers milled about the outside of the inn, casually walking in and out. Gavin's heart sank, fearing Colette had been captured. He rode around to the back of the inn and snuck into the stables to escape notice. He needed to determine what had happened without drawing attention to himself.

"Sir Gavin!" hissed Captain Perrine, hiding in a dark corner of the stable with the rest of Colette's soldiers.

"Captain Perrine, what happened here? Has Lady Colette been taken?"

"No. She is still upstairs in the inn. The English have chosen to stay at this establishment, a most inconvenient predicament."

Gavin took a breath in relief. "They are looking for a large party, so we must not appear suspicious," he whispered. "Take yer men and the wagons down to Bordeaux. Dismiss all of the stable hands and anyone else not absolutely essential. I'll slip out with Colette and we'll sail with the tide."

Gavin ensured the captain and his men left quietly and then packed his own saddlebag, changing back into breeches and an embroidered tunic. It might pass as the clothes of a merchant. Above all, it would not do to announce the fact that he was a Scot.

Gavin slipped into the common room and ordered refreshments, listening to the talk of the English soldiers, trying to gain as much information as he could. He sat at the table next to one party of soldiers and did not need to strain to hear their open conversation.

"We'll find her, make no mistake," a burly English soldier boasted, raising a tankard of ale to his lips and slamming it back down on the table for emphasis. "We know she's in the area. Only a matter of time before she's found. A woman like that, traveling heavy, with her dowry and her maids—she can't hide for long."

Gavin was relieved the maids had left and that he had sent the wagons ahead.

"What will they do once they find her?" asked a wiry man who needed two hands to raise his tankard.

"Supposed to give her to Major Thomas, maybe even send her to the Black Prince. But I reckon Captain Withers will take care of things for himself. Heard him talking about it. He figures once he gets her compromised, none of the others will want her and she'll be forced to marry him, giving him all of them wagons of dowry."

"I hear she's a beauty, she is," piped up another soldier.

"I hear that too. Not good for a woman to be too beautiful, makes them think too much of themselves. If I was her master, I'd slice her cheek just to get her attention, mind you. Good to let her know she ain't got nothing I can't take away. I bet Captain Withers does the same unless I'm much mistaken."

Gavin forced himself to remain seated, though it took every ounce of will not to rip out the man's throat for suggesting such a thing. Not trusting himself to look at them, Gavin slowly rose and walked up the stairs to find Marie Colette. There was no time to lose. They must leave now.

The door was opened by Pippa, who immediately stepped into the hall and closed it behind her, refusing to let him enter. "Go away with you."

Pippa was a changed woman. It was clear that Colette had taken the new maid in hand and the alteration was remarkable. Pippa's hair had been tamed and was now plaited into neat braids down her back. She wore a modest veil over her head as befitted her new station. Her dress was of fine blue linen, most assuredly the best she'd ever worn.

"I need to speak to Lady Marie Colette immediately."

"I've been told you're not to be alone with her," hissed Pippa, holding her head high. Clearly she was taking her new role seriously.

Gavin had no time to argue. "We must leave now. Is m'lady prepared for the journey?"

Pippa shrugged her shoulders. "She always looks good and smells nice. Not sure how she does it, but she always does. She tried to teach me how to take care of her hair, but there seemed to be an awful lot of rules about it."

Gavin had to clench his teeth together to prevent him from asking what color Colette's locks were. It seemed strange to him that he would have known her for so many days and still not know the color of her hair. "Please tell her we must leave at once." He lowered his voice. "English soldiers are downstairs."

"*Oui.*" Lady Marie Colette opened the door. "I am aware. But what of…?" Colette glanced behind her to the baby lying on the bed.

The baby. Gavin had forgotten about that little complication. "Have to bring her, for there is none who will care for her if we dinna do it ourselves. Besides, the landlady thinks her yers from a previous marriage. We canna leave the babe behind now," said Gavin in a low tone. "I'm sure once we reach my homeland my mother will be willing to care for her."

Colette gave a quick nod, accepting her fate of traveling with the infant. "But the landlady, it would be best to avoid her."

"She's not in the common room. Let us hope we can leave quickly wi'out anyone taking notice."

Colette nodded in agreement. "We will make all haste."

"I'll saddle yer horse and wait for ye in the common room."

Gavin moved as quickly as he could without arousing suspicion. They must escape the noose tightening around them. He prepared the horses in the stable and returned to the common room, standing at the bottom of the stairs, ready to swoop Colette out of the inn as soon as she emerged. As a matter of extra security, he strapped his broadsword on his back. If the English saw through their subterfuge, he would need to fight.

And fight he would.

Eighteen

THE ENGLISH WERE DRINKING HEAVILY IN THE COMMON room, but Gavin knew their kind too well to wager they would lose their wits to drink. These were Englishmen. They could drink all day and still stay razor sharp and twice as dangerous.

Gavin hoped Colette had not decided to dress in anything extravagant. Any display of wealth would certainly raise the suspicions of the soldiers who were well on their way toward raucous carousing in the public room. Finally, with an air of unruffled calm, Lady Marie Colette glided down the stairs of the inn, her maid preceding her.

Colette wore a relatively simple green silk kirtle and a modest headdress, but nothing could hide her beauty. The shimmering green of the silk exactly matched her striking, emerald eyes.

Gavin stepped forward to offer her his arm, with the ridiculous hope the soldiers in the public room would note that such a woman was with him. This was, of course, stupid since it was their intent not to be noticed by anyone. Yet she was so beautiful—her high cheekbones, her rosy lips, her thick, dark lashes—he wanted to soak in the moment and have it acknowledged by other men. A flash of jealousy toward her future husband came unwanted and unbidden. He pushed it brutally aside. He needed to focus on getting her out of the inn.

They were almost to the door when a man's voice called out behind them.

"Halt there!"

Gavin eyed the door and turned reluctantly. He considered making a run for it but doubted he could make it with Colette in tow.

"I am Captain Withers," said the man, striding forward on thick legs and folding equally thick arms across his chest. "State your name and your business." He took a keen interest in Colette when he spoke.

Gavin stepped forward, putting himself between Colette and their adversary. "I am Gavin Patrick, a humble merchant, at yer service." He bowed, never taking his eyes off the English captain. "Would ye be interested in some cloth or household goods?"

"I am interested in your traveling companion." Captain Withers gave a smile that was not at all friendly. "She is a fine thing. Very fine." He licked his lips.

"My *wife* is the delight of my life," said Gavin, trying to bluff his way out the door. Several English soldiers formed a semicircle around them. He backed up slowly, ready to push Colette out the door and fight them off, giving her time to escape.

"Your wife? I doubt that. You will need to come with us, *mademoiselle*," sneered Captain Withers.

"Ah, there you two are!" said the landlady, bustling forward in between Gavin and Captain Withers, which was either very brave or quite stupid, since it was clear things were about to turn violent. "Are you ready to go to church?"

"Church?" asked Gavin, his hand on the hilt of his undrawn sword.

"Why, yes, did you not tell me you wished to be married before departing?" She gave him a sidelong glance.

Bless her plump, rosy cheeks, their hostess was coming to their rescue. "Aye, church. Let us away now," said Gavin.

Colette did not move, but her hand on his arm squeezed tight.

Captain Wither's eyes narrowed. "Why would you call her your wife if you are not yet wed?" he asked in a suspicious tone.

"Our betrothal has been long planned and the marriage contract signed. We are as good as married." Colette spoke with remarkable poise and Gavin was relieved he stood beside a lady who was able to keep a cool head in times of trouble.

"But since you will be traveling a long ways in such close company, you decided to marry before leaving. A wise decision, for I have sailed on the *St. Olga*. It would be most unseemly for you to travel together without a proper chaperone," said the landlady.

"But my maid—" began Colette.

The landlady waved a hand to stop her. "That girl? No, it will not do. I know how it is with you young widows, but you are a mother now and you must think of propriety."

"I have always conducted myself with the highest level of propriety," stated Colette, her tone frigid.

Their disagreement was working to confuse Captain Withers, whose bushy eyebrows fell over narrow eyes. Gone was his self-assurance as he looked back and forth between the two women.

"Tsk, tsk, my dear, I meant no disrespect," said the landlady, ignoring the English captain. "But I understand how it is with young people. I can see how very much in love you are."

Gavin stilled. What emotion did the landlady see in Colette? Did Colette cherish feelings for him, or was this all part of the deception to escape Captain Withers? He shook his head quickly. "We do so wish to be married," said Gavin. "But we must make the evening tide. We canna tarry now."

"I'm under orders. No unmarried lady will leave these shores." Captain Withers was firm on that count.

"But the ship is leaving," pleaded Gavin. "There is no time."

"Of course you have time!" exclaimed the landlady in a loud voice. "I have seen to it. My brother, he will wait for you. Time to speak your vows at the door of the church, my dear ones."

Colette's hand held on to his arm with a death grip, but her face revealed no emotion. The English soldiers were closing in and there was no way to escape without either a fight or nuptials. His mind spun. He liked to solve problems with a sword. One always knew where you stood when the weapons came out to play. Subterfuge was not his strength, but any false move and Colette would be taken. He glanced at Colette, whose frozen expression told him she was out of ideas for how to extricate themselves from the situation. She took a breath and gave a barely perceptual nod.

"Aye, let's do it then," declared Gavin.

Without further ado, Gavin and Colette were escorted to the church in the middle of a group of English soldiers, the landlady triumphantly leading the way. The group walked a short distance to a monastery, where a priest was in residence. The village itself was too small to boast its own church or priest, so the locals were accustomed to walking to the monastery for their spiritual needs.

They arrived like some sort of strange parade and were greeted by two monks. The landlady must have prepared them for their arrival, for the monks nodded in a congenial sort of way and led them into the monastery.

One of the monks explained that Father Benedict would like to meet with the bride and groom alone in his cell prior to witnessing their vows. The group let them go, and Colette followed the monk as he led them down a narrow passage, past several closed doors, until they came to a small wooden door, which stood open. The monk motioned them inside, bowed, and closed the door, leaving them alone in the cell to await the priest.

Gavin pointed at a small window covered by a shutter. "Do ye ken ye could fit through the window?" he asked, focused on escape.

"Yes, I believe I could, but surely you could not."

"Aye." Gavin sighed.

"We must somehow get on that ship," said Colette. "Once we are at sea, we will be free from these English soldiers."

"I agree, m'lady. But how to do so wi'out getting married? If only there was a way to make them believe we are wed wi'out anything binding."

"Even if I wished to be married, I could not." Colette sighed. "I am formally betrothed. The marriage papers have been signed. I am not free to marry anyone but the Baron of Kintail."

Gavin frowned at her, tilting his head a bit to one side. "So if we were wed…"

Colette stared at him. "It would not be legal."

"So we could speak vows today and it would not be binding. If the marriage was never consummated, the union would be annulled." Gavin's thoughts raced, trying to find a problem with the hastily concocted plan, but his mind kept getting caught on the one act that could never occur.

"Vows are not considered binding if there is no… consummation." Colette's complexion, generally an even cream, blushed a becoming pink even as she stuttered over the word. The warm flush of her skin made her appear more alluring and alive. He forced himself to look away. Parts of his body were taking an unholy interest in the things he could *not* do.

"Good day, my children." Father Benedict chose that moment to open the door.

Gavin was not sure what he had expected, but what he saw before him was not at all what he'd thought he would see. Father Benedict was a tall, thin man with the darkest skin Gavin had ever seen on a man. He had heard that some knights in their travels had seen peoples with a skin color different than his own, but until this moment, Gavin had secretly suspected that it was all a bit of talk. Clearly, there was truth in it.

Gavin stole a look at Lady Colette to see if she was also similarly surprised to see a dark-skinned priest, but her face was utterly impassive. Perhaps it was not such a surprise to her as to him.

"It is very good to meet you both," said Father Benedict. "I understand you are desirous of becoming married. Or perhaps I should say that others quite insist on your nuptials. You must understand that I cannot perform the entire marriage office, since the bans have not been read, but I can certainly witness your vows at the door of the church. Either way, your marriage is just as binding."

Gavin and Colette exchanged a glance. *Binding* was the one thing they wished to avoid.

Father Benedict caught their reaction and raised his eyebrows slightly. "Sit down, my children." He motioned to a wooden bench and he sat across from them in a plain wooden chair. "So tell me, why do you to seek to be married?"

Colette and Gavin exchanged another glance. What to say? Gavin cleared his throat. "We are of age and we are traveling to Scotland. It seemed good to be wed before we left."

"Yes, that does seem wise. The long journey can be difficult. It is good to have your affairs in order before you commence," commented the priest.

"Have ye much experience with long journeys?" asked Gavin, trying to deflect attention away from their situation.

"Oh no, I was born in Bordeaux myself. But I have

heard from others that journeys can be quite arduous." His eyes twinkled as he spoke.

Gavin assumed the man had been born in foreign parts, so he was surprised by this answer.

"You are perhaps curious as to the reason for the color of my skin?" Father Benedict flashed them a smile, revealing a perfect row of dazzlingly white teeth.

Gavin floundered to find the right words, and it was Colette who ended the awkward silence. "Were your parents also from Bordeaux, or did they travel here from distant lands?"

"My parents did have a very long voyage to come here," confirmed the priest. "They had a bit of the wanderlust, I fear. They traveled with a group of Hospitaller Knights to France, and there they stayed. My mother served the church in Egypt, and my father was from Africa. It makes my skin very dark, no? It is usually the first thing that people notice about me. When I was younger, I did not appreciate the blessing of being different. But now, I understand that it helps me to see things others do not. You too are different from each other, and you go to a land quite different from your own." He looked at Colette as he spoke.

"*Oui*, it is true. I shall have to learn to adapt, as you have." Colette's face remained outwardly serene, but the slight tremble in her tone betrayed her emotion.

"You also have traveled here from a great distance, no?" The priest turned to Gavin.

"Aye, from the Highlands o' Scotland."

"Did you ever feel different from those around you?"

"Aye, there were times when I felt out of place with my comrades. One canna expect a Highlander to find a ready welcome in the polished society o' France." Gavin spoke lightly on the subject. In truth, he had sought to be accepted by his fellow knights and the French aristocracy, but soon learned that to most, he would always be a barbarian.

"It must have been difficult for you," said Father Benedict.

Gavin shrugged. "I have completed my mission here and can return wi' honor."

"*Oui*. But for those who do not plan to ever return to their homeland, it may be more difficult." Father Benedict directed his attention to Colette with compassion in his voice.

Colette did not move, but tears welled in her eyes. With a blink, one cascaded down her cheek. It was then Gavin recognized the totality of her loss. It wasn't about her things; it was about forever losing everything and everyone she had ever known.

"It must be difficult to leave everything ye ever knew for a strange and foreign land," said Gavin softly. He had a sudden recognition of just how difficult this journey was for her.

Colette blotted her eyes with a lace handkerchief and gave a small nod. She was going to an unknown land to give herself to an unknown man, with the full knowledge that she would never return.

Without thinking, Gavin reached out to hold her hand. He wished to spare her the difficulties her fate in life must surely bring.

"I know this is the thing I must do," said Colette finally. "But I do confess to some foreboding of going into an unknown future alone."

Father Benedict gave them a slow smile. "But you are not alone, my child. For the Lord who formed you before your birth has been with you every moment of your days and will continue to be ever present until that moment he brings you home. And you have your betrothed here, to walk beside you."

"I will do my utmost to protect her." Gavin gave her hand a slight squeeze, though with a twinge of guilt that he would only protect her until he handed her off to another man—a thought that rankled severely.

"Are you ready to be wed?" asked the priest evenly.

They both nodded.

"And what names shall I put on the register?" he asked.

"I am Gavin Patrick, o' Balquhidder," Gavin replied. He glanced at Colette and realized from her widening eyes they had a problem. She could not announce her true identity or the English would take her captive. She needed to give a false name.

"I am Marie Colette," she answered.

"Very good, and your father's name?" asked the priest.

Gavin tried to catch her eye; she needed to lie to the priest. He tried to speak for her, but his tongue refused to move. Lying to a priest, especially this priest, was no easy matter.

"Pierre," Colette answered in a small voice.

The priest smiled. "Is that his surname, my child?"

"It is Baudin," she whispered.

Gavin wondered if the English soldiers knew the family name of the duc de Bergerac. If they did, all was lost.

If Father Benedict understood the meaning of the name, he gave no inclination. He merely nodded and smiled. "It is time to be wed."

Nineteen

COLETTE WALKED TO THE DOOR OF THE CHURCH ON the arm of her knight and protector. She glanced up at Sir Gavin, who gave her a tense smile. She had given some thought to her wedding day, but this was not at all what she had anticipated. They stepped forward toward the church. It was of modest size but boasted a vaulted ceiling with flying buttresses extending from the walls.

More people arrived from the town, including Pippa with the baby and many townsfolk who simply followed the crowd to see what was happening. Colette held on to Gavin's arm and told herself that as long as he stood by her side, she could get through this travesty.

Gavin and Colette stood at the door of the church, as was tradition, while English soldiers and townsfolk surrounded them. Captain Withers stood close, his hand resting on the hilt of his sword. It was a situation fraught with danger. Clearly, she was suspected of being the lady they sought. She needed to appear to be a merchant's daughter marrying her love. If their ruse was discovered, she would be captured…and Gavin would be killed.

Gavin stood beside her, tall and confident. He gave her a small nod of encouragement and she took a deep breath. If Gavin was concerned for his fate, he kept it well hidden. He smiled down at her as if all was going according to plan and he was pleased with this wedding. It was all pretend, she knew, but she was still drawn to the warmth in his eyes. She could get lost in those deep brown eyes.

Gavin offered his right hand, and she placed her hand in his. Warmth spread through her at his touch. All she needed to do was say a few words and then proceed with their journey. It was just a few words. The marriage would not be valid unless they shared the intimacy of husband and wife, and of course that could never happen.

She took a deep breath, unable to look away from Gavin. If only her real husband could look like him, there would be no trouble giving herself in the marital bed. She swallowed compulsively at the thought, sweat trickling down the back of her gown. When had it grown so hot?

Father Benedict stood at the doorway to witness their vows, softly providing the words of the vow for Gavin to repeat. "Marie Colette, I take ye to be my wife and commit to ye the fidelity and loyalty o' my body…" He paused and Colette had a dreadful moment of picturing Gavin's body without his clothes.

Gavin gave a nervous cough and continued, "And my possessions; and I will keep ye in health and sickness and in any condition it please our Lord that ye should have, nor for worse or for better will I change towards ye until the end." He spoke the words reverently, sincerely, such that it caught her breath.

It was her turn and she spoke the words, intending them to remain nothing but words, but they seemed to break free from her control and became her true vow.

"Will there be a ring?" Father Benedict asked softly.

She had not thought of a ring and so shook her head no, but Gavin pulled something from beneath his tunic that hung on a gold chain around his neck.

"This is the ring my father gave my mother," said Gavin, holding up a simple gold band.

There was something surprisingly poignant about the simple, thin band of gold. She had seen much larger rings, rings festooned with glittering gems, rings that were worth a fortune. Yet she was unnerved by this simple band. This band was a wedding ring. This band…this band made it real.

She tried to give a subtle shake of her head. She should not wear his mother's ring, but Gavin had already taken her right hand.

"In the name of the father," he said, holding the ring over her thumb. "The son." The ring was held over her index finger. "And the Holy Ghost." It hovered over her middle finger. "Amen." He slid the simple band of gold onto her ring finger.

Chills ran up her spine. His eyes met hers, and she could no longer look anywhere else. He was here, larger and taller and more real than any of her worries or fears. At that moment, she forgot that it was all pretend, forgot everything, and became lost in his eyes.

Gavin met her gaze unwaveringly and encircled his fingers around her hands holding them closer. "With this ring, I thee wed; this gold and silver I thee give; with my body I thee worship; and with this dowry I thee endow."

Everything else faded away and it was Gavin and she only before the door of the church. Vaguely, she was aware the priest was giving his blessing, but all she could do was stare into Gavin's eyes. They had done it. They were married. Truly married. Could this be undone? Did she wish it to be?

Father Benedict cleared his throat, getting their attention. She wondered how long she'd been staring into the eyes of Sir Gavin in silence, like a fool. "Some of my more amorous couples choose this moment to seal their vow with a kiss," suggested the priest with a mischievous glint in his eye.

Before she could think of a response, Gavin leaned down and placed a chaste kiss on her cheek. She should have been shocked that he would take such liberties in public. Instead, she was annoyed he had not taken more. She forced herself to look away from him. She should not have these feelings for this man. It was wrong, and yet everything within her told her this was her true husband.

The priest made the sign of the cross over them, his kind eyes laughing with amusement. "I bless your journey. May it be a safe one and bring you great joy."

Marie Colette walked down the church steps on the arm of Sir Gavin, her new husband. She walked faster than normal, wanting to escape the confusing situation and think logically. Unfortunately, before she had gone far, she was subjected to a most unseemly hug from the landlady. She looked to Gavin for support against the attack, but he merely smiled benignly at the scene.

"Ah, what a lovely bride you make. I wish you all the best, my dears, all the best this world can offer. I cannot remember when I have seen a couple more in love. It reminds me of my dear Henri." She blotted her eyes with a handkerchief and gave Marie Colette another unwanted hug.

"See that English captain?" The landlady jerked her head toward Captain Withers. "He thought you was some fancy lady, but I told him you were not the high and mighty lady that they were looking for. They want some lady who is going to marry a Scottish lord. Of course, now they know you're not her—now that you've married our dear Sir Gavin."

"Thank you, madam," said Colette with all sincerity. Without the landlady's interference, she would have been taken captive.

"Yes, our great thanks, but now if we are going to make yer brother's ship, we should make haste to Bordeaux," said Gavin, eyeing the road ahead.

"Oh yes, listen to me prattle on when there's things to be done. You have a pleasant journey. My brother will take care of you. But how are you going to travel with your little one?" She gestured to Pippa, holding the baby.

"I am not certain," began Colette.

In a flash, the landlady, a most indomitable person, arranged for Pippa and the baby to be taken from the church by wagon to Bordeaux, while Gavin and

Colette would walk back to the village to ride their horses to town. Gavin had already arranged for the horses to be sold there.

The walk back to the village was only slightly less nerve-racking than the walk to the church. Colette would be glad to see the last of the English soldiers. As it was, the English were taking an unhealthy interest in her marriage. At least Captain Withers seemed satisfied she was not the lady he sought and saluted their health, making outrageous proclamations to the number of progeny he expected her to produce.

The walk seemed to go on forever, as she was forced to pretend not to hear several bawdy jokes regarding first-night jitters and bets as to how many babies the soldiers thought she was good for. Gavin had seemed to be in good humor when leaving the church, but even his patience was tried when the talk turned lewd.

Finally, they arrived back at the village and bid their English soldiers a firm farewell. They went to the stable and soon were on horseback, trotting into the main square to leave. Colette took a deep breath, the cool of the evening air filling her lungs. They had done it. They were going to escape. She turned her back to the inn just as she heard her name called in an insistent voice.

"Lady Marie Colette! Lady Marie Colette! Do not ride off, milady. I have a letter from your father, the duc de Bergerac!" the messenger, wearing the full livery of the duchy of Bergerac, proclaimed in a loud voice for all the village to hear.

Twenty

COLETTE FROZE, SCANNING THE VILLAGE SQUARE TO SEE who had heard such a loud pronouncement. Fortunately, it appeared her English friends were more interested in their drink and most had proceeded to the inn.

"Wheesht, man!" cried Gavin, riding up to the young messenger and grabbing the reins from his hands. "We are surrounded by English soldiers, ye fool," he hissed. "If we're caught, Lady Colette will be at their mercy and ye'll be killed."

The messenger's eyes widened so large Colette feared they might bug out from his face. "H-here," he stammered, holding out the missive to her.

"Thank you," said Colette quietly to the messenger. "Tell my father I am well and that we are making our escape. Tell him…tell him I will miss him." Her voice choked and she could say no more.

"Fly back to yer master, and quick." Gavin tossed the young lad his reins. The messenger did not hesitate and galloped from the square.

"Was he heard by anyone?"asked Colette in a whisper.

"I see none," said Gavin, his eyes narrowing. "But let us make haste."

They raced down the gentle sloping hill, away from the village. Colette pressed her mount to ride faster than she ever had before. She knew if she had any chance to make Scotland, she needed to get out of France before nightfall. Though she had many mixed feelings about joining her new husband in a land far away, it was preferable to being taken by the English. Surely, being a bride to a Scottish laird would be more agreeable than to live as a prisoner to an English captain.

Gavin motioned for her to go first and he followed behind, protecting her from any pursuers. She pressed forward, racing through the gloom of the early evening, brushing past the overgrown bushes along the path. They galloped past a grove of trees with sweeping branches that arced over the path like a leafy canopy.

It was a relief when she saw the outline of Bordeaux ahead and they reached a flat plain. She kicked her mount and raced even faster through the fields to Bordeaux. It was planting time, and the rich dark earth had been recently tilled into neat long rows, filling the air with the aroma of rich earth. She breathed deeply, wanting to hold on to her homeland for as long as she could.

They were forced to slow their mounts as they approached the town. It was a busy port and the gates were filled with people walking, peasants with carts of goods, and even English soldiers marching in and out at the city gate. Everyone wanted to get to their rightful places before the gates closed for the night.

They slowed to a brisk walk, not wanting to appear in too much of a rush, which might spark suspicion. Colette took the opportunity to break the seal of her missive from her father. Had anything changed? Was she not to proceed? She scanned the parchment.

"What is it?" asked Gavin. "Any change in our orders?"

"Oh, Father," murmured Colette. "He writes to say our ship has been taken and we must find an alternate route."

"Helpful," muttered Gavin.

A line of English soldiers stood by the city gates, causing her pulse to rise. Gavin pulled ahead of her, riding his horse at a walk past them with enviable cool. She followed, maintaining a serene expression, appreciative that her mother had instilled a strong commitment to maintaining a reserved appearance. She hoped her apprehension would not be reflected on her face.

More than one soldier turned to look at her, but she refused to turn her head, seeing them only out of the corner of her eye as her horse walked past them. She glanced behind her, taking one last look at the fields. This was her land, her home. And she was saying good-bye.

She pressed her lips together to avoid showing emotion, but still the feelings welled up inside her. She wished there was a way that she could serve her people and be faithful to her father that did not forever banish her from the home she loved. The urgent missive had seemed like her last lifeline to her homeland, the last chance she would be called back home. But there was no reprieve from her banishment.

A flash of steel from the far road behind them drew her attention. To her horror, a group of English soldiers were riding hard for the town, with the straight-backed form of Captain Withers leading the charge. They must have overheard her messenger.

They were coming for her.

She quickly rode up beside Gavin. "The English soldiers from the village, they have come for me," she whispered.

He looked around and gave a brief nod of understanding. He drew closer, riding right beside her, pointing up at Bordeaux Cathedral as if showing her the remarkable architecture. "We must get ye to the ship." He spoke in a low voice. "Whatever happens, ye go for the ship. I may have to keep them at bay. Dinna tarry. Get yerself to the *St. Olga*."

"I understand." What she understood was that Gavin was in grave danger. Her heart thumped wildly at her chest, but she kept her back straight and her head forward. They moved quickly through the narrow streets, Gavin taking the lead.

When they reached the docks along the Garonne River, Colette was relieved to see her own guards finishing loading the ship with her goods. Pippa was already on board, babe on her hip, and she waved to them from the deck.

The ship itself was about sixty feet in length and was of a traditional cog construction. It had one mast with a large, square sail, now furled in a neat bundle along the edge of the deck. At the stern of the ship was a raised deck made to look something like a square turret, complete with rectangle battlements at the top.

She guessed that during these tumultuous years of warfare, merchant ships had been adapted to defend themselves as necessary.

"Despite the help the landlady gave us, her brother is sympathetic to the English," whispered Gavin. "If the captain discovers yer identity, we shall no' travel."

Colette nodded in understanding.

Gavin dismounted in a single leap and reached up for her without ceremony. He lifted her off her saddle and touched her feet to the ground. His hands remained on her waist a moment longer than they needed to. His eyes gazed intently into hers, conveying all he could not say.

"Make yerself comfortable, my dear, and I will see to all the arrangements," he said loudly for the benefit of those around him and smiled at her like a doting newlywed, motioning for her to board the ship. He went over to the group of her guards to quietly alert them to their peril. It would not be long before the English would be upon them.

"I will see it done," said Captain Perrine with a grim face. He stepped to her and bowed a farewell, speaking in a low voice. "*Bonne chance* on your journey, my lady. It has been an honor to serve you."

"Thank you for your loyal service, my friend." She clasped his hand. "Be safe."

"I will join ye," said Gavin to the captain in a voice barely above a whisper. "Choose one o' yer men to guard Lady Colette. We must prevent the English from reaching the dock."

"No, you must be the one to see her safely to Scotland," whispered her captain. "Only you know the way, and the ship's captain would no doubt refuse to sail without you since he believes you to be wed." Captain Perrine clapped Gavin firmly on the shoulder. "It is here where we part ways. Good luck, my friend."

Colette could see Gavin was hesitant to leave the fight, but he had to admit it was the only chance they had. Gavin needed to be on that ship to serve as her guard and guide, and more than that, she needed him, more than anyone else, to be with her on this journey.

"Good luck, my friend. I wish ye well." Gavin and Perrine embraced the way men do, slapping each other on the back. Gavin turned and took a moment to rub behind the ear of his horse, whispering something to the mighty beast. He handed the reins to Captain Perrine, who mounted the great horse. Another guard claimed Colette's horse, and they raced into town with the remaining guards running behind.

Gavin plastered a smile on his face more false than any she had ever seen. He waved good-bye as if this were a normal occurrence and hustled her onto the ship.

"Greetings!" said a man with an abundance of sandy whiskers as they came on board. "I am Captain Dupont. What are your friends getting off to in such a hurry? They forget something they wanted to take, yes?"

"Nay," said Gavin, pausing only for a moment. "The lads decided to stay and not make the journey. They were racing to the pub. Last man buys the first round."

The captain laughed at this. "One way to make sure the men are fleet of foot, no?"

Gavin gave another forced smile. "I see that the tide has turned. Are we soon to set sail?"

"Eager to get on the seas, is it?" The captain smiled in a knowing way. "Or perhaps you are looking for an early evening to find yourself in bed with this beautiful young wife of yours."

Despite her strict training, Colette blushed straight down to her toes. How dare he speak of her in this manner, particularly in her presence?

"That obvious, am I?" Gavin played along. "Truth, I would like to be on our way."

"Well now, my lad, you will have a lifetime with this pretty young wife of yours, but I understand a young man's heart, I do. Make yourself at home and we'll shove off."

Colette could not stop watching the dock and the road beyond. Would her guards be able to hold off the English soldiers long enough for them to escape? What would happen to her guards? The minutes ticked by and still she saw no one. Every once in a while, she heard the faint noise of some commotion. She feared the soldiers were pressing closer and might soon be in view. She exchanged a glance with Gavin. Would they be able to leave fast enough?

"Let me help ye at yer work," said Gavin, stepping up to assist the small sailing crew in their duties. A few times, a definite clang of steel on steel was audible, causing more than a few sailors to stop their work and look around. Fortunately, Captain Perrine had so far held them off and the battle was not visible to anyone on board. Gavin took to humming a jaunty tune and then singing it outright, trying to prevent the good captain from hearing anything that might cause alarm.

"Get below," Gavin whispered to her as he passed.

He was right; she should not be seen from the dock, should the English soldiers break through. She found refuge in the raised wooden structure at the stern of the ship, which had been built to resemble a square castle turret. Inside was a narrow passageway leading to three doors, one on the left, one on the right, and one straight ahead. She chose the middle door and found herself in a neat little cabin. Opening a shutter, she could see the dock and hear the increasing noise from the battle.

She ran back to the narrow doorway to the deck, eager to see the square sail unfurl as it was raised up the mast. It was fastened to a long beam at the top and then secured on the lower edges by rigging it to the ship. Colette did not know if Gavin had any experience with sailing, but he certainly was jumping about, trying to be as helpful as possible.

The boat finally pulled away from the dock, the sailors helping with long oars until the sail caught the wind. They floated out into the river that would take them to the ocean itself. Colette sighed in relief, thinking they had escaped. She ran back to the cabin just as the English soldiers came into view. The clash between the English and her guards was now clearly visible on the dock if anyone was to look.

She ran back to the narrow door leading to the deck. "Gavin!" she hissed, pointing to their new problem.

Gavin grimaced for a second before putting his arm around Captain Dupont's shoulders and facing him out to sea. "So tell me, what's ahead of us and how long will be our journey?"

Colette's guards were making a good showing, holding a larger English force at bay, but they were greatly outnumbered. The English soldiers who had chased them from the village had joined with the foot soldiers from Bordeaux, and now they were all pressing her men hard. Her heart sank with the thought that they were protecting her with their very lives. She hoped they could hold out a little longer and return home to their families.

"What was that noise?" The captain paused, cocking his head to one side, listening carefully.

"Noise?" Gavin smiled, showing his teeth. "No' sure what ye mean, but I am enjoying the sound of the waves on the hull of the ship. 'Tis verra calming. Or mayhap ye mean the seagulls, though their squalling is less relaxing. Reminds me of a song I ken." Gavin loudly sang a jaunty tune in his native tongue.

The captain smiled but was undeterred, walking back along the railing of the ship, toward the dock and the sounds of the skirmish. Captain Withers and the English soldiers stood alone on the dock shouting and waving their arms.

Colette's stomach sank. Her guards had been defeated.

"Ah, look! They are waving us farewell. How verra kind." Gavin waved back and smiled boldly. "Farewell! We shall miss ye! Aye, we wish we could return, but we shall carry ye in our hearts!" Gavin yelled over the din of the soldiers who were far enough away to be difficult to hear.

Colette could tell they were yelling at them to stop, but she hoped their words and intent would not be clear to the captain.

Fortunately, the captain smiled and waved. "Farewell, my friends!"

"Stop your ship!" boomed the loud voice of Captain Withers. "You carry the daughter of the duc de Bergerac!"

Colette grabbed the door frame to keep herself standing. It was impossible Captain Dupont had not heard. The ship captain frowned and turned to look at her, sizing her up as though seeing her for the first time. The crew likewise stopped their work and stared at her, unsure what to do.

"Ye got nobility aboard wi' us?" Gavin asked the captain in a friendly manner.

"The only women aboard this ship are your wife and her maid," said the captain in a suspicious tone.

Gavin strolled boldly toward her. "So my wife is a fancy lady? Have ye been keeping secrets from me, my dear?" He laughed when he said it. He approached her with confidence and put an arm around her, snaking it up her back and pressing her toward him. "Tell yer English friends I'm kissing me a princess!"

"What are you doing?" she whispered, not sure if her heart was pounding from the danger of the situation or the closeness of the man.

Gavin leaned close to her, hissing in her ear. "They need to believe ye are my wife."

She knew what they must do. They needed to convince their captain she was not the lady they sought if they had any chance of escaping. What harm could a single kiss do?

He leaned forward, until his lips were only an inch

away from hers. "May I kiss ye, m'lady?" His whisper was so soft, she almost missed it on the wind.

"*Oui.*" A single word that would change everything.

His lips were surprisingly soft and inviting. He wrapped his arms around her slowly, drawing her in, allowing her body to melt slowly into his. The sensation was shocking yet warm and delicious. She moved her hands up his chest and wound her arms around his neck, soaking him in, wanting more.

A growl of pleasure emanated from him somewhere deep within his chest, a quiet rumble that told her he was not untouched by this kiss. He held her tighter and moved his lips along hers in a slow, sensuous dance. She could not help but press closer as he deepened the kiss.

Vaguely in the distance, she heard the sounds of cheering and she could only think it was her soul rejoicing in this powerful bonding of hearts. Suddenly, the connection was broken. Gavin ended the kiss abruptly and pulled away, keeping one arm around her shoulders. He faced the captain and crew, who were giving cheers and shouts of encouragement to Gavin. It turned a hallowed moment into something quite lurid, and her cheeks blazed in response.

"Verra well done, m'lady. We may get out o' here alive." Gavin spoke out of the corner of his mouth even as he smiled and waved to the crew.

"No duchess aboard this vessel!" the captain called back to the soldiers on the dock and, despite their protests, continued to set sail.

Colette forced a small smile. At least they had gotten away and Gavin thought it was all pretend. She would have to guard herself lest he discover her response was not at all feigned. The thing that disturbed her most was not the kiss they had shared, but the thought that it had not affected him as it had her.

Whatever happened now, his kisses would forever be seared upon her soul. She may have escaped France, but she would never escape the memory of Gavin's kiss.

Twenty-one

As the boat pulled away up the river, Colette's relief at having escaped Bordeaux turned to worry over the fate of her men. They had been on the docks and then they were gone. Had they been pushed into the river? Had they been killed and thrown aside?

She hurried down the corridor to the small cabin and looked out the window to view the dock slowly growing smaller as they floated away. Finally she saw them, not on the shore but in a large rowboat, rowing for all their might southward, toward the next port.

She waved at them from the window and they waved at her in return. She sighed and put a hand to her chest. They had done it. They were on the ship and her men had escaped the English.

She sank onto a small bed as the ship rocked gently from side to side. It had been an exhausting day. Despite her inner turmoil, the cabin was a cozy room with smooth, varnished woodwork. Much of the furniture was built into the walls, most likely to prevent it from tipping over in high seas. The cabin boasted a wardrobe, a small table, one wooden chair, and a firm bunk-style bed covered with a red wool blanket. Everything was stowed neatly away, giving the small space a tidy feel. The room was sparse yet homey.

The ship swayed gently as it caught the wind, and she put a hand on the windowsill to keep her balance. Outside the window, the shores of Bordeaux grew distant. She gazed with longing at the last vision of her homeland: the green fields, the red roofs of the town, and the church spire of Bordeaux Cathedral.

She had expected to be journeying with her guards and her maids, but she was now alone with only a Highland guide, an urchin for a maid, and an unwanted baby. If this was the new way the Lord was making for her in the wilderness, it was indeed a strange new road.

"Greetings, m'lady," said Gavin, leaning on the door frame of the small cabin.

Colette stood up fast, not wishing him to see her sitting on a bed, of all inappropriate things. Her heart fluttered at the sight of him after their performance on deck. The ship shifted several degrees to the port side, causing her to stumble slightly before regaining her balance.

"Careful there," said Gavin as he strolled into the cabin and held her elbow for a brief moment to steady her before letting go. "Might take a wee bit to get used to the shifting o' the boat."

The boat rocked and her knees, weak from all the momentous events of the past few days, gave way. At least, that was the rationale she told herself later. Whether by accident or design, she stumbled forward and once again Gavin was there to put his arm around her waist to steady her.

"Here, sit down, m'lady. I dinna wish ye to fall while ye're getting yer sea legs."

She allowed herself to be guided a few steps and sat down with Gavin beside her. She took another deep breath, filled with an emotion she could not name. Gavin gently gave her hand a squeeze in comfort, and the sensation that his fingers produced on her bare skin was something foreign to her.

"Forgive me." Colette breathed deep of the salty sea air mixed with the scent of varnished wood and fresh tar.

"'Tis been a difficult day for ye, I fear." Gavin gave her a bolstering smile and wrapped his arm around her shoulders, giving her a slight squeeze.

It was only then that she realized they were both sitting on one of the few pieces of furniture in the room. The bed. At this recognition, a jolt of something hot shot straight to her core. She was too tired to fight against it, and her head tipped naturally to his shoulder. "I had thought to have planned for everything along my journey, but never had I envisioned anything such as this."

Gavin rested his chin on the top of her head. It was a gesture of comfort and friendship, and Colette snuggled closer to Gavin, who embraced her with both arms. She allowed herself to be infused with his warmth and his strength. As long as she could remain in his arms, she felt secure.

Another moment's reflection brought the recognition that being in his arms was a mistake. A nagging part of her knew these were the pleasures that would forever be denied her. She was not free to choose her own partner in life. She should not accustom herself to finding comfort in the arms of a man. And yet he was warm and comforting, and no matter what was to come, she needed this moment of peace in the arms of Sir Gavin Patrick.

"Ah, the newlyweds." Captain Dupont strolled into the cabin with a wide grin, oblivious to the desperate fight on the dock to escape and the overall wrongness of finding Colette in Gavin's arms.

The captain was a large man, clearly built for a life of labor on the seas, with broad shoulders and large forearms. He removed his cap, revealing a bald head. His hair seemed to have migrated from the top of his head to his bushy, sandy-colored mustache. "You must take this, my cabin, for the duration of our journey. You will spend your wedding night in comfort, yes?" He waggled bushy eyebrows up and down.

"We woud'na presume to take yer own cabin, Captain Dupont," said Gavin, helping Colette to stand.

Fortunately, the captain insisted, saying he would take the cabin on the port side and Pippa the maid could have the cabin on the starboard with the baby. The captain smiled broadly under his bushy mustache, gave them both an obvious wink, and left them alone, closing the door behind him.

"I cannot stay with you," Colette said in a hushed tone. She understood why they needed to use subterfuge to get on the ship, but she had assumed that she would be staying in a cabin with Pippa, not the

Highland knight before her. "If you please, you must stay in the other cabin, and I will stay here with my maid."

Gavin looked at the ceiling and rubbed the back of his neck. "Aye, it would be the right thing to do." He shifted from one foot to the other and glanced around the small cabin as if he found the polished, honey-colored woodwork fascinating. "Trouble is, might raise some suspicions, ye ken. Especially since the captain thinks we were just married."

Colette suppressed a rising sense of panic. She could not stay here alone with a man. She could not. "I am to be married to Kenneth Mackenzie, the Baron of Kintail. If he discovers I spent my journey sailing unsupervised alone with a man…" It was simply unthinkable. Besides, she feared being alone with Gavin would inflame desires that could not be quenched.

"Aye, I see it would cause a stir. New husband woud'na care for that."

"Not care for it? He would refuse to wed me. He would send me back in shame, and everything that we have worked for, everything I sacrificed for, would be lost."

Gavin rubbed the back of his neck again. He had barely looked at her since this distressing topic had arisen. "Trouble is, if our good captain ever suspects us, he could verra easily put us to shore here in France or in England herself, and there would be verra little we could do about it."

"There must be another way." Colette kept her voice low and calm, hiding the growing sense of panic.

Gavin gave her his full attention, his rich brown eyes meeting hers and holding her gaze without wavering. "I swear to ye, Lady Marie Colette, that I winna force myself upon ye or make any unwanted advances."

She did not doubt it. She knew Sir Gavin was an honorable knight and would not press his advantage. His chivalry was not what troubled her. She did not doubt his ability to remain appropriately chaste, but she feared her own resolve was at risk. He was a handsome man, this Sir Gavin. She felt right in his arms, as if she belonged there, as if she'd been waiting her whole life to find this place, this man, this moment when she was fully alive and where she truly belonged.

Marie Colette shook her head vigorously, more to shake away her treacherous thoughts than to deny what Gavin said. "I trust you are an honorable knight, Sir Gavin. But some other arrangement must be made."

Gavin inspected the toes of his boots. He shrugged and nodded. "I can make up some excuse, I warrant."

"Very good, Sir Knight." She drank in one last look at his handsome body, his broad shoulders, and his muscular form that even his loose-fitting tunic garb could not hide. She preferred him in his native Highland attire, naked legs and all.

She forced herself to turn away, to the window, seeing nothing except the memory of Gavin, riding his destrier across the fields, his plaid hiked up to reveal a muscular thigh. He must not stay in her cabin, for she feared she could not make the same pledge to him that he had just made to her.

Twenty-two

THEY TRAVELED PEACEFULLY DOWN THE RIVER, TOWARD the setting sun and the great ocean. After collecting herself in the cabin, Colette emerged on deck, the gentle wind tugging at her headdress. She breathed deeply of the salty sea air. It was fresh and new and despite everything, she experienced a quiver of excitement.

It was the first time she had been on her own. Her ladies had been her constant companions since she had emerged from the nursery. She had lived a very public existence, always someone watching her, reporting her every movement. If she did anything unladylike, the tale would spread throughout the castle. She had been judged from the moment of her birth on her beauty and her ability to remain serene and demure. But now on this plain merchant vessel, she could say or do whatever she liked. Not that she had any great desire for misbehaving—except where a certain Highland knight was in question.

Colette smiled into the wind. She could be anybody. In fact, it was important for her not to act like

Lady Marie Colette, so she must behave in a manner different than her usual self. She was the hero of her own great adventure, just like the stories she loved to read.

The ship swayed, and the sail furled in the wind, catching a gust and pushing their craft forward. The captain was at the helm and the men pulled at thick ropes, singing a jaunty tune.

Colette walked carefully across the wood deck, conscious of how the ship swayed gently in the water and wishing not to embarrass herself by falling on her backside in front of all the crew. Gavin and Pippa, who still cradled the bundle of baby in her arms, were at the bow of the ship, facing the setting sun.

Gavin leaned closer to Pippa in a familiar manner that made Colette's jaw tight. Of course, he had every right to do so. If he wished, instead of taking the baby to his mother, he could marry Pippa and adopt the babe as his own. Colette ground her teeth at the thought.

Pippa turned to Gavin, her face in profile illuminated by the golden light of the setting sun. Despite her abrasive manner, Pippa was an attractive girl. Gavin reached up and touched a hand to her shoulder, rubbing it slightly in an affectionate manner. The gesture inflamed more than a twinge of jealousy and Colette had the sudden desire to tell Gavin to return to her cabin and remain there for the rest of the voyage. Not wanting to examine such uncharitable impulses, she strolled toward the bow and joined the pair by stepping boldly in between them.

Despite her brush with envy, Colette was momentarily transfixed by the beauty of the sight before her.

The sun dipped low on the horizon, creating a golden trail across the water from the bright ball of light to the bow of their ship. The sky was illuminated in orange and red as the edge of the sun touched the watery horizon before them. Orange and pink clouds brightened the horizon as if painted with a radiant brush. Colette caught her breath at its beauty. She had seen the sunsets over the hills by her castle but never over the ocean with the water reflecting the glory of the sun. It was indeed a splendid sight and she hoped one that foretold of good fortune and a safe passage along the seas.

Beside her, Pippa swallowed hard. "Good eve to you, m'lady." Her voice was not as sharp or confident as Colette was accustomed to hear from Pippa. A closer examination of the maid revealed that Pippa had gone a bit pale. The ship lurched a bit as it reached the mouth of the river and entered into the great ocean. Pippa responded by turning a pale shade of green.

"I fear our dear Pippa is experiencing a wee bit o' seasickness," said Gavin with a strong command of the obvious.

Pippa clutched the railing with one hand and pressed the swaddled baby to her shoulder.

"Here, let me take the babe," said Colette, not wishing that the infant be lost at sea by her unsteady maid.

Pippa readily handed over the child in favor of grasping the railing with both hands, as if she could hold the ship steady with sheer effort and determination. She swallowed again and took a deep breath.

Colette juggled the babe awkwardly, trying to imitate the easy manner with which Pippa held the tot. Colette had the impulse to hand the creature over to Gavin, but she did not wish to appear less capable than her seasick maid. Despite her compassion for the ill girl, she was secretly pleased to find Gavin's interest to be one of comforting the infirm and not flirtation.

The baby's eyes opened, and Colette held her breath lest the child begin a plaintive wail. Instead, the babe snuggled up to her and grabbed ahold of the hem of the bodice of her silk gown with one sticky hand.

Immediately, Colette attempted to move the offending chubby hand from her brocade silk, but only succeeded in the baby transferring her firm grasp from the fabric to Colette's index finger. The baby sighed contentedly, closed her eyes, and drew up Colette's finger into her slobbery mouth, happily gumming her fingertip.

Colette was about to pull back her molested finger, but Gavin spoke first. "Och, look how she's taken to ye." He smiled at her, the golden light of the setting sun glinting in his eyes.

"Yes, so it seems," said Colette, continuing to allow her finger to be maligned.

Colette looked down at the disfigured child, aware that this time when she saw the tot, the first thing she noticed was the child's eyes, not the red scar on her cheek. "She does have clear blue eyes," commented Colette, surprised she had never noticed them before.

Gavin smiled down at the infant, moving closer to touch the forehead of the baby. His gazed shifted from the infant to Colette. Their eyes met, his lips parting ever so slightly. "Truly lovely."

She wondered if the compliment was meant for her

or the baby. She had been complimented much in her life, fawned over by courtiers such that she stopped hearing the remarks. But these simple words touched her at her core.

Illuminated in the golden light of the setting sun, Gavin was more than handsome; he was the very image of the Greek gods of old. She wondered if he could read her thoughts and knew how her body longed to seek the comfort of his arms. She leaned toward him, and he slid his hand from the head of the infant to her shoulder and along her back, gently pulling her closer. She tilted her head up to look at him, her eyes traveling up his perfect form to his soft lips, seductive with promise. He leaned closer and everything else seemed to disappear. All that was left was her and Gavin and the setting sun…

Pippa heaved violently over the railing of the ship, jolting Colette back to reality. She jumped back from both Gavin and Pippa, though for different reasons.

"Oh dear, Pippa, you do not look at all well." It was Colette's turn to state the obvious.

"Sorry, my lady." Pippa held on to the railing, doubled over so that her cheek rested against the smooth wood. "Not feeling quite myself."

"Sometimes it takes a few days to get yer sea legs," said Gavin with sympathy. "Stand here and look at the horizon. Keep the wind in yer face if it helps."

In response, Pippa heaved again.

"Is there anything we can do to assist her?" It was a strange experience for Colette to be in a position to care for the needs of her maid. Everything on this journey seemed backward and now even the natural order of things was reversed, and instead of being waited on, she was the caretaker.

Strangely, it felt rather liberating. Somehow the implied message of always having other people look after her was that she was incompetent to care for even her own basic needs. Since the beginning of her journey, she had been pleased to find that this was not the case. She enjoyed the opportunity to take care of herself and others, though considering Pippa's current malady, Colette did not relish getting too close.

"No' much we can do but ride it out," said Gavin.

"Pippa." Colette took command. "Would you feel better here at the railing or would you like to lie down for a spell?"

"Think I'd like to lie down," said Pippa, doubled over at the waist.

"Come with me," said Colette, embracing her new role as caretaker. "Your cabin is this way." She glanced back at Gavin and almost stopped short from the sweetness of the smile on his face. She knew she needed to put more distance between them or she might do something delightfully regrettable.

"Perhaps you could find us a bucket," Colette called over her shoulder to Gavin. Nothing could chase away attraction so quick as the thought of the chamber pot.

"It would be my honor, m'lady." Gavin bowed at the waist as if she had sent him on an epic quest. Beside her, Pippa started to gurgle and Colette quickened her step, hoping that Gavin would complete the task with alacrity.

Pippa was soon seen to her tiny cabin, now sickroom, and reclined on her bunk, her eyes closed, her coloring a sickly hue of green. Colette placed the bucket within easy reach and lingered for a moment, wondering if there was anything more she could do. She reviewed what her own mother had said to her on the rare occasions on which she had become ill, but Colette doubted that being chastised for being overcome with sickness would help restore Pippa to health any more than it had helped her.

When she felt sickly or discouraged, she would turn to books. "Have you ever heard the story of the Trojan horse?" she asked, deciding to begin with a few Greek myths. She told the story of Helen of Troy and the giant horse until the room darkened and Pippa's eyes closed as she fell into a deep sleep.

Colette felt accomplished to have distracted her maid from her sickness until she slept. She left Pippa to recover as she could, closing the door behind her.

The ship rocked and swayed beneath her feet but far from being distressed by it, or made ill as it had her poor maid, Colette found the movement comforting, as if swinging in a bassinet like a baby. The baby in her arms had slept for a while but now glared at her, making slight whimpering and unhappy noises. Colette's first thought was to take the baby back to her maid, but of course Pippa could barely take care of herself at the moment. So what to do with the child?

Gavin. She had need of him.

Emerging back on deck, Colette found the sun had set and the moon was rising on the horizon. The sailors had lit lanterns along the side of the ship and continued to sail north, following the coastline in the distance off the starboard side. Gavin had returned to the bow and was looking out over the ocean as the stars began to appear in the clear night sky. The baby's soft noises of complaint grew ever louder as she approached until, in meeting Gavin, the child took a deep breath and let out a fearsome wail.

"Oh! You stop that noise at once, you naughty child," Colette reprimanded the tot. The child in question only began to wail louder. What was wrong with the thing?

"How does one make this noise stop?" she asked Gavin, hoping that he would have some insight into the matter. In truth, she hoped he would take over care of the squalling thing himself.

"When was the last time she was fed? Or given a fresh nappy?" Gavin did not seem at all fazed by the loud cries of the baby and instead was asking perfectly rational questions. How infuriating!

"I do not know. How would I know something like that? Shall I rouse Pippa?"

"Nay, I doubt Pippa would be a suitable caretaker for the bairn right now."

"Yes, I concede that you are correct in this matter." Colette paused, unsure what to do.

The baby however had no such qualms about causing a stir and proceeded to scream as if she was having her appendages pulled off.

"It sounds to me like the bairn is hungry. Why dinna ye go feed her?" Gavin did not seem particularly perturbed, though he watched her with a flicker of confusion on his face, as if trying to figure out why she did not attend to the much demanding infant.

Colette had no idea how to feed the infant without food being brought before her, and Pippa had mentioned something about milk, but how was that accomplished? However, she was reticent to admit the full extent of her lack of skill to Gavin. "Where Pippa has stored materials needed for the baby is not known to me."

"I believe everything is in yer trunks, which have been brought to yer cabin," said Gavin in a helpful tone, though he clearly did not understand the nature of the difficulty.

Darkness spread fast across the sky, the stars coming out in force, bright and twinkling, a stark contrast to the squalling infant in her arms. Colette cleared her throat. "In truth, I am not familiar with the feeding and care of infants." She hoped not to lose his good opinion with her confession.

A slow smile spread across Gavin's face. "Then ye must allow me to assist ye." He spoke in a tone that made her want to allow him to do just about anything. She had thought him a handsome man in the setting sun, but in the pale light of the ship's lantern, he looked like a different animal altogether. At night, there was a wildness about his eyes that drew her closer even as it warned her to stay away.

She held her back straight and gave him a brief nod, turning on her heel to march back to their cabin. *Their* cabin? Clearly Pippa could not be moved, so it would not be possible for Gavin to stay in the spare cabin. Pippa would not share her bedchamber tonight, of that Colette was certain. This left Colette with Gavin and the screeching infant. First things first, she needed to make the noise stop.

Back in the cabin, Gavin opened one of her trunks and quickly pulled out a leather bottle of milk. "This is the last of the cow's milk. From now on, we'll have to get milk from the goat in the hold below. She is also old enough to eat porridge and bread soaked in milk."

Much to Colette's relief, Gavin took the baby from her arms and helped the babe drink from the bottle by slowly pouring it drip by drip into her mouth. The baby warmed quickly to this exercise and gobbled up as much milk as she was provided. Colette was amazed the large Highlander could be so gentle with such a small creature. He held the babe easily in one arm and fed her with the other as natural as could be.

The babe was content with her meal, and Gavin handed the baby back to Colette. He then removed some pieces of wood and rope from the trunk. Colette watched in curious wonder as Gavin quickly put the pieces together to form a basket. Throwing the ropes over one of the main braces above them, he created a hanging bassinet for the baby.

Colette, wanting to show some small form of domesticity, found blankets for the bassinet, and soon the baby was sleeping peacefully in her new rocking cradle.

A knock on the door brought the ship's cook, who provided them with a simple supper of dried beef, bread, cheese, and wine. They set the simple fare on a small table, but there was only one chair in the cabin, so Colette perched herself as elegantly as she could manage on the edge of the bed and Gavin sat across from her on the chair.

They ate, breaking bread together. Alone together. Colette feared she was enjoying their time together in the quaint little cabin a bit too much.

"Thank you, good knight, you have proven your worth today. I cannot imagine what would have happened without you," she said, trying to remember how she used to make pleasant but distant conversation.

"Ye have done well yerself." Gavin gave her an easy smile. "What a day, eh? I tell ye the truth, I dinna ken we were going to make it." His words were warm and friendly.

She struggled to maintain her distance, her objectivity. She wished nothing more than to fall into the dream illusion they had created—the merchant and his new wife. What a happy life…if only it were hers to keep. But it wasn't, and she would do best to remember it.

"When we arrive at our destination, I will command my husband to provide you with some recompense for your efforts today." She would pay him. She knew it was an insult, but she did not know how else to reestablish the perspective she had lost.

The meaning of her words did not pass by Gavin unnoticed. He paused for a moment in his meal, his posture growing stiff. "A knight seeks no reward for doing his duty."

"Then you may sleep well tonight, knowing that you have behaved in a manner most becoming your knightly calling." She held her head high as if she were still seated at the head table beside her father.

A shadow fell over Gavin's eyes. She hated to see it, for she wanted the camaraderie of their friendship returned, but she knew she could not have it. Why tempt herself with something she could never have?

He may not thank her now, but in the end, it would be better for them both.

He rose stiffly and gave her a brief nod. "I'll check wi' Captain Dupont to ensure our journey proceeds well, m'lady."

"Very good." She rose to her feet and nodded to dismiss him. "As it is a pleasant night, perhaps you may remain on deck and ensure that our travels continue in a safe manner."

Gavin's eyes pierced through hers, blazing hot. She shifted slightly, hoping he could not read her wavering thoughts. "Ye wish to avoid me this evening, m'lady, and I'll grant ye yer wish. But know this, we canna avoid each other or be seen out of each other's good graces wi'out raising suspicion."

Gavin paused and his face softened a bit. He cocked his head to one side, looking slightly like an adorable puppy. She fought against the instant pull of attraction. She must remain aloof.

"Are ye afraid o' me?" Gavin asked.

"No, of course I am not!" she lied.

"Ye're afraid o' something. I can see it in yer eyes." A slow smile spread across his lips. "Ye woud'na be trying to purposely provoke me into anger, would ye?"

"No… I… Why would you say such a thing?" She was flustered.

He gave her a slow smile that slipped past her defenses and struck home in her heart. "Ye have yerself a good night, m'lady. I will see ye in the morn." He turned and left the cabin, shutting the door behind him before she could think of an appropriate response.

She stood there, shaking, not knowing how to feel. This was worse than anything she had anticipated. If he could see through her defenses, he could do what no one else ever had. She would be stripped naked before him.

What a delicious thought.

Twenty-three

IN THE WEE HOURS OF THE MORNING, COLETTE AWOKE
to the sound of her plans going completely awry. In her
desire to remove Gavin from her cabin, she had forgotten about one small thing—small but very, very loud.

The baby had awoken and was screaming at
the top of her little lungs. Colette sat bolt upright,
momentarily confused as to where she was. "See to
the infant," she called to her maids and lay back down.

The baby cried louder and her maids did not jump
to do her bidding. Colette sat up, looking for her
errant ladies-in-waiting, only to recall she was alone.
The baby screeched. *No, not alone.*

Colette struggled against the rolling ship to get out
of bed. If the baby was to be silenced, it would be up
to her. Clearly, chasing Gavin away had been a tactical
error on her part. She shuffled over to the squalling
child in nothing but her chemise and bare feet. "Well,
what is it you want?"

The baby quieted in anticipation, looking at her with
trembling lips. Colette had a sense she had but a moment
to figure out what the babe wanted before it would

unleash its piercing wail again. Colette's thick, wavy hair, usually bound up day and night, hung loose since there was no maid to tend to it and Colette had been too tired to bother with it last night. A strand fell in the bassinet, and the baby grabbed hold and pulled hard.

"Ow!" cried Colette, pulling back her long hair, out of the dangerous grasp of her tiny attacker.

The baby responded by howling all the more. Was it hungry? Gavin had mentioned something about a goat, but surely he did not intend for her to go into the hold of the ship and milk a goat in the wee hours of the morning.

Colette knew she had no option but to pick up the wailing thing before she woke the entire ship and possibly all the nautical inhabitants of the great ocean. She caught her breath. The baby smelled something horrible. She held the offending package at arm's length, not wanting to touch more of the slobbery thing than was absolutely necessary. She laid the unhappy bundle on the floor while she rummaged through one of the trunks, trying to find another bottle of milk.

As she feared, as soon as her hands left the infant, the tot began to scream. With no small amount of relief, Colette found what was left of the leather flask of milk and presented it triumphantly to the baby. The baby, however, batted at the leather bottle with tiny fists, wanting nothing to do with the peace offering.

"This is what Sir Gavin gave you and you liked it," she reasoned with the grumpy tot. It was not fair that the baby was responding differently to her then she had to Gavin. Colette thrust the milk into the child's face again. "Pray be reasonable. You liked this a few hours ago. Drink it and stop this caterwauling, I beg thee."

The baby was in no mood to be obliging. Colette picked up the little one once more, carefully holding her away from her nose. Ugh, the thing reeked. She must be utterly filthy. It suddenly occurred to Colette that if she smelled so bad, she would probably cry in a similar manner. Perhaps the baby did not wish to sit in her own excrement?

Of course, the only way to cleanse the infant would be to undress her, something Colette had never attempted. The baby was wrapped in some sort of long strip of linen. Colette searched for the proper place to begin unwrapping the crying package but was a little mystified. She rolled up her sleeves; this was going to be messy work. But if Pippa could do it, and Sir Gavin could do it, then she could take care of this noisy little thing too.

Finding ties in the back, she untied the tot and began to unwrap her. Far from being appreciative of her efforts, the baby only shrieked louder. The babe may not have enjoyed her current state of smelliness, but she protested loudly when her bare skin felt the cool night air. Colette was successful getting her out of the first layer of tightly bound swaddling clothes. She felt a swell of pride in her accomplishment, though she should not have looked to the baby to share in any such celebration.

"You should be pleased I have gotten this far," Colette chastised the tot for her emotional outburst. "My, but you are smelling something horrid."

Another long strip of solid swaddling clothes was wrapped tightly around the infant, which Colette quickly unwrapped. With her arms and legs now freed, the baby flapped her arms and legs about, free of her encumbrances.

"Now then, see here, if you would just stop that. Stop moving about so I can get at you." Her words had absolutely no effect on the baby, who must have thought of herself as some kind of windmill, moving her arms and legs wildly. "This is why you are bound tight, no?" reasoned Colette to the utterly recalcitrant baby.

The smell was growing worse, and Colette realized that she was getting near to the source of the problem. Thick flannel had been wrapped around the baby's bum, and Colette hesitated, not wanting to touch it for she could see it was utterly soaked through with urine and other unmentionable substances. She tucked her long hair behind her, ensuring it did not fall into something unpleasant. Taking a deep breath—and then regretting that decision for the smell was putrid—Colette carefully found a clean bit of the flannel and pulled off the repulsive nappy with one quick tug. The result brought tears to her eyes.

"Oh, oh, oh my word. Heaven protect me." How long had the baby sat in her own filth? She quickly wiped the baby's derriere clean with part of the linen strip and then stood, not knowing what to do with the offending mess in her hands. Out the window it went. Colette herself then leaned out the window and breathed deep of the clean sea air. Much better.

Turning back to the naked baby, she grabbed a flannel square from the trunk, dipped it into some water from a pitcher on the table and scrubbed the baby clean, once again tossing the flannel out the window when she was done. She had a vague sense she perhaps should not toss things overboard, but she could not think of what else to do with it.

The baby, naked but now quiet and happy, cooed at her and smiled. Colette smiled back. "Why did they have you all tied up?" she asked. "You do not like to be bound and restrained? Neither do I."

Colette washed her hands in the clean water, then rummaged through the trunk, finding a clean strip of linen for swaddling. She picked up the baby and placed her on the bed, trying to figure out how to dress her once more. Instead of swaddling the tot, she placed a thick flannel square around her bottom and then wrapped the swaddling strips just around her lower half, leaving the arms and legs free. Colette placed her in the bassinet and the baby laughed and kicked happily, pleased at her newfound freedom.

Colette was equally pleased at her success. She stood and glanced around the tidy cabin, but there were none present to share in her success. She wished Gavin could see her now, wanting to have his acknowledgment of her triumph. She realized the cabin door was slightly ajar and went to close it only to find Gavin standing in the tight passageway.

"You!" she cried.

Gavin shrugged his shoulders and gave a sheepish grin.

❧

Gavin could not sleep. He was trying to get some rest while partially hidden under some ropes, which smelled strongly of tar. He did not wish to draw attention to the fact he was not sharing the bed of his new wife, but his chosen spot was not at all comfortable. Yet the discomfort of his bed was not what was keeping him awake.

Every time he began to drift to sleep, unbidden thoughts of Marie Colette would come to him in his dreams, teasing him with her intoxicating perfume, winding her seductive hands around his neck, pressing her perfect body against his, moving in for the kiss... and then he would wake up with a start, the feel of her lips still tingling on his.

All he wanted was more, and he knew that was the one thing he could never have.

A loud wail of an unhappy baby pierced the night. Gavin lay still, waiting to see if she would quiet, but instead, the baby squalled louder. The baby's unpleasant howling no doubt disturbed the sleep of many a crewmen, and there did not seem to be any chance of Colette stopping the cries, so Gavin groggily made his way across the swaying deck to the cabins.

No doubt Colette would be upset at the disturbance to her sleep, particularly since she had no concept of how to care for a child. He had never known a woman so ill-equipped to handle children. He had thought the mothering instinct was inherent for all of the female species. Apparently, this was missing in Lady Colette.

Gavin entered the hatch and felt his way down the dark passageway to the center cabin. He opened it no more than a crack, his movements arrested by the vision before him. Marie Colette, wearing nothing more than a thin chemise, was carrying around the squalling infant. He had never before seen her in such

a state of disrobe. Most specifically, he had never seen
her before without her hair completely covered by
some sort of elaborate veil and headdress.

His jaw dropped. Her hair was a glossy, dark auburn
that shimmered in the lamplight, almost as if it was
wet. It fell over her shoulders and below her waist
in soft gentle rolling curls. It was beautiful. It was so
thick and rich, he had the sudden desire to sink his
hands into it and caress the soft curls. He wished to
ban her from ever veiling her hair again. And yet no,
he mentally amended, she should not share this beauty
with anyone but him; this would be his alone.

Colette stood, doing something for the baby, but
he could not bother to determine what. Whatever
she was doing, at least the baby had stopped the wild
screams. By the light of the single lantern, Colette's
body was perfectly silhouetted in her near-transparent
linen chemise. He sucked in his breath and held it,
afraid that if he moved, his presence would be noted
and the vision would vanish.

Her figure was sublime, a perfect, trim waist, rounded
hips, and a beautiful heart-shaped bottom. She moved,
and her full breasts swayed gently beneath the thin
fabric. He had never before wished to be a garment,
but, oh, if only he could be that chemise and cling to
her beautiful body, he would know heaven itself.

He knew he could not have her, yet the vows he
said ran through his mind. He had meant every word.
She was not meant for him, but he did not care. She
was his—somehow, she would be his.

He shook his head, banishing such disloyal thoughts,
ashamed of the direction they had taken. He had

promised to see her safely to the Baron of Kintail. He had to remain aloof. Besides, the lady could not even care for an infant without assistance. It was not the kindest musing, but he had to think of something to counter how her physical appearance stirred him.

He suddenly became aware that something had changed, something had stopped, and he realized it was the baby, who was now happily cooing in the bassinet. Somehow Lady Marie Colette had managed to take care of the infant by herself. Remarkable.

She walked to the door and her eyebrows flew up. He'd been spotted! He backed away, only to bump his head on a beam. The door opened and he leaned his shoulder on the wall, as if he was completely in control of himself and had not just smacked his own head.

"You! What are you doing here?" she demanded, grabbing a silk robe and hastily wrapping it around herself.

"Heard the cries, came to see if there was anything I could do," he said in a casual manner, hoping she did not realize he had been lusting after her perfect form.

"But do you help me? No! You watch me and offer nothing." Colette's perfectly formed eyebrows pressed together in an adorable frown. Even irritated, she was beautiful.

"Och, but ye looked to have the situation well under control. Though I've never seen swaddling such as this before." Gavin pushed past her into the room, desperately trying to change the topic. He inspected the baby, who was happily kicking her feet and waving her arms.

"She could not move and she did not care for it," defended Colette.

Gavin shrugged. "Most babies spend the first year o' their lives tightly bound. Helps their arms and legs to grow straight and keeps them from causing a mess." At least that is what he had been taught.

"But babies like to move about." Colette had a few minutes of practice and was now an expert.

"She does look happy," conceded Gavin. The baby gave him a wide smile and something melted inside him.

Colette smiled briefly at the compliment followed by another little frown. "Did you find the child's name when you searched for her family?"

Gavin slowly shook his head, remembering the sad scene at the church. "There were several families who took refuge in the church. None but this babe emerged alive. She was no doubt the bairn of one of the families, but no relations could be found."

"But she must have a name. We cannot continue to call her 'baby.'"

Gavin tilted his head slightly to one side. This was a new side of Colette. She was taking an interest in the tot beyond trying to be rid of her. "Aye, ye're right. She should have a name."

"What shall we name her?"

Gavin shook his head. "I ne'er named anyone or anything, except my horse."

"What did you name your horse?"

"Horse."

Colette raised an eyebrow at Gavin. "I shall name the child."

Gavin nodded in full agreement.

Colette paused and looked up at the ceiling, the warm light of the lantern forming a warm glow of a halo around her head. "I shall name her Marie Frances. For the saints, they must have been looking after her for her to have survived."

"Marie Frances." Gavin leaned over the child and held out a finger. Marie Frances grabbed on to his finger and held it tight with a smile. "Ah, look, she knows her name."

"She is a pretty thing," said Colette, apparently overlooking the ugly red scar marring her cheek. "She looks like a Marie Frances." Colette gazed down at the baby's face with an unguarded warmth that Gavin had never before seen. He would give much to have her look at him in the same manner.

"She does at that," he said, unable to disagree with anything she said. "Who would have thought ye would be such a good mother?"

"I am certainly not anyone's mother!" she protested.

"Good night, m'lady." Gavin turned and strolled from the room before his urge to take her into his arms and kiss her senseless could overpower him.

He walked out of the cabin and down the short passage, this time managing not to bang his head, and out onto the deck under a clear night full of twinkling stars. He rubbed his jaw, wondering how he was going to manage to live with this beautiful woman without revealing how deeply she touched him.

He curled back up with the ropes in the tar, trying to focus on manly things such as...such as... Och, he couldn't think of any manly things. The only thing he could think of was the curve of her body. And her hair—her luxurious amber hair.

It was a long voyage. And he was in trouble deep.

Twenty-four

COLETTE WAS HAVING THE STRANGEST DREAM. GAVIN was running toward her through a field of buttercups, his kilt flapping in the wind and somehow getting shorter and shorter with each approaching stride. Heedless of propriety, she ran to him, opening her arms wide. They met with a glorious crash, him wrapping his arms around her waist and twirling her around and around.

He set her down softly on the grass, his head bending down toward hers, his eyes simmering with anticipation. His lips hovered over hers for a moment, then lowered to her face, attaching themselves to her right cheek along the jawline, a wet, gooey, slobbery kiss.

Colette woke with a start, to find that she had fallen asleep on the bed with the baby in her arms, who was now using her jaw as some sort of teething ring.

"Oh, Marie Frances! What a naughty thing you are. Yes, you are. Yes, you are the cutest little beastie I have ever seen." She tickled the baby's tummy and was rewarded with a squeal of delight from the infant. She could not help but laugh herself. She tickled the baby again and was rewarded by another squeal of laughter. She had no idea how amusing babies could be. Why did people wish to avoid them until the babies were older?

Tickle. Laugh. Giggle.

Frances giggled again, then gave a hiccup, which caused her whole body to spasm and her eyes to fly open wide with surprise.

"It is the hiccups," said Colette, laughing at the baby's response.

The baby hiccuped, screwing her tiny face into an adorable grimace only to hiccup again. Again she was startled, with eyes open wide, and then scrunched her face together as if she was an old man. Colette laughed so hard she wiped tears from her eyes.

"Are ye well?" called Gavin from the other side of the door. Without waiting for her to answer, he opened the door.

"I am fine," said Colette, pulling the covers up. It was most indecent for him to see her in repose.

"Och, good. I thought ye were upset. I see ye've made a friend." Sir Gavin stood in the open doorway, his shoulder leaning on the door frame.

Colette scowled at him, making a mental note to figure out how to lock the door. "Were you in need of something?" she asked with as much authority as she could muster from her indecent position on the bed. Her dark hair fell around her, over her shoulder, and she pushed it back impatiently.

"Nay," said Gavin with a despicable twinkle in his eye. "Ye've given me everything I could've asked for this morn." The wretched man strolled from the cabin whistling a happy tune, no doubt pretending that he was coming from his marital bed a satisfied man.

"That man is an utter beast," she confided in the baby. Frances hiccuped in response.

❧

Colette expected, or more accurately hoped, that Pippa would emerge in the morning happy and well after a good night's sleep. The morning came and went, however, without any sign of Pippa. Thus, Colette was forced to attempt a new task—that of dressing herself.

It was not that she was a stranger to the process or that she did not possess the will to complete the task. It was simply that she did not possess the detachable arms required to lace up gowns in the back or secure elaborate headdresses. After much trial and error, she finally managed to dress in a simple linen gown with an emerald silk kirtle that laced in the front, masking whatever travesty had occurred trying to lace her gown behind her.

Her hair was another matter, and it took considerable time to sweep it all under a modest wimple and then attach a headdress of green and gold. It was a rather large headdress, for she had nothing in her collection that was small, and it took many pins to secure it.

It had been at her mother's insistence that she kept her hair hidden. In a world where she was on public display and her beauty was much commented upon, her hair was the one feature Colette felt was her own. Her hair was the one part of herself she could keep for herself, for no man would see it. Except her husband of course.

And Gavin.

Colette pushed thoughts of Sir Gavin Patrick aside and went about her work, putting the finishing touches on her costume and feeding the baby. She then removed the kirtle, which the baby spit up on, and replaced it with a fresh one. This is why maids wore aprons. She decided that tomorrow she would feed the baby first, before dressing, if Pippa had not recovered.

By midday, Pippa still had not reported for duty, and Colette decided it was time to check on the young woman. Bolstered with the success of caring for the infant, who was sleeping peacefully in the swaying cradle, Colette hoped she could similarly tend a seasick maid.

One step within the cabin revealed the drawbacks of being a caretaker. Pippa had not spent an easy night, and it was clear there had been difficulties finding the bucket.

"Pippa? Pippa, are you well?" Colette squinted into the dimly lit cabin, trying to ascertain if the maid had survived the night.

A piteous groan was the only response. At least Pippa was alive, which was good, though she doubted her maid thought so at the moment. "You poor dear. I did not realize you would be quite so ill. I do not think sea travel agrees with you."

"Throw me overboard and let me die," moaned Pippa.

"I am so sorry to disappoint, but I will not drown you today," said Colette briskly. She stuck her head out of the cabin to get a breath of fresh air. What should she do now?

"Pippa, I am going to get Sir Gavin." Colette did not know exactly what she expected Gavin to do or why she would seek him in such a situation, but it was to him that she turned. She strolled out of the cabin and onto the deck, her face to the wind and the sun.

It was a beautiful day and the wind was brisk. The ship rose and fell with the rolling waves. She could sense why someone might not enjoy the up-and-down motion, but it did not bother her. In truth, she quite enjoyed the ride. It reminded her of when, as a very little girl, she had been placed on a swing by a courtier. She had been pushed high on the swing, making her shriek with laughter. It had been the most fun of her life, and it ended very quickly when her maids insisted she stop making a spectacle of herself.

Colette staggered across the deck to find Gavin, the wind tugging at her headdress mercilessly. The large sail-like quality of the headdress made it tempting for the wind to think she should take flight. She fought against the wind, and the wind fought back, wanting to either throw her from the boat or rip the headdress from her hair. She was forced to hold on to it in a most unladylike fashion simply to get across the deck without having some sort of unfortunate incident.

Gavin was standing in the bow of the ship looking before them, toward his homeland. The wind teased his dark hair and his face was turned toward the sun, his eyes half-closed and a small smile playing about his mouth. She paused to admire him. She could not help herself.

Gavin turned at that moment, the amusement clear in his eyes. He put up a hand to hide a wide grin and closed his eyes for a moment as if trying to gain composure. He walked up to her, pressing his lips together to prevent himself from laughing out loud, but nothing could hide the twinkling in his eyes.

"You are laughing at me," Colette stated, trying to put her hands on her hips, but a strong gust required both hands to prevent the headdress from flying off her head.

"Nay, I—" Gavin dissolved into laughter.

Colette waited impatiently for his mirth to subside. "If you are quite finished enjoying your amusements, I wish to speak to you about a matter of great urgency."

Gavin sobered instantly. "What's the matter? Is Marie Frances no' well?"

"Frances is sleeping, but Pippa is still quite ill."

Gavin frowned. "Is she still sick? I had hoped she'd feel better on the second day o' the voyage."

"She remains ill and her cabin had taken quite the brunt of her illness."

Gavin swept her a bow. "I beg you would allow me to be of assistance."

Colette nodded her head indulgently, though the effect was ruined by having to hold on to her headgear. She was relieved at his offer and even more relieved to fight her way back to the cabin, where she could change into a more modest veil. She decided that at least for the sea voyage, she would take a more practical approach when it came to her head.

Colette removed the headdress and replaced it with the plain white veil and wimple she usually wore to bed. It felt as though she was insufficiently attired, but in truth, her hair was still completely covered.

She met Gavin at Pippa's cabin. He came armed with a bucket of water and a mop.

"Pippa?" Colette knocked on the door and opened it. Pippa moaned piteously.

"Why dinna ye take her outside for some fresh air? Mayhap it will revive her," suggested Gavin.

Colette nodded in agreement and it took both of them to help Pippa to the deck railing, where she clung desperately, a sickly shade of green.

"Is there anything I can do for you?" asked Colette.

Pippa shook her head but then looked up at her piteously. "Another story?"

"But of course. Have you heard *The Song of Roland*?" Colette was delighted to recount some of the stories she had surreptitiously read. Leaving behind her father's books had been a great loss, but if she could tell the tales, the stories would live on in her mind.

Colette leaned on the railing and told her tale. Soon she was caught up in the story, telling it with great enthusiasm. When she was finished, Pippa looked a bit revived.

"Ye tell a great tale, m'lady," commented Gavin.

Colette turned to see him leaning on the mast behind her, listening to her. In truth, Captain Dupont was there too, and a good portion of the crew all now turning to appear busy doing something.

"My story, have you all been listening?" asked Colette.

"How could we no'? Ye tell it so well," praised Gavin.

A wave of pure happiness flooded through Colette. Unlike her maids, who would have chastised her for reading books, he appreciated a good story. He appreciated *her* story. She cherished his compliment more than she should.

Whether it was due to the fresh air or her rousing tale, by the afternoon, Pippa seemed to be perking up a bit. She had changed position and was sitting at the bow of the ship, the wind in her face. She even felt well enough to take some bread and water followed by a little wine.

Colette should have been hoping that Pippa would feel well enough to take over the care of the baby. Strangely, however, she found that she did not mind taking care of the squalid little thing. In truth, Colette was enjoying all the little happy noises Marie Frances made.

Frances continued to delight in kicking her little legs. Despite Gavin's concerns that her arms and legs might not develop correctly if left to flail about, Colette did not have the heart to tie her down once more. She let the tot explore her environment and was rewarded by seeing her roll over onto her tummy and push her head up with a wide, toothless grin.

Colette even wrapped the little creature into a blanket, still letting her arms flail freely, and took her onto the deck for some sea air. Gavin noted her arrival on deck with a slow smile. A man next to him said something, but Gavin did not give any hint of hearing him and instead walked straight to Colette.

"How is our wee Marie Frances today?" he asked with a smile.

"Very well and happy," answered Colette, returning the smile.

"This is what I like to see. The happy couple together!" Captain Dupont strode up to them with a wide smile beneath his giant, sandy-colored moustache. "I am glad to see you well, m'lady, for now nothing will keep the two newlyweds apart tonight, eh?" He gave Gavin a knowing wink.

Gavin's eyes burned with intensity. "Aye, I am verra much looking forward to tonight."

Twenty-five

COLETTE RETREATED TO HER CABIN AND PACED THE floorboards, her mind whirling. The captain of the ship expected them to sleep in the same cabin. As they were traveling as newlyweds, there was little justification to sleep apart. But clearly they could not spend the night together. It would be unthinkable!

"What am I to do?" she asked Frances, who smacked her lips and cooed in response. Colette had found that by propping the baby up with rolls of folded clothing, forming pillows, the baby could sit on the bed without falling over.

Colette sat next to Frances on the bed and leaned close to the babe to tickle her tummy, a mistake because the babe grabbed a hold of her wimple and tugged mercilessly.

"Ow! Stop that at once!"

The baby pulled harder until the wimple was partially pulled off her head.

"Naughty baby. Very naughty baby!"

The baby laughed in response.

Colette removed the remainder of the wimple and

took up a brush to tame her long hair back into submission. "What am I to do with you?" she asked the tot. "And what am I to do with my hair?"

It was an age-old question. Though Colette had always worn headdresses of a most expensive variety, she knew that most unmarried ladies wore their hair loose or in plaits with a simple short veil over the top.

With encouraging coos from the baby, Colette began to style her own hair, a feat she had never before attempted. Always surrounded by maids, her hair had been their prerogative. She would sit for hours while they crafted intricate hairstyles, which were always entirely covered by some monstrous headdress. It was all very elaborate and rather unnecessary. After some trial and error, she parted her hair down the middle and plaited each side, tying it at the end with a silk ribbon.

"What do you think?" She showed her long plaits to the baby.

Marie Frances responded by grabbing the end of one of her braids and giggling uproariously, pulling on it, and then sticking it into her mouth. A few days before, Colette may have found it rather repulsive to have her glorious hair coated in baby slime, but now she accepted it as the baby's adoration of her newfound skill.

Colette picked up the baby and walked back and forth on the boards for a few minutes as the baby's eyelids drooped and she began to breathe softly and deeply. Colette placed the baby in the swinging bassinet and looked down on her fondly. It was strange, but the bright red scar on her cheek, which once seemed so garish, now seemed to matter not.

Colette paused by the cabin door, her hand on the latch. She wished to go out for a breath of fresh air, but she knew Gavin was out there, and on such a humble craft, there would be no avoiding him. Of course, the captain had made it perfectly clear that there would be no avoiding Gavin tonight. The fact sent a ripple of anticipation up her spine.

Colette rummaged through her trunks and found a gauzy veil, most likely one meant for one of her maids, and tied it tightly around her head with a ribbon, her long braids visible beneath the veil. She must look something of the peasant, but it was eminently more practical, and since she was supposed to be the wife of a tradesman, she now looked the part.

She boldly left the cabin and emerged on deck, her eyes searching for one man. Gavin was standing in conversation with Captain Dupont. He stopped mid-sentence when he saw her, his face brightening into a wide smile.

Colette turned from him to hide a blush, putting her attention on the glowing horizon. The light was dim and the sun would soon set behind the bright orange clouds. Her only hope for this evening was if Pippa would rally and be able to serve as a chaperone against the ever-pleasant Sir Gavin Patrick.

"Are you feeling any better?" Colette approached the seasick Pippa, who was still sitting where she had been left at the bow of the ship.

"A little, my lady," said Pippa slowly. Her eyelids looked heavy. She had most likely been awake all night getting sick. She had been able to take some nourishment but was clearly not entirely recovered.

"How is our patient this evening?" asked Gavin, joining the conversation.

Colette was uncomfortably aware of his presence. When he drew near, her senses became alive. She was drawn to the genuine warmth in his brown eyes and his easy smile.

"I might live" was all that Pippa could manage. She put a hand on her stomach and once again placed her cheek on the smooth wooden railing of the ship.

Gavin and Colette exchanged a glance. Pippa could clearly not yet return to her duties.

"Let us get you to bed. I hope most sincerely you will be feeling better by morn," said Colette.

She took one arm and Gavin the other, and together they helped an unsteady Pippa back to her small cabin. Colette helped her back into bed. Gavin brought an empty bucket and placed it beside the bed.

"I hope ye'll be well, Pippa," said Gavin cheerfully.

"I am never getting on a cursed boat again," moaned Pippa.

Gavin went to get their meal, and Colette returned to the cabin to wait for him. She set out the table and chair as she had before, with herself perching on the edge of the straw pallet as if ready to take flight. How was she to stay alone with this man?

Gavin returned with a modest meal of bread and some sort of stew. He flashed her a wide smile, as if nothing was out of the ordinary. Gavin said a quick prayer of blessing and they broke their bread and began to eat. Colette fought against the soothing notion that she was eating her meal with her husband and all was proper.

"Good day for sailing," said Gavin with a tight smile. Was he nervous too?

"Yes, lovely day," agreed Colette, not knowing what else to say.

They dissolved into silence and ate as the light faded. Gavin stood and lit a lantern to illuminate their meal. Colette wished the baby would scream or do something to dispel the awkwardness, but for once, the babe was happily sleeping.

Their meal complete, Colette tidied while Gavin paced the small space. It was a cozy cabin to begin with, but with the large form of Gavin Patrick, there was little space left to do anything but admire his perfectly formed physique.

Colette held her hands tightly together to ward off nerves. It was not that she was frightened of Gavin—he had proven himself a man of honor. No, she was afraid of herself. She was attracted to him in a way that defied explanation. She was sure she could manage if only she could avoid him, but stuck together in a cabin all night, she was not sure of herself.

"Sir Gavin…" she began but was not sure what to say.

"Aye?" His eyes were hopeful.

"We cannot stay together." Her words came out as a whisper.

His brown eyebrows fell over his eyes. "Do ye wish me to leave?"

"No, you cannot be seen leaving the cabin or the captain, he will grow suspicious."

"So I must no' stay and I must no' go. What would ye suggest I do, m'lady?"

"I have no idea," said Colette helplessly. "I am engaged to another man, so you cannot stay. And yet we cannot risk raising the doubts of our fine captain, so you cannot leave. I do not know what to do."

Gavin took a breath and sat down on the chair, motioning for her to return to her seat on the bed. "We are both adults. We know what we must do and"—he cleared his throat—"*not* do."

Colette nodded. Trouble was, she was giving the things she should not do more attention than the things she should.

"I shall simply sleep here in this chair and ye take the bed. We shall peacefully survive the night and all will be well." He made his ridiculous pronouncement as if it were a simple solution.

"You can sleep in the chair?" she asked.

"Aye, a Highlander can sleep anywhere." To prove his statement, he attempted to get comfortable by leaning the chair up against the wall. He managed to balance it and close his eyes when a wave rocked the ship and the chair slid down the wall, taking him to the floor.

"Gavin?" she cried, jumping up and looking down at him on the floor.

"I am well!" He scrambled up, rubbing the back of his head.

"That is not going to work, no?"

"I can do this. Dinna fear," said Gavin, looking around the sparse cabin for a safe place to sleep. "Aha!" he exclaimed. "This will work." He pulled two of her trunks together, end to end and attempted to lie on top. Unfortunately, the trunks had curved tops, making it difficult to balance. Also, Gavin was substantially longer than the trunks, so his legs dangled off of the end.

Colette thought he would topple over, but he remained atop the trunks. She waited, but he appeared to have mastered the delicate art. "I did not believe you capable of balancing on my trunks," commented Colette.

"Ha! Ye'll ne'er doubt my manly prowess again!" boasted Gavin. The ship tipped and Gavin was spilled onto the floor.

Colette put a hand to her mouth to prevent a bubble of mirth from emerging. "Your manly prowess seems to have fallen to the floor."

"All part o' my plan," said Gavin, his scowl turning into a grin. He grabbed a spare blanket from one of the trunks and lay down on the floor. "I am a Highlander, and if my mother is correct, there is a wee bit o' Viking in my bloodline."

"Do Vikings enjoy sleeping on the floor?"

"It is what Vikings do best. When they are no' pillaging the land, that is," said Gavin from the floor.

"It is not very comfortable, no?"

"Vikings love being uncomfortable."

"I am glad I am not a Viking then."

"I wish I wasna either," muttered Gavin.

"Sleep well, my Viking knight." Colette wanted to tell him to join her on the pallet bed but knew she could not.

Gavin was on the floor with his back to her, so she removed her kirtle and then attempted to remove her gown and slip under the blankets. It should have been an easy process, but in trying to untie the laces behind her, the strings became knotted and she became stuck in her gown.

Now what to do? She tried in vain to loosen the knot, but without seeing what she had done, it was impossible. Could she ask for assistance? *No. Yes. No.* She would be too embarrassed to admit being bested by her own gown.

She attempted to rub her back against the corner of the wardrobe without calling attention to herself. Maybe she could work something loose.

"What are ye doing? Scratching yer back like a bear?"

Heat flooded her cheeks. "No! I am only… I seem to be… A slight problem…"

Gavin jumped up off the floor. "How can I assist?"

"I fear I have become stuck in my gown. I am not practiced in doing the laces without help," she explained, her cheeks growing hotter with each word.

"I am at yer service," said Gavin, but the casual amusement was gone from his eyes, replaced by a simmering passion.

She turned for him to perform the office, and her heart pounded in response to his hands on her back. His hands were warm through the gown, making her itch for the feel of his hands on her bare skin. She was not sure how long it took him to untie the knot, but the moments stretched on with her heart pounding a dangerous beat, yet she did not wish him to stop.

"Do ye require assistance to remove the gown?" asked Gavin in a dry rasp.

"Yes, if you would," she responded huskily, though she knew she could remove the gown herself.

He pulled gently at the fabric, sliding his hands over the sides of her body. She knew she should stop him, yet instead she turned to face him, allowing him to remove the gown and view her in nothing but her thin chemise.

His hands reached for her, pulling her to him. He said nothing, but his lips parted and his eyes burned hot for her. She wound her arms around him, a most willing partner in their crime. She leaned close, drawn to his lips, ignoring the alarm bells of danger ringing through her mind.

He drew her closer, and their lips met as she knew they must. Her heart soared and she tasted heaven once more. She wrapped her arms around him, and this time it was she who deepened the kiss. This was the man for her. This was the man she loved.

"Oh!" She jumped back and put a hand on the wardrobe to steady herself, though her difficulties with balance had nothing to do with the rocking ship. She doubted she could ever right herself from the unwanted realization that Sir Gavin had touched her heart.

"I am sorry, m'lady," apologized Gavin, in a low voice that was more seductive than apologetic. "I shoud'na have taken liberties. I canna seem to help myself."

"No, 'twas my fault. I wanted to kiss you." She surprised herself with such an honest confession.

"I want to do more," said Gavin in a low voice, his eyes black in the dim light of the lantern.

"So do I," she whispered.

Gavin took a deep breath and blew it out again. "Canna do that, so we must take desperate measures."

A few minutes later, Colette was leaning out the window to talk to Gavin, keeping her voice low so as not to be overheard by the night watch. "Are you certain this will work?" she whispered anxiously.

Gavin had found a long coil of rope and somehow managed to tie himself horizontally, dangling from the windowsill, the ropes stringing across the room, anchored around the wardrobe that was bolted to the wall. The sloping edge of the ship and the battlements above the window made it impossible for him to be seen by the night watch. "Vikings did it all the time. Loved it, they did," he whispered cheerfully.

"But will you be safe?"

"Quite safe. I'll either be here by morning or in the belly o' the whale, like Jonah."

"Please do not tease me. Come inside before you drown."

"Nay, canna do it. I am no' a man to be trusted, I fear. I gave ye my word I would no' ravish ye tonight, and I am a man o' my word."

In the end, Colette had to admit he was right, for she could not be trusted either. As she finally drifted to sleep, her one thought was that he had promised not to touch her tonight…but the other nights of the journey were as yet unspoken.

Twenty-six

Gavin thought nothing could cool his ardor for Colette, but that was before he spent the night hanging outside her window, being splashed with cold salt water. By the time she helped haul him in, he had decided a life of celibacy would be for him.

"Did you survive? Oh, but you are cold as ice!" Colette helped him into the cabin and threw a blanket around his shoulders, squeezing him tight. He usually responded to her touch, but he was now too frozen. At least he had found a cure, though whether he could survive the treatment was less certain.

"I am well," he said—or tried to say as best he could through chattering teeth.

"You are mad, quite mad. If you should die of fever, I shall never in all my life forgive you." Colette stood with her hands on her hips. In her haste to pull him back into the ship, she had forgotten her robe and stood before him in her chemise, the fabric stretching over her ample bosom.

Life flickered within him and parts of his body he feared had frozen off during the night sparked to life. "Ye could rouse a dead man," he stammered, all thoughts of his life of celibacy forgot.

"You need hot water and something warm to eat. I do hope Pippa is well this morn and can be of use." She walked to the cabin door, but Gavin called her back.

"Ropes," he said in a hoarse voice, pointing at his handiwork. If the captain or any of the crew saw their cabin strung with ropes, they might come to a very interesting conclusion regarding the excitement of their marital bed.

"Oh my, yes." Colette helped Gavin untie the ropes and stow them away in the wardrobe. Their hands brushed together in the process and Colette stopped to hold his between her small warm ones. "You are so very cold." The warm sympathy in her brilliant green eyes was enough to stir life back into all extremities.

"I survived," he responded a bit more gruffly than he intended. The night had not passed well for him.

"You did it for me and I will forever be in your debt. You are a most honorable knight," she praised in her low, alluring tone.

"A pleasure, m'lady. Willing to do it again tonight if need be," promised Gavin, fervently hoping it would not prove necessary.

"You are very kind." She leaned closer, her chemise a seductive tease, revealing more than it hid. He could rip it from her in seconds. He shivered at the thought.

"Oh, but you are terribly cold." Colette frowned with concern. "And you are soaked through. You must get out of these clothes at once."

Colette began to strip off his tunic, and he allowed her to do so without comment, afraid one wrong move on his part would break the spell. If she wanted to strip him naked, he certainly had no complaints.

His tunic removed, she put her hands to his naked chest. "Saints above, but you are still so cold," she said briskly. "We need to get you into dry clothes." But she did not move. And her hands remained on his chest.

"I know what would warm me." He voiced thoughts he'd meant to keep to himself. He couldn't help himself. She was a half second away from being naked, and he was already half-undressed. He wanted her with a surging, burning passion that would not be denied.

"I have heard of using the heat of bodies to warm the cold-stricken soul." Her voice was low and halting. She met his eyes, not turning away.

Was she saying what he thought she was saying? "Aye." He wrapped his arms around her slowly, sliding one hand up her back and the other down, caressing her perfectly formed derriere. He could not help himself from tugging her close, engulfing her in his arms.

Her eyes widened. "Oh!" She stepped back, as if coming to her senses. "I…I think you are warm enough now."

Warm? No. Hot? Oh, heavens, yes. He cursed himself for pushing too hard too fast. And then cursed himself for wanting to seduce her. He stepped back, trying to gain some kind of objectivity. Hard to do with her still wearing her thin chemise. And he was still in wet breeches. It was a hard morning all around.

"Some refreshment might help me." He couldn't believe he was sending her away, but it was his only chance. "I'll change back into my plaid."

"Yes. Very good." She spun and put a hand to the latch.

"Put yer robe on, or ye'll tempt the entire crew!"

"Oh!" she gasped, clearly just realizing she was traipsing about in next to nothing. She grabbed a silk robe and donned it quickly, almost flying from the room without looking back.

He could do nothing but watch her go.

∽

Colette rushed down the narrow passage and out into the pale light of dawn, gulping air as if she had nearly suffocated. What was she about? She had lost her mind—it was her only excuse. She was not sure what she had offered Gavin, but she was reasonably certain it would have made her marriage to him good and legal. And nothing would be more disastrous.

She took a deep breath, trying to clear away the lingering slivers of desire. She needed to think clearly. She was going to get breakfast and act normally. Pretend none of this happened.

She walked back down the small passage and rapped on Pippa's door. "Are you well, Pippa? We would like breakfast if you can manage."

The muffled sounds emerging from the room did not inspire confidence, so she strode with purpose back down the small passage to go find something to break their fast. She was met by a stocky, red-faced fellow with something that might possibly resemble a breakfast tray.

"Sustenance to renew the strength of the newly-weds," he said with a toothy grin.

Colette cleared her throat and glared at him until the grin subsided. She did not care if she was a merchant's wife; she would not tolerate insolence—although the food tray was a kind gesture. "Thank you, you are very kind," she said, making amends for the glare, and was rewarded with another grin.

She took the tray and walked carefully down the passage, lifting the latch with an elbow and turning to push the door open with her back, so that she would not spill the contents of the tray. "Met a crewman who brought a meal for us." She set the tray on the small table.

"Err, I kenned ye would take longer. I'm no' quite dressed."

His warning came too late, for she had already turned around. The great plaid was stretched out on the floor and his was lying on top of it—utterly, completely naked. It was a good thing she had already set down the tray or she would surely have dropped it. In an instant, she took in his muscular chest, his powerful thighs, but she could not tear her gaze away from *him*, so, so naked. Hugely naked. Massively naked. Oh so very, very naked.

Nobody spoke. Nobody moved. She should scream and run out. Perhaps that was what he expected. Perhaps it was what he was waiting for. She was waiting for it too. Any second now, she would scream in horror and run.

But she didn't. She wasn't even properly horrified. She was intrigued. The flames of desire she had tried to squelch came roaring back to life. She either needed to dangle herself out the window or be in his arms, for nothing else would keep her away from him.

She took a step toward him, and he sat up. She glanced at the window and back at him. The window option was not going to win. What was she thinking? She needed to get herself under control. She turned and stepped to the door.

"Forgive me. I was just putting on the plaid. It's the only way, ye ken," he said in a rough rumble of a voice.

No she did not "ken." She stared at the open door for a moment longer, then kicked it closed with herself still inside. She turned slowly back toward him, just as he was standing up, his great plaid hastily wrapped around him. It didn't matter now. The image of him in all his naked glory would be forever etched in her mind.

"Under your plaid, you wear nothing?"

"Aye, m'lady. I hope I dinna shock ye."

Colette stepped closer. "Shocking, yes. Convenient too." She took another step closer.

It was his turn to open his eyes wide. "So…what is for our breakfast?"

"Are you hungry?" she purred.

Gavin's jaw went slack for a moment before he pulled himself together. "Colette, my lass, if ye're trying to seduce me, ye know it winna take much effort. I'm well past halfway there."

"Then for once we agree on something." She took another slow, deliberate step closer.

"But what about your father and Laird—"

She did not wish to hear what he was going to say so she kissed him. Truly, it was her only defense. She may have initiated the kiss, but Gavin was not slow to respond. He wrapped his arms around her and pressed her tight against his firm body, deepening the kiss. One of his hands held her closer, and the other slid down to cup her bottom, lifting her clean off the floor. She wound her arms around his neck and held on, pure molten desire coursing through her veins, drowning out all conscious thought.

It was the kiss she had been wanting since she had met him. And now that her one desire had been sated, it was replaced by several more. She was not entirely sure what happened between a man and a woman, but she was more than willing to find out in Gavin's arms.

"Lady Colette? Sir Gavin? I'm here as you asked," came Pippa's voice at the door.

"Ignore her," whispered Gavin, pulling Colette tighter.

"Lady Colette?" Pippa called louder, knocking sharply on the door.

"She'll go away," whispered Gavin.

Pippa knocked again, and Frances woke up with a whimper and a scream.

"Pippa might, but she won't," said Colette miserably. Reluctantly, she stepped back, and equally as unwillingly, Gavin let her go.

"We cannot do this. It is madness," said Colette, reality hitting her with the piercing cries of the baby. "We almost… The marriage would have been legal… and I am still promised to another!"

Gavin ran his fingers through his hair. "Ye ken how I feel about ye. Best thing is to avoid each other as much as possible, for I canna resist ye, Colette, and that is the honest truth."

"Agreed," said Colette over the din of the crying and the knocking. She felt like throwing a fit herself, for the one person she desired was forever forbidden.

She turned and opened the door to Pippa, who if she did not look completely well was at least a lighter shade of green and standing on her own feet. Pippa didn't waste time on pleasantries but instead picked up the baby, soothing her.

"I'll be moving into yer cabin, Pippa, and letting ye stay here with m'lady to care for the babe," announced Gavin in a resigned tone, his large, brown eyes sad.

He walked toward her at the door and paused beside Colette. "I shall miss ye always," he whispered.

"If I were free to choose…" she whispered back, allowing her words to trail off.

At the door, Gavin stole a quick kiss. "Fare thee well, my love. Ye may no' be free to love as ye will, but my heart beats true and only for ye."

Twenty-seven

By MUTUAL CONSENT, COLETTE AND GAVIN STAYED apart for the next several days. While they could not avoid seeing each other on the small ship, they could contrive never to be alone in each other's company. It was simply too dangerous. Colette needed to arrive in Scotland with the ability to dissolve the unconsummated marriage, not well and truly wed to the wrong man. Except Sir Gavin did not feel like the wrong man.

Not able to trust herself, Colette stuck to Pippa and never stirred from the cabin they now shared without her. If the crew was aware that Gavin had changed cabins, it was explained by him wanting a good night's sleep without the baby. He was still courteous and affectionate when they were together before others, and now Colette knew it was more than a ruse.

Several days into their journey, the wind picked up, and by late afternoon the seas were high and the ship began to pitch. Ominous black storm clouds rolled overhead, giving Colette an uneasy feeling. Gavin, never a man to remain still for long, lent a hand to the crew, fighting the stiff wind to keep the ship on course.

At the first raindrops hitting her nose, Colette went back inside to the cabin, having to take some care in walking across the rolling decks. In the cabin, Pippa was holding Marie Frances, looking a bit green once more.

"Are you well, Pippa?"

"This ship, it does not agree with me," groaned Pippa.

"Mayhap you should lie down for a while," said Colette. She had barely finished the sentence before Pippa handed her the baby and ran from the cabin, her hand over her mouth.

"Poor girl," said Colette to the baby, who only yawned in response. The tot seemed to get tired as the waves increased, and soon was happily asleep in her bassinet.

The rain pelted the top of her cabin so hard, it sounded like she was living inside a drum. The ship rolled back and forth, up and down, the wooden timbers groaning in complaint.

A short rap at the cabin door brought the entrance of Gavin followed by Captain Dupont, both shaking off the rain. "The captain says we've been blessed by a strong tailwind," said Gavin. "We may expect a wee bit o' weather this eve."

"Oh, but I am certain you have sailed through much weather, have you not?" Colette asked the captain, hoping for some reassurance. She was not pleased by the arrival of a storm, but she was not one to readily admit fear.

"Very true," agreed the hearty captain. "Me and the *St. Olga* have seen a storm or two in our time, that we have, my lady. We'll see it through and the storm will no doubt speed our journey."

"When do ye expect we'll reach the Scottish shore?" asked Gavin.

"Depends on the wind, my lad, but she's giving us a good push now. If this continues, I think we may see Scotland within several days' time. We've left our home shores now, and we are sailing in open seas toward England and beyond that Scotland."

Colette and Gavin exchanged glances. Though there was no way to reach Scotland without sailing up the coast of England, it was not a part of the journey either of them relished. They had every expectation of being able to slip by as an unremarkable merchant ship, but they would breathe easier when that part of the journey was behind them.

"Thank you, Captain Dupont. I hope we shall make good time," said Colette.

The captain wished them well and left them alone in the cabin.

Alone in the cabin.

"Pippa is feeling poorly again," said Colette, keeping to the safe topic of nausea. She was acutely aware of Gavin's presence.

"I am no' surprised. In truth, my own stomach is protesting a wee bit." Gavin stood near the door, as if ready to flee should she decide to throw herself at him.

The ship rocked and shuddered. Gone was the gentle sway Colette had found calming. Now the ship seemed to be intent on knocking her off her feet. The floor beneath her suddenly lurched, throwing her into Gavin. He was also thrown backward but braced himself on the side of the wall, holding her with one hand and keeping his own balance with the other.

"Are you all right?" he asked, his arm slipping around her waist like it belonged there.

Before she could answer, the ship rocked violently in the other direction, and they both fell backward onto the bed, with him on top of her. Even with the growing concern for their safety, Colette's body responded instantly. Tingles shot through her, and despite the fear, she had never felt so incredibly alive.

Gavin was breathing hard. The ship righted itself, but Gavin remained on top of her, his eyes black and smoldering. It was all in his face—his passion, his desire for her. The next instant, it was gone and Gavin pulled himself off and jumped back. "I beg yer pardon, m'lady. Are ye hurt?"

"No, a bit crumpled, but not hurt." Colette gradually sat up, smoothing her silk gown to hide her disappointment that Gavin's body was no longer pressed against hers. She was having enough difficulty managing her own desire without the storm conspiring against them. She considered standing, but given how much the ship was moving, she thought it better to remain where she was.

The ship pitched once again, this time hurling down as if they were falling down a huge slide only to reach the bottom and rise again. She was not quite queasy, but she was certain she left her stomach behind somewhere in the pitch and roll. "Is it normal for the ship to lurch in such a manner?" asked Colette. Fear was not the preferred method for reducing her desire for Gavin, but it did help to turn her attention.

"I'm sure it'll be fine. The captain's a good man and an experienced sailor. I'm certain he's sailed through many storms larger than this." Gavin's words may have been slightly more reassuring had the ship not pitched again at that moment, causing him to stumble forward. He caught himself, his arms braced on the bed on either side of her. He gulped air and stood up again. He was not unaffected either—by the storm or by her.

"Please, sit. This storm is making it difficult not to fall on top of each other, no?" Colette had meant the statement to be a simple fact, but even the thought of him falling on her made her pulse quicken. She knew what was hidden beneath the plaid.

"Aye. Rough seas." He tried to sit as far from her as possible, but the bunk was anything but spacious.

"I fear you must sleep here tonight," said Colette in her most reserved manner, as if her words were of little consequence. "Pippa is unwell and there can be no question of hanging you outside the window."

Gavin gave her a slow smile. "Ye're too kind. I thank thee for no' condemning me to a watery grave."

"I am benevolent this evening, no?" Colette returned in kind. She needed to stay aloof, if such a thing was possible sitting next to Gavin.

"Aye. I am fortunate ye are no' the person I thought ye were when we first met," he said lightly.

"What do you mean?" demanded Colette.

Gavin blinked and shifted a bit on the pallet. "I…I confess that when I first met ye, all I saw was yer beauty, which I must add is remarkable. I tell ye plain, ye're the most bonnie lass that has e'er lived." He gave her a wide smile.

"But you said you were fortunate I am not what you thought I was. What exactly did you think of me when we first met?" Colette was not to be distracted from this line of questioning.

Gavin bit his lip in a decidedly nervous manner but recovered quickly with a tight smile. "I may have thought ye a wee bit…overly aristocratic."

"Overly aristocratic! What does that even mean?" Colette would have put her hands on her hips if she did not require both hands to steady herself on the pallet of the swaying ship.

"In truth, it was yer beauty that captivated me most of all, but yer beauty is no' yer best feature."

Colette frowned in confusion. Everyone knew her worth was primarily in her appearance. "Are you in jest?"

"Nay, ye're not only attractive, ye're quick thinking as well."

Colette braced herself against the corner of the bunk to keep from falling as the ship rolled. Gavin's statement made her almost as off balance as the waves. "Of what good is that? Would a man ask a woman her opinion or seek her counsel? I have never heard of such a thing." Colette dismissed the comment with a wave of her hand.

"Ye think me so very shallow?" challenged Gavin with a gleam in his eye.

"I have met many knights and I can tell you they attend to beauty, not intelligence. I cast no judgment. I merely speak as I find. My mother taught me well to honor my father, most of which was best accomplished without speaking a word."

Gavin shook his head. "I have spent but little time in court. Forgive me, but wi'out conversation, it sounds verra dull."

"It was dull, for me at least," Colette admitted. "But it honored my father for me to be prized in court, so I did what was expected to please him. A daughter can be of little other use to her father."

The humor drained from Gavin's expression. "Seems to me yer father relies a great deal on ye and has asked a great sacrifice."

A lump formed in her throat. She had been asked to give much. Though if she had not met Gavin, she would never have known the extent of what she had forfeit. "I must do my duty to my father and my people, no matter my personal feelings on the matter," she said in a small voice.

"Yer willingness makes ye one o' the most admirable people o' my acquaintance, though I wish things could be different."

"Me too." Colette could not look at him. It was a dangerous confession.

A blinding white light blasted through the cracks in the shutters followed by the loudest crash she had ever heard. She flew to her feet, instinctively seeking escape, but had nowhere to run. Gavin stood and reached out his arms. She rushed into his embrace, soothed against the rising sense of panic. Her body responded to his with a rush of desire, mixed with the sorrow of being prevented from being together and the sheer fear of the storm. It was going to be a long, confusing night.

"'Tis well. Naught to fear. 'Twas only lightning," he murmured over the roar of thunder.

"I fear the sea, it is trying to kill us," she said shakily from the safety of his arms. Together they sat on the

bed, both holding on to each other. Colette clung to
him as if he could somehow make the wild rocking of
the ship stop.

"Aye, this ship does seem to be having troubles
making its mind up. First up, then down, then one
side, then the other. Reminds me o' my little brother
when he's fighting nature's call."

Colette started to laugh but a steep drop of the
ship drowned her mirth. She clung tighter to Gavin.
"Thank you, Sir Gavin. I would never have made it
this far without you."

"I intend to see ye all the way home, m'lady."

"I hope you will get the chance," said Colette in a
small voice.

"Surely, I will. And there's none I'd rather be wi'
in a storm than ye."

"If I am not too 'overly aristocratic' for you,"
grumbled Colette, still stinging from his comment.
No matter how unrealistic, she could not abide the
thought of Gavin not thinking well of her.

"Ye're no' going to let me forget this, are ye? Well,
wi' the ship rocking such, I feel I should let ye know
a few things while I have the chance."

Something in his lighthearted acknowledgment of
their potential danger tightened her stomach into an
aching knot. Yet, he continued to hold her in his arms
as the ship pitched and it gave her courage. "Yes?" She
encouraged him to continue.

"I said yer greatest feature is no' yer appearance and I stand by it, but I confess when I first
met ye—"

"You thought me very cold."

Gavin gave her a look of mock offense. "If ye could content yerself to hold yer tongue until I am finished wi' my confession, I'd be appreciative."

"Do continue." She smiled.

"Now, where was I? Aye, I was about to confess that I judged ye unfairly due to the amount of dowry ye wished to take with ye."

"Those things were my mother's," Colette began to protest. It was still a sore subject.

"I ken that now. Forgive me for saying, but ye make a most difficult confessor."

"Mayhap that is why all priests are male."

"I suppose, but I admit I am verra glad ye're not a male priest at this moment. Awkward, ye ken, to try to make confession while holding yer priest in yer arms."

Colette laughed out loud.

"Now, for my confession. If there will be no other untoward interruptions?" Gavin waited in mock severity.

"I suppose you would like to confess that you have decided I am not quite as pampered or spoiled as you once thought," suggested Colette.

"Aye, dinna steal my thunder!"

Another brilliant light and clap of thunder ripped through the night, but this time it only made Colette giggle at the timing. "Forgive me. Please do continue with your confession, Sir Knight."

"Now then, when yer way became difficult and yer ship was seized, I fully expected to take ye back to yer father. When yer maids abandoned ye, I thought our journey had come to an end. Ye're made of tougher stuff than I thought."

"I only seek to do my duty to my father," demurred Colette, but the compliment warmed her soul.

"In truth, I find ye brave, caring, loving, kind, intelligent…" Gavin cleared his throat. "The Laird Mackenzie is the luckiest man alive. I have never envied another man, but I do him. If ye were no' promised to another man, I would not hesitate to… Och, 'tis enough o' my confession."

Tears sprung to her eyes. It was the nicest compliment she had ever received. She knew he was attracted to her, that much was hard to miss, but if what he felt for her was based on her character and not her often-admired beauty, it would be a first. In that regard, it was perhaps the first true compliment she had ever been given.

"Thank you," she whispered. "You are a remarkable man, Sir Gavin."

Another wave hit hard, and the boat lurched, sending them rising and falling in a manner that made her stomach roll. She clung to Gavin and he held on right back. She held her breath for a moment, wondering if this would be her last, but the boat righted itself.

"Forgive me. I should not intrude upon your person." She held him closer.

"Ye may intrude upon my person anytime ye wish. Ye must know that." Gavin's eyes blazed warm and dark.

She rested her head upon his shoulder. She wanted him, needed him. But she could not have him. With painful self-control, she released her grip on him and forced herself to move at least a few inches away.

Gavin cleared his throat and stood up. "Ye're right. We must keep our heads. Ye get some rest, m'lady. I can sit in the chair."

"The chair, it does not seem restful. Besides, I'm not sure how much sleep we will be able to get tonight. Bit of a rocky evening." She tried to keep her tone light, though she doubted she was fooling anyone.

In truth, she was growing concerned about the increased movement of the ship. It was rocking more harshly from side to side and up and down. The tilting and the sudden lurches were most disconcerting. Had she the option, she would have most definitely gotten off on dry land and not continued bobbing about in such a wild manner.

A sharp rap at the door got their attention. Captain Dupont burst through the door, wearing a coat of oiled canvas, dripping wet from the rain.

"We've got ourselves a real storm," said the good captain, his face grim. "Sorry, but it's too rough to feed you. I advise you to stay in the cabin. Might get worse."

"Is there anything I can do to help?" asked Gavin, stepping forward as best he could.

"Not much we can do but ride it out. I hope to cross the channel soon, but even when we reach the other side, we are in danger from the rocks, so we need to steer clear."

Colette's mind was racing to try to understand. "You mean if we get too close to shore, we could end up crashing on the rocks?"

He gave a sharp nod. "We will stay out where it is deep and hope to avoid the rocks."

"But if you stay far from the shore, how will you know where to go in this storm? How do you know in what direction to sail?"

The captain said nothing for a moment and rocked with the movement of the ship as the water dripped off of his coat and pooled around his feet. "Well, that's why, as a God-fearing man, I pray that the Lord will guide us. Wherever we are, we will still be in his hands. It is times like these we must pray all the more."

"Thank ye, Captain. We shall do so," said Gavin.

"A word outside, if I may?" the captain asked Gavin in a tone that was not so much a request as a command.

Gavin left the cabin with him, leaving her alone. She stared after them, holding on to the side of the bed to keep from falling as the ship pitched. A pool of liquid fear grew in the pit of her stomach. Whatever the captain wished to talk to Gavin about in private could not be good.

Gavin returned to the cabin, his face grim, his lips pressed together in a thin line. Colette knew—she simply knew.

"Our captain fears we may not survive the storm," she said.

Gavin met her gaze but said nothing.

Twenty-eight

GAVIN HELD ON TO THE DOORWAY TO KEEP FROM FALL-ing as the ship pitched sharply one way and then another. The captain had indeed given him bad news, which Colette, her eyes wide and vulnerable, had accurately guessed. She was scared. *He* was scared. He must say something to ease her fear, but what?

The boat rolled awkwardly to one side and he grit-ted his teeth, wondering if it would go over entirely, but it righted itself only to roll onto the other side. The truth was, no matter how scared Colette looked, he was more so. He tried to put a grin on his face, pretending that this was utterly normal and that storms did not bother him in the least. It could not have been further from the truth. He was a man who belonged on the land, a farmer at heart, not a sailor.

"The captain needs to lighten the ship," said Gavin, entering the cabin and closing the door behind him. "He asked if he could throw over some o' yer heavier items." It was her dowry—or what was left of it.

"Yes, tell the captain he must do what he thinks best." Colette sighed.

"I already have." Her dowry meant nothing if it took them to the bottom of the ocean.

Suddenly, a white flash blinded them, followed by a booming roar of thunder, causing Colette to shriek in fright. He flew to her and pulled her into his arms, though whether to comfort her or himself, he did not wish to know.

They fell back, sitting on the pallet as the ship tipped up once more. "We should pray, as the good captain suggested," said Gavin.

"Yes, let us do so." She reached into the pocket of her kirtle and pulled out her Book of Hours, flipping through the pages. "Oh, but I cannot find a prayer to calm high seas."

"Are the only prayers ye've ever said the ones ye read in yer prayer book?"

"But of course. Is there any other way?"

Gavin reached out and held her as the ship pitched. "Ye can pray to the Lord wi' yer own words. Ye dinna need to memorize a prayer in order to speak to God."

Colette looked at him in wonderment. "Will you show me?"

"Dear Lord," prayed Gavin, "please put yer hand o' protection upon us, rebuke the wind and waves, and let us travel in safety. Amen."

Colette lifted her head and met his eyes with her large green ones. Even frightened, she was beautiful. "That is how you pray?"

"Aye."

"And the Good Lord, He hears such a prayer?"

"I hope so most fervently."

Colette's trembling lips curved into a small smile. "Do you think we shall reach the shores of your homeland?"

Gavin did not know. The captain had not given him much hope. "'Tis late. Why dinna ye get some sleep? I'm sure the storm will be gone by morn." It was the biggest bluff he had ever told.

Colette raised her eyebrows. "How could you think of sleep at a time like this?"

"There is naught we can do. What will be will be. 'Tis in the Lord's hands."

"But if these are to be our last hours"—she paused as the ship lurched to one side and then violently to the other—"should we not choose carefully our last moments?"

Gavin stared at her, unsure if his heart was pounding from the peril they were in or the desire that could not be restrained for this woman. He knew exactly what he would do if he had only a few hours left to live. And all of it would be with Colette. Despite the prospect that they could be sent to a watery grave at any moment—or perhaps because of it—Gavin responded to Colette in an elemental manner. All the plans and obligations they had for the future washed away in the high waves.

"Forgive me for the remembrance if it is unwanted," whispered Gavin, "but we are legally wed. As husband and wife, we could give ourselves some allowance to comfort each other through the storm."

"You are right." The light returned to her eyes, giving her face an expression somewhere between desire and fear. "I am obligated to marry the Baron of Kintail." She took a deep breath and her voice dropped lower. "But if we never reach the Scottish shore…"

"If we never arrive to the land o' Kintail, we are free to consummate this marriage and enter heaven as man and wife." Gavin's voice shook. He was facing a watery grave, yet his impending death gave him the right to call this woman his wife. The ship rocked violently and the timbers groaned in protest. Gavin did not know how much longer they had before the entire thing broke apart.

"I fear our forever may not be very long," whispered Colette, her eyes wide with fear.

Gavin reached out and held her tight. The ship lurched again, and he knew they were not likely to live through the night. The awareness heightened his senses and made every word, every action important. He would not waste what little time he had left by pretending. "Even if it is just for tonight," he whispered into her ear, "I am honored to be yer husband."

"And I your wife." She tilted her head up and their lips met. The waves rocked them closer together and he deepened the kiss. He did not want to think about the ship breaking apart or how the end would come. No, he would drown himself in her and think only of Marie Colette, his wife for the night.

His wife for the rest of his life.

"Hold me," breathed Colette, an unnecessary request since he was already embracing her as tight as he could. "Make me forget."

He kissed away her words. He did not want to think either. He wished only to hold her close and be lost in her arms, not lost at sea. His life may soon come to an end, yet he had never felt more alive. The exhilarating thrill of the power of the wind and waves coursed through him, piquing his already inflamed desire. He had been given this most holy gift, and it was only because he was moments from death. His fingers fumbled at the ties of her gown in the back. He needed to feel her, to be as close as husband and wife could be.

"Hurry." She pressed herself closer to him, almost squeezing the breath from his lungs, though he hardly had a mind to complain. They must make every moment count. He managed to untie the strings and remove the embroidered silk gown. He tossed it aside and soaked in the beauty of Colette in her white chemise. Her hair was next. He pulled off the gauzy veil and loosed her braided hair, running his fingers through her silky locks. He gloried in burying his hands into her thick, dark auburn hair, a forbidden pleasure that had taunted him in his dreams.

The ship lurched again, and they both slid until they were lying down on the bed, him above her. At least for once the ship had helped him. He paused for a moment, but she did not hesitate.

She pulled at his plaid and he unpinned it. She unwrapped it with swift hands and he pulled it over them, using it now as a blanket. She began to pull up his shirt, but he held her hands in his.

"This is all I wear."

The corner of her mouth twitched up. "I know." She pulled his shirt up and over his head, revealing to her the full extent of his body. Somehow, facing death had only heightened his response. He could not remember when he had been more fully aroused.

Her eyes widened. "I think when Marie Claude told me all she thought I should know about the marriage bed, she left out a few things."

"I dinna wish to rush ye into anything."

"But of course we must rush. How many more moments do we have? I never expected the chance to give myself fully to the man I chose and not the one chosen for me. We are married, at least for a few minutes more. And with those minutes, I choose you."

"Colette." He breathed her name like a prayer and kissed her thoroughly with all the life left within him.

The ship fell again from what felt like a huge height, only to bob back up again, breaking their kiss. His stomach rolled like the high seas. He needed to focus on something else. He needed to focus on Colette. When he looked into her eyes, everything else drifted away.

He kissed her until he forgot anything other than her long fingers trailing up and down his back. He found the edge of her chemise and slowly worked it up, his hand skimming over her thigh, hip, belly, and coming to rest on her ample breast. It was glorious. She inhaled sharply and he bent down to kiss her into full attention, being rewarded with another sharp inhalation.

He paused, hesitant to pluck such forbidden fruit. As if sensing his uncertainty, she reached down and grabbed his backside, banishing all thoughts entirely from his brain. He slid the chemise up higher, and she helped him pull it over her head and toss it aside. He wanted to get a good look at her, but in his current position, he would have to content himself with touch. He was more than pleased. Her skin, soft and inviting, seemed to melt into his.

This was what he had wanted since he'd met her, and yet it was so much more than physical. She was his wife—not just for the night but forever. This was right. She was his and he was hers, in a union that went beyond written contract. They were designed for each other. It was a power he could not fight and he submitted willingly to its demands.

❧

Colette was alive and free. Despite the terrifying rocking of the ship and the fear of capsizing at any moment, she had never felt more filled with the power of life. Her skin tingled with energy as she pressed herself against Gavin's perfect form.

She had not known exactly what to expect, but his chiseled features, each muscle rippling with prominence, had been her utter undoing. She wanted him with a burning desire she could not describe. She was swept up in its power, knowing she could not stop now.

Far from being helpless, she had never felt more in control. Her body was hers. For the first time in her life, she was truly in command of her own person, not flaunted before courtiers or given in marriage to a man her father chose.

Marriage. With a signature on parchment, her father controlled who would have unmitigated rights to her body. She'd ventured on this ill-fated journey knowing that at the end of it, she would be compelled to give herself to a man she had never met. But no more. She was claiming her body as her own, to be given to the one whom she desired.

He pressed closer, his naked body covering hers, and she felt whole, complete, and fully alive. How long had she hidden her feelings and emotions behind a facade of detachment? She had never truly lived. Now her flesh was alive and fully engulfed in the flesh of another—her husband. It was only right to consummate the vows they had spoken.

She wrapped her arms around him, demanding he bring himself closer to her, though not exactly sure what it all meant. Her nursemaid had told her some of what happened between a man and woman, but most of the talk was about flowers and pollinating bees and strange unknown objects, such as inflamed members and private caves. It had all sounded entirely baffling, but now she was most willing to learn.

Gavin kissed an ear, trailing down her neck to her left breast while caressing the other with his hand. Something was coiling within her, growing tighter and tighter, demanding release, though she had no idea how to accomplish this end. His hand traveled lower until he was touching her in a place that made her gasp in pleasure. She was lost in this strange new experience but trusted Gavin implicitly.

"Gavin," she gasped.

"My heart, my wife," he murmured in her ear. "Ye are my bride, now and forever."

The tension he was building inside her was beyond anything she had experienced, and she pressed herself forward, wanting more. Even the rolling of the waves and the shifting of the bed seemed to move in concert with the rhythm building within her. Her heart pounded within her chest and her breath came in short, fast pants. Most confusing, her body moved beneath him of its own accord. She wanted, needed more.

"I want—" She did not know how to finish the sentence. She did not know what she wanted, but she knew she needed it from him and she needed it now, before the ship broke apart or she herself splintered into shards of pleasure.

"I need you." It was all she needed to say. He whispered something in his native tongue and moved even closer. The ship rolled again, pitching sharply to one side. She cried out in fear and pain until the ship righted itself again, and she realized they were joined together. Husband and wife. Now and forever—or for as many minutes as forever was for them.

Gavin began to move in rhythm with the waves as the ship rolled. He rocked, and she moved in concert with the primitive dance. As they moved together, rolling with the ship, something once again began to coil within her, tightening and tightening, narrowing her awareness to him and him only.

She held on to him, pressing herself closer, reaching for something until heat and power and pleasure burst within her, pulsing through her. He cried out and they clung to each other as waves of pleasure crashed over her. The ship sank and rose again and slid down at such an odd angle that they both tumbled from the bed, a mass of blankets and arms and legs.

"Are ye well?" asked Gavin.

Colette laughed. She could not help herself. She had just experienced something for which she had no name, and she felt more alive than she ever had before, trapped on a ship that was almost assuredly going to go to the bottom of the ocean. Perhaps she had lost her senses, for all she could do was laugh.

Gavin scooped her back onto the bed and straightened the tangled blankets as best he could so that they could cuddle close. He chuckled with her in a deep baritone sound, much like the roar of the wind and the rain.

She did not think that she could possibly sleep in such a storm, but her eyelids grew heavy and she snuggled toward his warmth. Despite everything, she was filled with a sense of security and belonging. Whatever happened, they would meet it together.

Twenty-nine

THE STORM RAGED ON FOREVER. COLETTE GAVE UP ALL hope of ever seeing land again, even as she found comfort in Gavin's arms. It was impossible to tell how many days the storm raged or how long they were together in that small cabin, but she had given them up for lost entirely. They were truly married now, their vows well and truly consummated. Resigned to her fate, she experienced a strange sense of calm, knowing that they were together as they were meant to be.

So it was a complete surprise when one morning she opened her eyes to sunlight streaming through the window so bright, she had to hold up a hand to protect her eyes from the glaring sun.

"Gavin, wake up! The storm, it has passed. I believe we have survived."

"Are ye sure we have no' passed over into heaven?" Gavin drew an arm around her and snuggled close to her. They had spent much of the past several days riding out the storm in bed. Other than tending to the needs of the baby, who thankfully had slept through much of the storm, they had not left the relative

security of their bed. Standing was difficult and walking near impossible, so lying in bed was the only
suitable answer, comforting each other as they might.

Truth be told, they had comforted each other a lot.
They had expected to arrive at the gates of heaven
hand in hand.

But if they were to live...

"I am in earnest. The storm is gone and we are
alive," persisted Colette.

Gavin raised his head to the window and squinted
into the sunlight. At first, a smile brightened his face.
He shifted his gaze to her and the smile faded, replaced
by a crease appearing between his eyebrows. What
were they going to do now?

"I should go see the captain," murmured Gavin.
He pulled on his shirt and laid out his plaid, quickly
belting it around his waist, throwing the end over one
shoulder. Colette watched as he dressed but he did not
meet her eyes. He threw her an awkward half smile
before leaving the cabin, shutting the door behind him.

As glad as Colette was to be alive, she recognized
their survival was going to make things difficult. How
was she going to become Laird Mackenzie's wife when
she was married to another? She sighed and drew her
knees up to her chin, wrapping her arms around her
legs. Their marriage was very, very consummated.
The strange sense of calm she had experienced in
Gavin's arms during the storm was shattered.

Colette lay back down, covering her head with the
blankets, not wanting to face the torrent of emotions
that swirled around her. She could not give herself to
another man—not now. It was impossible. Yet she

knew what she was required to do. Laird Mackenzie had already sent warriors to France. How could she not honor the agreement now?

She was drawn from her hiding place by the cries of Marie Frances, who, after surviving the storm, had decided she was hungry and loudly requested her breakfast. Colette dragged herself out of bed and tended to the baby's needs, finding her something to eat.

The baby laughed and cooed, as if all was right in her world. Colette smiled in return. They had lived. It was reason to smile. Colette dressed herself in a plain linen gown and draped a blue veil around her head. She smoothed her skirts and waited anxiously for Gavin to return. There was much to discuss.

After some time, a knock came at the door. She wondered at why Gavin would feel the need to be so formal now as to knock after all they had shared together.

"Enter," called Colette.

A man entered the cabin, but instead of Gavin, it was one of the sailors, holding a tray of something to eat. It was simple fair, biscuits and dried pork with a bottle of wine. "Here you are. Something to eat after the long storm."

"Thank you," said Colette, realizing how hungry she actually was. "Will my husband be joining me this morning?"

"No, madam. He ate with the captain." The sailor turned and left the cabin.

Gavin had eaten without her. She sat down hard on the bed and then jumped up again as if the memories of all that they shared had poisoned the very bed itself. The message was clear enough. It was over. All they

had shared had only occurred when they were knocking on death's door, but now that they'd lived, they
must be apart.

She steeled herself against any display of emotion.
This is why her mother kept herself removed. A lump
formed in her throat, but she swallowed it back down.
She would not cry. He was right to stay away. This
was how it must be. Somehow, she must toss aside
all that she had experienced and return to the cold
detachment that protected her from harm.

A tear ran down her cheek. How could she forget
everything, now that a whole new world had been
opened to her? It was more than simply the physical
comfort she had found in Gavin's arms—it was so much
more. In his arms, she had felt safe, protected…loved.

Colette sat on the wooden chair and slumped down
over the table. Realization hit her like a physical blow.
Love—powerful, strange, dangerous. It could have no
place in her life, and yet it had snuck in, taking up
permanent residence in her heart.

She loved Gavin Patrick.

Colette stood quickly, putting a hand to the wall
to regain her balance, and wiped the tears from her
eyes. It would not do to succumb to the emotion that
threatened to drown her more surely than the sea. She
had to remain strong. And yet…

She found herself on her knees, unsure how to
proceed. Gavin had said she could speak to her maker
in words not constructed by a priest. Perhaps it was
time to try such a strange notion. "Lord, I may fool
the world, but you see my heart. It is broken. I cannot
see a way for me to remain with my husband, Gavin,

though my heart longs to be his wife. Yet your will be done. Amen."

Colette stood and breathed deep. A new sense of peace came to her. She picked up the Book of Hours and read again the verses promising a future for her, a way through the unknown wilderness. She had no idea what to do, but she was content to let the matter reside in the hands of the Lord. Besides, she had business to attend to. Poor Pippa had no doubt fared ill during the storm. It was time to see if she had survived.

❧

Gavin did not know what to think. He had never felt more alive than when he was with Colette—a bit ironic since they had both thought they were about to die, and yet with her by his side, he had the courage to face anything. Colette had been by his side, under him, on top of him—he put a hand to the wall to steady himself as the memories flashed through him.

While he could not say he had never before known the intimacy of a woman, what he had shared with Colette went far beyond anything he had ever experienced or even imagined. They had clung to each other on the verge of destruction, and he had given himself in a way he never had before. They had consummated their marriage vows utterly and completely. He was her husband and she his wife. Surely, such a bond could never—*should* never be broken.

He wandered out into the bright sunlight on the deck of the ship. Amazingly, the bright sun sparkled off the gray-blue ocean. The wind was brisk and the sail was full. The crew was whistling and singing as they worked. Despite a broken railing and some ripped rigging, the ship appeared to have weathered the storm without major damage.

"Bless my soul, the Lord has saved us!" The captain sauntered up to him and gave him a wide smile and a sharp clap on the back. "I do not mind telling you, I never thought I'd see the sun again this side of heaven."

"It was quite a storm," agreed Gavin. "Thought we were going down many a time."

"In all my years of sailing, I've never seen the wind and waves more determined to sink my ship. But come and join me to break our fast. Haven't been able to eat properly for days."

"Forgive me, but I need to return to my wife."

"But how can this be? You spent days with her cooped up in a cabin. No, take it from a man who's been married twenty years—give her some time to freshen herself. A man needs to know when he's been too long at the hearth."

Since Gavin was already in a quandary as to what to say to Colette, he decided to follow the captain's advice. Maybe the captain knew better than Gavin did in this matter. "Can we arrange to have some food brought in for her?"

"But of course." Captain Dupont roared with laughter. "One must keep the wife fed at all costs."

Gavin followed the captain as he led him belowdecks to the hold.

The captain stopped and shook his head. "Had a table and benches here, but we tossed them over in the storm." He looked away and added. "Much of your cargo went as well, I fear."

"Ye kept us alive, Captain Dupont, and for that we will forever be in yer debt."

"Like to say I saved you, but I confess it must have been the hand of God. Here now, let's get some food and take it to the deck to eat in the sun."

Captain Dupont and Gavin carried biscuits, dried beef, and wine to the bow of the ship, where they leaned on the railing and ate their fill. Gavin ate greedily, not realizing how hungry he had been until he began to eat.

"When do ye ken we will arrive? I fear I've lost track o' time."

"Not too much longer now, a few days at most. We are sailing up the coast now. A miracle we were not blown off the edge of the world." The captain smiled at him and Gavin did his best to return it. Two or three days. Soon they would reach their destination and then what? He was supposed to present Lady Marie Colette to the Mackenzie laird for marriage.

Could he do it? Could he let Colette marry another? Could he let her go to the bed of another man? Gavin slammed his fist onto the railing. He would fight before he let his wife be handed over to another man. She was his, and he would never let her go!

The captain stared at him with wide eyes, and Gavin realized he must appear quite odd. "Forgive me. I…I was thinking o' something else."

The captain stared at him in a moment of confusion, then gave him an easy smile. "Of course, you must be tired from the storm. Too long indoors makes a man go mad. Stay here and get some fresh air to revive your soul."

"Aye. I dinna ken what I'm about this morn. Some air will do me good."

The captain left him, and Gavin stared out over the sparkling water. *Please, Lord, let me keep her. Let me keep my wife.* The waves danced in the sun before him, yet Gavin's heart was filled with pain. He could not let her go. She was his wife.

And he loved her.

The realization cut through to his core, taking up permanent residence. Nothing he could do about it now. Colette would forever hold his heart. He turned to go speak with her only to see her striding up the deck toward him.

"Pippa has been quite ill, but she has survived," said Lady Marie Colette in a reserved tone.

He stepped forward to embrace her but stopped short. Something in her eyes was different. Actually, in her expression was the same distance, the same cold reserve that had been there when they had first met. He gritted his teeth, pained to see the wall between them had been rebuilt so quickly.

"I'm glad she is recovering." Everything he wanted to say seemed barred to him. Did she wish to forget the past few days ever happened? Perhaps it would be best if they both forgot what happened in the storm.

"Yes, she is quite relieved that the storm is past, but she is weak from her illness. Fortunately, she was able to eat this morning." Colette was speaking to him in a formal manner, as if nothing untoward had transpired between them.

"It must be relief to ye that yer maid is well. I hope she can return to her duties soon," he responded to her in kind, though something died in his heart to remain so distant.

"Yes, I would like her to stay in the room with me to ensure she recovers from her ordeal, by your leave of course." Her eyes slid to the side, noting the crew members who were within earshot. He had no doubt she only added the last obligatory request to keep up appearances of the happily wedded couple. He was being dismissed. Something within his very soul splintered. It was painful—this loss was something he was never supposed to have.

"As you wish."

She gave him a formal curtsy, turned, and returned to her cabin. Gavin turned to the railing and stared out at the horizon. The wind was brisk and brought tears to his eyes more than once. He rubbed his eyes with a fist. They were alive and that was all that truly mattered. Whatever happened in the cabin while they faced death, it was best to leave it where it was. He had agreed to see her safely to her affianced husband and he was honor bound to continue to perform his duty.

He needed to let her go.

Thirty

COLETTE RETURNED TO HER CABIN AND COLLAPSED ON her bed. She was exhausted from pretending her heart was not breaking. Tears sprung to her eyes and she let them fall. She took a shaky breath against the pain of loss. She felt like she had just begun to live, like a seed that had just pushed a tender green sprout up through the dirt, searching for the sun, only to be pulled out of the ground and thrown on the trash heap.

"Are you unwell, m'lady?" asked Pippa, standing in the doorway. As soon as the waves calmed and she had a bit of food, Pippa had declared herself much improved.

Colette hastily wiped away the tears. "I am quite well, thank you."

"You don't look well." Pippa stepped inside and shut the door behind her, sliding into a chair on legs still wobbly from her ordeal. "You've been crying," she accused.

"It is nothing. A little wind in my eyes."

Pippa raised an eyebrow. "It is a very windy cabin, no?"

Colette sighed. Her new maid did not know how to take a hint about subjects that were not to be discussed. "Yes, quite," she said dryly.

Pippa frowned. "This is about Sir Gavin, isn't it?"

"Pippa, this is not a subject open to discussion." Colette had tried subtle. Now it was time to be direct.

"Why not?" asked Pippa, unable to be dissuaded.

"Because it is none of your concern," snapped Colette.

Pippa's eyes widened. "Forgive me, my lady. I was concerned for you is all."

"Yes, of course. Forgive me my sharp words. It has been a trying couple of days." Actually it had been the best few days of her life. The trying part was now that they were over.

"I thought I was going to die, lying there all alone," said Pippa with a dramatic sigh.

"Me too," confessed Colette.

"Was not Sir Gavin with you?" asked Pippa with innocent eyes.

Colette took a breath. If Pippa were to say such thing to anyone once they arrived at Kintail, all would be lost. "I am intended to wed Mackenzie, the Baron of Kintail."

"But you married Sir Gavin, no?"

"I have explained that to you. It was only a ruse to allow us to travel to Scotland. When I arrive, my marriage to Sir Gavin will be annulled, for I have a marriage contract with the Baron of Kintail. We must pretend this never happened. It would be most awkward for you to mention that I was ever alone with Sir Gavin. Do you understand?"

Pippa frowned at her. "But why would you want to marry someone else?"

"I do not wish to. I must. My father has a contract with—"

"So you have to marry someone just because your father says so?" Pippa was incredulous.

"But of course."

"Why?" Pippa demanded. "Should you not be able to choose who you go to bed with?"

"Pippa! You shall not speak to me in such a manner!" Anger surged through her, though Pippa was only a scapegoat. She was angry that she was required to sacrifice her freedom and even her own body, especially after experiencing the freedom she found in Gavin's arms.

Pippa was not easily cowed. She shook her head at Colette as if chastising a child. "It is all nonsense if you ask me. Anyone can see that you and Sir Gavin are meant to be together."

"I have a dreadful headache," said Colette. It was the truth. And she could take no more of the conversation.

Pippa took the baby and left the cabin without another word.

⁓

The next few days, Colette kept to herself, or at least she kept to the cabin. Pippa acted as her maid, though she never perfected the art of obsequiousness. She said what she thought and, though never intentionally disrespectful, showed deference to no one. She was a most unsuitable maid, but Colette found her demeanor refreshing. The one thing on which Colette had been adamant was that Sir Gavin was never to be mentioned.

Of Gavin, she saw little. He ate his meals with the captain and slept either in the spare cabin or beneath the stars. They spoke but rarely and only of benign pleasantries. It was as if the connection between them had never existed. Colette began to wonder if she had dreamed it all in some storm-induced haze. And yet her heart knew the truth, and her heart was broken.

The weather remained favorable, with strong winds and sunny skies, and they sailed a few days without incident. Although Captain Dupont had originally planned to travel to Glasgow, an additional bag of coins induced him to take them north as far as he dared. At last, the captain announced that they had reached the mouth of Loch Hourn.

Colette headed out to the deck to see her first glimpse of her new homeland, Pippa right behind her. The loch itself was a deep blue, surrounded by lush green shrubs and trees. Everything was green and swaying softly in the breeze. The sun was rising, casting a warm hue over the landscape. Despite all her misgivings of leaving her homeland to come here, Colette had to admit, it was an appealing vantage.

"It is very beautiful, no?" asked Pippa beside her.

"Aye," said Gavin, strolling up beside them. "'Tis the green o' the Highlands. Ye'll ne'er see this green anywhere but the Highlands."

Colette felt like she must say something but did not know what. Every subject she wished to discuss with Gavin was banned to her. She was saved from the awkward silence by the arrival of the captain.

"We are almost at your destination," he said in his booming voice. "We will sail as far up the Kylerhea

River as we can, so you will be close to your destination. I wish you all well in your journey. A pleasure sailing with you."

"Thank ye, Captain, for seeing us safe thus far," said Gavin with an easy smile, as if he had not a care in the world. Had he truly forgotten her so quickly?

Colette forced herself to look away from the pleasing features of Sir Gavin to the wonder of the sight before her. She was resigned. She would go and do her duty to her family, her father, and her people. She had known it would be a sacrifice—it was no different now. She told herself that whatever had happened with Sir Gavin made no difference. A small voice within her wondered if her womb had been receptive to his seed. But even if it were so, she would be married to the Baron of Kintail as soon as she arrived and no one would be the wiser, though the thought came with a shiver of sorrow she could not name.

"Are ye cold?" Gavin put a hand on her shoulder. His warmth burned through her gown and melted straight through to her heart. It was all she could do to shake her head in response.

"Colette," he whispered into her ear. "I wish to speak to ye… I need to speak to ye. I beg yer indulgence for a private word."

Colette's heart thumped heavily as if it was trying to escape. She put a hand to her chest to keep the unruly organ contained. She held her head high and struggled to keep the cool mask in place. "Do you wish to speak about the arrangements for our journey?" She feared what he was going to say and hoped if she gave him an alternative topic of conversation, she could steer him into safer waters.

"Aye, I wish to speak about our arrangements but not about travel, and no' here on deck," he whispered in her ear, his breath hot on her neck.

Colette knew she should not allow him a private audience. It was too dangerous. And yet she could deny him nothing.

"Pippa, would you mind—"

"I'll stay here on deck for as long as you need." Pippa gave them an impertinent wink.

Unable to chastise her maid in public, Colette walked to the cabin, followed by Gavin. Once shut inside, Gavin took a breath as if gathering up his courage to speak. He paced back and forth in the small cabin, his long gait taking only a few strides to cross the room before needing to turn back again.

"I ken yer reticence in speaking to me after what we shared during the storm," began Gavin, finding it hard to look directly at her. "I have tried to remain silent to respect yer feelings and yer wishes in this manner. But I canna keep silent any longer."

Colette's hands clenched, crushing the silk fabric of her gown. She held her breath, waiting for Gavin to continue.

"I ne'er meant for this to happen." He sighed. "After traveling wi' ye and seeing how ye have given o' yerself to care for everyone around ye, I was attracted to yer very soul, yer essence, yer being. I ken we took the wedding vows intending to have the marriage annulled. And yet, now that those vows have been…" He paused, cleared his throat, and continued,

"Now that our vows have been consummated, I find I canna so easily forget them."

"Please, Sir Gavin." Her voice was barely above a whisper, as if she could hardly stand to speak of such things out loud. She had spent the last few days trying to forget all that he was now dragging out into the bright light of day. It was all too much. "We made an error in judgment. It is best to let the past fade away."

"'Tis true we both made a wrong assumption regarding the sea worthiness o' this vessel. Despite her excellent crew, the ferocity o' the storm did not inspire confidence. I am surprised she managed to stay afloat."

"In truth," said Colette in a weary voice, "it would have been more convenient for all of us if it had gone down."

Gavin rushed to her and took both her hands in his. "Dinna speak that way, m'lady. Ye must no' speak that way. We've been saved for a purpose. It must be so."

"Yes, but I fear my purpose is to serve my father and my people by presenting myself as a bride to the Baron of Kintail."

Gavin's eyebrows fell over blazing eyes. "Nay, there must be another way." Gavin closed his eyes and bowed his head so that his forehead touched hers. "I canna lose ye. I canna watch ye wed another."

"And what would you have me do?" Her voice cracked and the mask of cool detachment shattered. "My people are depending on the soldiers to protect their very lives. My hand in marriage is the price for this protection. If I do not become his wife, it is my people who will suffer as a consequence. This you cannot ask me to do."

"Nay, but I canna allow my wife to marry another. Ye canna ask this o' me." His voice shook as he spoke and he gently squeezed her hands.

Colette tilted her face toward his, needing to feel the warmth of his lips. He leaned down, his lips brushing against hers. It was so right but so wrong.

"No!" she cried and jumped back. "No, we must not. Pray, you must leave."

Gavin opened his mouth to say something but she interrupted him, not giving him the chance to speak.

"I beg you, you must leave me," cried Colette. "For if you do not leave me, I will never leave you, and my people will pay a harsh price for my own happiness."

Gavin gave her a deep bow. "As you wish." He left the cabin, taking her heart with him.

A few minutes later, a sharp rap came at the door, causing Colette's heart to race as she hoped Gavin had returned. Instead, Pippa entered the room.

"Why did you chase him away?" she chastised in a brash manner.

"Pippa, please mind your work," said Colette, hoping to redirect Pippa. She was in no mood to be questioned by her maid.

"Why do you not tell him you love him?"

"Pippa! That is an impertinence."

Pippa cocked her head to one side, confusion spreading across her face. "Is impertinence another word for the truth?"

Thirty-one

IT HAD BEEN A LONG JOURNEY, BUT NOW THAT SHE WAS at the end of it, Colette did not wish to leave the tiny world of their sailing ship and face the reality of her life. But time kept moving forward, and she prepared to disembark from the stalwart *St. Olga*. Colette was relieved with the thought of putting her feet back on dry land, but she did not wish to continue the journey. How many days would it be before she met her future husband? The mere thought made her ill.

Colette was accustomed to directing Pippa's movements, but when it came to packing to leave the ship, Pippa was more than efficient. There was no one who looked forward to leaving the ship more than Pippa.

Satisfied that all was going according to plan, at least where packing was concerned, Colette walked out onto the deck, trying to portray confidence she did not feel. This was it. This would be her new home. She paused a moment, her face to the sun, enjoying the warmth kissing her cheeks without servants running to protect her from the elements. She had come a long way since she first began her journey.

Gavin stood at his accustomed post in the bow of the ship, looking forward. He did not turn to her, but she knew from the growing tension in his shoulders when she approached that he was aware of her presence. She wished to heal this breach between them, but she knew she could not. They were apart, and they were intended to remain this way.

Instead of approaching him, she leaned on the railing, looking out at the shore. This was no sandy beach. Large, jagged rocks plunged into the ocean and angry waves battled against them, shooting up spray. It was springtime in Scotland, and the shore was awash in different colors of green—bright green fields, darker green trees, and bushes of various sizes and shapes in every shade of green imaginable.

She took a deep breath, relishing the aroma of growing things and not only salt water. She smiled in spite of herself. The prospect was so fair, she was at least relieved that her new homeland made for a lovely setting. Her tranquillity was interrupted by the arrival of Gavin. Just one glance at his approach and her heart fluttered and her palms started to sweat. It was intolerable.

"Are ye ready?" he asked, his eyes simmering with unspoken emotion.

Was she? "I must be" was her answer.

Gavin gave her a short nod, his lips pressed into a thin line. "I've been talking wi' the captain and he doubts his ability to sail all the way up Kylerhea River to Loch Duich. I've suggested he dock at Glenelg, where we should be able to hire transport to Eilean Donan Castle."

"How long will the journey be to the castle?" she asked, wondering how many precious days she had left with Sir Gavin.

"'Tis no more than a half day's walk. We could be there before supper."

"So soon!" she gasped. Despite many times wishing for an end to her arduous journey, she had not expected it to be over so quickly. She had hoped for more time, more opportunity to think of some escape from her fate, more time with the man beside her. It now seemed very foolish of her to have pushed him away these last few precious days.

"Mayhap the roads will be bad with the spring rains," suggested Gavin hopefully.

"Indeed, it is likely," agreed Colette.

They stood in silence and watched the distant shore grow ever nearer.

"I am not ready," whispered Colette.

Without a word, Gavin took her hand in his.

◈

Gavin took a step onto dry land and breathed deeply. He was home. He had always wondered if he would fall to the sword or some other peril while adventuring in France, as his father had, but now his feet stood on Scottish soil. He might still die of the sword—the Highlands could be a dangerous place—but at least he would die in his homeland.

Glenelg was a small village that served as the main connection between the mainland and the Isle of Skye. Otherwise, it was not notable; yet to Gavin's eyes, nothing could be better. Everything from the crofter's huts to the smell of the heather in the hills above was familiar to him. It smelled of home.

For Colette, however, everything was different. She was assisted off the ship and stood on the shore, looking out of place. Her style of dress and speech marked her as an outsider. It was a different world for her. He longed to shield her from any difficulties, but he knew he could not. She had made her choice. And her choice did not include him.

Gavin forced himself to turn away. He had a job to do, and he needed to complete it. He walked into the village, surprised to find it vacant. He expected the curious to come and see what ship had arrived, but no one could be found. It appeared that people may soon return, with chickens running free in the yard and clothes out on the line. Strange.

Finally, he found an elderly man in the stable, nursing a bottle of golden liquid. "Where are the villagers?" he asked the man.

The man blinked at him and rose shakily to his feet. "Out! Damn thieves! Ye'll no' get past me!" He wobbled on unsteady feet and finally collapsed to the ground. "Och! Ye killed me!"

"I've no' touched ye. Where did everyone go?"

"They be gone," agreed the man.

"Aye, but where?"

"Dinna ken." The man shrugged and took another swig.

"I ken ye've had about enough o' this bottle." Gavin plucked the bottle from the man's grasp, ignoring the howl of protest. "I need to purchase horses and a cart."

"Got none!" The inebriated man folded his arms over his chest.

"Ye've got two horses and a cart right here." Gavin pointed to them. "Now name yer price."

The man eyed the bottle.

After a brief negotiation involving a few coins and a returned bottle, Gavin was in possession of two modest horses and a cart.

"Dinna travel at night" was the old man's parting. "Woods full o' beasties."

"Thank ye for the warning," said Gavin, wondering about the man's overall sanity.

Gavin walked the horse and cart back down to the shore. Pippa was running up and down the beach, laughing in a manner that made her appear quite mad. Colette was sitting on one of her trunks. She appeared smaller than usual, holding the edges of a cloak about the baby on her lap, protecting Frances against the brisk sea wind.

"That cart is all you could find?" asked Colette.

Gavin nodded.

"We shall have to take several trips, or mayhap the Mackenzies can send for the things that do not fit in the cart."

Gavin ran his fingers through his hair, unsure what to say. "I dinna ken we'd be needing more than one cart."

"But my dowry will require more than one cart when my trunks are fully unloaded from the ship."

Captain Dupont was already pulling up the anchor to leave.

"My dowry!" Colette stood.

"It is all here on the beach, m'lady."

"But…" Colette looked around at the few trunks and canvas bags.

"Recall the storm," said Gavin gently, remembering more about the storm than he could now express. "We had to lighten the ship to stay afloat."

"Oh." Colette stared at the few things she had left. "Yes, of course," she added briskly.

Pippa slowed down enough to make comment. "Is that all you have left? Not much of what you had when you started."

Gavin glared at Pippa for her unnecessary comment. She noted his look and shut her mouth. "You still have the treasury box containing the coin, which should be the most pressing concern," said Gavin, trying to ease the blow.

"And you have your clothes and look—a bag full of iron," said Pippa, trying to be helpful but unable to hide her disappointment when the canvas bag she opened had nothing but iron cooking implements.

Fortunately, Colette was more pleased to see the iron spoons than Pippa. "My father's wedding gift. I am glad to have it at least. Come, Pippa, let us pack the cart."

"Nay, I will see to it," said Gavin. He was impressed that she had taken the news so well. She had lost nearly all her inheritance, and yet she still held her head high like a queen. It did not take long for him to load the cart and get them started on their journey. Gavin decided Colette had enough to worry over without burdening her with his concerns over the lack of villagers.

He scanned the road ahead as he led Colette on the last leg of the journey—before he would leave her forever. He carried his large claymore on his back, within easy grasp. He could not fix everything, but he was prepared for anything.

Thirty-two

PIPPA ROLLED HER EYES IN DISGUST. WATCHING LADY Colette and Sir Gavin was insufferable. Colette rode ahead of her, on the horse pulling the cart in which Pippa now sat. Gavin rode on another horse, trotting alongside Colette's mount. They stole meaningful glances at each other. They sighed. Between them were longing gazes enough to make Pippa's stomach feel as if she had never left the ship. They even slowed to a stop on more than one occasion and just stared at each other.

Pippa had a good mind to throw cow pies at them to get them moving again. Clearly, they were desperately, repulsively in love with each other. She had never seen any two people act more ridiculous. Why they were traveling to hand Colette off to marry another man was utterly beyond Pippa's understanding.

Colette and Gavin were married. She had witnessed it herself. To make matters worse, they were hopeless for each other. All this rubbish about marriage con- tracts and duty held as much worth to Pippa as one of those cow pies she considered flinging. They should have ridden off together and been happy.

"They are very silly, no?" Pippa whispered to the baby, who babbled in return. Pippa had to content herself with appreciating the many different greens of the passing countryside as they rode around the loch to reach their destination. It was a pleasant day, and Pippa made herself comfortable sitting on one of Colette's few remaining trunks, while the goat, tied to the back of the cart, trotted along behind them.

After a few hours, they came to a small rise, giving a clear vista of Eilean Donan Castle in the distance. It was built on a small island, close enough to the shore to be reached by a stone bridge. The castle was a large fortress, beautifully reflected in the still waters of the loch. Pippa grinned in satisfaction. Such a prospect made the entire wretched boat ride worth the misery. She was to live in such luxury? She could hardly believe her good fortune.

Her delight in the castle was clearly not shared by her two companions. Gavin's lips were set tight and his complexion had gone gray. Colette's lips trembled in an expression of mournful beauty.

"So close," said Colette as one led to the slaughter.

Gavin looked like he wanted to hurt something—or maybe he looked like he was being hurt. It was hard to tell. One thing was clear—these two needed someone to help them.

"The baby is fatigued by this journey," said Pippa, though the baby was cooing happily and chewing on her own fist. "I wonder if we may stop here for the night." It was a preposterous notion, since it was only midafternoon and they had no more than an hour to travel before they would reach their destination.

"I would not wish to distress the baby," said Colette, quickly clinging to any excuse to stop.

"I agree. It would be good to stop here for the night." Gavin's color began to return. He led them back down the rise and into the forest, out of sight of the castle. He found a flat space a bit off the road and began to make camp. A tent or two were among the remaining items of her dowry, along with the basic necessities to make camp.

Pippa watched as Sir Gavin constructed a tent for Colette. She soon recognized he intended the tent for Colette, the baby, and herself, which of course would never do.

"I was thinking, my lady," Pippa said to Colette. "The baby, she seems a bit fussy. I fear she may keep you up at night. Mayhap we should put up another tent, and I will stay there with the babe while you get some sleep."

Colette regarded Pippa carefully, and Pippa did her best to appear innocent, even though the baby was now sleeping like an angel.

"Pippa, you know it would not be appropriate for me to stay in the tent by myself."

"True, I had forgot. I know, why do you not ask Sir Gavin to spend the night at the entrance of your tent? Then you will be safe, for none shall reach you if Sir Gavin is your protector." Pippa glanced away, unable to look at Lady Colette and keep a straight face.

Lady Colette was silent for a moment, and though her face revealed nothing, Pippa knew she was thinking hard. "Yes, let us do as you suggest."

Pippa nodded with a grin. They were being delightfully easy to manage. Maybe another night together would clarify everything they needed to know. At the very least, Pippa had given them the opportunity to spend one last night together. It was the least she could do to repay Lady Colette for the kindness she had shown her.

Lady Colette reached out and touched Pippa's hand in an unusual gesture. "Thank you, Pippa." Her eyes were deep with understanding.

"Forgive me for saying, but why must you go on at all? Why not stay with Sir Gavin?" Pippa had pressed too far; she knew by the sudden cloud that came over Colette's eyes.

"I must go on, you know that. Even if my duty is not clear to you, it is to me." Colette held herself rigid and tall.

"I know. You've told me before. But you love him and he loves you. You would be a fool to throw it away. And I know, it's an impertinence, but it's the truth and I don't mind saying it."

Instead of chastising her, Colette stared at her with large green eyes. "Sir Gavin in love?"

"With you." Pippa was emphatic. "I confess I know little of it, but I have never seen a man look at anyone the way Sir Gavin looks at you. I never knew a man like Sir Gavin could exist. I thought they were all worse than devils. If I met someone like Sir Gavin, I would never let him go!"

Pippa turned to stomp off, remembered herself, and turned back to curtsy and then spun to continue her retreat. Lady Colette did not know what a rare gift she had been given. Pippa had a low opinion of men to begin with, but Gavin was a different sort of man than she had ever met. He took care of Lady Colette. He held the baby. He even emptied a chamber pot half-full of vomit without a word of complaint. No, this Sir Gavin was an entirely different breed of man. If all Highlanders were like that, she could only hope to find one herself.

❧

Colette pondered Pippa's words. Did Gavin love her? No! Yes? Did it matter? She did not know her own mind anymore. She knew her maid was giving them the flimsiest of excuses to spend one more night together, but she was weak and clung to the offered reprieve.

Colette retired early to her bed, with Gavin remaining on guard outside her tent. Thick clouds rolled in, obscuring all light from moon and stars. Colette lay awake, knowing that Gavin would come to her. She waited for the soft rustle of the tent flap, her body alive with anticipation.

"Colette?" Gavin whispered, barely audible over the wind that rustled the canvas of the tent.

"I am here," she whispered in return.

In a moment, he bumped into her cot and sat beside her on her pallet. "Colette," he said again, his voice a rasp.

She sat up and reached for him, and suddenly she was in his arms and they were kissing their hellos and their good-byes. She could not keep the tears from running down her face. She did not want to marry another. She could not imagine leaving him.

"Say the word," whispered Gavin, "and I will take ye away from here. Somewhere ye'll ne'er be found and we can be together forever."

Colette clung to him, much within her wanting to say yes. She wished to give up everything for the sake of this powerful love. But she could not. For love, true love, could not hurt those around it.

"I wish to say yes," said Colette, her heart breaking. "But you know it cannot be. I cannot leave my father, my people, unprotected."

"I'll gather forces myself. I'm o' Clan MacLaren, and my uncle the laird has once before fought for friends in France. I will gather warriors and take them myself to defend yer father and yer people."

Colette shook her head. She could never allow Gavin to return to the dangers in France. "To return to danger, I cannot ask you. You have already fought for us at great personal risk. I cannot have you risk yourself and your clan to save mine."

When Gavin opened his mouth to protest, she put a finger to his lips, silencing his objections. "Never could I live with myself if you returned to France and were hurt or killed. No, it cannot be. On this matter I am absolutely resolute."

"There must be a way," whispered Gavin in the dark. "There must be a way for me to keep ye."

"There is no way." The words were like gravel in her mouth. "Tomorrow I must go to my future husband. The past must be the past."

Gavin held her close as if he never meant to let her go. "Know this: ye are my wife. There will be no other wife for me but ye. In truth..." He paused and held her so close, she could feel his heart beating on her chest. "In truth, I love ye. I love ye wi' my whole heart. And none o' this will ever change my love for ye." He sealed his proclamation with a kiss.

She clung to him, not wanting to let him go. They reclined onto the pallet together, still in each other's embrace, neither willing to let go. They kissed away everything but their love. This was their last night together. This was their last chance.

Finally, she broke the kiss to speak the words she needed to say. "Gavin, I need you to know." She swallowed hard. "I have never said this to anyone, but you I do love."

Gavin pulled her even tighter, which suited her well because Colette wanted to be as close to him as she could. Her husband, her lover, the man to whom she'd given her heart, was hers now but only for a few hours more.

She reached for her chemise and flung it off over her head without a thought, needing her whole body to feel him. He must have agreed with the sentiment for he too threw aside his clothes, covering them both with his thick plaid. They lay together in each other's embrace, not moving, not speaking, not wanting the moment to end.

Gavin kissed her on the cheek, then trailed kisses to her lips and down to the hollow of her neck. He continued his sensuous path until his face was buried in her bosom. She pulled him even closer as he demanded more of her. Heat radiated from her core, tingling up her spine, to her fingers and toes. Tension was building within her. She needed him, wanted him, and held on to him with arms and legs.

He once more caressed her lips with his even as he claimed her for his own. She opened herself to him, needing to be united to him. She closed her eyes as the tension built. The ground moved beneath her and he above her, spinning, rocking, until she cried out as pleasure ripped through her.

They laid together, holding on to each other even as ripples of pleasure continued to course through them. "I love you." It was the only thing she could say.

"I love ye too."

She fought sleep, not wanting to waste a moment with him. Holding him close but knowing he was already lost to her was a pleasure fractured with the deepest pain—but one that she would not deny herself. This was life. This was true. She had loved, and she had lost.

So be it.

Thirty-three

GAVIN LEFT THE TENT WHEN THE SUN WAS BEGINNING to rise. They had slept little that night, but Colette had finally succumbed to fatigue, and he would not wake her for anything. He walked across the road and climbed the small rise, gazing out toward their final destination. The castle of the Mackenzies was lit with an orange glow as the rays of the rising sun touched the ethereal wisps of mist. Somewhere behind the secure stone walls, the Baron of Kintail smugly awaited the arrival of his bride.

In a moment of cowardice, Gavin considered stealing away and letting Colette travel the final distance herself, so he would not have to face the final farewell. How could he willingly hand over his wife to become another man's bride? No, it was impossible.

Gavin swallowed down gall and ran his fingers through his hair, trying to inspire some grand thought, some rationale that would allow him to keep Colette for himself that would not hurt her kin. He took a deep breath of the damp, cool morning air. He knew what needed to happen. There was nothing to be done but the inevitable. She must become the wife of the Baron of Kintail, and he must let her go.

As Gavin watched the castle, he became curiously aware that no banner had been raised to greet the morn. Were the Mackenzies not in residence? Even more odd, there were no farmers or tradesmen beginning their day or coming down the road toward the castle. He had picked a spot off the road so as not to be disturbed, but no one had passed them at all. In truth, all looked abandoned.

He strained to see past the fog. Was that a breach in one of the walls? A cold chill that had nothing to do with the damp morning air crept up his spine. Gavin did not know what had happened to the castle or even if anything was wrong, but he wanted to be the one to find out, not Colette.

He walked back to their campsite, surveying it with fresh eyes. They were well off the road, but the tops of the tents were visible. He needed to get them down, which meant waking Colette. He walked into the canvas tent and was stopped in his tracks. Colette lay sleeping on the pallet, her beautiful, deep auburn hair splayed about her, a small, secret smile playing on her lips. She was a beautiful creature.

Once again he fought the impulse to take her away and keep her for himself. Instead, he sat on the edge of the pallet and gently shook her shoulder. Her eyelids fluttered open, and she gave him a wide, sleepy grin. It was all he could do not to crawl under the blankets and join her one last time.

"Forgive me, but I must wake ye now."

"Is something the matter?" Colette sat up, her hair falling about her in a seductive manner.

Gavin forgot what he wanted to say. All he could consider was how her hair covered her breasts, but if she tilted just a bit to the left...

"Gavin?" she repeated, looking quizzically at him. "What is wrong?"

The only thing wrong was that he could not join her once more. Gavin cleared his throat, trying to remember what had brought him into the tent. "The castle is quiet this morning. I will scout ahead, but I wish to take down the tents before I go."

Colette's eyebrows fell as she considered his words. He had tried to convey nothing to worry her, but she was too clever to be easily fooled. "What do you think has happened to the castle?" she asked.

"I dinna ken, but I'll find out. Mayhap 'tis naught, but I've learned to be cautious."

"I will go with you," began Colette.

"Nay! Ye need to stay safe." His voice was loud with the intensity of this sentiment. He paused and spoke it in a softer tone. "Yer safety is one thing I can protect. It is the one service I can still give ye. Let me do this."

She nodded slowly, a crease forming between her eyebrows. "Call in Pippa and I shall dress quickly."

❧

Marie Colette stood by the side of the road and watched Gavin ride away until he turned back and motioned for her to conceal herself in the brush. It was probably unnecessary at this point, since none had traveled the path since they had arrived. Yet Colette backed off the road to please him.

With a sigh, she walked back to where the tents had been, now packed neatly into the wagon. Soon she would meet her new husband. Her eye caught the simple band of gold around her finger. Her heart sinking, she realized she would need to take off her ring and return it to Gavin. She pulled at it, but it wouldn't budge.

An unpleasant noise interrupted her focus. Pippa was holding a fussy Marie Frances, trying to soothe her baby whimpers.

"What is wrong with Frances?" asked Colette, twisting the ring painfully on her finger.

"Hungry, I warrant. She's not eaten since last night."

"Then by all means, let us feed her. By the saints, I cannot get this off." Colette gave one more yank on the ring, but it was well and stuck on her finger.

"'Tis a sign," said Pippa with wide eyes.

Was it? Colette wished she could believe it were true. Frances, however, was less than impressed and increased her cries.

"I believe Frances would like some milk," said Colette, changing the subject.

"Which means I need to milk the goat," said Pippa.

Colette nodded in agreement and took a whimpering baby, so Pippa could attend to her work. She walked with the baby, she bounced the baby, she tried to reason with the baby, attempted to give her a biscuit to eat, but the baby would have none of it. Marie Frances wanted her milk and nothing else would do.

The baby's whimpers increased until her cries could not be silenced, and the tot began to wail. "Pippa?" called Colette. "How much longer will it take to milk the goat?"

"*Milking* the goat does not take too long," called Pippa from somewhere in the thick brush. "*Finding* the goat is another matter."

"You lost the goat?"

"I did not lose it. It wandered off!" defended Pippa.

"Why did you not tie the goat last night?" Colette asked with an edge to her voice.

"I did tie it, but it chomped right through the rope."

The baby's screams were becoming more insistent. If they could not settle the infant, anyone within earshot would know they were there, whether or not they stayed out of sight.

"I shall help you look," said Colette. She began to march through the brush, looking for a white goat with black spots. Or was it a black goat with white spots?

"Hush, Frances. Everyone in all the Highlands will hear you," she reasoned, but the baby was determined to make her wishes known. Loudly. She walked through another thicket and came to an abrupt halt. She was back on the road. And she was not alone.

Five men on horseback had stopped on the road, clearly drawn by the baby's squalls. They were Highlanders, all wearing various forms of the great plaid. Several had overgrown, unkempt beards, and all looked grimy and rough. Far from the polished courtiers she was accustomed to, these were wild men who all looked as if they were kin to the massive rocks and crags of this untamed land.

It was pointless to try to run now, and though she hardly liked the look of the men who stood before her, she did not know if they meant her any harm. She told herself to calm her nerves and hold her head high, as if standing by the side of the road with a squalling infant was a completely normal event.

"Who are ye, and what do ye have there?" one of the men asked gruffly, pulling on a long beard that appeared to hold the contents of several past meals.

"The baby is hungry," Colette said simply.

"Then feed it," said another man, as if the conclusion was obvious. Of course it was a natural response, but Colette felt it best not to get into the details of the missing goat.

"I shall shortly, thank you, kind sir."

"Ye be French?" The bearded man narrowed his eyes at her, taking an unwelcome interest in her. To her dismay, some of the horsemen began to edge their way around her, forming a half circle.

She did not doubt Gavin would be displeased with this turn of events. She glanced around, unsure of what to do. There was no escape, not holding a squalling infant, and even if she put Marie Frances down, she wasn't about to outrun five men on horseback.

In the bushes toward her left, something caught her eye. It was Pippa, peeking at her through a bush.

"Ye're going to need to come wi' us," said one of the Highlanders in a gruff voice. Two of them dismounted and approached her with dark looks.

Her mind spun, trying to think of something to say to get her out of this predicament. "Come no farther!"

she demanded. She held up the squalling infant. "For I hold a changeling."

The men stopped cold, their eyes growing wide.

"I was here, alone, to find a flat stone to lay this changeling out with the hopes that the healthy baby that was stolen would be returned to her mother," said Colette ominously. Everyone knew that fey creatures would exchange their own sickly brats for healthy human babies. The only way to get the babe back was to leave the sickly changeling out in the elements and hope that it would be exchanged once more.

Colette backed away from the men, toward the bush where Pippa was hiding. She turned so that her back was to the man and caught a glimpse of one of Pippa's eyes through the thick, leafy branches. "Take care of her," she mouthed to Pippa, who gave her a small nod in understanding.

Colette placed the whimpering baby on a flat rock, placing her hand over her chest, not wanting to let go. "Be well, my little one." She pressed a kiss on the baby's forehead, wondering if she would ever see the child again.

Of course, Colette would never have been able to keep the child anyway, but she had not considered her feelings when it came time to say good-bye. It hurt, this pain of loss. She was already grieving the loss of Gavin, and now she realized there would be other losses. She was getting right tired of being in pain. She turned to the men and narrowed her eyes at them.

"What do you want from me? And who are you to demand that I go anywhere?" Colette faced down the rough men.

"Ye trespass on the land o' the Baron o' Kintail," declared one of the men with long greasy hair. "We'll take ye to him, and he'll decide yer fate."

Colette held her head high and stared at the men with as much regal hauteur as she could muster. If these were the men her future husband chose to be his emissaries along the road, it did not bode well for the likelihood of a happy future together. Still, it was not her choice to make, and even if her future husband chose to employ ruffians, she would still be married to him.

"I am on my way to visit the Baron of Kintail," declared Colette. "You may have the honor of being my escort."

If Colette had hoped one of the men would offer his mount to her, she was sadly mistaken. So she marched down the road on foot, with five dubious guards surrounding her. It was hardly the way she had anticipated entering the keep as the mistress of the castle, but she had long learned to let go of expectations and allow life to roll along as it pleased. Despite being led to her future husband, one thought alone dominated her mind.

Where was Sir Gavin?

Thirty-four

GAVIN APPROACHED THE CASTLE, STRUCK BY THE LACK of activity outside. No crofters were attending their crops. No tradesmen were setting up shop. The little village outside the Eilean Donan Castle was strangely vacant. He wished there was someone he could ask what the signs meant. But there was no one about. He slowed the horse to walk and slowly ambled toward the gate, which was barred to him.

He came to a stop before the gates and wondered what to do next. Had something happened to the Mackenzies? Was Marie Colette not to marry him after all? He tried to sweep away hope, but it stubbornly remained, clinging to any reason that would allow Colette to remain his.

His thoughts were interrupted by a loud barking from the top of the wall. "Who goes there? State yer name and yer purpose at this here castle," called a man with slightly slurred speech.

Gavin stepped back to see the man more clearly. He had not been standing at his post when Gavin approached. It appeared he may have just woken to attend to his duty. Gavin was wary. Something was not right, but there was only one way to find out what was going on, and that was to talk to the laird himself.

"I am Sir Gavin Patrick. I have traveled far to visit the Baron o' Kintail. Please tell yer master I would speak to him."

"The Baron o' Kintail, eh?" The man spoke in a sarcastic tone as if there was some joke about the request. "Och, we have the Baron o' Kintail here. Come in, come in, and sup wi' him."

Gavin dismounted and walked his horse into the castle as the gates were opened for him. Things were not in good repair. Debris littered the courtyard, along with several men who still appeared to be asleep. If the groggy stupor in which a few men staggered forward was any indication, their condition was enhanced by liberal doses of alcohol. They must have drunk heavily the night before.

"Where is the Baron o' Kintail?" asked Gavin suspiciously. His great sword on his back was within easy reach, but none of the men about him appeared to be in any condition to attack.

"He is here. He is here in the great hall. But ye must wait here until my master is ready to receive ye."

Gavin waited outside the doors of the great hall. The Highlanders who were beginning to wake up in the courtyard were a surly lot. Never had he seen a more slovenly group. They staggered around and swore and went in search of more whiskey.

Just when Gavin was beginning to consider leaving the castle altogether, the door swung open, and he was heralded inside. Within the walls were more men in various states of groggy stupor. He wondered at what must have transpired the night before. This was no place he would allow Marie Colette to enter, marriage contract or no.

He scanned the room for the master of the castle, to hopefully get some answers, but no one was on the raised dais. In the corner of the room, a man was relieving himself on the rushes. "Are ye Sir Gavin Patrick?" the man asked midstream.

Gavin was itching to grab his sword at the disrespect this man was showing him, but he stayed his hand and answered through gritted teeth. "Aye, and what manner o' man are ye?"

The man finished his business and strolled back into the middle of the hall stepping up on the raised dais and sitting in the master's chair. He was a large man, even compared to Gavin, who was a tall man himself. The man before him was practically a giant. He stood at least a foot taller than any man around him. His square shoulders and muscular arms gave Gavin no doubt he was addressing a warlord. His legs were large and muscular, about the diameter of tree trunks. Most fearsome of all was his flaming red hair, which stuck out at all angles around his head, merging into his bushy red beard.

"Do ye ken who I am?" The large man narrowed his eyes and gave him a wicked grin.

Gavin had never met him, but he knew the man by reputation. "Ye're Red Rex, the Scourge o' the Highlands."

The man smiled, showing his blackened teeth. "Aye, 'tis so nice to be recognized for one's work."

Gavin was relieved he had Colette and Pippa wait in safety. He wanted to return immediately, but he needed to know how this warlord knew his name. "And what has happened to the Baron o' Kintail?"

"I am the Baron o' Kintail! Ye may address any business wi' the Baron o' Kintail to me." Red Rex sat smugly on the raised chair.

"And what o' the man who formally held this title?" Gavin wanted information but glanced at the exit, preparing himself for a hasty departure when things went bad, as they undoubtedly would.

"Now where did we put him?" Red Rex looked to the high ceiling as if deep in thought. "I do believe he is watching over our gardens. Or more accurately, buried in our gardens." He gave Gavin another wide smile.

Gavin refused to show any emotion. Red Rex had an infamous reputation. He was a warlord, strong and smart. He knew how to pick a vulnerable target and pillage it for everything he could. He was known for robbing and stealing and conquering weak lairds, taking over their castles until he tired of it and moved on. But the Baron of Kintail should not have been an easy target.

"But how is it that ye have ascended to this lofty title?" asked Gavin.

"The former Baron o' Kintail made a poor bargain wi' them French bastards. When he was parted from a large force o' his warriors and then the castle was beset with sickness, I knew my time had come. And strike we did."

Gavin balled his fists at his side. So this snake waited for Mackenzie to send troops to help defend Colette's people, only to be plundered himself, his castle taken, his life forfeit. Gavin realized he needed to be wary. Red Rex knew more about this business with Colette than Gavin wished.

"And now, young Gavin, tell me what business ye have with my predecessor. What brings ye here today?"

The slovenly men were beginning to wake, taking a keen interest in the conversation. Some even moved between him and the door, blocking his escape. Red Rex knew Gavin's name, but how much more did he know? Gavin took a breath, knowing that whatever he said now would most likely make the difference as to whether he walked out alive or not. "I have recently returned from France, and I come to bring tidings of the war to the Baron o' Kintail."

"Ye may give me yer report, soldier." An odd smile played on the lips of Red Rex not unlike that of a cat toying with a caught mouse.

"The English grow stronger and more bold. They have taken the port o' Bordeaux."

"And how is it that ye have escaped to give this report?"

Gavin was not sure how far this man's sphere of influence went and how much he already knew. To be caught in a lie could be fatal—to provide more information than necessary equally so. He decided to keep as close to the truth as possible, with one major omission. "I sailed in a merchant vessel to Glenelg."

Red Rex leaned forward, his eyes glittering not unlike that of the snake about to strike. "I heard a vessel stopped there. And what o' Lady Marie Colette, the one the Baron o' Kintail was promised to wed?"

Gavin's heart sunk at the mention of her name. Red Rex must have come in possession of Laird Mackenzie's papers, which told him of the arrangement. Gavin looked him straight in the eye. "'Tis the other unfortunate tiding I have to give. Lady Marie Colette was captured by the English along with all her dowry. I fear 'tis verra likely she has by now been forced to wed another." It was Gavin's intention to make Marie Colette appear as distant as possible. Now if he could only get out of the castle alive, they might have a chance.

"How disappointing." Red Rex gave no indication as to whether or not he believed Gavin's story.

Gavin tensed, ready to draw his sword if need be. He would fight his way free if it came to it, though he hoped to be allowed to walk out without the need for swordplay. He bowed to Red Rex. "That is all I have to report. Good day to ye."

Red Rex waved a hand at him like swatting away a fly. Gavin had been dismissed.

He turned to go. He was almost free. He got no more than a few steps when a group of men walking in stopped him cold. A prisoner was led into the great hall, escorted on either side by gruff guards, even by Highlander standards.

It was Marie Colette.

❧

Colette knew as soon as she entered the great hall of the castle something was wrong. Gavin was standing near the entrance, and when he saw her, all the color drained from his face. She was in danger. They both were. Though how or from whom she did not know. Beyond Gavin sat a large man with shocking red hair sticking out at all angles. He had wild eyes and a self-satisfied smile. She sincerely hoped that this was not her husband to be.

"Who is this ye bring before me?" demanded the man with the red hair.

"We found her a few miles up the road. She be French," said one of the ruffians who had marched her into the great hall.

"Ah, what a beautiful creature ye are. Ye must be the lovely Lady Marie Colette. I've been waiting for ye to arrive," said the man with red hair. He rose and strode to her.

Gavin's lips pressed into a thin line; every muscle in his body appeared to be tensed, ready to run or strike. "Nay," said Gavin through gritted teeth. "As I said before, Lady Marie Colette was taken by the English in France."

"But ye must be mistaken," said the imposingly large man, standing and walking toward her. Colette's heart dropped lower with dread at every approaching step. "For the Baron o' Kintail was promised in marriage the most beautiful woman who had ever lived in exchange for warriors. And this creature before me can be none other than Lady Marie Colette." He gave her a slippery smile that left a bad taste in her mouth.

Gavin flashed his eyes in warning, but there was no denying who she was. She would have to concoct a story in which she would be some other French lady wandering about who was not Lady Marie Colette. All of which stretched credibility beyond the breaking point. She feared telling a falsehood to this man, which could have unhappy consequences for either her or Gavin. Her main concern now was to prevent Gavin from being caught in a lie.

"This man, he is correct. I was taken by the English, but when they were transporting me to one of their strongholds, my father's soldiers attacked and they were able to free me. We found a sympathetic captain and sailed away even as my guards fought off the English soldiers."

"What a tale ye tell," said the large man walking around her slowly, inspecting her person in a crude manner.

Colette held her head high and would not allow him to make her cower. "And to whom am I addressing, sir?"

"I am the Baron o' Kintail." He stood before her, his massive hands fisted at his waist.

Colette gasped. Surely, this could not be the man her father intended her to marry.

"He is Red Rex," growled Gavin. "He defeated Laird Mackenzie and has taken his castle and his title."

Now Colette understood. This was not the man her father chose, but rather a usurper who'd taken the man's title by force. "And the previous lord of this land?"

"Dead." Red Rex smiled as if the word was delicious on his lips. "And now, by a contract signed by yer father pledging ye in marriage to the Baron o' Kintail, ye belong to me."

Thirty-five

IT WAS ONLY THROUGH THE PRACTICE OF CONTROLLING her emotions over many years that Colette was able to prevent herself from screaming and trying to run from the hall. She felt an absolute obligation to the man her father chose, but to this warlord, she felt no allegiance whatsoever. She glanced at Gavin. If only she had taken his offer to run away when he had proposed it.

Anger surged inside her, swallowing the fear. She had tried to do what was right, but it had ended in disaster. She was always pushing aside her own thoughts, feelings, and desires so she could serve the demands of others. And what had it gotten her? Now she was pledged in marriage to some heinous monster.

"You wish to marry me?" she asked politely, as if questioning his preference in meals.

"What I want is yer dowry." All pretense of nicety drained from the face of Red Rex, vicious intensity blazing in his eyes.

"If a weighty dowry is what you wish, then I advise you to choose another," said Colette coolly. "I fear my dowry was captured and will never leave France now."

"Yer father will fix the trouble with yer dowry, have no fear."

"My father has nothing more to give."

"Ye best hope he can. He will be sent a missive, telling him that I am keeping ye comfortable…for a time." His voice dropped and the humorless smile once again marred his countenance. "I'm sure, wi' the right incentive, yer father will find a replacement dowry for ye."

Colette looked again at Gavin, but he refused to turn her way.

"I plan to return to France soon," said Gavin, stepping in between Red Rex and Colette as though the proceedings between them were of little consequence to him. "I would be willing to transport a missive from ye to the duc de Bergerac."

Colette's heart stopped. Would he abandon her to this warlord?

Red Rex turned his attention to Gavin, as if he'd forgotten he was still in the room. "Aye, tell the duke I will feed his daughter for six months, waiting for the dowry promised in the marriage contract. If it doesna arrive in that time, I will consider the marriage forfeit and give her to my men to do with as they may."

Colette balled her fists at her sides. Evil man.

"Aye, my lord," said Gavin, though Colette wondered how he could speak with his jaw so tight.

Red Rex turned and walked back toward the raised dais, calling for a scribe to write a letter to the duc de Bergerac. Gavin waited only for his back to turn before he drew his sword. He swung it around menacingly, causing the ruffians around them to stumble back. Gavin grabbed her hand and they bolted for the door.

"Get them!" raged Red Rex.

Colette hiked up her skirts and ran with all her might, half drug by Gavin as he sprinted ahead of her. Shouts sprang up around them and the courtyard that had seemed almost abandoned when she'd entered now sprung to life with grim-faced knaves popping up from every direction. Gavin launched himself onto his horse, gaining his seat in one leap. He reached down and clasped her wrist to pull her up behind him.

Colette jumped toward Gavin, but someone wrapped their hands around her waist and pulled her back, jerking her hand from Gavin's. Colette screamed in surprise and Gavin spun, sword in hand, and with one mighty thrust, dispatched the man who had grabbed her.

Colette reached again for Gavin, even as he leaned down toward her. Something sliced through the air just inches beyond her own nose and she realized the ruffians were shooting at them from the ramparts above.

"Hurry!" Gavin reached for her hand, but she was once again brought down from behind. This time she was thrown to the sand of the courtyard and held down by a burly man with a knife pointed menacingly at her neck. Arrows continued to rain down as Gavin spun his horse toward her. One arrow glanced off his harness and another stuck into the saddle. They were going to kill him.

"Go!" she screamed at him. "Leave me and get help."

"Never!" He charged the men who stood before her but was intercepted by Red Rex, who rushed into the fray, brandishing his sword. Gavin engaged, clashing steel on steel. The only reprieve was from the bowmen who stopped shooting so as not to hit their master. More rough men poured out of the main keep. Gavin was a skilled warrior, but he could not last long against such an onslaught.

"Go now! I command you to go or all will be lost!" Colette screamed at him, hoping he would heed her words. It was her fault he was here. He needed to escape and she needed to know he would be safe.

He met her eyes for only the briefest moment, but the anguish in his face was clear and palpable. He swung once more at the mighty Red Rex. "Ye winna hurt her. Ye winna harm her in any manner."

"Ye ken what I want. Bring me the dowry. The lass is o' little consequence," Red Rex sneered at him.

"I will go and seek the ransom ye demand. But know this, harm her in any way and ye will die."

Red Rex smiled as only a man accustomed to threats of violence could do. "Stand down! Let him go." The warriors stopped and stood aside.

Gavin shouted something at them in his Gaelic tongue that could only be something of a curse, gave her one last longing look, and galloped out of the courtyard.

Colette was lifted roughly to her feet. She watched as Gavin galloped down the road, becoming smaller and smaller in the distance. At least he had escaped. Now she needed to keep herself safe until he returned, for she had no doubt that he would come for her.

"Let us show ye our best hospitality," said Red Rex in a silky voice. He strolled up to her and ran a finger down the side of her face, along the edge of her veil.

Colette shuddered at his touch, not wanting any part of him to be near to her.

"Afeared o' me? Dinna tremble, my dear," said Rex, mistaking her aversion for fear. "My, ye're a beauty. I shall enjoy ye."

"I shall never marry you," declared Colette in a loud voice.

Red Rex shrugged as if it was of little consequence. Colette realized with an unpleasant turn of her stomach that he intended to enjoy her with or without the formality of marriage.

"Take her to the tower," he commanded his men. He gave her an oily smile. "I will come to ye soon." The threat in his deep voice was clear.

Colette held her back straight and her chin up, giving him one of her most regal glares. He could abduct her, he could lock her in a tower, but he could not own her.

Colette was led up to the tower, with two large warriors on either side. There would be no escape. She was marched up the circular stone stairs to a private bedchamber. She was ushered inside and the door locked behind her. There was nothing more she could do but wait.

Gavin would come for her. Somehow, he would come.

&

Pippa sat on a large rock with the baby in her arms. Several rough-looking men had taken Lady Colette to the castle, where Gavin had gone earlier. If anyone could keep her safe, it would be Sir Gavin. But what to do now?

"Naaaaaaa!" bleated the goat, who apparently had decided to make a belated appearance.

"You have caused us all measure of ill," she berated the goat, who merely attempted to take a bite of the hem of her gown. Pippa secured the goat and milked the animal, giving the milk to the baby. At least the goat and the babe were content.

She decided it would be good to take the wagon farther into the forest. She did not trust the men who had grabbed Colette and she feared they might return. So she hitched the wagon to the remaining horse and walked the wagon with all their belongings deeper into the trees, looking for a good hiding place to stash it. She heard the babbling of rushing water and followed the sound, interested in a fresh drink.

Sunlight filtered down through the green leaves, making a mosaic of bright patches of light on the forest floor. It was a pleasant wood, fresh with the new buds of spring. She was accustomed to trees, but here in the Highlands, they also grew rocks—rocks covered in bright green moss, rocks the size of boulders, rocks the size of a crofter's huts. She knew her mistress had not been pleased to leave France, but Pippa could not have been more content to leave her homeland behind. She closed her eyes and breathed deep of the fresh forest. This was home.

"Halt! State yer name and yer purpose!"

Pippa was startled out of her happy reverie by the angry male voice. She looked around the forest but saw nothing but trees.

"Who calls me? Show yourself."

"Answer the question if ye value yer life!"

"I shall not! How do I know you are not a faerie? For this place could be enchanted, no? Step out and show yourself if you be a man." Pippa was not in the habit of bending to anyone's will. If someone wished to threaten her, she needed more proof than a disembodied voice's word on the matter.

A Highlander emerged from behind a large boulder to her left. He was a tall, trim man, young and clean shaven. He was wearing the plaid wrap that appeared to be the fashion of the Highlands, but on him it looked particularly well. He stepped forward slowly, a sword slung across his back within easy reach.

"Are ye satisfied I am a man?" he asked in a low voice. He was a stunning contrast in features with black, neatly trimmed hair and bright, blue eyes.

Was she satisfied? Not by half. She swallowed on a dry throat. "I have heard that the fey folk, they can take the image of a man. How do I know if I can trust you?"

The man stepped closer. "I am a man, no more or less. What would ye have me do?"

Pippa could think of a few things, but none that would meet the approval of her mistress. She generally had little regard for the male of the species, but this handsome lad made her forget. Besides, if he was anything like the version of man she had met in Sir Gavin, she was definitely interested in learning more about him. "What is your name, sir man?"

The man smiled slowly at her. "I have demanded yer name, and now ye convince me to part wi' mine. I am Ronan Mackenzie, the Baron o' Kintail since my father quit the title."

"Mackenzie? We have been looking for you!"

"Ye're French, are ye no'?" His eyes opened wide. "Ye must be Lady Marie Colette, the one we have been waiting for. Surely, the description of yer beauty has no' been overstated, for ye are a bonnie lass."

Pippa stared at the man. No one had ever thought her beautiful. Could this man truly have confused her with Lady Colette? It was shocking. A strange warmth spread across her face. It was amazing. "I...I..."

"Forgive me, m'lady, for challenging ye. And here I have made ye stand before me. Please do come here and sit. My men will attend yer horse." At a gesture, men appeared from the trees, lowering their bows.

Pippa swallowed hard. She'd had no idea she had been surrounded. She followed Ronan Mackenzie around the boulder and down a narrow path. The path widened into a clearing around a lagoon, where a small waterfall cascaded down large boulders into a crystal clear pool.

Crates of supplies were stacked around the pool and Pippa surmised this was where they had made camp. Ronan motioned to a flat rock, and she sat down beside the pool, her host sitting on a stone beside her. The rushing water was a peaceful sound and a rainbow formed in the mist brought up by the spray of the water.

"This place, it is quite beautiful," said Pippa. "Are you hunting?" she asked, trying to guess what they were doing making camp outside the castle.

"Nay. In truth, ye have found us in sad times. Soon after my father sent many of his warriors to France to fight the English for the duc de Bergerac, we were beset by a fever that afflicted many. At our weakest, we were attacked by a warlord, Red Rex." Ronan spit on the ground at the mention of his name. "The castle was taken and my father killed."

"I am so sorry." Pippa touched his hand without thinking.

He held her hand in his. "In truth, I had not thought to marry soon." He spoke softly, his clear blue eyes meetings hers. "Yet wi' the death o' my father, I am honor bound to fulfill the marriage contract. I hope ye will accept this change." He squeezed her hand. "I hope ye will accept me."

"You wish for me to be your wife?" Pippa stared at him in shock. The Baron of Kintail wanted to *marry* her?

The sound of a baby's cry had her jumping to her feet. "The baby!" She ran back to the cart and scooped up the little one, who was just waking from her nap. They turned to face Ronan Mackenzie, who stared at the infant with a confused frown.

"Ye have a bairn?"

"No, oh no, this child, she is not mine. She belongs to my mistress. That is to say, we found the baby abandoned, her kin killed, and none would care for her, so we kept her with us until we could find for her a proper home." Pippa took a breath, realizing she was babbling.

"I see," said the young Ronan Mackenzie in a voice that said he did not understand at all.

It was time for the truth. "I confess I am not the Lady Marie Colette. I am her maid. Sir Gavin Patrick is our guide, and he went to the castle alone to scout it out, but then Lady Colette was discovered by some mean-looking knaves and was taken to the castle as well."

Ronan took a moment to absorb this new information. He shook his head sadly. "If Lady Colette and her guide have fallen into the hands o' Red Rex, all is lost."

Pippa's stomach sank. "Sir Gavin, he is a sharp one. Mayhap he can save my lady? If they could escape, they would try to find me and the cart by the road from the direction in which I came."

"I shall post men to watch for them," said Ronan, and with another wave of his hand, several warriors left the clearing to attend to the master's request.

Pippa was left with Ronan, standing beside him in the forest. He was a handsome man, there was no denying, but he was meant for Colette. And Colette was meant for Gavin. And Pippa? She was meant for no one.

Thirty-six

GAVIN RACED DOWN THE ROAD, KNOWING THAT HE could not spare a single second in trying to save Colette. His mind raced faster than his horse, trying to devise a plan to rescue her. His stomach rolled at the thought of Colette trapped with the warlord.

He slowed only when he reached the place where they had camped the night before. He wondered if Pippa would be there with the baby or if she had been captured too.

"Pippa?" He called in a loud voice. "Are ye there, lass?"

He waited for a moment, hoping that she would make herself known, but all was quiet. He pressed forward into the brush and found the small clearing where they had made camp, but no one was about. The wagon was gone and there was no sign of Pippa or the baby. They must have been taken, and with the loss of the wagon, Gavin had no hope of ransoming Colette before nightfall.

Gavin slid off his horse to the ground. What was he to do? He had no army of men to attack Red Rex. He had no treasure to tempt Red Rex. He had no way to save Colette. She was trapped with that monster, who might be molesting her even at that moment. He sank to his knees, an anxious despair welling up within him. He bowed his head and prayed. *Lord, show me a way. Help me, please.*

"Are ye Sir Gavin?"

Gavin leaped to his feet and stared at the Highlander before him. "I am."

Several more men emerged from the brush, ready for battle. Gavin did not know whether they were friend or foe, yet none drew a weapon. "We've come looking for ye. Come wi' us. The Mackenzie wishes to speak wi' ye."

"Laird Mackenzie? I feared he was dead."

"The master is dead, but his son lives on." The men turned and disappeared into the brush, and Gavin hastened to grab the reins of his horse and follow them.

"Thank ye," Gavin whispered to the heavens. It was not often his prayers were answered so quickly.

Gavin followed the men deeper into the woods, where no path was visible. The sound of rushing water grew louder as they approached. It was a struggle to keep his thoughts on the events around him and not Colette trapped in the castle unprotected, but there was nothing he could do about her now except pray for her safety, and pray he did. He hoped the Lord would answer all his prayers as quickly as the last.

The men led him to a river beside a pool of water beneath a small waterfall. He was relieved to see Pippa, with the baby in her arms, and beyond her the wagon and the treasure the warlord sought. Pippa was deep in conversation with a young man who looked barely older than Pippa herself. So focused were they on each other that it took a moment before they realized he approached.

"I seek the son of Kenneth Mackenzie," called Gavin. "'Tis a matter o' great urgency."

"Sir Gavin!" Pippa gave him a wide smile. "You are not dead. How good of you."

"I am Ronan Mackenzie," said the young man, stepping forward. "And the Baron o' Kintail now that my father has gone to his rest."

"Forgive me, but I met another man today who has taken the title o' the Baron o' Kintail."

"Red Rex," Ronan growled, and he spat for emphasis. "That usurper shall pay for what he has done."

"Bastard." Gavin spat to show solidarity with the young man.

"But where is Lady Marie Colette? Pippa told me she was taken. Please tell me she has no' fallen into the hands o' that demon," said Ronan.

"She has. She has been taken by Red Rex. He only let me go because he heard she traveled with a great dowry and he wishes it for himself. I am to bring him the treasure for her exchange."

Ronan shook his head. "Once he gets what he wants, he will most likely kill ye all. He will no' stay his hand, no' for ye, no' for Lady Marie Colette."

Gavin nodded in understanding. He feared Rex was not a man to be trusted. "Then our only choice is to attack him. I hope to find men o' stout hearts who will be willing to help me. This demon must be stopped. His actions canna go unanswered."

"We have sent up the cry for help among our neighbors and beyond. We hope to gather some o' the clans and, within two months, have enough men to launch an attack," responded Ronan.

"Two *months*?" Gavin's heart sank. "Two months is two months too long. Have ye no' heard me? Lady Colette is even now at the mercy o' that fiend. We must save her now!"

"I understand yer wishes, Sir Gavin, for I share them." Ronan stepped forward, his blue eyes bright with intensity. "But we are too few to mount an attack against the castle. We would no' save Lady Colette. We would only achieve our own demise."

Gavin did not want to admit it, but the man was right. They did not have the warriors to fight the man directly.

"What about the secret passageways?" asked Pippa, joining the conversation.

"Pippa, this is no' yer fight," said Gavin, the fatigue catching up with him. He knew Pippa wished only to help, but there was nothing she could do.

Pippa stood her ground. "Lady Colette was the only one who was ever nice to me, except for you, Sir Gavin. I cannot do nothing. Truth, sir, she must be saved."

"Unfortunately," said Ronan, "there are no secret passages in or out o' the castle."

"Oh," said Pippa with some disappointment. "I thought all castles had secret passageways. They did in the stories she told me."

"There's a difference between real life and a made-up story," grumbled Gavin.

"But Lady Colette always said stories could help," Pippa persisted. "Like when I was so sick and she told me the story of people of Greece who wore sheets instead of clothing."

"Pippa, this is no time for stories," Gavin said, dismissing her. "We need to find a way to rescue yer mistress."

"But that is what I am trying to say," demanded Pippa, refusing to be brushed aside. "What we need is a big horse that is hollow inside."

"Pippa, yer brain's addled. Go tend to the baby and let us figure out how to save Lady Colette." Gavin's concern for Colette had made him short-tempered; he did not have time to waste.

"Wait," said Ronan, turning to Pippa. "What do ye mean we need a hollow horse?"

"We could get into the castle like how they tricked the people of Troy into opening their gates," said Pippa, smiling at the young laird.

"A Trojan horse?" asked Gavin, now interested in the conversation. His mind spun and a new idea emerged. "Pippa, ye're brilliant!"

❧

Colette surveyed the large bedchamber, looking for something that could aid in escape or, if that failed, could be used as a weapon. It was a fine chamber, with a large bed, curtained with the heavy, wine-colored drapes, now drawn. The furniture pieces were finely wrought, stained the color of warm amber. Intricate tapestries hung from the walls, their bright colors inviting one into their scenes of battle and adventure.

Animal skins instead of rushes graced the floor and
much of the woodwork had been decorated with
intricate designs in gold paint.

Clearly, the room had been decorated by someone
with an eye for fine things. No doubt this was the
chamber for the master, the former Baron of Kintail,
who now rested in eternal repose. Ironically, it was the
kind of room that made her feel comfortable and at
home. She wondered if the previous Baron of Kintail
had taken pains to make the master's bedchamber a
comfortable home for her.

She had never before thought of this man to whom
she had been pledged to marry as a real person, someone who may have anxiously awaited her arrival and
tried to make her comfortable. She had considered her
intended as some sort of monster, but the man who
had lived in this chamber had been no barbarian. She
gritted her teeth as a wave of anger swept over her at
the true barbarian who had murdered him. She was all
the more determined to escape.

The room boasted a great stone fireplace on one
side and a window built into the thick stone wall on
the other. Colette ran to the window, hoping it could
be a method of escape. The shuttered window was
large enough to fit through, but the drop was at least
fifty feet down to the courtyard below. Even if she
could lower herself on some sort of rope, she would
be in plain sight to everyone in the courtyard.

Colette sighed. She sat down on the stone bench
built into the wall by the window and closed her eyes.
Lord, help me to escape! Her prayer was nothing like
the lengthy formal recitations she had heard from her

priest, but no prayer had ever been more heartfelt. A slight rustle caught her attention, and she opened her eyes to find a young man sneaking out from behind the drapes of the poster bed.

Colette shrieked in surprise and fear, but the figure merely dashed for the door. He grabbed at the latch and banged it several times, trying to open the door, but of course, it was locked.

Colette backed away from him, scanning the room for something she might use as a weapon. The man, however, did not appear to be a threat. In truth, he seemed to be scanning the room himself, looking for some manner of escape. He pressed hard against the door as if he could somehow push his way through the lock. He was an ungainly lad, with long arms and legs, unruly brown hair, and glinting dark eyes.

"Who are you?" she demanded in a bold voice.

"Wheesht!" The lad held up a hand as if to quiet her.

"You will tell me who you are at once," she said in a tone that brooked no opposition.

"Aye," he whispered. "Only keep yer voice down, m'lady. I am Cormac MacLean."

"Well, Monsieur MacLean, I know why I am locked into this room, but why are you?"

"I dinna intend to get locked in the room, did I? I was merely trying to…" And here his already soft voice lowered to such a low tone that Colette could no longer hear him.

"I beg your pardon?"

He stepped toward her, his eyes darting from side to side as if afraid that the walls might overhear. "I wished to read a book," he whispered with great significance.

A book? Shocking indeed. From the look on his face, he might as well have admitted to a heinous crime or a mortal sin. "What book are you reading?"

"I dinna get the chance to begin. I'd only seen it in the room when we first came. But when I came today to try to steal a look, I found it destroyed." He pointed toward the fireplace. Stepping toward the hearth, Colette saw the remnants of several leather book covers.

"Who would burn a book?" she cried, truly outraged. Everyone knew books were highly prized and of great value. Even if Red Rex was not the reading kind, and this was no surprise to Colette, he did strike her as motivated by profit. It was shocking he would burn something he could sell at a high price.

"My father hates books," sighed the young man.

"Your *father*? Your father is Red Rex?"

Cormac MacLean shrugged. "Aye, my sire is Red Rex."

"But you…" It was Colette's turn to have her voice trail off into nothing. She wished to ask if the lad was certain as to his parentage because his lanky frame was so much different from his monstrous father.

"I ken I dinna look much like my father," admitted the lad with another sigh. "'Tis not uncommonly remarked upon."

"Yes, well, perhaps you take after your mother's side of the family," said Colette, trying to be of help to the dejected lad before her.

"Aye, my father accuses me of it often, as if I could choose a different form. Truth is, I have it on good authority I am his son. My mother was even married to him," he added as if it made it only worse.

"Is your mother with you?" Colette asked, hoping to find a sympathetic soul.

"Nay, she was a fragile thing and died bringing me into the world. I was raised by monks and taught to read, but my father says all that reading while I was growing up made me scrawny. I came to sneak just a chapter or two, but it seems my father anticipated me and destroyed the books."

Colette stared at the ashes. She already felt for Red Rex such a vehement hatred that it was hard for her opinion of him to sink lower—but it did. Burning books was unforgivable. Most of the books had been burned beyond recognition but there was one leather cover she recognized.

"This one I know. I read it many times," commented Colette.

"Did ye?" Cormac's eyes grew large, and he took another step toward her, but far from being intimidating, he now appeared more like an eager puppy, wanting a go at some new toy. "Do ye remember the story?"

"Yes, of course. It was one of my favorites."

"Could ye tell me?"

Colette surveyed him, a new plan emerging. "I could. But I wonder if you might be able to help me as well."

Cormac's countenance fell. "If ye're going to ask me to help ye escape from my father, dinna bother. I canna do it. My life would be forfeit. He's been looking for a reason to kill me and that would be more than enough."

"I cannot believe a man would kill his own son." The words were out of her mouth before she remembered of whom she was speaking. A man who burned books was capable of anything.

Cormac raised an eyebrow and Colette knew he was right. She couldn't help herself; she felt sorry for the young man. "Fine, do not help me. Just promise not to stand in my way."

The man shrugged one shoulder. "That's what I do most o' the time anyway."

"Good. But do you know a way out of the tower? For I imagine you would not wish to be here when your father returns."

Cormac made a strangled sound. "Nay, that would be fatal." He looked around the room once more until his eyes fixed on the door and a smile came to his face. "Aye, it will be easy enough. Remove the hinges and the door will fall off."

"Can this be done? Can you take the door off the hinges?"

The man narrowed his eyes at her, and for the first time, she could see the likeness between him and his wretched father. "I could…"

"I shall tell you the story while you work," Colette said to entice him.

Cormac smiled. "Aye, 'tis a deal."

Colette returned the smile. "*La Chanson de Roland.*"

Thirty-seven

THE PLAN WAS SHEER MADNESS. IT HAD SEEMED LIKE A good idea—in truth, it seemed like the only idea—but now, rolling along as the sun was setting, Gavin feared the plan was going to end quite badly. The risks were irrelevant, however, since it was their only hope to free Colette. He held tight to his sword. This had to work.

The wagon rattled along until he feared his teeth might shake free. He wished to move to a more comfortable position, but he was shoulder to shoulder with the other men hidden in the false bottom they had quickly constructed in the wagon. The Mackenzie master of arms was on his left side, and the son of the slain Laird Mackenzie was on his right. A few other warriors packed them in, tight and hot in the small, dark space. They had incorporated another wagon as well, dividing the dowry and trying to make it look larger while concealing more men.

The wagons slowed to a halt. "We bring the dowry o' Lady Marie Colette," cried the driver, chosen for the role as being an older member of the party and less

threatening. "Send forth Lady Marie Colette, and ye
may have yer reward."

"Give us the goods, or we'll cut the verra life from
ye!" The shouts of the ruffians grew louder as they
charged the wagons.

The driver kicked the wagon twice. It was the
signal. They expected foul play, and the men of Red
Rex did not disappoint. The plan was for the drivers
to jump down from the carts and run away. So far,
it sounded like all was going according to plan. But
would the thieves bring the wagons into the courtyard?

All was quiet for a few minutes. Sweat ran down
Gavin's forehead from the heat of the confined
space. He longed to break free but held quiet. A few
shouts were heard as the thieves climbed through the
wagons, exclaiming over the riches they had found.
Ironic that Gavin had often tried to convince Lady
Colette to travel with fewer possessions, but now he
was grateful they had at least something left to tempt
the thieves.

With another shout, the wagons once again began
to roll. The gates were opened with a loud squawk,
and the wagons rattled on the cobblestones of the
gatehouse. They were being brought into the walls of
the castle.

～⌘～

Colette snuck down the darkened spiral staircase,
keenly aware of the slightest sound. The sun had
set, casting the castle into deep shadow, lit only by
an occasional torch. She hoped the dark would ease
her escape, but the black shadows only increased her

anxiety. Her heart was beating so loudly she feared it would give her away.

She had managed, with help from the son of Red Rex and her rendition of the *Song of Roland*, to escape from the bedchamber. Yet now she was at a loss as to how to escape the rest of the castle. Her unlikely benefactor, once he had managed to remove the door from its hinges, had merely saluted her and wandered off, not getting in her way but not helping her either. She should not have been ungrateful, but she did believe her inspired version of the *Song of Roland* had earned her a little more assistance.

The sounds of feasting came from the great hall. She hoped they were all passed out, drunk as sin, thus facilitating her escape. At the bottom of the stairs, she paused at the doorway. The door was not locked, but she did not know what was on the other side. Somehow, she needed to make it out the door, across the courtyard, and out the gate without anyone noticing her. She lifted a prayer and gathered her courage.

She opened the great wooden door a crack, peeking outside. She could see little in the dimly lit corridor. She opened the door farther, but only stone walls greeted her. She slunk into the corridor, picking up her skirts to prevent them from brushing against the stone floor. She had dressed that morning with the expectation of meeting her new husband, not with the anticipation that she would have to sneak through the castle without being seen or heard. She had always prided herself on being appropriately dressed for any situation, but her burgundy velvet gown was only a hindrance in her current plight.

The sound of voices rolled down the corridor, and she pressed herself into a dark corner to avoid being seen. She prayed she would not be discovered, but the voices grew ever closer as her heart beat against her rib cage harder and harder. The voices grew louder with every step she took until she realized they were coming right at her. She pressed herself against the cold, dark wall and held her breath, praying she would not be found.

Three men walked past, laughing at a crude joke and already stumbling from an excess of drink, even though the night was young. They passed her without notice and gradually the voices faded away. It felt like an eternity before she could no longer hear them, and she finally took a breath, gasping for air.

"I wondered how long ye could go wi'out breathing," said a cold voice from behind her. A hand grabbed her shoulder and spun her around.

She was face-to-face with Red Rex.

⁓

The hardest part about the plan was waiting. Gavin took a stifled breath, trying to suppress the growing feeling of being buried alive. He knew for the plan to work they needed to wait until the thieves and ruffians had lost interest in the wagons and sought more interesting sport. From the state of the men Gavin had seen that morning, he knew the whiskey ran freely and would win half the battle for them if they were patient.

Yet he also knew that somewhere in the castle, Marie Colette was alone, unprotected, and in danger at every moment. Gavin's hand tightened around the hilt of his sword. Any man who laid a finger on his wife would die, starting with that bastard Red Rex.

He tried to calm his mind, but all that came to mind was Colette in danger, and he was lying there doing nothing to save her. They must sneak out at some point, but when? How would he know when to spring the trap?

Lord, give me a sign. Help me to know when to act.

A panicked scream shattered the quiet of the night. It was Colette.

❧

Colette jumped in fright, staring up at the gleaming eyes of the warlord. She opened her mouth to scream, but no sound would emerge.

"Coud'na wait to see me? Felt neglected, did ye?" Red Rex mocked her.

His mockery subdued her fear with anger. "I am the daughter of the duc de Bergerac. You will release me at once," demanded Colette, though she knew it was a pointless command. She needed to speak now, before she lost all courage.

"Ye'll learn to stay where I put ye. Ye belong to me now." He sneered down at her, menacing in his sheer size and the coldness of his voice. He released her and pointed to the door that led back up to the tower bedchamber. She knew there was little point in resisting. Rex was a monstrously large man. There was no way to overpower him or outrun him.

Most unwillingly, she walked up the stairs, back to her prison. He followed along behind, his thunderous footsteps echoing off the stone stairs behind her, sending slivers of fear through her.

He stopped at the door propped up against the wall. "Ye're more clever than I gave ye credit." He glared at her. "I dinna care for wenches what thinks themselves above their place." He backed her into the bedchamber and easily lifted the heavy oak door, slamming it back on its hinges with a bang that made her jump.

She scanned the room for some way to subdue the barbarian before her. It was pointless.

"Wenches are good fer only one thing, and it's time ye found out what that is." He strode toward her with a sickening smile.

Her heart pounded and her breath came in gasps. Fear gripped her, strangling her with its power. She backed away from the warlord, desperately trying to think of some way to escape. "If it is money you seek, my father will pay more with the assurance that I am untouched."

"Then I'll be sure to tell that to yer father." He took one large stride toward her and grabbed her shoulders with both hands.

She screamed with all her might. It may be a useless gesture, but she would not relent without a fight.

"Shut up!" Rex raised his hand to strike, but suddenly a loud bang stopped him in his tracks. His eyes crossed, and he fell to the floor unconscious.

Colette stared at the large heap of Red Rex on the floor, confused as to what had happened until she noted Cormac, holding a frying pan.

"Is he…" she asked, looking at Rex.

"Och, he's no' dead. Got the hardest head o' any Highlander what ever lived. But swiftly now if ye wish to escape."

"Thank you, but why are you doing this for me?" she asked as she followed him out of the room and down the stone stairs.

"I've been thinking o' what Roland would do. He'd ne'er cower before his father. Ye told a good tale, m'lady," praised Cormac, leading her through a corridor until he reached a cluttered storeroom at the bottom of one of the towers, with a side door leading to the courtyard outside. Vaguely, strange, muffled noises could be heard coming from the courtyard, and she hoped this time she could escape the castle unnoticed.

"Thank you for helping me. I cannot begin to say how much I appreciate it," said Colette warmly.

Cormac waved off her thanks. He peeked out the door and turned back to her with a small smile. "I wager ye've been telling stories yer entire journey, including some ancient tales from Greece, am I correct?"

"Yes, but how did you know?"

Cormac shrugged but gave no explanation. "I believe I shall go hunting today. Probably be gone for a while before I return. Whatever happens, I would request one boon from ye."

"Name it."

"I wish to hear yer version of that Trojan horse." He gave her a sly smile, slung a bow over one shoulder, and casually strolled out the tower door, leaving Colette to ponder what to do next. Though unsure what adventures awaited for her outside the door,

Colette was certain she would fare better with a bow
in her hand.

Within the storeroom, supplies had been tossed
about, and all manner of weaponry littered the floor in
a haphazard manner. She stepped gingerly over several
spears and picked up a bow and quiver of arrows. She
had limited practice with the bow, but she had seen
it shot many times. This was a different bow than she
was used to, but how hard could it be to pull back on
a string?

Just as she was wondering how she would manage
to sneak across the courtyard, shouts erupted from the
courtyard. At first, she thought Cormac had given
the alarm as to her escape, but the sudden clanging
of steel on steel made her realize a battle was at hand.
She nocked an arrow and opened the door a sliver to
peek outside. A battle was raging between a small but
fierce band of Highlanders and the warlord's men. She
scanned the men until she found him.

It was Gavin, fighting bravely. He had come back
for her! How Gavin and his men had gotten past the
gates or even who these men were, she did not know,
but they were hopelessly outnumbered.

She attempted to pull back on her bowstring but
found it surprisingly hard to do. With great effort, she
pulled back on her bow, but the arrow slipped and
fell to the ground instead of flying through the air.
Determined not to give up, she nocked another arrow
and pulled back only to have her elbow grabbed,
swinging her around.

Red Rex snarled down at her, grabbing her bow
and throwing it to the floor. "Ye're becoming most

inconvenient. Let's see how much trouble ye can cause after I've broken yer face." He grabbed her shoulder and slung her up against a stone wall. She screamed and tried to pull away, but he easily held her fast. He raised his massive clenched fist above her. He was so large, she feared he could kill her with a single blow.

"Let her go!" Gavin charged in the room, swinging his sword at Red Rex.

The warlord threw her to the ground, quickly drawing his own broadsword, the ring of steel on steel reverberating in her ears. "I was a fool to let ye live, boy," snarled Rex, the spittle flying from his mouth. "I winna make that mistake again."

Gavin did not waste his energy in conversation with the warlord. He ran between Colette and Red Rex, protecting her. "Run!" he commanded, but she grabbed her bow.

Gavin could not protest; he was too busy defending himself from the attacks coming from the warlord in a furious wave. Red Rex attacked him as a man possessed, and Gavin defended valiantly, backing out of the storeroom, into a corridor. Gavin was quick and light on his feet, which was fortunate since the blows came fast, each one intended to kill. Red Rex was a master swordsman, clearly benefitting from a lifetime of practice in the warrior arts.

Colette nocked an arrow and tried to find a clear shot, but the men circled and scrambled about, making it impossible to shoot without the risk of hitting Gavin. Red Rex backed them both out of the storeroom, into the corridor and up a spiral stone staircase, leading to one of the towers. She sprinted up several stone steps, so she could have a better vantage and take her mark.

She aimed at the warlord and let fly, but it bounced off the wall. She tried again, and it flew within inches of his nose. Another bounced off Gavin's helm. She nocked another arrow, but both men paused in their fight to glare at her.

"Stop shooting!" they both commanded.

"I am trying to help," defended Colette.

"Well, stop helping before ye kill me!" demanded Gavin.

"That's my job," sneered Rex.

Red Rex struck again, clashing sword on sword. Colette didn't know how much longer Gavin could hold out against his larger opponent. Rex's comfortable smile showed he knew it was inevitable he would win. Gavin's face was a cool mask. If there was any way for him to win, it was not readily apparent. Sooner or later, Gavin would surely fall.

"I love you, Gavin," Colette called. She wanted the last words he heard to be hers, to be her declaration of love for him. A single tear rolled down her cheek. She would love him forever and remember how valiantly he fought to protect her. She would never forget how he had come back for her and given the ultimate sacrifice to try to protect her.

Gavin stilled, his shoulders sagging. He looked at her, his brown eyes warm. "I love ye too, Colette. No matter what happens next, I'm glad I was able to tell ye one last time o' my love."

"Time to die now, boy," snarled the warlord, turning his back to Colette to face Gavin.

Gavin bowed his head and dropped his sword with an ominous clank on the stone floor. Rex raised his sword parallel to his shoulders and Colette realized he was going to swing his weapon, cutting Gavin's head from his neck. Red Rex howled a battle cry and began the swing. Colette screamed, unable to look away.

Gavin dropped quickly and somersaulted through Red Rex's legs, jumped up the stairs, grabbed the bow from her hands, and shoved it down, over Red Rex's head, choking him with the bowstring. Gavin was so fast, Rex was just completing what should have been the fatal swing of his sword when Gavin was behind him, choking the life from him. The sword flung out of the warlord's hands, and his hideous battle cry was cut short into a gurgle. Rex pulled at the bowstring with all his might, but Gavin looped his arms around the bow and put his foot in the small of the man's back, pulling the bow even tighter.

"Surrender or I swear I will kill ye where ye stand." Gavin pulled back harder to make good his threat.

Colette stared at Gavin, seeing him in an entirely new light. Who was this man who could defeat such a fearsome enemy? He was her man, that was who he was.

Red Rex stumbled to his knees, and Colette thought for a moment that the big man was dead. But Gavin released the bow, allowing the man to take a shattered breath. Still holding on to the bow with one hand, with the other, he pulled a knife from his boot and pointed it at the base of the man's neck, letting him feel his steel.

"Call off yer army, or ye will die here," commanded Gavin.

The warlord was spared having to call out by the arrival of some of his men through the door. They stopped short at the scene of their master on his knees and Gavin with a knife to his neck.

"Call the men. Tell them to lay down their arms," said Rex in a gravelly voice. A man fighting for an honest cause may have told his men to continue the fight, even if it meant his own death. But Red Rex was interested in power and profit, not honor. When there was no longer any chance of winning, he was no longer interested in the fight.

The ruffians at the door continued to gawk at them, not moving.

"Do as your master says," said Colette with all authority, "and we may be willing to show mercy." The warlord's men stared at her, openmouthed, but then bowed and left the room.

Gavin shook his head at her. "Just by giving the command, ye can make any man do yer bidding."

"Not any man." She gestured at him.

"Ye mean our friend Red Rex here?" asked Gavin, able to be magnanimous now that he had won.

"No, I mean you. I thought I told you to take my dowry and escape."

"And I thought I told ye to remain hidden beside the road," countered Gavin.

"You are blaming me for being captured by ruffians?"

"Aye! If ye'd remained hidden, none o' this would've happened."

"How dare you! I suppose you are going to blame me for this entire adventure. I know you had no interest in taking this journey from the start."

"'Tis naught but the truth. If yer father had no' manipulated me into gaining my assent, I surely would never have done it."

"Manipulated?" Colette put her hands on her hips. "My father manipulated no one. It is hardly my fault you put yourself at risk to rescue me. I told you to leave!"

"Enough sweet talk. Just kiss her already," growled Red Rex. Colette almost forgot he was still there and glared at his back, he was an unwarranted intrusion in their conversation.

Gavin, however, smiled at her. "I'm glad we are both here to argue. I dinna ken what I would do without ye."

Colette smiled back at him and took a deep breath. She couldn't believe it was over. They had done it.

Some of Ronan Mackenzie's men arrived and took command of their prisoner. It took one on each side of the big man, another with a sword at his back, and a fourth with a bow in order to ensure Red Rex did not escape. They marched him out of the tower and into the courtyard.

Before Colette could say another word, Gavin swept her into his arms. "Are ye hurt? Did he touch ye? If he touched ye, I'll kill the bastard, prisoner or no'."

"You came in time," she whispered. "I am fine."

"Praise the saints. I was sick thinking ye were being hurt." He held her closer.

"I did have help from an unlikely young man. If you meet a Cormac MacLean, the son of Red Rex, please do treat him with kindness."

Gavin said no more but kissed his greeting, hot and demanding. All the anxiety and fear she had experienced all day pulsed through her, heightening every nerve, awakening her senses. She was suddenly alive and aroused. She wanted him right there, right now.

"Gavin, I need you," she panted.

Gavin growled in response. He tried to pull back, but she clung to him. He grabbed her and swung her around until her back was to the cold stone wall. It was a relief, for she was burning inside. She needed him.

"I love ye," Gavin said, gasping as he pressed closer. "I was so afraid I lost ye. I was so afraid." He buried his face on her shoulder, but not before she saw a tear fall.

"I love you too." She clung to him as relief of their escape washed over her.

Gavin kissed her again, the sweet passion speaking more clearly than words. When breathing became necessary, Gavin touched his forehead to hers. "Ye are my wife, now and forever."

"Yes, now we can finally be together," murmured Colette.

"Sir Gavin?" someone called from outside in the courtyard.

Gavin staggered back and took a deep breath. He gave her a nod and offered his arm to her. "Are ye ready?" he asked.

"No, but I suppose we must," said Colette, trying to smooth her hair. She felt most unequal to public viewing and was sure she looked a sight. She was not sure when she had lost her veil, but it was long gone.

Gavin led her out the side door, into the courtyard. It was a clear night. Thousands of stars twinkled in the black night sky. Torches had been lit along the ramparts and flickered in the soft breeze.

Colette took a deep breath of the early summer night. It was done. It was over. The warlord had been captured and now nothing stood between her and being with the man she loved.

The ruffians who had served Red Rex had all been disarmed and were standing in a surly pack at one end of the courtyard, a group of Highlanders guarding them. Cormac, she noted, was not among them. Red Rex was standing in the middle of the courtyard, glowering at all he saw.

"So who are these men you found to fight for us?" asked Colette, linking arms with Gavin and leaning her shoulder on his to help her stay on her feet.

Before Gavin could answer, a young man walked up to her. "Ye must be the renowned beauty, Lady Marie Colette."

"I am Lady Marie Colette," said Colette. "I must extend my sincere gratitude for your assistance in capturing these knaves. May I know to whom I am indebted?"

"I am Ronan Mackenzie and gratified to be o' service to ye. I hope despite the poor welcome ye received, ye may be comfortable in yer new home."

Colette stilled. "New home?"

"Aye, for since my father's death, I am now the Baron o' Kintail, and as such, yer affianced husband."

Thirty-eight

WITH RED REX IN THE DUNGEON AND HIS FOLLOWERS safely locked in one of the barracks, the Mackenzie clan retook the castle and feasted in celebration of their victory. Colette watched it all transpire as though in a dream. She could not lose Gavin now. She could not. She clung to Gavin's arm and refused to be separated. She asked about Pippa, and a runner was sent to bring her and the babe from their hiding place.

Gavin asked for a private audience with Ronan Mackenzie. He seemed a good sort, and Colette had nothing against him, but she could not marry him. And yet how could she deny him, knowing that his father and many others had been killed because of their ill-fated agreement?

Ronan led Colette and Gavin up to his private solar. More books had been burned and parchments and maps were scattered everywhere. He shook his head at the disarray the ruffians had left behind. "What a waste."

"Not a man o' enlightenment I see," said Gavin, stepping into the room, helping the young man by picking up some of the papers.

"I canna believe a man such as he was able to take the castle from us." Ronan sighed as if still in shock over what had transpired. "And tonight I was even more surprised we could take it back. I owe ye much, Sir Gavin. Ye have but to name yer reward and ye shall have it."

Gavin and Colette glanced at each other.

"In truth, there is something I desire, though I have no right to ask," said Gavin.

"Ask for anything ye wish. If it is my power to grant ye, it shall be given, for I would have naught wi'out ye."

Colette's hopes were raised. She once again shared a glance with Gavin.

"It is about the agreement ye had wi' the duc de Bergerac," began Gavin.

"Aye, dinna fear. I will uphold our end o' the agreement. I winna let my father's legacy be tarnished by no' following through on the last agreement he put his name to."

Colette's hopes fell. "But, sir, I must inform you that my journey here has been most arduous and much of my dowry has been lost."

"Ye still have the chest o' treasure and a few other items. It may no' be the full dowry we agreed upon, but I shall ne'er hold it against ye," said Ronan.

"So you wish to follow all the terms of the agreement?" asked Colette nervously. She appeared to be several years older than him, though he was old enough for marriage.

"Aye, we shall be married as soon as may be."

Gavin cleared his throat. "With all due respect to yer excellent father and to yerself, I must pray yer indulgence to express my feelings on this matter."

Colette's pulse raced. What was he going to say?
What could he say? Was there any way out of this?

The door opened and Pippa rushed in, a squalling
baby on her hip. "There you are! I'm so glad you are
both alive. I was beginning to despair. Marie Frances
will have none but you. Here, take her." Pippa shoved
the child into Colette's arms.

As soon as she took the baby into her arms, Marie
Frances stopped her crying and gave her a watery smile.

Ronan Mackenzie noted the obvious preference of
the babe and tilted his head to one side in thought.
"The babe is attached to ye."

Colette gathered her courage, a flash of a plan
coming to her mind. "This is my child, Marie
Frances." She held the baby close.

"Yer child?" gasped Ronan. "Ye said it was a babe
ye found in yer travels," he directed this at Pippa.

Pippa shrugged, and Colette wondered if she would
give her away. "It is difficult to remember right,"
Pippa said vaguely.

"Ye have a child? How did this happen? There was
no mention of a previous marriage. What is wrong
with it?" sputtered Ronan.

Colette held the babe closer, protecting her from
critical eyes. She realized she no longer saw the red
scar that marred the baby's face. Appearances were
only the outer layer. Could he not look beyond the
deformed skin to the precious child within? "I claim
this child as mine." She stood defiantly next to Gavin,
who placed his arm around her.

"We had intended to send the child to live with
my mother," said Gavin in a soft apology. Colette

noticed that though he spoke the truth, the meaning the young laird heard was something else. In normal circumstances, she would have never insinuated that she had borne a child out of wedlock, but now it seemed her only hope.

"I see." Ronan Mackenzie sat hesitantly down on a bench. Colette felt sorry for the young man. It was hardly his fault. He had lost much in this arrangement.

"I understand if you no longer feel the marriage would be quite appropriate," said Colette. "Though I must insist you keep the dowry."

"Aye, the marriage canna be now. 'Twas all for naught." Ronan sighed.

"Do not be so sad." Pippa sat next to him, putting a hand on his shoulder. "You've defeated a monstrous enemy and the dowry of my mistress is yours. Begging your pardon, but anybody who has been with my mistress and Sir Gavin for more than a few minutes could tell they belong together. They fought it for as long as they could, but in the end, fate, she is a demanding mistress."

Ronan took Pippa's hand in his. "I must thank ye for the idea o' how to retake the castle."

"Philippa has traveled with me on this long journey and proved her worth many times." Colette added to the praise of Pippa.

"Philippa." Her name was a caress on the young laird's lips. "Ye must come from a prestigious family o' court. Considering the situation…would it be too much if I was to ask…could ye ever consider…"

"Consider what?" asked Pippa, wide-eyed and breathless.

"Would ye agree to fulfill the agreement my father had with the duc de Bergerac?"

Pippa's jaw dropped. "You wish to marry me?"

"Yes, of course," said Colette, relief flooding through her. "Pippa would make you a most excellent wife."

"What say ye?" Ronan leaned closer to Pippa, ignoring anyone else in the room.

"I wish to say yes, but…" Pippa hesitated, glancing at Colette and Gavin.

"Ye're no' sure ye would like to live in the Highlands?" asked Ronan.

"No, I love it here. I would wish to live here my whole life. It is only that…"

Colette could see Pippa doubted herself, doubted her worth to accept marriage to this young man. She could also plainly see that Pippa was quite along the way of falling in love with this man. Pippa needed to forget her past and believe in her worth.

"Our journey was quite difficult," said Colette. "When accommodations at sea were not what my ladies expected, they abandoned me and refused to travel farther. It was only Pippa who stood by me. She has proven her worth to be much greater than any lady I have ever known."

Ronan broke into a bright smile. "Then ye're the lass for me! If ye'll have me."

Pippa gave him an honest smile, her eyes dancing. She truly was a handsome girl when she smiled. "To marry you, it would be a dream."

Relief rushed through Colette and she took a long breath. Gavin reached for one of her hands, then the other, squeezing them gently and smiling down on her. His warm eyes drew her closer, and she trailed her fingers up his arms and entwined her hands around the back of his neck, reaching up on the tips of her toes so she could claim his lips for her own. He wrapped his arms around her and pulled her close, deepening the kiss. Something akin to pure joy radiated through her and she felt weightless and free.

"We did it," Gavin whispered in her ear. "Praise the good Lord who has blessed me wi' ye."

Colette could think of only one response and kissed him again.

"I see what ye mean. They must be meant for each other," said Ronan to Pippa.

Colette jumped back, shocked at her own behavior. How could she be so brazen as to kiss Gavin in the company of others?

Gavin merely laughed. "It has been a long day, has it no'? What are ye going to do wi' Red Rex and his band?"

"Lock them away until we can hold a trial," replied Ronan. "Should no' take long to decide on their guilt."

"Seems a waste to toss them into the dungeon, where they are no earthly good to anyone," commented Gavin.

"It is too bad they have such criminal proclivities," said Colette. "For my father is in desperate need of trained warriors."

"Aye, it does seem a waste. But why no' give them the choice o' making an honest life for themselves by joining the French forces?" asked Gavin with sudden insight.

"Do you think they would actually be of some service to my father's knights?" asked Colette.

"'Tis no' so much of them being a service to the French, as being trouble to the English. They are still Scots and clearly have a penchant for mischief. Let them take their rabble-rousing ways and bedevil the English," said Gavin.

"It sounds a worthy plan, though Red Rex must stand trial for his crimes. He killed my father, and for that he must pay," said Ronan in a definitive tone.

"Aye, I am more than agreed," said Gavin.

"And if we send more warriors to France, mayhap some of our men could be spared to return to us, as we also are in considerable need," suggested Ronan.

"Yes, that would be a help for us all." Colette extended a hand to the young Mackenzie. "This is not the outcome either of our fathers expected, but I hope we can part in peace and as friends."

The young Mackenzie took her hand and pressed it briefly to his lips. "Aye, 'tis my honor to consider ye both my friends." Ronan smiled at Colette and Gavin, and they returned it.

❧

Everything was planned. Ronan Mackenzie did not wish to tarry, so the wedding was set for the morrow. Pippa lay awake in a large bed in an even larger bedchamber, all by herself. Despite all the excitement of the day and the lateness of the hour, she could not sleep. She had never slept in such a large room by herself, but more than that, her conscience would not give her peace.

With a sigh, she pushed back the soft linen sheets and climbed out of the tall bed. She could not do this.

She could not marry Ronan under false pretenses. He thought her a nobly born lady, and she was anything but.

She crept down the hall on bare feet, the cold of the stones seeping into her bones, freezing her feet. It did not matter. She was freezing her heart, so the rest of her might as well be frozen too. Maybe then it wouldn't hurt so much.

She stopped at the door to his bedchamber. A lady would never enter in the middle of the night. A lady would not have taken note of which bedchamber was his. But she was no lady. She knocked softly and pulled the latch; the door swung open.

She closed the door behind her and paused, scanning the tower chamber. The room was dark, illuminated only by beams of moonlight filtered through the shutters. He was there, asleep in the bed.

She took a few silent steps forward, but he sat up suddenly. "Who goes there?" his voice rang out, strong and sure.

"It is only me," said Pippa, stepping closer so he could see her.

Ronan's frown broke into a look of bemusement, and he placed his knife back under his pillow. "Should ye no' be sleeping?"

"Yes, but there is something I must tell you, a reason why we cannot wed." Pippa stepped forward until she stood by his bed. He was naked from the chest up, and probably below as well, though covered by the blankets. Her mind took a little detour, and she lost what she was going to say.

"What reason?" prompted Ronan.

Pippa blinked at him. He was so handsome, and a laird, and half-naked. Why was she ruining this? She closed her eyes and tried to remember why she had come. "I am not what you think I am. I am no highborn maid. In truth, I am but an orphan who stole for my supper many a time. I met Lady Colette and Sir Gavin on the road and only accompanied them as her maid because all others had left."

Ronan stared at her for a moment. It was clear her words surprised him. His warm hand sought hers, and he held it gently. "Why would ye tell me this? Ye could proceed wi' the wedding tomorrow and no one would ever ken the truth."

"But I would know the truth. And I would feel like a fraud my whole life. I may be a baseborn thief but I'm an honest one. I cannot play you false."

"To be a Highland bride, 'tis more important to have honor and courage than a genteel birth."

Pippa stared at him. What was he saying?

"My offer o' marriage is yers if ye will have me. We can be an unruly lot, and I prefer a lass wi' some pluck, if truth be told."

"You still wish to marry me?" Pippa's heart, which moments before was crushed, now leaped back to life, surging heat through her body. Even her toes were no longer cold.

"Aye, ye're brave and honest and true and..." He opened his mouth to continue his pretty speech, but whatever he was about to say was swallowed up by Pippa, who was so excited she grabbed his face with both hands and planted a kiss straight on his lips.

Ronan wrapped his arms around her, pulling her

onto the bed. "So ye'll be my wife?" he asked in a low, seductive tone.

Pippa answered him with a kiss.

Thirty-nine

COLETTE AND GAVIN WITNESSED THE MARRIAGE OF Philippa and Ronan Mackenzie. Colette provided a sumptuous gown for the affair, and Pippa was transformed into the most beautiful of brides for her wedding. Word spread among the Mackenzie clan that he had defeated the ruthless warlord, and his people returned with great joy. Everyone knew the former Baron of Kintail had traded warriors for a French lady of exquisite beauty. No one who looked upon the beaming face of Pippa doubted for one moment that she was not the most beautiful lady of the land.

The warriors who had followed Red Rex easily agreed to the prospect of fighting in France, rather than face trial. Colette felt sure these ruffians would cause the English more trouble than any of her gently bred brethren and wished them all a fond farewell.

The only dark cloud on the proceedings was the unwelcome news that Red Rex had overpowered his guards and escaped, disappearing into the Scottish Highlands. Colette knew he would never repent of his murderous ways, but hoped that he would be less troublesome now, deprived of so many of his followers. Cormac, the unlikely son of Red Rex, never came back for his promised story, though Colette made sure to tell Laird Mackenzie of the service he gave her, so he might be safe if he ever returned.

The next day, it was time for Gavin and Colette to travel home. It was a brisk morning in the Highlands, with a bright sun and a stiff breeze to help them along their way. Colette woke early and watched for a moment as Gavin slept—her husband that none could ever take from her.

Odd how things had transpired along the way. She had begun her journey burdened with many things and ended with the one thing she had not realized she even wanted. It was more than a fair trade.

She rose and sat in the window seat of their tower chamber. It would most likely be the last time she slept in a castle. She ran her hand along the smooth stones, but there was no sadness in the knowledge. She was ready to move on.

She opened her Book of Hours and read a passage from the book of Romans. *Et sicut non probaverunt Deum habere in notitia, tradidit illos Deus in reprobum sensum.* Colette closed the book and leaned her head back to rest on the stones. The sun rose over the hills, and she smiled into the new day. It was true. "We know that in all things, God works for the good of those who love him."

Colette bounded off the bench and shook Gavin awake. "Arise, my love! For I am eager to get on the road to see my new home."

Gavin opened a sleepy eye and smiled lazily at her. "Are ye certain ye wish to leave the comforts o' castle life?"

"This drafty place? Let us be gone from here. I have always thought a farmhouse to be more comfortable." She met his eye, daring him to challenge her bold claim.

He merely raised an eyebrow but wisely held his tongue.

They dressed and prepared for the journey, both ready to begin their life together. Gavin packed two large horses for their journey overland. They met Pippa and Ronan in the courtyard to say their farewells.

"Please do take good care of yourself and your new husband," said Colette to Pippa, smiling at her warmly. "And thank you. I do not know what I would have done had you not had the courage to stand by me."

"It is I who must thank you," returned Pippa with more confidence and grace than Colette had ever thought possible when they'd first met. "You gave me a chance and helped me through my miserable seasickness. If it was not for you, I may have thrown myself off the boat, but now look at me. I am the mistress of a castle, no?"

"*Oui*! And you are a lady."

"I suppose it is true, now that I have married a laird."

Colette gave Pippa a warm embrace. "You were a lady long before you were married," she whispered in her ear.

Pippa gave Colette a watery smile. "*Merci*." She wiped away a tear with the back of her hand. "But it is nonsense, this talk of us keeping your dowry. It is yours. I shall not be the one to take it."

"No, dear Pippa, there is a contract and it must be honored. The warriors have already been sent to my father at what has been great sacrifice for the Mackenzie clan. The dowry belongs here. Besides, we must continue on our journey, and Sir Gavin does not like to carry more than what can be shoved into a saddlebag, is that not right, my love?"

"Verra true," announced Gavin. "Our journey is long, and we must travel light."

"Is there naught we can give ye to thank ye for all ye have done for us?" asked Ronan, his eyes only for Pippa.

"I hope this will not sound too sentimental," said Colette slowly, "but my father gave me a special wedding gift. It is some iron kitchen utensils. My father made me promise I would cook a meal for my new husband and I would like to honor this request."

"Aye, take anything ye wish wi' my blessing," said Ronan, who was paying little heed to all around him in favor of gazing into Pippa's eyes.

The heavy utensils were soon found and tied to a pack mule along with what remained of Colette's personal belongings. Someone called for a mounting block for Lady Colette, but Gavin waved it off. Instead, he knelt before Colette, his hands open before her.

She smiled down at him and placed her foot in his hands, allowing him to toss her into the saddle. A jolt of tingly awareness shot through her at his touch. He was still the most handsome man she had ever known and had the power to send chills down her spine at a mere touch.

Gavin and Colette traveled by horseback over the countryside to his homeland. There was no question of leaving the baby, so Colette wore her in a sling. The goat and the pack mule followed along behind.

It was summer, and they were able to make good time to reach their destination. Throughout the journey, Colette never felt more alive. Unlike her journey to Scotland, which had been fraught with danger and anxiety, traveling with Gavin as husband and wife was a joy. They rode through verdant forests dripping with bright green moss, galloped over windswept fields of purple heather, and climbed over rocky passes.

Finally, the road led into a fertile valley bordered by tall, craggy cliffs. They arrived in the evening when the sun's rays touched the high peaks, setting them aglow with fiery light. It was a formidable and impressive site, the rocks, harsh and jagged, against the valley, lush and green.

Gavin turned to her and gave her a wide smile. "Welcome to yer new home, m'lady. Those high peaks are the Braes o' Balquhidder. The tower house built into the rock there is Creag an Tuirc, the seat of the MacLaren clan, where my uncle is laird." He glanced at Colette with uncharacteristic nervousness, as if concerned she would be displeased.

"It is the most beautiful place I have ever seen," said Colette, hoping to appease his fears. "You told me the day we met that your homeland was more beautiful than any lavish great hall. Faith, sir, you spoke the truth."

"I'm so glad it pleases ye." His face lit up with honest pleasure. "Ahead is the village o' Balquhidder by the shores of Loch Voil. 'Tis good fishing this time o' year. They will all be surprised to see me, I warrant."

The dirt path meandered past fields, swaying in the gentle breeze. Before them was a modest farmhouse, nestled comfortably into the landscape as if it belonged there as much as any tree or boulder. Gavin dismounted and opened the gate, leading their horses through. He latched the gate behind the horses and reached up and helped her down.

She expected him to set her down, but instead he took her easily into his arms and carried her over the threshold, into the farmhouse. Finally, he set her down, saying somewhat anxiously, "Well, here we are. This is my home. I ken it is no castle."

The farmhouse was larger than the crofters' huts, but certainly of modest, albeit well-built construction. The front room boasted a wooden floor and large stone hearth. A table and benches were in the middle of the room. A doorway to the side led to the kitchen, another door led to what was probably a bedchamber, and a steep staircase, more akin to a ladder, led to what must have been a loft. Though smaller than any place she had lived, it had a pleasant feel.

"It is home," said Colette with a smile. She walked around, noting the furnishings that had been stored along the walls, waiting for the return of the master. She even found a cradle and placed the sleeping baby inside.

"Can I help ye, sir?" asked an elderly man, shuffling into the farmhouse. He stopped short when he saw Gavin. "Well, bless my soul. 'Tis Gavin Patrick. How are ye, my boy?"

"Verra well and glad to be home. Could ye tell Laird MacLaren I've returned?"

"That I will, and yer mother and Sir Chaumont as well, for they are a'visiting." He left at a fast clip before Gavin had a chance to introduce his bride.

Gavin gestured around at the humble wooden furnishings. "I canna give ye what ye deserve," he began, rubbing the back of his neck.

"You have given to me your whole heart, a gift I do not deserve and only hope to repay you by giving you my heart in return. The first day we met, you tempted me with the gift of freedom. It has been a long journey, but you have given me this gift, this freedom, which means more to me than any item listed on my dowry. And best of all, I am with the man I love."

Gavin gave her a wide smile, wrapped her up in his arms, and swung her around the cozy main room.

"Gavin!" A middle-aged, buxom woman stood in the doorway with tears in her eyes.

Gavin set Colette down and opened his arms wide. "Mother!" They ran to greet each other with a warm embrace.

Colette smoothed her hair and made sure her veil was in place and proper. She was nervous to meet her mother-in-law for the first time and hoped to make a good impression.

"I was so scared I'd ne'er see ye again. Ye stayed so long," chastised Gavin's mother, but then she pulled him into an embrace once more. "I'm so glad ye're home."

More people entered the farmhouse: a tall, handsome, distinguished gentleman and a large, barrel-chested Highlander followed by a lovely lady with flaming red hair.

"Mother," said Gavin, once he was able to break free of her warm embrace. "Please allow me to introduce my wife, Lady Marie Colette, the daughter o' the duc de Bergerac. May I present my mother, Lady Mary Patrick and my stepfather, Sir Chaumont." The tall, handsomely dressed knight bowed and gave her a winning smile.

"My dear boy is married! Welcome, my love!" Mary embraced Colette with as much enthusiasm as she had her son. "I am so pleased to meet ye." Any anxiety Colette might have felt in being accepted melted in Mary's loving arms.

"Daughter of a duke, eh?" said Sir Chaumont with a decidedly French accent. "Glad I made an impression on you in the choice of your marriage partner. Well done, my lad!"

"Please let me also introduce my uncle, Laird MacLaren, and his wife, Lady Aila," continued Gavin, once his mother had finally released Colette.

Laird MacLaren, a large and fearsome man with a wicked scar down his cheek, gave her a quick nod. "Glad the lad chose well. Welcome to Clan MacLaren."

Lady Aila was next to greet her. She gave Colette a shy smile. "I am so glad ye've come. I'm sure we shall be the best o' neighbors."

Relief flooded through Colette at the warm reception.

"Now we should leave the two newlyweds alone to settle in," said Chaumont with a mischievous wink.

They all began to leave but stopped short when little Marie Frances chose that moment to wake from her nap, greeting the world with a lusty cry. Colette turned to pick up the tot and then faced her new family, who stared at her, then all slowly turned to Gavin, their eyes asking for explanation. Colette's heart sank. Would they understand?

"We found a baby in our travels, orphaned and left for dead by the English," said Gavin.

"Bastard Sassenach!" growled MacLaren.

"And ye rescued this wee babe? What a kindhearted lass ye are," cried Mary, giving Colette and Frances another hug. "What a day! Let me know if I can help ye in any way," she called as Chaumont led her back out the door.

When the door swung closed, Colette collapsed onto a bench. "I was so nervous they would not accept me."

"Not accept ye? They will love ye as I do and that's the end of it!" stated Gavin in complete confidence.

"In that case"—Colette laughed, regaining her feet and her confidence—"I believe I need to act in obedience to my father and make you a meal in our new home."

"My love, I am no' the richest man, but I'm not entirely impoverished. These lands belong to me, so dinna fear ye must live wi'out the benefits of a cook and maid."

"'Tis good to know, but my father instructed me to do it myself and I shall see it done. At least," she added with a rueful smile, "on this, our first night together."

"Do ye ken how to cook?" asked Gavin hopefully. It was a fair question, since on their journey he had done all the outdoor cooking when they had not been able to stay at an inn.

"Not in the least. I suspect you will no doubt wish to employ a cook in the future, but tonight I shall try on my own."

Gavin relented and unpacked the goods and the heavy iron given to her by her father, bringing it into the kitchen. Colette found a large iron pot and, after several failed attempts and an embarrassing request for assistance from Gavin, lit the fire. Soon she had water boiling in the hanging cauldron over the fire. She carefully chopped a parsnip and threw it into the pot, followed by a carrot and some cabbage, hoping to make something edible.

She took one of the heavy, long-handled spoons her father had given to her and stirred the pot with it. As she stirred, she realized with horror that her entire stew had turned black. Could she have possibly burned it? She pulled out the spoon and screamed.

Gavin came running into the kitchen. "What is it? Are ye all right? Are ye hurt?"

"My spoon!" She held up the common utensil that was no longer common. The handle was still black, but where it had been in the hot soup it had turned bright yellow gold.

"Holy Saint Andrew," breathed Gavin and he inspected the strange spoon. "'Tis gold! Yer father must have painted it over with black paint. No wonder it was so heavy." He looked at Colette in astonishment. "But why would he do it? Why give ye a fortune in gold when ye already were carrying a king's ransom in the form o' yer dowry?"

Tears sprang to Colette's eyes. "He must have wanted to give me something of my own, something that would not be counted as my dowry to go to my husband, something that would not even be listed as my inheritance. It was his way of giving me something for myself. He was protecting me to the very end. My dear, sweet father, how I miss him."

"Does this mean ye wish to return?" asked Gavin, his voice a rasp.

Colette merely smiled at him and shook her head. "I fear you are stuck with me."

"Good." He sighed in relief. "I fear I woud'na let ye go. Especially now that ye're rich," he teased with a wide grin.

Colette laughed, and they threw their arms around each other for a kiss, while the golden spoon dropped to the table, forgotten. Colette relaxed into the warmth of his embrace until her stomach growled in protest.

"Oh dear," she said. "The stew is ruined, full of black paint."

"No matter," said Gavin with a hungry look in his eye. "I have a better idea of how to welcome ye home." He scooped her up into his arms, carrying her to the small bedchamber. "I hope ye are in the mood for a warm Highland welcome. We are a friendly lot, we are."

Colette laughed and Gavin joined her, their joy complete.

Author's Note

During the fourteenth century, the Book of Hours was a relatively common book at a time when books were uncommon. An abbreviated form of the breviary, the Book of Hours was the ancestor of the more modern-day prayer book. It contained a form of the Divine Office, which was practiced in monasteries. It was so named because it held specific Scriptures and prayers for the different hours of the day and different seasons of the Church calendar. The hours followed the monastic division of prayer times, including Matins, Lauds, Prime, Terce, Sext, Nones, Compline, and Vespers. Though each Book of Hours was unique, most included a calendar of the Church feasts, excerpts from the gospels and the Psalms, the Litany of Saints, the Office of the Dead, the Hours of the Cross, and various other prayers.

Before the invention of the printing press, these books were each painstakingly created by hand, often by monks transcribing the texts on thin vellum pages. A Book of Hours might be commissioned by a member of the aristocracy or by a wealthy merchant.

Many books were actually created for women, some given as a wedding present to a bride. These books came in many sizes, from huge volumes with multiple pages of brilliant illustrations, to pocket-sized volumes smaller than a modern-day paperback. Some had many full-page illustrations and many had an elaborately decorated first letter of the text. The language of the work was almost always Latin.

Though a fictional character, in *The Highlander's Bride*, Colette's mother, a member of the French nobility, would have been the type of fourteenth-century lady to own a Book of Hours. Further, it would not have been unusual for the book to be passed down from mother to daughter. Thus, it was fun to incorporate this beautiful book into the story.

Acknowledgments

No book is written without considerable help and support and *A Highlander's Bride* is no exception. I greatly appreciate my beta reader, Laurie Maus, who has supported me and corrected all my numerous typos. Special thanks to my editor, Deb Werksman, and my agent, Barbara Poelle, who continue to support and encourage my growth as a writer. And to my husband I extend my most sincere thanks for giving me the time and support I need to be able to write. You remain my hero.

A Sword for His Lady
by Mary Wine

A *Publishers Weekly* Top 10 Pick for Spring 2015

— ❧ —

He'd defend her keep…

After proving himself on the field of battle, Ramon de Segrave is appointed to the Council of Barons by Richard the Lionheart. But instead of taking his most formidable warrior on his latest Crusade, the king assigns Ramon an even more dangerous task—woo and win the Lady of Thistle Keep.

If only she'd yield her heart

Isabel of Camoys has fought long and hard for her independence, and if the price is loneliness, then so be it. She will not yield…even if she does find the powerful knight's heated embrace impossible to ignore. But when her land is threatened, Isabel reluctantly agrees to allow Ramon to defend the keep—knowing that the price may very well be her heart.

— ❧ —

Praise for Mary Wine:

"I always find the emotional and philosophical tugs of war interesting between Wine's characters. Her main characters are always admirable and there are always some true baddies to root against." —*For the Love of Books*

For more Mary Wine, visit:
www.sourcebooks.com

First Time with a Highlander
by Gwyn Cready

❧

She needs a man—but only for one night

What do you get when you imbibe centuries-old whiskey—besides a hangover the size of the Highlands? If you're twenty-first-century ad exec Gerard Innes, you get swept back to eighteenth-century Edinburgh and into the bed of a gorgeous, fiery redhead. Gerard has only a foggy idea what he and the lady have been up to…but what he does remember draws him into the most dangerous and exhilarating campaign of his life.

Be careful what you wish for…

Serafina Seonag Fallon's scoundrel of a fiancé has left her with nothing, and she's determined to turn the tables. If she can come up with a ringer, she can claim the cargo he stole from her. But the dashing man she summons from the future demands more than one night, and Serafina finds it easier to command the seas under her feet than the crashing waves he unleashes in her heart.

❧

Praise for Gwyn Cready:

About the Author

Amanda Forester holds a PhD in psychology and worked for many years in academia before discovering that writing historical romance was decidedly more fun. Whether in the rugged Highlands of medieval Scotland or the decadent ballrooms of Regency England, her novels offer fast-paced adventures filled with wit, intrigue, and romance. Amanda lives with her family in the Pacific Northwest. You can visit her at www.amandaforester.com.